THE WORLD OF O. HENRY

STRICTLY BUSINESS

and other stories

THE WORLD OF O. HENRY

STRICTLY BUSINESS

and other stories

HODDER AND STOUGHTON
LONDON SYDNEY AUCKLAND TORONTO

73

Introduction

"Pull up the shades," he enjoined a nurse. "I don't want to go home in the dark."

O. Henry had been taken ill two days earlier in the Caledonian Hotel, New York: he died his sunny death at the age of forty-eight, departing as suavely as a character in one of his own stories. He'd been a lonely man, making do with acquaintances where others demand friends, twice married, and on his own reckoning the daily consumer of two quarts of whisky. He haunted the New York streets and bars, endlessly listening to the stories of other people's lives: the world was grist to his typewriter, and towards the end of his life he lived for nothing else.

He was born William Sydney Porter in Greensboro, N.C., in 1862, the son of a doctor whose practice of medicine took second place to his interest in perpetual motion. When he was three, William Sydney's mother died. At fifteen, he left school to work in an uncle's drug store, and a few years later he became a teller in the First National Bank in Austin. Summoned to stand trial for embezzlement, he fled—and at once became involved with Al and Henry Jennings, whose methods of extracting money from banks were swifter and more direct than months of patient appropriation.

He travelled to Mexico with thirty thousand dollars, the proceeds of a Jennings robbery, but having "knocked around with refugees and consuls" for some years, he returned to Austin and was awarded three years' incarceration in the Ohio State Penitentiary. Here, it seems, there was a prison guard named Orrin Henry, whom William Sydney Porter, small-town crook and model prisoner, immortalised as O. Henry.

7

There's the whiff of some bad, black joke about all that, some wry O. Henry comment that wryly bore its final fruit twenty-odd years later when the citizens of Greensboro built the O. Henry Hotel in honour of their safely-dead reprobate. An extraordinary tribute this, and a rare one for a man of letters: in one grandiloquent American gesture it established him as the Henry Ford of the short story, and since that time his creations have to some extent shared the vicissitudes of the Tin Lizzie. O. Henry's collected works published in 1913 ran into twelve volumes. Once considered classics of their kind, they fell from grace when popular American magazines became fashionably sophisticated. But their decline and resurrection parallels the decline and resurrection of the short story itself, which is a starting point in any assessment of their quality.

O. Henry's stories are the stories people tell one another. They are anecdotes with a beginning, a middle and an end. It is the end that contains the punch or often the winning trick, and because of their construction a certain similarity carries from story to story. Like the stories of Saki and unlike those of, say, Thomas Hardy, they are true to the form: they could not, by any stretch of the Henry imagination, have been novels. Most of Hardy's could, and many of the fashionable short stories that have led the way since O. Henry's day are chapters from some unwritten novel rather than stories in their own right. Novels themselves during that same period have become shorter, more confused, and emptier of content.

But now, as the mid-seventies approach, the story and the novel are finding their length and their shape again. Frank O'Connor, one of the best short-story writers of this century, was an appallingly bad influence because what O'Connor could get away with lesser writers emphatically could not. This is all too patently true, far more so than the argument that magazine outlets for the short story dried up and in so doing almost killed it. What *did* seriously affect its health since the days when writers thrived on popular demand was the fashion for slight, formless little bits and pieces, addressed

8

to an intelligentsia—O'Connor without the genius. To quote
Alan Ross, who as the editor of the *London Magazine* did so
much for the short story during its wilderness years by publish-
ing stories that represented: "a necessary reaction against
shapeless impressionism, against the post Denton Welch
period in which china bric-a-brac and a young man's
relationship with his mother appeared controlling forces."
The story, in short, had become inbred, precious, self-
consciously literary and often self-congratulatingly in-
comprehensible.

O. Henry is rather the opposite of all that, and those who
seek to denigrate his works might perhaps consider them the
contents of a cracker-barrel. There is an ordinariness about
his ordinary people that could well be too much for those
who require characters of a nobler cut. There is a precision
about his plotting that may offend those who believe that
plots have no place in art. But in his style and in the crisp
naturalness of his dialogue and his wit there is little that anyone in full possession of senses and sensibility could object to.
With the economy that is, above all, the essence of the thing
he creates characters with real life in them and draws from
their lips words that start the machinery of drama immediately
moving. But it's his own prose, set in the succinct style of a
primitive who's a comedian and a professional as well, that
distinguishes most of his pages. And the familiar ring it
sometimes has is because it has been endlessly imitated since
the days when it was fresh and new.

The first time my optical nerves were disturbed by the
sight of Buckingham Skinner was in Kansas City. I was
standing on a corner when I see Buck stick his straw-
coloured head out of a third-story window of a business
block and holler, "Whoa, there! Whoa!" like you would
in endeavouring to assuage a team of runaway mules.

I looked around; but all the animals I see in sight is a
policeman, having his shoes shined, and a couple of
delivery wagons hitched to posts. Then in a minute down-

stairs tumbles this Buckingham Skinner, and runs to the corner, and stands and gazes down the street either at the imaginary dust kicked up by the fabulous hoofs . . . .

"Was that your team broke away and run just now?" I asks him, polite. "I tried to stop 'em," says I, "but I couldn't. I guess they're half-way back to the farm by now."

"Gosh blame them darned mules," says Strawtop, in a voice so good that I nearly apologized . . .

Con-men, street-men, grafters, bar-flies, vaudeville players, soap kings, bread kings, scrub-women, dice-shakers, captains of adventure, girls who are strictly business, loiterers in Bogle's Chop House, where the pepper is tasteless and melancholy: the failings of all of them flow as the blood of the O. Henry world.

They have not lost their lustre and at a time when the short story can again hold up its head it seems right that, being so much part of the history of the form in America, they should again be presented. Their stories are one kind of story. They are not classic and they are not the only kind. But a renaissance is a varied movement, and I believe this present one would be incomplete without its O. Henry tribute.

William Trevor

Contents

THE WORLD OF O. HENRY

STRICTLY BUSINESS

and other stories

1

Strictly Business

I SUPPOSE you know all about the stage and stage people. You've been touched with and by actors, and you read the newspaper criticisms and the jokes in the weeklies about the Rialto and the chorus girls and the long-haired tragedians. And I suppose that a condensed list of your ideas about the mysterious stageland would boil down to something like this:

Leading ladies have five husbands, paste diamonds, and figures no better than your own (madam) if they weren't padded. Chorus girls are inseparable from peroxide, Panhards and Pittsburg. All shows walk back to New York on tan oxford and railroad ties. Irreproachable actresses reserve the comic-landlady part for their mothers on Broadway and their step-aunts on the road. Kyrle Bellew's real name is Boyle O'Kelley. The ravings of John McCullough in the phonograph were stolen from the first sale of the Ellen Terry memoirs. Joe Weber is funnier than E. H. Sothern; but Henry Miller is getting older than he was.

All theatrical people on leaving the theatre at night drink champagne and eat lobsters until noon the next day. After all, the moving pictures have got the whole bunch pounded to a pulp.

Now, few of us know the real life of the stage people. I we did, the profession might be more overcrowded than it is. We look askance at the players with an eye full of patronizing superiority—and we go home and practise all sorts of elocution and gestures in front of our looking-glasses.

Latterly there has been much talk of the actor people in a new light. It seems to have been divulged that instead of being motoring bacchanalians and diamond-hungry *loreleis* they are businesslike folk, students and ascetics with childer and homes and libraries, owning real estate, and conducting their private affairs in as orderly and unsensational a manner as any of us good citizens who are bound to the chariot wheels of the gas, rent, coal, ice, and ward men.

Whether the old or the new report of the sock-and-buskiners be the true one is a surmise that has no place here. I offer you merely this little story of two strollers; and for proof of its truth I can show you only the dark patch above the cast-iron handle of the stage-entrance door of Keetor's old vaudeville theatre made there by the petulant push of gloved hands too impatient to finger the clumsy thumb-latch—and where I last saw Cherry whisking through like a swallow into her nest, on time to the minute, as usual, to dress for her act.

The vaudeville team of Hart & Cherry was an inspiration. Bob Hart had been roaming through the Eastern and Western circuits for four years with a mixed-up act comprising a monologue, three lightning changes, with songs, a couple of imitations of celebrated imitators, and a buck-and-wing dance that had drawn a glance of approval from the bass-viol player in more than one house—than which no performer ever received more satisfactory evidence of good work.

The greatest treat an actor can have is to witness the pitiful performance with which all other actors desecrate the stage. In order to give himself this pleasure he will often forsake the sunniest Broadway corner between Thirty-fourth and Forty-fourth to attend a matinée offering by his less gifted brothers. Once during the lifetime of a minstrel joke one comes to scoff and remains to go through with that most difficult exercise of Thespian muscles—the audible contact of the palm of one hand against the palm of the other.

One afternoon Bob Hart presented his solvent, serious, well-known vaudevillian face at the box-office window of a rival attraction and got his d.h. coupon for an orchestra seat.

A, B, C, and D glowed successively on the announcement

16

spaces and passed into oblivion, each plunging Mr. Hart deeper into gloom. Others of the audience shrieked, squirmed, whistled and applauded; but Bob Hart ,"All the Mustard and a Whole Show in Himself'", sat with his face as long and his hands as far apart as a boy holding a hank of yarn for his grandmother to wind into a ball.

But when H came on, "The Mustard" suddenly sat up straight. H was the happy alphabetical prognosticator of Winona Cherry in Character Songs and Impersonations. There were scarcely more than two bites to Cherry; but she delivered the merchandise tied with a pink cord and charged to the old man's account. She first showed you a deliciously dewy and ginghamy country girl with a basket of property daisies who informed you ingenuously that there were other things to be learned at the old log schoolhouse besides cipherin' and nouns, especially "When the Teach-er Kept Me in." Vanishing, with a quick flirt of gingham apron-strings, she reappeared in considerably less than a "trice" as a fluffy "Parisienne"—so near does Art bring the old red mill to the Moulin Rouge. And then——

But you know the rest. And so did Bob Hart; but he saw somebody else. He thought he saw that Cherry was the only professional on the short order stage that he had seen who seemed exactly to fit the part of "Helen Grimes" in the sketch he had written and kept tucked away in the tray of his trunk. Of course, Bob Hart, as well as every other normal actor, grocer, newspaper man, professor, kerb broker, and farmer, has a play tucked away somewhere. They tuck 'em in trays of trunks, trunks of trees, desks, haymows, pigeon-holes, inside pockets, safe-deposit vaults, handboxes, and coal cellars, waiting for Mr. Frohman to call. They belong among the fifty-seven different kinds.

But Bob Hart's sketch was not destined to end in a pickle jar. He called it "Mice Will Play". He had kept it quiet and hidden away ever since he wrote it, waiting to find a partner who fitted his conception of "Helen Grimes". And here was "Helen" herself, with all the innocent abandon, the youth,

17

the sprightliness, and the flawless stage art that his critical taste demanded.

After the act was over Hart found the manager in the box office, and got Cherry's address. At five the next afternoon he called at the musty old house in the West Forties and sent up his professional card.

By daylight, in a secular shirt waist and plain *voile* skirt, with her hair curbed and her Sister of Charity eyes, Winona Cherry might have been playing the part of Prudence Wise, the deacon's daughter, in the great (unwritten) New England drama not yet entitled anything.

"I know your act, Mr. Hart," she said after she had looked over his card carefully. "What did you wish to see me about?"

"I saw you work last night," said Hart. "I've written a sketch that I've been saving up. It's for two; and I think you can do the other part. I thought I'd see you about it."

"Come in the parlour," said Miss Cherry. "I've been wishing for something of the sort. I think I'd like to act instead of doing turns."

Bob Hart drew his cherished "Mice Will Play" from his pocket, and read it to her.

"Read it again, please," said Miss Cherry.

And then she pointed out to him clearly how it could be improved by introducing a messenger instead of a telephone call, and cutting the dialogue just before the climax while they were struggling for the pistol, and by completely changing the lines and business of Helen Grimes at the point where her jealousy overcomes her. Hart yielded to all her strictures without argument. She had at once put her finger on the sketch's weaker points. That was her woman's intuition that he had lacked. At the end of their talk Hart was willing to stake the judgment, experience, and savings of his four years of vaudeville that "Mice Will Play" would blossom into a perennial flower in the garden of the circuits. Miss Cherry was slower to decide. After many puckerings of her smooth young brow and tappings on her small, white teeth with the end of a lead pencil she gave out her dictum.

"Mr. Hart," said she, "I believe your sketch is going to win out. That Grimes part fits me like a shrinkable flannel after its first trip to a handless hand laundry. I can make it stand out like the colonel of the Forty-fourth Regiment at a Little Mothers' Bazaar. And I've seen you work. I know what you can do with the other part. But business is business. How much do you get a week for the stunt you do now?"

"Two hundred," answered Hart.

"I get one hundred for mine," said Cherry. "That's about the natural discount for a woman. But I live on it and put a few simoleons every week under the loose brick in the old kitchen hearth. The stage is all right. I love it; but there's something else I love better—that's a little country home, some day, with Plymouth Rock chickens and six ducks wandering around the yard.

"Now, let me tell you, Mr. Hart, I am STRICTLY BUSINESS. If you want me to play the opposite part in your sketch, I'll do it. And I believe we can make it go. And there's something else I want to say: There's no nonsense in my make-up; I'm *on the level*, and I'm on the stage for what it pays me, just as other girls work in stores and offices. I'm going to save my money to keep me when I'm past doing my stunts. No Old Ladies' Home or Retreat for Imprudent Actresses for me.

"If you want to make this a business partnership, Mr. Hart, with all nonsense cut out of it, I'm in on it. I know something about vaudeville teams in general; but this would have to be one in particular. I want you to know that I'm on the stage for what I can cart away from it every pay-day in a little manila envelope with nicotine stains on it, where the cashier has licked the flap. It's kind of a hobby of mine to want to cravenette myself for plenty of rainy days in the future. I want you to know just how I am. I don't know what an all-night restaurant looks like; I drink only weak tea; I never spoke to a man at a stage entrance in my life, and I've got money in five savings banks."

"Miss Cherry," said Bob Hart in his smooth, serious

19

tones, "you're in on your own terms. I've got 'strictly business' pasted in my hat and stencilled on my make-up box. When I dream of nights I always see a five-room bungalow on the north shore of Long Island, with a Jap cooking clam broth and duckling in the kitchen, and me with the title deeds to the place in my pongee coat pocket, swinging in a hammock on the side-porch, reading Stanley's *Explorations into Africa*. And nobody else around. You never was interested in Africa, was you, Miss Cherry?"

"Not any," said Cherry. "What I'm going to do with my money is to bank it. You can get four per cent on deposits. Even at the salary I've been earning, I've figured out that in ten years I'd have an income of about $50 a month just from the interest alone. Well, I might invest some of the principal in a little business—say, trimming hats or a beauty parlour, and make more."

"Well," said Hart, "you've got the proper idea all right, anyhow. There are mighty few actors that amount to anything at all who couldn't fix themselves for the wet days to come if they'd save their money instead of blowing it. I'm glad you've got the correct business idea of it, Miss Cherry. I think the same way; and I believe this sketch will more than double what both of us earn now when we get it shaped up."

The subsequent history of "Mice Will Play" is the history of all successful writings for the stage. Hart & Cherry cut it, pieced it, remodelled it, performed surgical operations on the dialogue and business, changed the lines, restored 'em, added more, cut 'em out, renamed it, gave it back the old name, rewrote it, substituted a dagger for the pistol, restored the pistol—put the sketch through all the known processes of condensation and improvement.

They rehearsed it by the old-fashioned boarding-house clock in the rarely used parlour until its warning click at five minutes to the hour would occur every time exactly half a second before the click of the unloaded revolver that Helen Grimes used in rehearsing the thrilling climax of the sketch.

Yes, that was a thriller and a piece of excellent work. In the act a real 32-calibre revolver was used loaded with a real cartridge. Helen Grimes, who is a Western girl of decidedly Buffalo Billish skill and daring, is tempestuously in love with Frank Desmond, the private secretary and confidential prospective son-in-law of her father, "Arapahoe" Grimes, quarter-million-dollar cattle king, owning a ranch that, judging by the scenery, is in either the Bad Lands or Amagansett, L.I. Desmond (in private life Mr. Bob Hart) wears puttees and Meadow Brook Hunt riding trousers, and gives his address as New York, leaving you to wonder why he comes to the Bad Lands or Amagansett (as the case may be) and at the same time to conjecture mildly why a cattleman should want puttees about his ranch with a secretary in 'em.

Well, anyhow, you know as well as I do that we all like that kind of play, whether we admit it or not—something along in between "Bluebeard, Jr.", and "Cymbeline" played in the Russian.

There were only two parts and a half in "Mice Will Play". Hart and Cherry were the two, of course; and the half was a minor part always played by a stage hand, who merely came in once in a Tuxedo coat and a panic to announce that the house was surrounded by Indians, and to turn down the gas-fire in the grate by the manager's orders.

There was another girl in the sketch—a Fifth Avenue society swelless—who was visiting the ranch and who had sirened Jack Valentine when he was a wealthy clubman on lower Third Avenue before he lost his money. This girl appeared on the stage only in the photographic state—Jack had her Sarony stuck up on the mantel of the Amagan—of the Bad Lands droring-room. Helen was jealous, of course.

And now for the thriller. Old "Arapahoe" Grimes dies of angina pectoris one night—so Helen informs us in a stage-ferryboat whisper over the footlights—while only his secretary was present. And that same day he was known to have had $647,000 in cash in his (ranch) library just received

21

for the sale of a drove of beeves in the East (that accounts for the prices we pay for steak!). The cash disappears at the same time. Jack Valentine was the only person with the ranchman when he made his (alleged) croak.

"Gawd knows I love him; but if he has done this deed——" you sabe, don't you? And then there are some mean things said about the Fifth Avenue girl—who doesn't come on the stage—and can we blame her, with the vaudeville trust holding down prices until one actually must be buttoned in the back by a call-boy, maids cost so much?

But, wait. Here's the climax. Helen Grimes, chaparralish as she can be, is goaded beyond imprudence. She convinces herself that Jack Valentine is not only a falsetto, but a financier. To lose at one fell swoop $647,000 and a lover in riding trousers with angles in the sides like the variations on the chart of a typhoid-fever patient is enough to make any perfect lady mad. So, then!

They stand in the (ranch) library, which is furnished with mounted elk heads (didn't the Elks have a fish fry in Amagansett once?), and the dénouement begins. I know of no more interesting time in the run of a play unless it be when the prologue ends.

Helen thinks Jack has taken the money. Who else was there to take it? The box-office manager was at the front on his job; the orchestra hadn't left their seats; and no man could get past "Old Jimmy", the stage doorman, unless he could show a Skye terrier or an automobile as a guarantee of eligibility.

Goaded beyond imprudence (as before said), Helen says to Jack Valentine: "Robber and thief—and worse yet, stealer of trusting hearts, this should be your fate!"

With that out she whips, of course, the trusty 32-calibre.

"But I will be merciful," goes on Helen. "You shall live— that will be your punishment. I will show you how easily I could have sent you to the death that you deserve. There is *her* picture on the mantel. I will send through her more beautiful face the bullet that should have pierced your craven heart."

And she does it. And there's no fake blank cartridges or assistants pulling strings. Helen fires. The bullet—the actual bullet—goes through the face of the photograph—and then strikes the hidden spring of the sliding panel in the wall— and lo! the panel slides, and there is the missing $647,000 in convincing stacks of currency and bags of gold. It's great. You know how it is. Cherry practised for two months at a target on the roof of her boarding-house. It took good shooting. In the sketch she had to hit a brass disk only three inches in diameter, covered by wall-paper in the panel; and she had to stand in exactly the same spot every night, and the photo had to be in exactly the same spot, and she had to shoot steady and true every time.

Of course old "Arapahoe" had tucked the funds away there in the secret place; and, of course, Jack hadn't taken anything except his salary (which really might have come under the head of "obtaining money under"; but that is neither here nor there); and, of course, the New York girl was really engaged to a concrete house contractor in the Bronx; and, necessarily, Jack and Helen ended in a half-Nelson—and there you are.

After Hart and Cherry had gotten "Mice Will Play" flawless, they had a try-out at a vaudeville house that accommodates. The sketch was a house wrecker. It was one of those rare strokes of talent that inundates a theatre from the roof down. The gallery wept; and the orchestra seats being dressed for it, swam in tears.

After the show the booking agents signed blank cheques and pressed fountain pens upon Hart and Cherry. Five hundred dollars a week was what it panned out.

That night at 11.30 Bob Hart took off his hat and bade Cherry good night at her boarding-house door.

"Mr. Hart," said she thoughtfully, "come inside just a few minutes. We've got our chance now to make good and to make money. What we want to do is to cut expenses every cent we can, and save all we can."

"Right," said Bob. "It's business with me. You've got your scheme for banking yours; and I dream every night of that bungalow with the Jap cook and nobody around to raise trouble. Anything to enlarge the net receipts will engage my attention."

"Come inside just a few minutes," repeated Cherry, deeply thoughtful. "I've got a proposition to make to you that will reduce our expenses a lot and help you work out your own future and help me work out mine—and all on business principles."

* * *

"Mice Will Play" had a tremendously successful run in New York for ten weeks—rather neat for a vaudeville sketch —and then it started on the circuits. Without following it, it may be said that it was a solid drawing card for two years without a sign of abated popularity.

Sam Packard, manager of one of Keetor's New York houses, said of Hart & Cherry:

"As square and high-toned a little team as ever came over the circuit. It's a pleasure to read their names on the booking list. Quiet, hard workers, no Johnny and Mabel nonsense, on the job to the minute, straight home after their act, and each of 'em as gentlemanlike as a lady. I don't expect to handle any attractions that give me less trouble or more respect for the profession."

And now, after so much cracking of a nutshell, here is the kernel of the story:

At the end of its second season "Mice Will Play" came back to New York for another run at the roof gardens and summer theatres. There was never any trouble in booking it at the top-notch price. Bob Hart had his bungalow nearly paid for, and Cherry had so many savings-deposit bank books that she had begun to buy sectional bookcases on the instalment plan to hold them.

24

I tell you these things to assure you, even if you can't believe it, that many, very many of the stage people are workers with abiding ambitions—just the same as the man who wants to be president, or the grocery clerk who wants a home in Flatbush, or a lady who is anxious to flop-out of the Count-pan into the Prince-fire. And I hope I may be allowed to say, without chipping into the contribution basket, that they often move in a mysterious way their wonders to perform.

But, listen.

At the first performance of "Mice Will Play" in New York at the new Westphalia (no hams alluded to) Theatre, Winona Cherry was nervous. When she fired at the photograph of the Eastern beauty on the mantel, the bullet, instead of penetrating the photo and then striking the disk, went into the lower left side of Bob Hart's neck. Not expecting to get it there, Hart collapsed neatly, while Cherry fainted in a most artistic manner.

The audience, surmising that they viewed a comedy instead of a tragedy in which the principals were married or reconciled, applauded with great enjoyment. The Cool Head, who always graces such occasions, rang the curtain down, and two platoons of scene shifters respectively and more or less respectfully removed Hart & Cherry from the stage. The next turn went on, and all went as merry as an alimony bell.

The stage hands found a young doctor at the stage entrance who was waiting for a patient with a decoction of Am. B'ty roses. The doctor examined Hart carefully and laughed heartily.

"No headlines for you, Old Sport," was his diagnosis. "If it had been two inches to the left it would have undermined the carotid artery as far as the Red Front Drug Store in Flatbush and Back Again. As it is, you just get the property man to bind it up with a flounce torn from any one of the girls' Valenciennes and go home and get it dressed by the parlour-floor practitioner on your block, and you'll be all right. Excuse me; I've got a serious case outside to look after."

After that Bob Hart looked up and felt better. And then to where he lay came Vincente, the Tramp Juggler, great in his line. Vincente, a solemn man from Brattleboro, Vt., named Sam Griggs at home, sent toys and maple sugar home to two small daughters from every town he played. Vincente had moved on the same circuits with Hart & Cherry, and was their peripatetic friend.

"Bob," said Vincente in his serious way, "I'm glad it's no worse. The little lady is wild about you."

"Who?" asked Hart.

"Cherry," said the juggler. "We didn't know how bad you were hurt; and we kept her away. It's taking the manager and three girls to hold her."

"It was an accident, of course," said Hart. "Cherry's all right. She wasn't feeling in good trim or she couldn't have done it. There's no hard feelings. She's strictly business. The doctor says I'll be on the job again in three days. Don't let her worry."

"Man," said Sam Griggs severely, puckering his old smooth, lined face, "are you a chess automaton or a human pincushion? Cherry's crying her heart out for you—calling 'Bob, Bob,' every second, with them holding her hands and keeping her from coming to you."

"What's the matter with her?" asked Hart, with wide-open eyes. "The sketch'll go on again in three days. I'm not hurt bad, the doctor says. She won't lose out half a week's salary. I know it was an accident. What's the matter with her?"

"You seem to be blind, or a sort of a fool," said Vincente. "The girl loves you and is almost mad about your hurt. What's the matter with *you*? Is she nothing to you? I wish you could hear her call you."

"Loves me?" asked Bob Hart, rising from the stack of scenery on which he lay. "Cherry loves me? Why, it's impossible."

26

"I wish you could see her and hear her," said Griggs.

"But man," said Bob Hart, sitting up, "it's impossible. It's impossible, I tell you. I never dreamed of such a thing."

"No human being," said the Tramp Juggler, "could mistake it. She's wild for love of you. How have you been so blind?"

"But, my God," said Bob Hart, rising to his feet, *"it's too late.* It's too late, I tell you, Sam; *it's too late.* It can't be. You must be wrong. It's *impossible.* There's some mistake."

"She's crying for you," said the Tramp Juggler. "For love of you she's fighting three, and calling your name so loud they don't dare to raise the curtain. Wake up, man."

"For love of me?" said Bob Hart with staring eyes. "Don't I tell you it's too late? It's too late, man. Why, *Cherry and I have been married two years!*"

2

The Love-philtre of Ikey Schoenstein

THE Blue Light Drug Store is down-town, between the
Bowery and First Avenue, where the distance between
the two streets is the shortest. The Blue Light does not consider that pharmacy is a thing of bric-à-brac, scent and ice-
cream soda. If you ask it for a pain-killer it will not give you
a bonbon.

The Blue Light scorns the labour-saving arts of modern
pharmacy. It macerates its opium and percolates its own
laudanum and paregoric. To this day pills are made behind
its tall prescription desk—pills rolled out on its own pill-tile,
divided with a spatula, rolled with the finger and thumb,
dusted with calcined magnesia and delivered in little round,
pasteboard pill-boxes. The store is on a corner about which
coveys of ragged-plumed, hilarious children play and
become candidates for the cough-drops and soothing syrups
that wait for them inside.

Ikey Schoenstein was the night clerk of the Blue Light
and the friend of his customers. Thus it is on the East Side
where the heart of pharmacy is not *glacé*. There, as it should
be, the druggist is a counsellor, a confessor, an adviser, an
able and willing missionary and mentor whose learning is
respected, whose occult wisdom is venerated and whose
medicine is often poured, untasted, into the gutter. Therefore
Ikey's corniform, bespectacled nose and narrow, knowledge-
bowed figure was well known in the vicinity of the Blue
Light, and his advice and notice were much desired.

Ikey roomed and breakfasted at Mrs. Riddle's, two squares
away. Mrs. Riddle had a daughter named Rosy. The circumlocution has been in vain—you must have guessed it—Ikey

adored Rosy. She tinctured all his thoughts; she was the compound extract of all that was chemically pure and officinal—the dispensatory contained nothing equal to her. But Ikey was timid, and his hopes remained insoluble in the menstruum of his backwardness and fears. Behind his counter he was a superior being, calmly conscious of special knowledge and worth; outside, he was a weak-kneed, purblind, motorman-cursed rambler, with ill-fitting clothes stained with chemicals and smelling of socotrine aloes and valerianate of ammonia.

The fly in Ikey's ointment (thrice welcome, pat trope!) was Chunk McGowan.

Mr. McGowan was also striving to catch the bright smiles tossed about by Rosy. But he was no out-fielder as Ikey was; he picked them off the bat. At the same time he was Ikey's friend and customer, and often dropped in at the Blue Light Drug Store to have a bruise painted with iodine or get a cut rubber-plastered after a pleasant evening spent along the Bowery.

One afternoon McGowan drifted in in his silent, easy way, and sat, comely, smoothed-faced, hard, indomitable, good-natured, upon a stool.

"Ikey," said he, when his friend had fetched his mortar and sat opposite, grinding gum benzoin to a powder, "get busy with your ear. It's drugs for me if you've got the line I need."

Ikey scanned the countenance of Mr. McGowan for the usual evidences of conflict, but found none.

"Take your coat off," he ordered. "I guess already that you have been stuck in the ribs with a knife. I have many times told you those Dagoes would do you up."

Mr. McGowan smiled. "Not them," he said. "Not any Dagoes. But you've located the diagnosis all right enough— it's under my coat, near the ribs. Say! Ikey—Rosy and me are goin' to run away and get married to-night."

Ikey's left forefinger was doubled over the edge of the mortar, holding it steady. He gave it a wild rap with the

29

pestle, but felt it not. Meanwhile Mr. McGowan's smile faded to a look of perplexed gloom.

"That is," he continued, "if she keeps in the notion until the time comes. We've been layin' pipes for the gateway for two weeks. One day she says she will; the same evenin' she says nixy. We've agreed on to-night, and Rosy's stuck to the affirmative this time for two whole days. But it's five hours yet till the time, and I'm afraid she'll stand me up when it comes to the scratch."

"You said you wanted drugs," remarked Ikey.

Mr. McGowan looked ill at ease and harassed—a condition opposed to his usual line of demeanour. He made a patent-medicine almanac into a roll and fitted it with unprofitable carefulness about his finger.

"I wouldn't have this double handicap make a false start to-night for a million," he said. "I've got a little flat up in Harlem all ready, with chrysanthemums on the table and a kettle ready to boil. And I've engaged a pulpit pounder to be ready at his house for us at 9.30. It's got to come off. And if Rosy don't change her mind again!"—Mr. McGowan ceased, a prey to his doubts.

"I don't see then yet," said Ikey shortly, "what makes it that you talk of drugs, or what I can be doing about it."

"Old man Riddle don't like me a little bit," went on the uneasy suitor, bent upon marshalling his arguments. "For a week he hasn't let Rosy step outside the door with me. If it wasn't for losin' a boarder they'd have bounced me long ago. I'm makin' $20 a week and she'll never regret flyin' the coop with Chunk McGowan."

"You will excuse me, Chunk," said Ikey. "I must make a prescription that is to be called for soon."

"Say," said McGowan, looking up suddenly, "say, Ikey, ain't there a drug of some kind—some kind of powders that'll make a girl like you better if you give 'em to her?"

Ikey's lip beneath his nose curled with the scorn of superior enlightenment; but before he could answer, McGowan continued:

30

"Tim Lacy told me once that he got some from a croaker up-town and fed 'em to his girl in soda water. From the very first dose he was ace-high and everybody else looked like thirty cents to her. They was married in less than two weeks."

Strong and simple was Chunk McGowan. A better reader of men than Ikey was could have seen that his tough frame was strung upon fine wires. Like a good general who was about to invade the enemy's territory he was seeking to guard every point against possible failure.

"I thought," went on Chunk hopefully, "that if I had one of them powders to give Rosy when I see her at supper to-night it might brace her up and keep her from reneging on the proposition to skip. I guess she don't need a mule team to drag her away, but women are better at coaching than they are at running bases. If the stuff'll work just for a couple of hours it'll do the trick."

"When is this foolishness of running away to be happening?" asked Ikey.

"Nine o'clock," said Mr. McGowan. "Supper's at seven. At eight Rosy goes to bed with a headache. At nine old Parvenzano lets me through to his backyard, where there's a board off Riddle's fence, next door. I go under her window and help her down the fire-escape. We've got to make it early on the preacher's account. It's all dead easy if Rosy don't balk when the flag drops. Can you fix me one of them powders, Ikey?"

Ikey Schoenstein rubbed his nose slowly.

"Chunk," said he, "it is of drugs of that nature that pharmaceutists must have much carefulness. To you alone of my acquaintance would I entrust a powder like that. But for you I shall make it, and you shall see how it makes Rosy to think of you."

Ikey went behind the prescription desk. There he crushed to a powder two soluble tablets, each containing a quarter of a grain of morphia. To them he added a little sugar of milk to increase the bulk, and folded the mixture neatly in a

31

white paper. Taken by an adult this powder would ensure several hours of heavy slumber without danger to the sleeper. This he handed to Chunk McGowan, telling him to administer it in a liquid, if possible, and received the hearty thanks of the backyard Lochinvar.

The subtlety of Ikey's action becomes apparent upon recital of his subsequent move. He sent a messenger for Mr. Riddle and disclosed the plans of McGowan for eloping with Rosy. Mr. Riddle was a stout man, brick-dusty of complexion and sudden in action.

"Much obliged," he said briefly to Ikey. "The lazy Irish loafer! My own room's just above Rosy's. I'll just go up there myself after supper and load the shot-gun and wait. If he comes in my backyard he'll go away in an ambulance instead of a bridal chaise."

With Rosy held in the clutches of Morpheus for a many-hours' deep slumber, and the blood-thirsty parent waiting, armed and forewarned, Ikey felt that his rival was close, indeed, upon discomfiture.

All night in the Blue Light Store he waited at his duties for chance news of the tragedy, but none came.

At eight o'clock in the morning the day clerk arrived and Ikey started hurriedly for Mrs. Riddle's to learn the outcome. And, lo! as he stepped out of the store who but Chunk McGowan sprang from a passing street-car and grasped his hand—Chunk McGowan with a victor's smile and flushed with joy.

"Pulled it off," said Chunk with Elysium in his grin. "Rosy hit the fire-escape on time to a second, and we was under the wire at the Reverend's at 9.30¼. She's up at the flat—she cooked eggs this mornin' in a blue kimono—Lord! how lucky I am! You must pace up some day, Ikey, and feed with us. I've got a job down near the bridge, and that's where I'm heading for now."

"The—the powder?" stammered Ikey.

"Oh, that stuff you gave me!" said Chunk, broadening his grin; "well, it was this way. I sat down at the supper table last night at Riddle's, and I looked at Rosy, and I says to myself, 'Chunk, if you get the girl get her on the square—don't try any hocus-pocus with a thoroughbred like her.' And I keeps the paper you give me in my pocket. And then my lamps falls on another party present, who, I says to myself, is failin' in a proper affection toward his comin' son-in-law, so I watches my chance and dumps that powder in old man Riddle's coffee—see?"

3

Mammon and the Archer

OLD Anthony Rockwall, retired manufacturer and proprietor of Rockwall's Eureka Soap, looked out the library window of his Fifth Avenue mansion and grinned. His neighbour to the right—the aristocratic clubman, G. Van Schuylight Suffolk-Jones—came out to his waiting motorcar, wrinkling a contumelious nostril, as usual, at the Italian renaissance sculpture of the soap palace's front elevation.

"Stuck-up old statuette of nothing doing!" commented the ex-Soap King. "The Eden Musee'll get that old frozen Nesselrode yet if he don't watch out. I'll have this house painted red, white, and blue next summer and see if that'll make his Dutch nose turn up any higher."

And then Anthony Rockwall, who never cared for bells, went to the door of his library and shouted "Mike!" in the same voice that had once chipped off pieces of the welkin on the Kansas prairies.

"Tell my son," said Anthony to the answering menial, "to come in here before he leaves the house."

When young Rockwall entered the library the old man laid aside his newspaper, looked at him with a kindly grimness on his big, smooth, ruddy countenance, rumpled his mop of white hair with one hand and rattled the keys in his pocket with the other.

"Richard," said Anthony Rockwall, "what do you pay for the soap that you use?"

Richard, only six months home from college, was startled a little. He had not yet taken the measure of this sire of his, who was as full of unexpectednesses as a girl at her first party.

"Six dollars a dozen, I think, dad."

"And your clothes?"

"I suppose about sixty dollars, as a rule."

"You're a gentleman," said Anthony decidedly. "I've heard of these young bloods spending $24 a dozen for soap, and going over the hundred mark for clothes. You've got as much money to waste as any of 'em, and yet you stick to what's decent and moderate. Now I use the old Eureka—not only for sentiment, but it's the purest soap made. Whenever you pay more than ten cents a cake for soap you buy bad perfumes and labels. But fifty cents is doing very well for a young man in your generation, position and condition. As I said, you're a gentleman. They say it takes three generations to make one. They're off. Money'll do it as slick as soap grease. It's made you one. By hokey! it's almost made one of me. I'm nearly as impolite and disagreeable and ill-mannered as these two old Knickerbocker gents on each side of me that can't sleep of nights because I bought in between 'em."

"There are some things that money can't accomplish," remarked young Rockwall rather gloomily.

"Now, don't say that," said old Anthony, shocked. "I bet my money on money every time. I've been through the encyclopædia down to Y looking for something you can't buy with it; and I expect to have to take up the appendix next week. I'm for money against the field. Tell me something money won't buy."

"For one thing," answered Richard, rankling a little, "it won't buy one into the exclusive circles of society."

"Oho! won't it?" thundered the champion of the root of evil. "You tell me where your exclusive circles would be if the first Astor hadn't had the money to pay for his steerage passage over?"

Richard sighed.

"And that's what I was coming to," said the old man less boisterously. "That's why I asked you to come in. There's something going wrong with you, boy. I've been noticing it for two weeks. Out with it. I guess I could lay my hands on eleven millions within twenty-four hours, besides the real estate. If it's your liver, there's the *Rambler* down in the bay, coaled, and ready to steam down to the Bahamas, in two days."

"Not a bad guess, dad; you haven't missed it far."

"Ah," said Anthony keenly; "what's her name?"

Richard began to walk up and down the library floor. There was enough comradeship and sympathy in this crude old father of his to draw his confidence.

"Why don't you ask her?" demanded old Anthony. "She'll jump at you. You've got the money and the looks, and you're a decent boy. Your hands are clean. You've got no Eureka soap on 'em. You've been to college, but she'll overlook that."

"I haven't had a chance," said Richard.

"Make one," said Anthony. "Take her for a walk in the park, or a straw ride, or walk home with her from church. Chance! Pshaw!"

"You don't know the social mill, dad. She's part of the stream that turns it. Every hour and minute of her time is arranged for days in advance. I must have that girl, dad, or this town is a blackjack swamp for evermore. And I can't write it—I can't do that."

"Tut!" said the old man. "Do you mean to tell me that with all the money I've got you can't get an hour or two of a girl's time for yourself?"

"I've put it off too late. She's going to sail for Europe at noon day after to-morrow for a two years' stay. I'm to see her alone to-morrow evening for a few minutes. She's at Larchmont now at her aunt's. I can't go there. But I'm allowed to meet her with a cab at the Grand Central Station to-morrow evening at the 8.30 train. We drive down Broadway to Wallack's at a gallop, where her mother and a box party will be waiting for us in the lobby. Do you think she would listen to a declaration from me during those six or eight minutes under those circumstances? No. And what chance would I have in the theatre or afterward? None. No, dad, this is one tangle that your money can't unravel. We can't buy one minute of time with cash; if we could, rich people would live longer. There's no hope of getting a talk with Miss Lantry before she sails."

"All right, Richard, my boy," said old Anthony cheerfully. "You may run along down to your club now. I'm glad it ain't your liver. But don't forget to burn a few punk sticks in the joss-house to the great god Mazuma from time to time. You say money won't buy time? Well, of course, you can't order eternity wrapped up and delivered at your residence for a price, but I've seen Father Time get pretty bad stone bruises on his heels when he walked through the gold diggings."

That night came Aunt Ellen, gentle, sentimental, wrinkled, sighing, oppressed by wealth, in to brother Anthony at his evening paper, and began discourse on the subject of lovers' woes.

"He told me all about it," said brother Anthony, yawning. "I told him my bank account was at his service. And then he began to knock money. Said money couldn't help. Said the rules of society couldn't be buckled for a yard by a team of ten millionaires."

"Oh, Anthony," sighed Aunt Ellen, "I wish you would not think so much of money. Wealth is nothing where a true affection is concerned. Love is all-powerful. If he only had spoken earlier! She could not have refused our Richard. But now I fear it is too late. He will have no opportunity to address her. All your gold cannot bring happiness to your son."

At eight o'clock the next evening Aunt Ellen took a quaint old gold ring from a moth-eaten case and gave it to Richard.

"Wear it to-night, nephew," she begged. "Your mother gave it to me. Good luck in love, she said it brought. She asked me to give it to you when you had found the one you loved."

Young Rockwall took the ring reverently and tried it on

his smallest finger. It slipped as far as the second joint and
stopped. He took it off and stuffed it into his vest pocket, after
the manner of man. And then he 'phoned for his cab.

At the station he captured Miss Lantry out of the gadding
mob at 8.32.

"We mustn't keep mamma and the others waiting," said
she.

"To Wallack's Theatre as fast as you can drive!" said
Richard loyally.

They whirled up Forty-second to Broadway, and then
down the white-starred lane that leads from the soft meadows
of sunset to the rocky hills of morning.

At Thirty-fourth Street young Richard quickly thrust up
the trap and ordered the cabman to stop.

"I've dropped a ring," he apologized, as he climbed out.
"It was my mother's, and I'd hate to lose it. I won't detain
you a minute—I saw where it fell."

In less than a minute he was back in the cab with the ring.

But within that minute a cross-town car had stopped
directly in front of the cab. The cabman tried to pass to the
left, but a heavy express wagon cut him off. He tried the right,
and had to back away from a furniture van that had no
business to be there. He tried to back out, but dropped his
reins and swore dutifully. He was blockaded in a tangled
mess of vehicles and horses.

One of those street blockades had occurred that sometimes
tie up commerce and movement quite suddenly in the big
city.

"Why don't you drive on?" said Miss Lantry impatiently.
"We'll be late."

Richard stood up in the cab and looked around. He saw
a congested flood of wagons, trucks, cabs, vans and street-
cars filling the vast space where Broadway, Sixth Avenue and
Thirty-fourth Street cross one another as a twenty-six-inch
maiden fills her twenty-two-inch girdle. And still from all
the cross-streets they were hurrying and rattling toward
the converging point at full speed, and hurling themselves

into the struggling mass, locking wheels and adding their drivers' imprecations to the clamour. The entire traffic of Manhattan seemed to have jammed itself around them. The oldest New Yorker among the thousands of spectators that lined the sidewalks had not witnessed a street blockade of the proportions of this one.

"I'm very sorry," said Richard, as he resumed his seat, "but it looks as if we are stuck. They won't get this jumble loosened up in an hour. It was my fault. If I hadn't dropped the ring we——"

"Let me see the ring," said Miss Lantry. "Now that it can't be helped, I don't care. I think theatres are stupid, anyway."

At eleven o'clock that night somebody tapped lightly on Anthony Rockwall's door.

"Come in," shouted Anthony, who was in a red dressing-gown, reading a book of piratical adventures.

Somebody was Aunt Ellen, looking like a grey-haired angel that had been left on earth by mistake.

"They're engaged, Anthony," she said softly. "She has promised to marry our Richard. On their way to the theatre there was a street blockade, and it was two hours before their cab could get out of it.

"And oh, brother Anthony, don't ever boast of the power of money again. A little emblem of true love—a little ring that symbolized unending and unmercenary affection—was the cause of our Richard finding his happiness. He dropped it in the street, and got out to recover it. And before they could continue the blockade occurred. He spoke to his love and won her there while the cab was hemmed in. Money is dross compared with true love, Anthony."

"All right," said old Anthony. "I'm glad the boy has got what he wanted. I told him I wouldn't spare any expense in the matter if——"

"But, brother Anthony, what good could your money have done?"

"Sister," said Anthony Rockwall, "I've got my pirate in a

devil of a scrape. His ship has just been scuttled, and he's too good a judge of the value of money to let drown. I wish you would let me go on with this chapter."

The story should end here. I wish it would as heartily as you who read it wish it did. But we must go to the bottom of the well for truth.

The next day a person with red hands and a blue polka-dot necktie, who called himself Kelly, called at Anthony Rockwall's house, and was at once received in the library.

"Well," said Anthony, reaching for his cheque-book, "it was a good bilin' of soap. Let's see—you had $5,000 in cash."

"I paid out $300 more of my own," said Kelly. "I had to go a little above the estimate. I got the express wagons and cabs mostly for $5; but the trucks and two-horse teams mostly raised me to $10. The motor-men wanted $10, and some of the loaded teams $20. The cops struck me hardest—$50 I paid two, and the rest $20 and $25. But didn't it work beautiful, Mr. Rockwall? I'm glad William A. Brady wasn't on to that little outdoor vehicle mob scene. I wouldn't want William to break his heart with jealousy. And never a rehearsal, either! The boys was on time to the fraction of a second. It was two hours before a snake could get below Greeley's statue."

"Thirteen hundred—there you are, Kelly," said Anthony, tearing off a cheque. "Your thousand, and the $300 you were out. You don't despise money, do you, Kelly?"

"Me?" said Kelly. "I can lick the man that invented poverty."

Anthony called Kelly when he was at the door.

"You didn't notice," said he, "anywhere in the tie-up, a kind of a fat boy without any clothes on shooting arrows around with a bow, did you?"

"Why, no," said Kelly, mystified. "I didn't. If he was like you say, maybe the cops pinched him before I got there."

"I thought the little rascal wouldn't be on hand," chuckled Anthony. "Good-bye, Kelly."

4

From the Cabby's Seat

THE cabby has his point of view. It is more single-minded, perhaps, than that of a follower of any other calling. From the high, swaying seat of his hansom he looks upon his fellow-men as nomadic particles, of no account except when possessed of migratory desires. He is Jehu, and you are goods in transit. Be you President or vagabond, to cabby you are only a fare. He takes you up, cracks his whip, joggles your vertebræ and sets you down.

When time for payment arrives, if you exhibit a familiarity with legal rates, you come to know what contempt is; if you find that you have left your pocket-book behind you, you are made to realize the mildness of Dante's imagination.

It is not an extravagant theory that the cabby's singleness of purpose and concentrated view of life are the results of the hansom's peculiar construction. The cock-of-the-roost sits aloft like Jupiter on an unsharable seat, holding your fate between two thongs of inconstant leather. Helpless, ridiculous, confined, bobbing like a toy mandarin, you sit like a rat in a trap—you, before whom butlers cringe on solid land—and must squeak upward through a slit in your peripatetic sarcophagus to make your feeble wishes known.

Then, in a cab, you are not even an occupant; you are contents. You are a cargo at sea, and the "cherub that sits up aloft" has Davy Jones's street and number by heart.

One night there were sounds of revelry in the big brick tenement-house next door but one to McGary's Family Café. The sounds seemed to emanate from the apartments of the Walsh family. The sidewalk was obstructed by an assortment of interested neighbours, who opened a lane from time to time for a hurrying messenger bearing from McGary's goods pertinent to festivity and diversion. The sidewalk contingent was engaged in comment and discussion from which it made no effort to eliminate the news that Norah Walsh was being married.

In the fullness of time there was an eruption of the merry-makers to the sidewalk. The uninvited guests enveloped and permeated them, and upon the night air rose joyous cries, congratulations, laughter and unclassified noises born of McGary's oblations to the hymeneal scene.

Close to the kerb stood Jerry O'Donovan's cab. Night-hawk was Jerry called; but no more lustrous or cleaner hansom than his ever closed its doors upon point lace and November violets. And Jerry's horse! I am within bounds when I tell you that he was stuffed with oats until one of those old ladies who leave their dishes unwashed at home and go about having expressmen arrested, would have smiled yes, smiled—to have seen him.

Among the shifting, sonorous, pulsing crowd glimpses could be had of Jerry's high hat, battered by the winds and rains of many years; of his nose like a carrot, battered by the frolicsome, athletic progeny of millionaires and by contuma-cious fares; of his brass-buttoned green coat, admired in the vicinity of McGary's. It was plain that Jerry had usurped the functions of his cab, and was carrying a "load". Indeed, the figure may be extended and he be likened to a bread-wagon if we admit the testimony of a youthful spectator, who was heard to remark "Jerry has got a bun".

From somewhere among the throng in the street or else out of the thin stream of pedestrians a young woman tripped and stood by the cab. The professional hawk's eye of Jerry caught the movement. He made a lurch for the cab, over-turning three or four onlookers and himself—no! he caught the cap of a water-plug and kept his feet. Like a sailor shinning up the ratlins during a squall, Jerry mounted to his professional seat. Once he was there McGary's liquids were baffled. He seesawed on the mizzen-mast of his craft as safe as a steeplejack rigged to the flagpole of a skyscraper.

"Step in, lady," said Jerry, gathering his lines.

The young woman stepped into the cab; the doors shut with a bang; Jerry's whip cracked in the air; the crowd in the gutter scattered, and the fine hansom dashed away 'cross-town.

When the oat-spry horse had hedged a little his first spurt of speed Jerry broke the lid of his cab and called down through the aperture in the voice of a cracked megaphone trying to please:

"Where, now, will ye be drivin' to?"

"Anywhere you please," came up the answer, musical and contented.

"'Tis drivin' for pleasure she is," thought Jerry. And then he suggested as a matter of course:

"Take a thrip around in the park, lady. 'Twill be ilegant cool and fine."

"Just as you like," answered the fare pleasantly.

The cab headed for Fifth Avenue and sped up that perfect street. Jerry bounced and swayed in his seat. The potent fluids of McGary were disquieted and they sent new fumes to his head. He sang an ancient song of Killisnook and brandished his whip like a baton.

Inside the cab the fare sat up straight on the cushions, looking to right and left at the lights and houses. Even in the shadowed hansom her eyes shone like stars at twilight.

When they reached Fifty-ninth Street Jerry's head was bobbing and his reins were slack. But his horse turned in through the park gate and began the old familiar, nocturnal round. And then the fare leaned back entranced, and breathed deep the clean, wholesome odours of grass and leaf and bloom. And the wise beast in the shafts, knowing his ground, struck into his by-the-hour gait and kept to the right of the road.

Habit also struggled successfully against Jerry's increasing torpor. He raised the hatch of his storm-tossed vessel and made the inquiry that cabbies do make in the park.

"Like shtop at the Cas-sino, lady? Gezzer r'freshm's, 'n lish'n the music. Ev'body shtops."

"I think that would be nice," said the fare.

They reined up with a plunge at the Casino entrance. The cab doors flew open. The fare stepped directly upon the floor. At once she was caught in a web of ravishing music and dazzled by a panorama of lights and colours. Someone slipped a little square card into her hand on which was printed a number—34. She looked around and saw her cab twenty yards already lining up in its place among the waiting mass of carriages, cabs and motor-cars. And then a man who seemed to be all shirt-front danced backward before her; and next she was seated at a little table by a railing over which climbed a jessamine vine.

There seemed to be a wordless invitation to purchase; she consulted a collection of small coins in a thin purse, and received from them licence to order a glass of beer. There she sat, inhaling and absorbing it all—the new-coloured, new-shaped life in a fairy palace in an enchanted wood.

At fifty tables sat princes and queens clad in all the silks and gems of the world. And now and then one of them would look curiously at Jerry's fare. They saw a plain figure dressed in a pink silk of the kind that is tempered by the word "foulard", and a plain face that wore a look of love of life that the queens envied.

Twice the long hands of the clocks went round. Royalties thinned from their *al fresco* thrones, and buzzed or clattered away in their vehicles of state. The music retired into cases of wood and bags of leather and baize. Waiters removed cloths pointedly near the plain figure sitting almost alone.

Jerry's fare rose, and held out her numbered card simply:

"Is there anything coming on the ticket?" she asked.

A waiter told her it was her cab check, and that she should give it to the man at the entrance. This man took it, and called the number. Only three hansoms stood in line. The driver of one of them went and routed out Jerry, asleep in his cab. He swore deeply, climbed to the captain's bridge and steered his craft to the pier. His fare entered, and the cab whirled into the cool fastnesses of the park along the shortest homeward cuts.

At the gate a glimmer of reason in the form of sudden suspicion seized upon Jerry's beclouded mind. One or two things occurred to him. He stopped his horse, raised the trap and dropped his phonographic voice, like a lead plummet, through the aperture:

"I want to see four dollars before goin' any further on th' thrip. Have ye got th' dough?"

"Four dollars!" laughed the fare softly, "dear me, no. I've only got a few pennies and a dime or two."

Jerry shut down the trap and slashed his oat-fed horse. The clatter of hoofs strangled but could not drown the sound of his profanity. He shouted choking and gurgling curses at the starry heavens; he cut viciously with his whip at passing vehicles; he scattered fierce and ever-changing oaths and imprecations along the streets, so that a late truck driver, crawling homeward, heard and was abashed. But he knew his recourse, and made for it at a gallop.

At the house with the green lights beside the steps he pulled up. He flung wide the cab doors and tumbled heavily to the ground.

"Come on, you," he said roughly.

His fare come forth with the Casino dreamy smile still on her plain face. Jerry took her by the arm and led her into the police station. A grey-moustached sergeant looked keenly across the desk. He and the cabby were no strangers.

"Sargeant," began Jerry in his old raucous, martyred, thunderous tones of complaint. "I've got a fare here that——"

Jerry paused. He drew a knotted, red hand across his brow. The fog set up by McGary was beginning to clear away.

"A fare, sargeant," he continued, with a grin, "that I want to inthroduce to ye. It's me wife that I married at ould

45

man Walsh's this avening. And a divil of a time we had, 'tis thrue. Shake hands wid th' sargeant, Norah, and we'll be off to home."

Before stepping into the cab Norah sighed profoundly.

"I've had such a nice time, Jerry," said she.

5

The Romance of a Busy Broker

PITCHER, confidential clerk in the office of Harvey Maxwell, broker, allowed a look of mild interest and surprise to visit his usually expressionless countenance when his employer briskly entered at half-past nine in company with his young lady stenographer. With a snappy "Good morning, Pitcher," Maxwell dashed at his desk as though he were intending to leap over it, and then plunged into the great heap of letters and telegrams waiting there for him.

The young lady had been Maxwell's stenographer for a year. She was beautiful in a way that was decidedly unstenographic. She forwent the pomp of the alluring pompadour. She wore no chains, bracelets or lockets. She had not the air of being about to accept an invitation to luncheon. Her dress was grey and plain, but it fitted her figure with fidelity and discretion. In her neat black turban hat was the gold-green wing of a macaw. On this morning she was softly and shyly radiant. Her eyes were dreamily bright, her cheeks genuine peachblow, her expression a happy one, tinged with reminiscence.

Pitcher, still mildly curious, noticed a difference in her ways this morning. Instead of going straight into the adjoining room, where her desk was, she lingered, slightly irresolute, in the outer office. Once she moved over by Maxwell's desk, near enough for him to be aware of her presence.

The machine sitting at that desk was no longer a man; it was a busy New York broker, moved by buzzing wheels and uncoiling springs.

"Well—what is it? Anything?" asked Maxwell sharply. His opened mail lay like a bank of stage snow on his crowded desk. His keen grey eye, impersonal and brusque, flashed upon her half impatiently.

"Nothing," answered the stenographer, moving away with a little smile.

"Mr. Pitcher," she said to the confidential clerk, "did Mr. Maxwell say anything yesterday about engaging another stenographer?"

"He did," answered Pitcher. "He told me to get another one. I notified the agency yesterday afternoon to send over a few samples this morning. It's nine forty-five o'clock, and not a single picture hat or piece of pineapple chewing gum has showed up yet."

"I will do the work as usual, then," said the young lady, "until someone comes to fill the place." And she went to her desk at once and hung the black turban hat with the gold-green macaw wing in its accustomed place.

He who has been denied the spectacle of a busy Manhattan broker during a rush of business is handicapped for the profession of anthropology. The poet sings of the "crowded hour of glorious life". The broker's hour is not only crowded, but the minutes and seconds are hanging to all the straps and packing both front and rear platforms.

And this day was Harvey Maxwell's busy day. The ticker began to reel out jerkily its fitful coils of tape, the desk telephone had a chronic attack of buzzing. Men began to throng into the office and call at him over the railing, jovially, sharply, viciously, excitedly. Messenger boys ran in and out with messages and telegrams. The clerks in the office jumped about like sailors during a storm. Even Pitcher's face relaxed into something resembling animation.

On the Exchange there were hurricanes and landslides and snowstorms and glaciers and volcanoes, and those elemental disturbances were reproduced in miniature in the broker's offices. Maxwell shoved his chair against the wall and transacted business after the manner of a toe-dancer. He jumped from ticker to 'phone, from desk to door with the trained agility of a harlequin.

In the midst of this growing and important stress the broker became suddenly aware of a high-rolled fringe of golden hair under a nodding canopy of velvet and ostrich tips, an imitation sealskin sacque and a string of beads as large as hickory nuts, ending near the floor with a silver heart. There was a self-possessed young lady connected with these accessories; and Pitcher was there to construe her.

"Lady from the Stenographer's Agency to see about the position," said Pitcher.

Maxwell turned half around, with his hands full of papers and ticker tape.

"What position?" he asked, with a frown.

"Position of stenographer," said Pitcher. "You told me yesterday to call them up and have one, sent over this morning."

"You are losing your mind, Pitcher," said Maxwell. "Why should I have given you any such instructions? Miss Leslie has given perfect satisfaction during the year she has been here. The place is hers as long as she chooses to retain it. There's no place open here, madam. Countermand that order with the agency, Pitcher, and don't bring any more of 'em in here."

The silver heart left the office, swinging and banging itself independently against the office furniture as it indignantly departed. Pitcher seized a moment to remark to the bookkeeper that the "old man" seemed to get more absent-minded and forgetful every day of the world.

The rush and pace of business grew fiercer and faster. On the floor they were pounding half a dozen stocks in which Maxwell's customers were heavy investors. Orders to buy and sell were coming and going as swift as the flight of swallows. Some of his own holdings were imperilled, and the man was working like some high-geared, delicate, strong machine—strung to full tension, going at full speed, accurate, never hesitating, with the proper word and decision and act ready and prompt as clockwork. Stocks and bonds, loans and mortgages, margins and securities—here was a world of finance, and there was no room in it for the human world or the world of nature.

When the luncheon hour drew near there came a slight lull in the uproar.

Maxwell stood by his desk with his hands full of telegrams and memoranda, with a fountain pen over his right ear and his hair hanging in disorderly strings over his forehead. His window was open, for the beloved janitress Spring had turned on a little warmth through the waking registers of the earth.

And through the window came a wandering—perhaps a lost—odour—a delicate, sweet odour of lilac that fixed the broker for a moment immovable. For this odour belonged to Miss Leslie; it was her own, and hers only.

The odour brought her vividly, almost tangibly before him. The world of finance dwindled suddenly to a speck. And she was in the next room—twenty steps away.

"By George, I'll do it now," said Maxwell, half aloud. "I'll ask her now. I wonder I didn't do it long ago."

He dashed into the inner office with the haste of a short trying to cover. He charged upon the desk of the stenographer.

She looked up at him with a smile. A soft pink crept over her cheek, and her eyes were kind and frank. Maxwell leaned one elbow on her desk. He still clutched fluttering papers with both hands and the pen was above his ear.

"Miss Leslie," he began hurriedly, "I have but a moment to spare. I want to say something in that moment. Will you be my wife? I haven't had time to make love to you in the ordinary way, but I really do love you. Talk quick, please— those fellows are clubbing the stuffing out of Union Pacific."

"Oh, what are you talking about?" exclaimed the young lady. She rose to her feet and gazed upon him, round-eyed.

"Don't you understand?" said Maxwell restively. "I want you to marry me. I love you, Miss Leslie. I wanted to tell you, and I snatched a minute when things had slackened up a bit. They're calling me for the 'phone now. Tell 'em to wait a minute, Pitcher. Won't you, Miss Leslie?"

The stenographer acted very queerly. At first she seemed overcome with amazement; then tears flowed from her wondering eyes; and then she smiled sunnily through them, and one of her arms slid tenderly about the broker's neck.

"I know now," she said softly. "It's this old business that has driven everything else out of your head for the time. I was frightened at first. Don't you remember, Harvey? We were married last evening at eight o'clock in the Little Church Around the Corner."

6

The Ransom of Red Chief

IT looked like a good thing: but wait till I tell you. We
were down in South, in Alabama—Bill Driscoll and
myself—when this kidnapping idea struck us. It was, as
Bill afterward expressed it, "during a moment of temporary mental apparition"; but we didn't find that out till
later.

There was a town down there, as flat as a flannel-cake,
and called Summit, of course. It contained inhabitants of as
undeleterious and self-satisfied a class of peasantry as ever
clustered around a Maypole.

Bill and me had a joint capital of about six hundred
dollars, and we needed just two thousand dollars more to
pull off a fraudulent town-lot scheme in Western Illinois with.
We talked it over on the front steps of the hotel. Philo-
progenitiveness, says we, is strong in semi-rural communities;
therefore, and for other reasons, a kidnapping project ought
to do better there than in the radius of newspapers that send
reporters out in plain clothes to stir up talk about such things.
We knew that Summit couldn't get after us with anything
stronger than constables and, maybe, some lackadaisical
bloodhounds and a diatribe or two in the *Weekly Farmers'
Budget*. So, it looked good.

We selected for our victim the only child of a prominent
citizen named Ebenezer Dorset. The father was respectable
and tight, a mortgage fancier and a stern, upright collection-
plate passer and forecloser. The kid was a boy of ten, with
bas-relief freckles, and hair the colour of the cover of the
magazine you buy at the news-stand when you want to
catch a train. Bill and me figured that Ebenezer would melt

down for a ransom of two thousand dollars to a cent. But wait till I tell you.

About two miles from Summit was a little mountain, covered with a dense cedar brake. On the rear elevation of this mountain was a cave. There we stored provisions.

One evening after sundown, we drove in a buggy past old Dorset's house. The kid was in the street, throwing rocks at a kitten on the opposite fence.

"Hey, little boy!" says Bill, "would you like to have a bag of candy and a nice ride?"

The boy catches Bill neatly in the eye with a piece of brick.

"That will cost the old man an extra five hundred dollars," says Bill, climbing over the wheel.

That boy put up a fight like a welter-weight cinnamon bear; but at last, we got him down in the bottom of the buggy and drove away. We took him up to the cave, and I hitched the horse in the cedar break. After dark I drove the buggy to the little village, three miles away, where we had hired it, and walked back to the mountain.

Bill was pasting court-plaster over the scratches and bruises on his features. There was a fire burning behind the big rock at the entrance of the cave, and the boy was watching a pot of boiling coffee, with two buzzard tailfeathers stuck in his red hair. He points a stick at me when I come up, and says:

"Ha! cursed paleface, do you dare to enter the camp of Red Chief, the terror of the plains?"

"He's all right now," says Bill, rolling up his trousers and examining some bruises on his shins. "We're playing Indian. We're making Buffalo Bill's show look like magic-lantern views of Palestine in the town hall. I'm Old Hank, the Trapper, Red Chief's captive, and I'm to be scalped at daybreak. By Geronimo! that kid can kick hard."

Yes, sir, that boy seemed to be having the time of his life. The fun of camping out in a cave had made him forget that he was a captive himself. He immediately christened me

Snake-eye, the Spy, and announced that, when his braves returned from the warpath, I was to be broiled at the stake at the rising of the sun.

Then we had supper; and he filled his mouth full of bacon and bread and gravy, and began to talk. He made a during-dinner speech something like this;

"I like this fine. I never camped out before; but I had a pet 'possum once, and I was nine last birthday. I hate to go to school. Rats ate up sixteen of Jimmy Talbot's aunt's speckled hen's eggs. Are there any real Indians in these woods? I want some more gravy. Does the trees moving make the wind blow? We had five puppies. What makes your nose so red, Hank? My father has lots of money. Are the stars hot? I whipped Ed Walker twice, Saturday. I don't like girls. You dassent catch toads unless with a string. Do oxen make any noise? Why are oranges round? Have you got beds to sleep on in this cave? Amos Murray has got six toes. A parrot can talk, but a monkey or a fish can't. How many does it take to make twelve?"

Every few minutes he would remember that he was a pesky redskin, and pick up his stick rifle and tiptoe to the mouth of the cave to rubber for the scouts of the hated paleface. Now and then he would let out a war-whoop that made Old Hank the Trapper shiver. That boy had Bill terrorized from the start.

"Red Chief," says I to the kid, "would you like to go home?"

"Aw, what for?" says he. "I don't have any fun at home. I hate to go to school. I like to camp out. You won't take me back home again, Snake-eye, will you?"

"Not right away," says I. "We'll stay here in the cave a while."

"All right!" says he. "That'll be fine. I never had such fun in all my life."

We went to bed about eleven o'clock. We spread down some wide blankets and quilts and put Red Chief between us. We weren't afraid he'd run away. He kept us awake for three hours, jumping up and reaching for his rifle and screeching, "Hist! pard," in mine and Bill's ears, as the fancied crackle of a twig or the rustle of a leaf revealed to his young imagination the stealthy approach of the outlaw band. At last, I fell into a troubled sleep, and dreamed that I had been kidnapped and chained to a tree by a ferocious pirate with red hair.

Just at daybreak, I was awakened by a series of awful screams from Bill. They weren't yells, or howls, or shouts, or whoops, or yawps, such as you'd expect from a manly set of vocal organs—they were simply indecent, terrifying, humiliating screams, such as women emit when they see ghosts or caterpillars. It's an awful thing to hear a strong, desperate, fat man scream incontinently in a cave at daybreak.

I jumped up to see what the matter was. Red Chief was sitting on Bill's chest, with one hand twined in Bill's hair. In the other he had the sharp case-knife we used for slicing bacon; and he was industriously and realistically trying to take Bill's scalp, according to the sentence that had been pronounced upon him the evening before.

I got the knife away from the kid and made him lie down again. But, from that moment, Bill's spirit was broken. He laid down on his side of the bed, but he never closed an eye again in sleep as long as that boy was with us. I dozed off for a while, but along toward sun-up I remembered that Red Chief had said I was to be burned at the stake at the rising of the sun. I wasn't nervous or afraid; but I sat up and lit my pipe and leaned against a rock.

"What you getting up so soon for, Sam?" asked Bill.

"Me?" says I. "Oh, I got a kind of pain in my shoulder. I thought sitting up would rest it."

"You're a liar!" says Bill. "You're afraid. You was to be burned at sunrise, and you was afraid he'd do it. And he would, too, if he could find a match. Ain't it awful, Sam? Do you think anybody will pay out money to get a little imp like that back home?"

"Sure," said I. "A rowdy kid like that is just the kind that parents dote on. Now, you and the Chief get up and cook breakfast, while I go up on the top of this mountain and reconnoitre."

I went up on the peak of the little mountain and ran my eye over the contiguous vicinity. Over toward Summit I expected to see the sturdy yeomanry of the village armed with scythes and pitchforks beating the country-side for the dastardly kidnappers. But what I saw was a peaceful landscape dotted with one man ploughing with a dun mule. Nobody was dragging the creek; no couriers dashed hither and yon, bringing tidings of no news to the distracted parents. There was a sylvan attitude of somnolent sleepiness pervading that section of the external outward surface of Alabama that lay exposed to my view. "Perhaps," says I to myself, "it has not yet been discovered that the wolves have borne away the tender lambkin from the fold. Heaven help the wolves!" says I, and I went down the mountain to breakfast.

When I got to the cave I found Bill backed up against the side of it, breathing hard, and the boy threatening to smash him with a rock half as big as a coconut.

"He put a red-hot boiled potato down my back," explained Bill, "and then mashed it with his foot; and I boxed his ears. Have you got a gun about you, Sam?"

I took the rock away from the boy and kind of patched up the argument. "I'll fix you," says the kid to Bill. "No man ever yet struck the Red Chief but what he got paid for it. You better beware!"

After breakfast the kid takes a piece of leather with strings wrapped around it out of his pocket and goes outside the cave unwinding it.

"What's he up to now?" says Bill anxiously. "You don't think he'll run away, do you Sam?"

"No fear of it," says I. "He don't seem to be much of a home body .But we've got to fix up some plan about the ransom. There don't seem to be much excitement around Summit on account of his disappearance; but maybe they haven't realized yet that he's gone. His folks may think he's

THE RANSOM OF RED CHIEF

spending the night with Aunt Jane or one of the neighbours. Anyhow, he'll be missed to-day. To-night we must get a message to his father demanding the two thousand dollars for his return."

Just then we heard a kind of war-whoop, such as David might have emitted when he knocked out the champion Goliath. It was a sling that Red Chief had pulled out of his pocket, and he was whirling it around his head.

I dodged, and heard a heavy thud and a kind of a sigh from Bill, like a horse gives out when you take his saddle off. A niggerhead rock the size of an egg had caught Bill just behind his left ear. He loosened himself all over and fell in the fire across the frying-pan of hot water for washing the dishes. I dragged him out and poured cold water on his head for half an hour.

By and by, Bill sits up and feels behind his ear and says: "Sam, do you know who my favourite Biblical character is?"

"Take it easy," says I. "You'll come to your senses presently."

"King Herod," says he. "You won't go away and leave me here alone, will you, Sam?"

I went out and caught that boy and shook him until his freckles rattled.

"If you don't behave," says I, "I'll take you straight home. Now, are you going to be good, or not?"

"I was only funning," says he sullenly. "I didn't mean to hurt Old Hank. But what did he hit me for? I'll behave, Snake-eye, if you won't send me home, and if you'll let me play the Black Scout to-day."

"I don't know the game," says I. "That's for you and Mr. Bill to decide. He's your playmate for the day. I'm going away for a while, on business. Now, you come in and make friends with him, and say you are sorry for hurting him, or home you go, at once."

I made him and Bill shake hands, and then I took Bill aside and told him I was going to Poplar Cove, a little village three miles from the cave, and find out what I could about how the kidnapping had been regarded in Summit. Also, I thought it best to send a peremptory letter to old man Dorset that day, demanding the ransom and dictating how it should be paid.

"You know, Sam," says Bill, "I've stood by you without batting an eye in earthquakes, fire and flood—in poker games, dynamite outrages, police raids, train robberies and cyclones. I never lost my nerve yet till we kidnapped that two-legged skyrocket of a kid. He's got me going. You won't leave me long with him, will you, Sam?"

"I'll be back some time this afternoon," says I. "You must keep the boy amused and quiet till I return. And now we'll write the letter to old Dorset."

Bill and I got paper and pencil and worked on the letter while Red Chief, with a blanket wrapped around him, strutted up and down, guarding the mouth of the cave. Bill begged me tearfully to make the ransom fifteen hundred dollars instead of two thousand. "I ain't attempting," says he, "to decry the celebrated moral aspect of parental affection, but we're dealing with humans, and it ain't human for anybody to give up two thousand dollars for that forty-pound chunk of freckled wildcat. I'm willing to take a chance at fifteen hundred dollars. You can charge the difference up to me."

So, to relieve Bill, I acceded, and we collaborated a letter that ran this way:

EBENEZER DORSET, ESQ.:

We have your boy concealed in a place far from Summit. It is useless for you or the most skilful detectives to attempt to find him. Absolutely the only terms on which you can have him restored to you are these: We demand fifteen-hundred dollars in large bills for his return; the money to be left at midnight to-night at the same spot and in the same box as your reply—as hereinafter described. If you agree to these terms, send your answer in writing by a solitary messenger to-night at half-past eight o'clock. After crossing Owl Creek, on the road to Poplar Cove, there are three large trees about a hundred yards apart, close to the fence of the wheat-field on the right-hand side. At the bottom of the fence-post, opposite the third tree, will be found a small pasteboard box.

The messenger will place the answer in this box and return immediately to Summit.

If you attempt any treachery or fail to comply with our demand as stated, you will never see your boy again.

If you pay the money as demanded, he will be returned to you safe and well within three hours. These terms are final, and if you do not accede to them no further communication will be attempted.

TWO DESPERATE MEN.

I addressed this letter to Dorset, and put it in my pocket. As I was about to start, the kid comes up to me and says: "Aw, Snake-eye, you said I could play the Black Scout while you was gone."

"Play it, of course," says I. "Mr. Bill will play with you. What kind of a game is it?"

"I'm the Black Scout," says Red Chief, "and I have to ride to the stockade to warn the settlers that the Indians are coming. I'm tired of playing Indian myself. I want to be the Black Scout."

"All right," says I. "It sounds harmless to me. I guess Mr. Bill will help you foil the pesky savages."

"What am I to do?" asks Bill, looking at the kid suspiciously.

"You are the hoss," says Black Scout. "Get down on your hands and knees. How can I ride to the stockade without a hoss?"

"You'd better keep him interested," said I, "till we get the scheme going. Loosen up."

Bill gets down on his all fours, and a look comes in his eye like a rabbit's when you catch it in a trap.

"How far is it to the stockade, kid?" he asks in a husky manner of voice.

"Ninety miles," says the Black Scout. "And you have to hump yourself to get there on time. Whoa, now!"

The Black Scout jumps on Bill's back and digs his heels in his side.

"For Heaven's sake," says Bill, "hurry back, Sam, as soon as you can. I wish we hadn't made the ransom more than a thousand. Say, you quit kicking me or I'll get up and warm you good."

I walked over to Poplar Cove and sat around the post office and store, talking with the chaw-bacons that came in to trade. One whiskerando says that he hears Summit is all upset on account of Elder Ebenezer Dorset's boy having been lost or stolen. That was all I wanted to know. I bought some smoking tobacco, referred casually to the price of black-eyed peas, posted my letter surreptitiously and came away. The postmaster said the mail-carrier would come by in an hour to take the mail on to Summit.

When I got back to the cave Bill and the boy were not to be found. I explored the vicinity of the cave, and risked a yodel or two, but there was no response.

So I lighted my pipe and sat down on a mossy bank to await developments.

In about half an hour I heard the bushes rustle, and Bill wabbled out into the little glade in front of the cave. Behind him was the kid stepping softly like a scout, with a broad grin on his face. Bill stopped, took off his hat and wiped his face with a red handkerchief. The kid stopped about eight feet behind him.

"Sam," says Bill, "I suppose you'll think I'm a renegade, but I couldn't help it. I'm a grown person with masculine proclivities and habits of self-defence, but there is a time when all systems of egotism and predominance fail. The boy is gone. I have sent him home. All is off. There was martyrs in old times," goes on Bill, "that suffered death rather than give up the particular graft they enjoyed. None of 'em ever was subjugated to such supernatural tortures as I have been. I tried to be faithful to our articles of depredation; but there came a limit."

"What's the trouble, Bill?" I asks him.

"I was rode," says Bill, "the ninety miles to the stockade, not barring an inch. Then, when the settler was rescued, I was given oats. Sand ain't a palatable substitute. And then, for an hour I had to try to explain to him why there was nothin' in holes, how a road can run both ways and what makes the grass green. I tell you, Sam, a human can only stand so much. I takes him by the neck of his clothes and drags him down the mountain. On the way he kicks my legs black-and-blue from the knees down; and I've got to have two or three bites on my thumb and hand cauterized.

"But he's gone"—continues Bill—"gone home. I showed him the road to Summit and kicked him about eight feet nearer there at one kick. I'm sorry we lose the ransom; but it was either that or Bill Driscoll to the madhouse."

Bill is puffing and blowing, but there is a look of ineffable peace and growing content on his rose-pink features.

"Bill," says I, "there isn't any heart disease in your family, is there?"

"No," says Bill, "nothing chronic except malaria and accidents. Why?"

"Then you might turn around," says I, "and have a look behind you."

Bill turns and sees the boy and loses his complexion and sits down plump on the ground and begins to pluck aimlessly at grass and little sticks. For an hour I was afraid of his mind. And then I told him that my scheme was to put the whole job through immediately and that we would get the ransom and be off with it by midnight if old Dorset fell in with our proposition. So Bill braced up enough to give the kid a weak sort of a smile and a promise to play the Russian in a Japanese war with him as soon as he felt a little better.

I had a scheme for collecting that ransom without danger of being caught by counterplots that ought to commend itself to professional kidnappers. The tree under which the answer was to be left—and the money later on—was close to the road fence with big, bare fields on all sides. If a gang of constables should be watching for anyone to come for the note they could see him a long way off crossing the fields or in the road. But no, sirree! At half-past eight I was up in that tree as well hidden as a tree toad, waiting for the messenger to arrive.

Exactly on time, a half-grown boy rides up the road on a bicycle, locates the pasteboard box at the foot of the fence-post, slips a folded piece of paper into it and pedals away again back toward Summit.

I waited an hour and then concluded the thing was square. I slid down the tree, got the note, slipped along the fence till I struck the woods, and was back at the cave in another half an hour. I opened the note, got near the lantern and read it to Bill. It was written with a pen in a crabbed hand, and the sum and substance of it was this:

Two Desperate Men.

Gentlemen—I received your letter to-day by post, in regard to the ransom you ask for the return of my son. I think you are a little high in your demands, and I hereby make you a counter-proposition, which I am inclined to believe you will accept. You bring Johnny home and pay me two hundred and fifty dollars in cash, and I agree to take him off your hands. You had better come at night, for the neighbours believe he is lost, and I couldn't be responsible for what they would do to anybody they saw bringing him back.

Very respectfully,
Ebenezer Dorset.

"Great pirates of Penzance!" says I; "of all the impudent——"

But I glanced at Bill, and hesitated. He had the most appealing look in his eyes I ever saw on the face of a dumb or a talking brute.

"Sam," says he, "what's two hundred and fifty dollars,

after all? We've got the money. One more night of this kid will send me to a bed in Bedlam. Besides being a thorough gentleman, I think Mr. Dorset is a spendthrift for making us such a liberal offer. You ain't going to let the chance go, are you?"

"Tell you the truth, Bill," says I, "this little ewe lamb has somewhat got on my nerves too. We'll take him home, pay the ransom and make our get-away."

We took him home that night. We got him to go by telling him that his father had bought a silver-mounted rifle and a pair of moccasins for him, and we were going to hunt bears the next day.

It was just twelve o'clock when we knocked at Ebenezer's front door. Just at the moment when I should have been abstracting the fifteen hundred dollars from the box under the tree, according to the original proposition, Bill was counting out two hundred and fifty dollars into Dorset's hand.

When the kid found out we were going to leave him at home he started up a howl like a calliope and fastened himself as tight as a leech to Bill's leg. His father peeled him away gradually, like a porous plaster.

"How long can you hold him?" asks Bill.

"I'm not as strong as I used to be," says old Dorset, "but I think I can promise you ten minutes."

"Enough," says Bill. "In ten minutes I shall cross the Central, Southern and Middle Western States, and be legging it trippingly for the Canadian border."

And, as dark as it was, and as fat as Bill was, and as good a runner as I am, he was a good mile and a half out of Summit before I could catch up with him.

7

The Barber Talks

THE Post Man slid into the chair with an apologetic manner, for the barber's gaze was superior and scornful. He was so devilish, cool and self-possessed, and held the public in such infinite contempt.

The Post Man's hair had been cut close with the clippers on the day before.

"Haircut?" asked the barber in a quiet but thoroughly dangerous tone.

"Shave," said the Post Man.

The barber raised his eyebrows, gave his victim a look of deep disdain, and hurled the chair with a loud rattle and crash back to a reclining position.

Then he seized a mug and brush and, after bestowing upon the Post Man a look of undying contumely, turned with a sneer to the water faucet. Thence he returned, enveloped the passive victim in a voluminous cloth, and with a pitiless hand daubed a great brushful of sweetish-tasting lather across his mouth.

Then he began to talk.

"Ever been in Seattle, Washington Territory?" he asked.

"Blub-a-lub-blub," said the Post Man, struggling against the soap, and then he shook his head feebly.

"Neither have I," said the barber, "but I have a brother named Bill who runs an orange orchard nine miles from St. John, Fla. That's only a split hair on your neck; it's growing the wrong way. They are caused by shaving the neck in the wrong direction. Sometimes whisky will make them go that way. Whisky is a terrible thing. Do you drink it?"

The Post Man only had one eye of all his features uncovered

by lather and he tried to throw an appealing expression implying negation into this optic, but the barber was too quick for him and filled the eye with soap by a dextrous flap of his brush.

"My brother Bill used to drink," continued the barber. "He could drink more whisky than any man in Houston, but he never got drunk. He had a chair in my shop, but I had to let him go. Bill had a wonderful constitution. When he got all he could hold he would quit drinking. The only way he showed it was in his eyes. They would get kind of glazed and fishy and wouldn't turn in his head. When Bill wanted to look to one side he used to take his fingers and turn his eyeballs a little the way he wanted to see. His eyes looked exactly like those little round windows you see in the dome of the post office. You could hear Bill breathe across the street when he was full. He could shave people when he was drunk as well as he could sober.—Razor hurt you?"

The Post Man tried to wave one of his hands to disclaim any sense of pain, but the barber's quick eye caught the motion and he leaned his weight against the hand, crushing it against the chair.

"I kept noticing," went on the barber, "that Bill was getting about four customers to my one, even if he did drink so much. People would come in three or four at a time and sit down and wait their turns with Bill when my chair was vacant. I didn't know what to make of it. Bill had all he could do, and he was so crowded that he didn't have time to go out to a saloon, but he kept a big jug in the back room, and every few minutes he would slip in there and take a drink.

"One day I noticed a man that got out of Bill's chair acting queer, and he staggered as he went out. A day or two afterwards the shop was full of customers from morning till night, and one man came back and had a shave three different times in the forenoon. In a couple of days more there was a crowd of men in the shop, and they had a line formed outside two or three doors down the sidewalk. Bill made $9.00 that day. That evening a policeman came in and jerked me up for running a saloon without a licence. It seems that Bill's breath was so full of whisky that every man he shaved went out feeling pretty hilarious and sent his friends there to be shaved. It cost me $300 to get out of it, and I shipped Bill to Florida pretty soon afterward."

*   *   *

"I was sent for once," went on the barber, as he seized his victim by the ear and slammed his head over on the other side, "to go out on Piney street and shave a dead man. Barbers don't much like a job of that kind, although they get from $5 to $10 for the work. It was 1908 Piney street. I started about eleven o'clock at night. I found the street all right and I counted from the corner until I found 1908. I had my razors, soap and mug in a little case I use for such purposes. I went in and knocked at the door. An old man opened it and his eye fell on my case.

"'You've come, have you?' he asked. 'Well, go up stairs; he's in the front room to your right. There's nobody with him. He hasn't any friends or relatives in town; he's only been boarding here about a week.'

"'How long since he—since it occurred?' I asked.

"'About an hour, I guess,' says the old man. I was glad of that because corpses always shave better before they get good and cold. I went in the room and turned up the lamp. The man was laid out on the bed. He was warm yet and he had about a week's growth of beard on. I got to work and in half an hour I had given him a nice clean shave that would have done his heart good if he had been alive. Then I went down stairs and saw the old man.

"'What success?' he asked.

"'Good,' says I. 'He's fixed up all right. Who's to pay?'

"'He gave me $30 to send his folks in Alabama yesterday,' says the old man. 'I guess your fee will have to come out of it.'

"'It'll be five,' I said.

"The old man handed me a five-dollar bill and I went home very well satisfied."

Here the barber seized the chair, hurled it upright, snatched off the cloth, buried his hands in the Post Man's hair and tore out a handful, bumped and thumped his head, shook it violently and hissed sarcastically:

"Bay rum?"

The Post Man nodded stupidly, closed his eyes and tried unsuccessfully to recall a prayer.

"Next day," said the barber, "I heard some news. It seems that a man had died at 1908 Piney street and just a little while before a man in the next house had taken poison. The folks in one house sent for a doctor and the ones in the other sent for a barber. The funny part is the doctor and I both made a mistake and got into the wrong house. He went in to see the dead man and found the family doctor just getting ready to leave. The doctor didn't waste any time asking questions, but got out his stomach pump, stuck it into the dead man and went to work pumping the poison out. All this time I was busy shaving the man who had taken poison. And the funniest part of it all is that after the doctor had pumped all the other doctor's medicine out of the dead man, he opened his eyes, raised up in bed and asked for a steak and potatoes.

"This made the family doctor mad, and he and the doctor with a stomach pump got into a fight and fell down the stairs and broke the hat rack all to pieces."

"And how about your man who had taken poison?" asked the Post Man timidly.

"Him?" said the barber, "why, he died, of course, but he died with one of the beautifulest shaves that ever a man had. —Brush!"

An African of terrible aspect bore down upon the Post Man, struck him violently with the stub of a whisk broom, seized his coat at the back and ripped it loose from its collar.

"Call again," growled the barber in a voice of the deepest menace, as the scribe made a rush for the door and escaped.

8

Barber Shop Adventure

WHEN the Post Man entered the shop yesterday the chairs were full of customers, and for a brief moment he felt a thrill of hope that he might escape, but the barber's eye, deadly and gloomy, fixed itself upon him.

"You're next," he said, with a look of diabolical malevolence, and the Post Man sank into a hard chair nailed to the wall, with a feeling of hopeless despair.

In a few moments there was a rattle and a bang, the customer in the chair was thrown violently on his feet, and fled out of the shop pursued by the African who was making vicious dabs at him with a whisk broom full of tacks and splinters.

The Post Man took a long look at the sunlight, pinned a little note to his tie with his scarf pin, giving his address, in case the worst should happen, and settled into the chair.

He informed the barber, in answer to a stern inquiry, that he did not want his hair cut, and in turn received a look of cold incredulity and contempt.

The chair was hurled to a reclining position, the lather was mixed, and as the deadly brush successively stopped all sense of hearing, sight and smell, the Post Man sank into a state of collapse, from which he was aroused by the loud noise of a steel instrument with which the barber was scraping off the lather and wiping it on the Post Man's shirt sleeve.

*   *   *

"Everybody's riding bicycles now," said the barber, "and it's going to be very difficult for the fashionable people to keep it an exclusive exercise. You see, you can't prevent anybody from riding a bicycle that wants to, and the streets are free for every one. I don't see any harm in the sport, myself, and it's getting more popular every day. After a while, riding will become so general that a lady on a wheel will not create any more notice than she would walking. It's good exercise for the ladies, and that makes up for their looking like a bag full of fighting cats slung over a clothes line when they ride.

"But the pains they do take to make themselves mannish! Why can't a lady go in for athletics without trying to look and dress tough? If I should tell you what one of them did the other day you wouldn't believe it."

The barber here glared so fiercely at the Post Man that he struggled up to the top of the lather by a superhuman effort and assured the artist that anything he said would be received with implicit faith.

"I was sent for," continued the barber, "to go up on McKinney Avenue and was to bring my razor and shaving outfit. I went up and found the house.

"A good-looking young lady was riding a bicycle up and down in front of the gate. She had on a short skirt, leggings, and a sack coat, cut like a man's.

"I went in and knocked and they showed me into a side room. In a few minutes the young lady came in, sat down on a chair and an old lady whom I took to be her ma dropped in.

"'Shave,' said the young lady. 'Twice over, and be in a hurry; I've an engagement.'

"I was nearly knocked down with surprise, but I managed to get my outfit in shape. It was evident that that young lady ruled the house. The old lady said to me in a whisper that her daughter was one of the leaders among the girls who believed in the emancipation of women, and she had resolved to raise a moustache and thus get ahead of her young lady companions.

"The young lady leaned back in the chair and closed her eyes.

"I dipped my brush in the lather and ran it across her upper lip. As soon as I did so she sprang to her feet, her eyes flashing with rage.

"'How dare you insult me!' she stormed, looking as if she would like to eat me up. 'Leave the house, immediately,' she went on.

"I was dumbfounded. I thought perhaps she was a trifle flighty, so I put up my utensils and started for the door. When I got there, I recovered my presence of mind enough to say:

"'Miss, I am sure I have done nothing to offend you. I always try to act a gentleman whenever it is convenient. In what way have I insulted you?'

"'Take your departure,' she said angrily. 'I guess I know when a man kisses me.'

"And so I left. Now, what do you think of that?" asked the barber, as he pushed about an ounce of soap into the Post Man's mouth with his thumb.

"I think that's a pretty tough story to believe," said the Post Man, summoning up his courage.

The barber stopped shaving and bent a gaze of such malignant and cool ferocity upon his victim that the Post Man hastened to say:

"But no doubt it occurred as you have stated."

"It did," said the barber. "I don't ask you to take my word for it. I can prove it. Do you see that blue mug on the shelf, the third from the right? Well, that's the mug I carried with me that day. I guess you'll believe it now."

"Speaking of bald heads," went on the barber, although no one had said a word about bald heads, "reminds me of how a man worked a game on me once right here in Houston. You know there's nothing in the world that will make hair grow on a bald head. Lots of things are sold for that purpose, but if the roots are dead nothing can bring them to life. A man came into my shop one day last fall and had a shave. His head was as bald and smooth as a tea cup. All the tonics in the world couldn't have started one hair growing there. The

70

man was a stranger to me, but said he ran a truck garden out on the edge of town. He came in about three times and got shaved and then he struck me to fix him up something to make his hair grow."

The barber here reached back upon a shelf and got a strip of sticking plaster. Then he cut a gash along the Post Man's chin and stuck the plaster over it.

"When a man asks for a hair tonic," continued the barber, "in a barber shop he always gets it. You can fix up a mixture that a man may use on his head for a long time before he finds it is doing him no good. In the meantime he continues to shave in your shop.

"I told my customer that I had invented a hair tonic that if its use were persisted in would certainly cause the hair to grow on the smoothest head. I sat down and wrote him out a formula and told him to have it prepared at a drug store and not to give away the information, as I intended after a while to have it patented and sell it on a large scale. The recipe contained a lot of harmless stuff, some salts of tartar, oil of almonds, bay rum, rose water, tincture of myrrh and some other ingredients. I wrote them down at random just as they came into my head, and half an hour afterwards I couldn't have told what it was composed of myself. The man took it, paid me a dollar for the formula and went off to get it filled at a drug store.

"He came back twice that week to get shaved, and he said he was using it faithfully. Then he didn't come any more for about two weeks. He dropped in one afternoon and hung his hat up, and it nearly knocked me down when I saw the finest kind of a suit of hair had started on his head. It was growing splendidly, and only two weeks before his head had been as bald as a door knob.

"He said he was awfully pleased with my tonic, and well he might be. While I was shaving him I tried to think what the ingredients were that I had written down for him to use, but I couldn't remember the quantities or half the things I had used. I knew that I had accidentally struck upon a tonic

71

that would make the hair grow, and I knew furthermore that that formula was worth a million dollars to any man if it would do the work. Making hair grow on bald heads, if it could be done, would be better than any gold mine ever worked. I made up my mind to have that formula. When he was about to start away I said carelessly:

" 'By the way, Mr. Plunket, I have mislaid my memorandum book that has the formula of my tonic in it and I want to have a bottle or two prepared this morning. If you have the one I gave you I'd like to make a copy of it while you are here.'

"I must have looked too anxious, for he looked at me for a few minutes and then broke out into a laugh.

" 'By Jiminy,' he said, 'I don't believe you've got a copy of it anywheres. I believe you just happened to hit on the right thing and you don't remember what it was. I ain't half as green as I took. That hair grower is worth a fortune, and a big one, too. I think I'll just keep my recipe and get somebody to put the stuff up and sell it.'

"He started out, and I called him into the back room and talked to him half an hour.

"I finally made a trade with him and bought the formula back for $250 cash. I went up to the bank and got the money which I had there saving up to build a house. He then gave me back the recipe I had given him and signed a paper relinquishing all rights to it. He also agreed to sign a testimonial about the stuff having made his hair grow out in two weeks."

The barber began to look gloomy and ran his fingers inside the Post Man's shirt collar, tearing out the button hole, and the collar button flew out the door across the sidewalk into the gutter.

"I went to work next day," said the barber, "and filed application at Washington for a patent on my tonic and arranged with a big drug firm in Houston to put it on the market for me. I had a million dollars in sight. I fixed up a room where I mixed the tonic—for I wouldn't let the druggists or anybody else know what was in it—and then the druggists bottled and labelled it.

"I quit working in the shop and put all my time into my tonic.

"Mr. Plunket came into the shop once or twice within the next two weeks and his hair was still growing finely. Pretty soon I had about $200 worth of the tonic ready for the market, and Mr. Plunket was to come in town on Saturday and give me his testimonial to print on advertising dodgers and circulars with which I was going to flood the country.

"I was waiting in the room where I mixed my tonic about eleven o'clock Saturday when the door opened and Mr. Plunket came in. He was very much excited and very angry.

"'Look here,' he cried, 'what's the matter with your infernal stuff?'

"He pulled off his hat, and his head was as shiny and bare as a china egg.

"'It all came out,' he said roughly. 'It was growing all right until yesterday morning, when it commenced to fall out, and this morning there wasn't a hair left.'

"I examined his head and there wasn't the ghost of a hair to be found anywhere.

"'What's the good of your stuff,' he asked angrily, 'if it makes your hair grow and then all fall out again?'

"'For heaven's sake, Mr. Plunket,' I said, 'don't say anything about it or you'll ruin me. I've got every cent I've got in the world invested in this hair tonic, and I've got to get my money back. It made your hair grow, give me the testimonial and let me sell what I've got put up, anyway. You are $250 ahead on it and you ought to help me out of it.'

"He was very mad and cut up quite roughly and said he had been swindled and would expose the tonic as a fraud and a lot of things like that. Finally he agreed that if I would pay him $100 more he would give me the testimonial to the effect that the tonic had made his hair grow and say nothing about its having fallen out again. If I could sell what I had put up at $1.00 per bottle I would come out about even.

"I went out and borrowed the money and paid it to him and he signed the testimonial and left."

*　　*　　*

"Did you sell your tonic out?" asked the Post Man, trying to speak in a tone calculated not to give offence.

The barber gave him a look of derisive contempt and then said in a tone of the utmost sarcasm:

"Oh, yes, I sold it out. I sold exactly five bottles, and the purchasers, after using the mixture faithfully for a month, came back and demanded their money. Not one of them that used it ever had a new hair to start on his head."

"How do you account for its having made the hair grow on Mr. Plunket's head?" asked the Post Man.

"How do I account for it?" repeated the barber in so dangerous a tone that the Post Man shuddered. "How do I account for it? I'll tell you how I account for it. I went out one day to where Mr. Plunket lived on the edge of town and asked for him.

"'Which Mr. Plunket?' asked a man who came out to the gate?

"'Come off,' I said, 'the Plunket that lives here.'

"'They've both moved,' said the man.

"'What do you mean by "both"?' I said, and then I began to think, and I said to the man:

"'What kind of looking men were the Plunkets?'

"'As much like as two peas,' said the man. 'They were twins, and nobody could tell 'em apart from their faces or their talk. The only difference between 'em was that one of 'em was as bald-headed as a hen egg and the other had plenty of hair.'"

"Now," said the barber as he poured about two ounces of bay rum down the Post Man's shirt front, "that's how I account for it. The bald-headed Plunket would come in my

shop one time and the one with hair would come in another'
and I never knew the difference."

When the barber finished the Post Man saw the African
with the whisk broom waiting for him near the front door,
so he fled by the back entrance, climbed a brick wall and
escaped by a side street.

9

Hearts and Crosses

BALDY WOODS reached for the bottle, and got it. Whenever Baldy went for anything he usually—but this is not Baldy's story. He poured out a third drink that was larger by a finger than the first and second. Baldy was in consultation; and the consultee is worthy of his hire.

"I'd be king if I was you," said Baldy, so positively that his holster creaked and his spurs rattled.

Webb Yeager pushed back his flat-brimmed Stetson, and made further disorder in his straw-coloured hair. The tonsorial recourse being without avail, he followed the liquid example of the more resourceful Baldy.

"If a man marries a queen, it oughtn't to make him a two-spot," declared Webb, epitomizing his grievances.

"Sure not," said Baldy, sympathetic, still thirsty, and genuinely solicitous concerning the relative value of the cards. "By rights you're a kins. If I was you, I'd call for a new deal. The cards have been stacked on you. I'll tell you what you are, Webb Yeager."

"What?" asked Webb, with a hopeful look in his pale blue eyes.

"You're a prince consort."

"Go easy," said Webb, "I never blackguarded you none."

"It's a title," explained Baldy, "up among the picture cards; but it don't take no tricks I'll tell you, Webb. It's a brand they've got for certain animals in Europe. Say that you or me or one of them Dutch dukes marries in a royal family. Well, by and by our wife gets to be queen. Are we king? Not in a million years. At the coronation ceremonies we march between little casino and the Ninth Grand Custo-

dian of the Royal Hall Bedchamber. The only use we are is
to appear in photographs, and accept the responsibility for
the heir-apparent. That ain't any square deal. Yes, sir,
Webb, you're a prince consort; and if I was you, I'd start an
interregnum or a habeas corpus or somethin'; and I'd be
king if I had to turn from the bottom of the deck."

Baldy emptied his glass to the ratification of his Warwick
pose.

"Baldy," said Webb solemnly, "me and you punched
cows in the same outfit for years. We been runnin' on the
same range, and ridin' the same trails since we was boys. I
wouldn't talk about my family affairs to nobody but you.
You was line-rider on the Nopalito Ranch when I married
Santa McAllister. I was foreman then; but what am I now?
I don't amount to a knot in a stake rope."

"When old McAllister was the cattle king of West Texas,"
continued Baldy with Satanic sweetness, "you was some
tallow. You had as much to say on the ranch as he did."

"I did," admitted Webb, "up to the time he found out I
was tryin' to get my rope over Santa's head. Then he kept
me out on the range as far from the ranch-house as he could.
When the old man died they commenced to call Santa the
'cattle queen'. I'm boss of the cattle—that's all. She 'tends to
all the business; she handles all the money; I can't sell even
a beef-steer to a party of campers, myself. Santa's the 'queen';
and I'm Mr. Nobody."

"I'd be a king if I was you," repeated Baldy Woods, the
royalist. "When a man marries a queen he ought to grade
up with her—on the hoof—dressed—dried—corned—any
old way from the chaparral to the packing-house. Lots of
folks thinks it's funny, Webb, that you don't have the say-so
on the Nopalito. I ain't reflectin' none on Miz Yeager—she's
the finest little lady between the Rio Grande and next
Christmas—but a man ought to be boss of his own camp."

The smooth, brown face of Yeager lengthened to a mask
of wounded melancholy. With that expression, and his
rumpled yellow hair and guileless blue eyes, he might have

been likened to a schoolboy whose leadership had been usurped by a youngster of superior strength. But his active and sinewy seventy-two inches, and his girded revolvers forbade the comparison.

"What was that you called me, Baldy?" he asked. "What kind of a concert was it?"

"A 'consort,'" corrected Baldy—"a 'prince consort'. It's a kind of short-card pseudonym. You come in sort of between Jack-high and a four-card flush."

Webb Yeager sighed, and gathered the strap of his Winchester scabbard from the floor.

"I'm ridin' back to the ranch to-day," he said half-heartedly. "I've got to start a bunch of beeves for San Antone in the morning."

"I'm your company as far as Dry Lake," announced Baldy. "I've got a round-up camp on the San Marcos cuttin' out two-year-olds."

The two *compañeros* mounted their ponies and trotted away from the little railroad settlement, where they had foregathered in the thirsty morning.

At Dry Lake, where their routes diverged, they reined up for a parting cigarette. For miles they had ridden in silence save for the soft drum of the ponies' hoofs on the matted mesquite grass, and the rattle of the chaparral against their wooden stirrups. But in Texas discourse is seldom continuous. You may fill in a mile, a meal, and a murder between paragraphs without detriment to your thesis. So, without apology, Webb offered an addendum to the conversation that had begun ten miles away.

"You remember, yourself, Baldy, that there was a time when Santa wasn't quite so independent. You remember the days when old McAllister was keepin' us apart, and how she used to send me the sign that she wanted to see me? Old man Mac promised to make me look like a colander if I ever come in gunshot of the ranch. You remember the sign she used to send, Baldy—the heart with a cross inside of it?"

"Me?" cried Baldy, with intoxicated archness. "You old

sugar-stealing coyote! Don't I remember. Why, you dad-blamed old long-horned turtle-dove, the boys in camp was all cognoscious about them hiroglyphs. The 'gizzard and crossbones' we used to call it. We used to see 'em on truck that was sent out from the ranch. They was marked in char-coal on the sacks of flour and in lead pencil on the newspapers. I see one of 'em once chalked on the back of a new cook that old man McAllister sent out from the ranch—danged if I didn't."

"Santa's father," explained Webb gently, "got her to promise that she wouldn't write to me or send me any word. That heart-and-cross sign was her scheme. Whenever she wanted to see me in particular she managed to put that mark on somethin' at the ranch that she knew I'd see. And I never laid eyes on it but what I burnt the wind for the ranch the same night. I used to see her in that coma mott back of the little horse corral."

"We knowed it," chanted Baldy; "but we never let on. We was all for you. We knowed why you always kept that fast paint in camp. And when we see that gizzard and cross-bones figured out on the truck from the ranch we knowed old Pinto was goin' to eat up miles that night instead of grass. You remember Scurry—that educated horse-wrangler we had—the college fellow that tangle-foot drove to the range? Whenever Scurry saw that come-meet-your-honey brand on anything from the ranch, he'd wave his hand like that, and say, 'Our friend Lee Andrews will again swim the Hell's point to-night'."

"The last time Santa sent me the sign," said Webb, "was once when she was sick. I noticed it as soon as I hit camp, and I galloped Pinto forty mile that night. She wasn't at the coma mott. I went to the house; and old McAllister met me at the door. 'Did you come here to get killed?' says he; 'I'll disoblige you for once. I just started a Mexican to bring you. Santa wants you. Go in that room and see her. And then come out here and see me.'

"Santa was lyin' in bed pretty sick. But she gives out a

kind of a smile, and her hand and mine lock horns, and I sets down by the bed—mud and spurs and chaps and all. 'I've heard you ridin' across the grass for hours, Webb,' she says. 'I was sure you'd come. You saw the sign?' she whispers. 'The minute I hit camp,' says I. ''Twas marked on the bag of potatoes and onions.' 'They're always together,' says she, soft like—'always together in life.' 'They go well together,' I says, 'in a stew.' 'I mean hearts and crosses,' says Santa. 'Our sign—to love and to suffer—that's what they mean.'

"And there was old Doc Musgrove amusin' himself with whisky and a palm-leaf fan. And by and by Santa goes to sleep; and Doc feels her forehead; and he says to me: 'You're not such a bad febrifuge. But you'd better slide out now; for the diagnosis don't call for you in regular doses. The little lady'll be all right when she wakes up.'

"I seen old McAllister outside. 'She's asleep,' says I. 'And now you can start in with your colander work. Take your time; for I left my gun on my saddle-horn.'

"Old Mac laughs, and he says to me: 'Pumpin' lead into the best ranch-boss in West Texas don't seem to me good business policy. I don't know where I could get as good a one. It's the son-in-law idea, Webb, that makes me admire for to use you as a target. You ain't my idea of a member of the family. But I can use you on the Nopalito if you'll keep outside of a radius with the ranch-house in the middle of it. You go upstairs and lay down on a cot and when you get some sleep we'll talk it over.'"

Baldy Woods pulled down his hat, and uncurled his leg from his saddle-horn. Webb shortened his rein, and his pony danced, anxious to be off. The two men shook hands with Western ceremony.

"*Adios*, Baldy," said Webb, "I'm glad I seen you and had this talk."

With a pounding rush that sounded like the rise of a covey of quail, the riders sped away toward different points of the compass. A hundred yards on his route Baldy reined in on the top of a bare knoll, and emitted a yell. He swayed on his horse; had he been on foot, the earth would have risen and conquered him; but in the saddle he was a master of equilibrium, and laughed at whisky, and despised the centre of gravity.

Webb turned in his saddle at the signal.

"If I was you," came Baldy's strident and perverting tones, "I'd be king!"

At eight o'clock on the following morning Bud Turner rolled from his saddle in front of the Nopalito ranch-house, and stumbled with whizzing rowels towards the gallery. Bud was in charge of the bunch of beef-cattle that was to strike the trail that morning for San Antonio. Mrs. Yeager was on the gallery watering a cluster of hyacinths growing in a red earthenware jar.

"King" McAllister had bequeathed to his daughter many of his strong characteristics—his resolution, his gay courage, his contumacious self-reliance, his pride as a reigning monarch of hoofs and horns. *Allegro* and *fortissimo* had been McAllister's tempo and tone. In Santa they survived, transposed to the feminine key. Substantially, she preserved the image of the mother who had been summoned to wander in other and less finite green pastures long before the waxing herds of kine had conferred royalty upon the house. She had her mother's slim, strong figure and grave, soft prettiness that relieved in her the severity of the imperious McAllister eye and the McAllister air of royal independence.

Webb stood on one end of the gallery giving orders to two or three sub-bosses of various camps and outfits who had ridden in for instructions.

"'Morning," said Bud briefly. "Where do you want them beeves to go in town—to Barber's, as usual."

Now, to answer that had been the prerogative of the queen. All the reins of business—buying, selling, and banking —had been held by her capable fingers. The handling of the cattle had been entrusted fully to her husband. In the days of "King" McAllister, Santa had been his secretary and helper; and she had continued her work with wisdom and profit.

But before she could reply, the prince consort spake up with calm decision—

"You drive that bunch to Zimmerman and Nesbit's pens. I spoke to Zimmerman about it some time ago."

Bud turned on his high boot-heels.

"Wait!" called Santa quickly. She looked at her husband with surprise in her steady grey eyes.

"Why, what do you mean, Webb?" she asked, with a small wrinkle gathering between her brows. "I never deal with Zimmerman and Nesbit. Barber has handled every head of stock from this ranch in that market for five years. I'm not going to take the business out of his hands." She faced Bud Turner. "Deliver those cattle to Barber," she concluded positively.

Bud gazed impartially at the water-jug hanging on the gallery, stood on his other leg, and chewed a mesquite leaf.

"I want this bunch of beeves to go to Zimmerman and Nesbit," said Webb, with a frosty light in his blue eyes.

"Nonsense," said Santa impatiently. "You'd better start on, Bud, so as to noon at the Little Elm water-hole. Tell Barber we'll have another lot of culls ready in about a month."

Bud allowed a hesitating eye to steal upward and meet Webb's. Webb saw apology in his look, and fancied he saw commiseration.

"You deliver them cattle," he said grimly, "to——"

"Barber," finished Santa sharply. "Let that settle it. Is there anything else you are waiting for, Bud?"

"No, m'm," said Bud. But before going he lingered while a cow's tail could have switched thrice; for man is man's ally; and even the Philistines must have blushed when they took Samson in the way they did.

"You hear your boss!" cried Webb sardonically. He took off his hat, and bowed until it touched the floor before his wife.

"Webb," said Santa rebukingly, "you're acting mighty foolish to-day."

"Court fool, your Majesty," said Webb, in his slow tones, which had changed their quality. "What else can you expect? Let me tell you. I was a man before I married a cattle queen. What am I now? The laughing-stock of the camps. I'll be a man again."

Santa looked at him closely.

"Don't be unreasonable, Webb," she said calmly. "You haven't been slighted in any way. Do I ever interfere in your management of the cattle? I know the business side of the ranch much better than you do. I learned it from Dad. Be sensible."

"Kingdoms and queendoms," said Webb, "don't suit me unless I am in the pictures, too. I punch the cattle and you wear the crown. All right. I'd rather be High Lord Chancellor of a cow-camp than the eight-spot in a queen-high flush. It's your ranch; and Barber gets the beeves."

Webb's horse was tied to the rack. He walked into the house and brought out his roll of blankets that he never took with him except on long rides, and his "slicker", and his longest stake rope of plaited raw-hide. These he began to tie deliberately upon his saddle. Santa, a little pale, followed him.

Webb swung up into the saddle. His serious, smooth face was without expression, except for a stubborn light that smouldered in his eyes.

"There's a herd of cows and calves," said he, "near the Hondo water-hole on the Frio that ought to be moved away from timber. Lobos have killed three of the calves. I forgot to leave orders. You'd better tell Simms to attend to it."

Santa laid a hand on the horse's bridle, and looked her husband in the eye.

"Are you going to leave me, Webb?" she asked quietly.

"I am going to be a man again," he answered.

"I wish you success in a praiseworthy attempt," she said, with a sudden coldness. She turned and walked directly into the house.

Webb Yeager rode to the south-east as straight as the topography of West Texas permitted. And when he reached the horizon he might have ridden on into blue space as far as knowledge of him on the Nopalito went. And the days, with Sundays at their head, formed into hebdomadal squads; and the weeks, captained by the full moon, closed ranks into menstrual companies carrying "Tempus fugit" on their banners; and the months marched on toward the vast campground of the years; but Webb Yeager came no more to the dominions of his queen.

One day a being named Bartholomew, a sheepman—and therefore of little account—from the lower Rio Grande country, rode in sight of the Nopalito ranch-house, and felt hunger assail him. *Ex consuetudine* he was soon seated at the midday dining-table of that hospitable kingdom. Talk like water gushed from him: he might have been smitten with Aaron's rod—that is your gentle shepherd when an audience is vouchsafed him whose ears are not overgrown with wool.

"Missis Yeager," he babbled, "I see a man the other day on the Rancho Seco down in Hidalgo County by your name —Webb Yeager was his. He'd just been engaged as manager. He was a tall, light-haired man, not saying much. Maybe he was some kin of yours, do you think?"

"A husband," said Santa cordially. "The Seco has done well. Mr. Yeager is one of the best stockmen in the West."

The dropping out of a prince consort rarely disorganizes a monarchy. Queen Santa had appointed as *mayordomo* of the ranch a trusty subject, named Ramsay, who had been one of her father's faithful vassals. And there was scarcely a ripple on the Nopalito ranch save when the gulf breeze created undulations in the grass of its wide acres.

For several years the Nopalito had been making experiments with an English breed of cattle that looked down with aristocratic contempt upon the Texas long-horns. The experiments were found satisfactory; and a pasture had been set apart for the blue-bloods. The fame of them had gone forth into the chaparral and pear as far as men ride in saddles.

84

Other ranches woke up, rubbed their eyes, and looked with new dissatisfaction upon the long-horns.

As a consequence, one day a sunburned, capable, silk-handkerchiefed, nonchalant youth, garnished with revolvers, and attended by three Mexican *vaqueros*, alighted at the Nopalito ranch and presented the following business-like epistle to the queen thereof—

Mrs. Yeager—The Nopalito Ranch—
DEAR MADAM—
I am instructed by the owners of the Rancho Seco to purchase 100 head of two and three-year-old cows of the Sussex breed owned by you. If you can fill the order please deliver the cattle to the bearer; and a cheque will be forwarded to you at once.

Respectfully,
WEBSTER YEAGER,
Manager the Rancho Seco.

Business is business, even—very scantily did it escape being written "especially"—in a kingdom.

That night the 100 head of cattle were driven up from the pasture and penned in a corral near the ranch-house for delivery in the morning.

When night closed down and the house was still, did Santa Yeager throw herself down, clasping that formal note to her bosom, weeping, and calling out a name that pride (either in one or the other) had kept from her lips many a day? Or did she file the letter in her business way, retaining her royal balance and strength?

Wonder, if you will; but royalty is sacred; and there is a veil. But this much you shall learn—

At midnight Santa slipped out of the ranch-house, clothed in something dark and plain. She paused for a moment under the live-oak tree. The prairies were somewhat dim, and the moonlight was pale orange, diluted with particles of an impalpable flying mist. But the mock-bird whistled on every

85

bough of vantage; leagues of flowers scented the air; and a kindergarten of little shadowy rabbits leaped and played in an open space near by. Santa turned her face to the southeast and threw three kisses thitherward; for there was none to see.

Then she sped silently to the blacksmith-shop, fifty yards away; and what she did there can only be surmised. But the forge glowed red; and there was a faint hammering such as Cupid might make when he sharpens his arrow-points.

Later she came forth with a queer-shaped, handled thing in one hand, and a portable furnace, such as are seen in branding-camps in the other. To the corral where the Sussex cattle were penned she sped with these things swiftly in the moonlight.

She opened the gate and slipped inside the corral. The Sussex cattle were mostly a dark red. But among this bunch was one that was milky white—notable among the others.

And now Santa shook from her shoulder something that we had not seen before—a rope lasso. She freed the loop of it, coiling the length in her left hand, and plunged into the thick of the cattle.

The white cow was her object. She swung the lasso, which caught one horn and slipped off. The next throw encircled the forefeet and the animal fell heavily. Santa made for it like a panther; but it scrambled up and dashed against her, knocking her over like a blade of grass.

Again she made the cast, while the aroused cattle milled around the four sides of the corral in a plunging mass. This throw was fair; the white cow came to earth again; and before it could rise Santa had made the lasso fast around a post of the corral with a swift and simple knot, and had leaped upon the cow again with the raw-hide hobbles.

In one minute the feet of the animal were tied (no record-breaking deed) and Santa leaned against the corral for the same space of time, panting and lax.

And then she ran swiftly to her furnace at the gate and brought the branding-iron, queerly-shaped and white-hot.

The bellow of the outraged white cow, as the iron was applied, should have stirred the slumbering auricular nerves and consciences of the near-by subjects of the Nopalito, but it did not. And it was amid the deepest nocturnal silence that Santa ran like a lapwing back to the ranch-house and there fell upon a cot and sobbed—sobbed as though queens had hearts as simple ranchmen's wives have, and as though she would gladly make kings of prince consorts, should they ride back again from over the hills and far away.

In the morning the capable revolvered youth and his *vaqueros* set forth, driving the bunch of Sussex cattle across the prairies to the Rancho Seco. Ninety miles it was; a six days' journey, grazing and watering the animals on the way.

The beasts arrived at Rancho Seco one evening at dusk; and were received and counted by the foreman of the ranch.

The next morning at eight o'clock a horseman loped out of the brush to the Nopalito ranch-house. He dismounted stiffly, and strode, with whizzing spurs, to the house. His horse gave a great sigh and swayed foam-streaked, with down-drooping head and closed eyes.

But waste not your pity upon Belshazzar, the flea-bitten sorrel. To-day, in Nopalito horse pasture he survives, pampered, beloved, unridden, cherished record-holder of long-distance rides.

The horseman stumbled into the house. Two arms fell around his neck, and someone cried out in the voice of woman and queen alike: "Webb—oh, Webb!"

"I was a skunk," said Webb Yeager.

"Hush," said Santa, "did you see it?"

"I saw it," said Webb.

What they meant God knows; and you shall know, if you rightly read the primer of events.

"Be the cattle-queen," said Webb; "and overlook it if you can. I was a mangy, sheep-stealing coyote."

"Hush!" said Santa again, laying her fingers upon his mouth. "There's no queen here. Do you know who I am? I

87

am Santa Yeager, First Lady of the Bedchamber. Come here."

She dragged him from the gallery into the room to the right. There stood a cradle with an infant in it—a red, ribald, unintelligible, babbling, beautiful infant, sputtering at life in an unseemly manner.

"There's no queen on this ranch," said Santa again. "Look at the king. He's got your eyes, Webb. Down on your knees and look at His Highness."

But jingling rowels sounded on the gallery, and Bud Turner stumbled there again with the same query that he had brought, lacking a few days, a year ago.

"'Morning. Them beeves is just turned out on the trail. Shall I drive 'em to Barber's, or——"

He saw Webb and stopped, open-mouthed.

"Ba-ba-ba-ba-ba-ba!" shrieked the king in his cradle, beating the air with his fists.

"You hear your boss, Bud," said Webb Yeager, with a broad grin—just as he had said a year ago.

And that is all, except that when old man Quinn, owner of the Rancho Seco, went out to look over the herd of Sussex cattle that he had bought from the Nopalito ranch, he asked his new manager—

"What's the Nopalito ranch brand, Wilson?"

"X Bar Y," said Wilson.

"I thought so," said Quinn. "But look at that white heifer there; she's got another brand—a heart with a cross inside of it. What brand is that?"

10

Vanity and Some Sables

WHEN "Kid" Brady was sent to the ropes by Molly
McKeever's blue-black eyes he withdrew from the
Stovepipe Gang. So much for the power of a colleen's
blanderin' tongue and stubborn true-heartedness. If you are a
man who read this, may such an influence be sent you before
two o'clock to-morrow; if you are a woman, may your
Pomeranian greet you this morning with a cold nose—a sign
of dog-health and your happiness.

The Stovepipe Gang borrowed its name from a sub-
district of the city called the "Stovepipe", which is a narrow
and natural extension of the familiar district known as "Hell's
Kitchen". The "Stovepipe" strip of town runs along Eleventh
and Twelfth avenues on the river, and bends a hard and sooty
elbow around little, lost, homeless DeWitt Clinton park.
Consider that a stovepipe is an important factor in any
kitchen and the situation is analysed. The chefs in "Hell's
Kitchen" are many, and the Stovepipe Gang wears the
cordon blue.

The members of this unchartered but widely known
brotherhood appeared to pass their time on street corners
arrayed like the lilies of the conservatory and busy with nail
files and pen-knives. Thus displayed as a guarantee of good
faith, they carried on an innocuous conversation in a 200-
word vocabulary, to the casual observer as innocent and
immaterial as that heard in the clubs seven blocks to the
east.

But off exhibition the "Stovepipes" were not mere street-
corner ornaments addicted to posing and manicuring. Their
serious occupation was the separating of citizens from their

coin and valuables. Preferably this was done by weird and singular tricks without noise or bloodshed; but whenever the citizen honoured by their attentions refused to impoverish himself gracefully his objections came to be spread finally upon some police-station blotter or hospital register.

The police held the Stovepipe Gang in perpetual suspicion and respect. As the nightingale's liquid note is heard in the deepest shadows, so along the "Stovepipe's" dark and narrow confines the whistle for reserves punctures the dull ear of night. Whenever there was smoke in the "Stovepipe" the tasselled men in blue knew there was fire in "Hell's Kitchen".

"Kid" Brady promised Molly to be good. "Kid" was the vainest, the strongest, the wariest and the most successful plotter in the gang. Therefore the boys were sorry to give him up.

But they witnessed his fall to a virtuous life without protest. For, in the Kitchen it is considered neither unmanly nor improper for a guy to do as his girl advises.

Black her eye for love's sake, if you will; but it is all-to-the-good business to do a thing when she wants you to do it.

"Turn off the hydrant," said the Kid, one night when Molly, tearful, besought him to amend his ways. "I'm going to cut out the gang. You for mine, and the simple life on the side. I'll tell you, Moll—I'll get work; and in a year we'll get married. I'll do it for you. We'll get a flat and a flute, and a sewing machine, and a rubber plant, and live as honest as we can."

"Oh, Kid," sighed Molly, wiping the powder off his shoulder with her handkerchief, "I'd rather hear you say that than to own all of New York. And we can be happy on so little!"

The Kid looked down at his speckless cuffs and shining patent leathers with a suspicion of melancholy.

"It'll hurt hardest in the rags department," said he. "I've kind of always liked to rig out swell when I could. You know how I hate cheap things, Moll. This suit set me back sixty-five. Anything in the wearing apparel line has got to be just so, or it's to the misfit parlours for it, for mine. If I work I won't have so much coin to hand over to the little man with the big shears."

"Never mind, Kid. I'll like you just as much in a blue jumper as I would in a red automobile."

Before the Kid had grown large enough to knock out his father he had been compelled to learn the plumber's art. So now back to this honourable and useful profession he returned. But it was as an assistant that he engaged himself; and it is the master plumber and not the assistant, who wears diamonds as large as hailstones and looks contemptuously upon the marble colonnades of Senator Clark's mansion.

Eight months went by as smoothly and surely as though they had "elapsed" on a theatre programme. The Kid worked away at his pipes and solder with no symptoms of backsliding. The Stovepipe Gang continued its piracy on the high avenues, cracked policemen's heads, held up late travellers, invented new methods of peaceful plundering, copied Fifth Avenue's cut of clothes and neckwear fancies and comported itself according to its lawless by-laws. But the Kid stood firm and faithful to his Molly, even though the polish was gone from his finger-nails and it took him fifteen minutes to tie his purple silk ascot so that the worn places would not show.

One evening he brought a mysterious bundle with him to Molly's house

"Open that, Moll!" he said in his large, quiet way. "It's for you."

Molly's eager fingers tore off the wrappings. She shrieked aloud, and in rushed a sprinkling of little McKeevers, and Ma McKeever, dishwashy, but an undeniable relative of the late Mrs. Eve.

Again Molly shrieked, and something dark and long and sinuous flew and enveloped her neck like an anaconda.

"Russian sables," said the Kid pridefully, enjoying the

sight of Molly's round cheek against the clinging fur. "The real thing. They don't grow anything in Russia too good for you, Moll."

Molly plunged her hands into the muff, overturned a row of family infants and flew to the mirror. Hint for the beauty column. To make bright eyes, rosy cheeks and a bewitching smile: Recipe—one set Russian sables. Apply.

When they were alone Molly became aware of a small cake of the ice of common sense floating down the full tide of her happiness.

"You're a bird, all right, Kid," she admitted gratefully. "I never had any furs on before in my life. But ain't Russian sables awful expensive? Seems to me I've heard they were."

"Have I ever chucked any bargain-sale stuff at you, Moll?" asked the Kid, with calm dignity. "Did you ever notice me leaning on the remnant counter or peering in the window of the five-and-ten? Call that scarf $250 and the muff $175 and you won't make any mistake about the price of Russian sables. The swell goods for me. Say, they look fine on you, Moll."

Molly hugged the sables to her bosom in rapture. And then her smile went away little by little, and she looked the Kid straight in the eye sadly and steadily.

He knew what every look of hers meant; and he laughed with a faint flush upon his face.

"Cut it out," he said, with affectionate roughness. "I told you I was done with that. I bought 'em and paid for 'em all right, with my own money."

"Out of the money you worked for, Kid? Out of $75 a month?"

'Sure. I been saving up."

"Let's see—saved $425 in eight months, Kid?"

"Ah, let up," said the Kid, with some heat. "I had some money when I went to work. Do you think I've been holding 'em up again? I told you I'd quit. They're paid for on the square. Put 'em on and come out for a walk."

Molly calmed her doubts. Sables are soothing. Proud as a

queen she went forth in the streets at the Kid's side. In all that region of low-lying streets Russian sables had never been seen before. The word sped, and doors and windows blossomed with heads eager to see the swell furs Kid Brady had given his girl. All down the street there were "Oh's" and "Ah's", and the reported fabulous sum paid for the sables was passed from lip to lip, increasing as it went. At her right elbow sauntered the Kid with the air of princes. Work had not diminished his love of pomp and show, and his passion for the costly and genuine. On a corner they saw a group of the Stovepipe Gang loafing, immaculate. They raised their hats to the Kid's girl and went on with their calm, unaccented palaver.

Three blocks behind the admired couple strolled Detective Ransom of the Central Office. Ransom was the only detective on the force who could walk abroad with safety in the Stovepipe district. He was fair dealing and unafraid, and went there with the hypothesis that the inhabitants were human. Many liked him, and now and then one would tip off to him something that he was looking for.

"What's the excitement down the street?" asked Ransom of a pale youth in a red sweater.

"Dey're out rubberin' at a set of buffalo robes Kid Brady staked his girl to," answered the youth. "Some say he paid $900 for de skins. Dey're swell all right enough."

"I hear Brady has been working at his old trade for nearly a year," said the detective. "He doesn't travel with the gang any more, does he?"

"He's workin', all right," said the red sweater, "but—say, sport, are you trailin' anything in the fur line? A job in a plumbin' shop don't match wid dem skins de Kid's girl's got on."

Ransom overtook the strolling couple on an empty street near the river bank. He touched the Kid's arm from behind.

"Let me see you a moment, Brady," he said, quietly. His eye rested for a second on the long fur scarf thrown stylishly back over Molly's left shoulder. The Kid, with his old-time police-hating frown on his face, stepped a yard or two aside with the detective.

"Did you go to Mrs. Hethcote's on West 7th Street yesterday to fix a leaky waterpipe?" asked Ransom.

"I did," said the Kid. "What of it?"

"The lady's $1,000 set of Russian sables went out of the house about the same time you did. The description fits the ones this lady has on."

"To h—Harlem with you," cried the Kid angrily. "You know I've cut out that sort of thing, Ransom. I bought them sables yesterday at——"

The Kid stopped short.

"I know you've been working straight lately," said Ransom. "I'll give you every chance. I'll go with you where you bought the furs and investigate. The lady can wear 'em along with us and nobody'll be on. That's fair, Brady."

"Come on," agreed the Kid hotly. And then he stopped suddenly in his tracks and looked with an odd smile at Molly's distressed and anxious face.

"No use," he said grimly. "They're the Hethcote sables, all right. You'll have to turn 'em over, Moll, but they ain't too good for you if they cost a million."

Molly, with anguish in her face, hung upon the Kid's arm.

"Oh, Kiddy, you've broke my heart," she said. "I was so proud of you—and now they'll do you—and where's our happiness gone?"

"Go home," said the Kid wildly. "Come on, Ransom—take the furs. Let's get away from here. Wait a minute—I've a good mind to—no, I'll be d——if I can do it—run along, Moll—I'm ready, Ransom."

Around the corner of a lumber-yard came Policeman Kohen on his way to his beat along the river. The detective signed to him for assistance. Kohen joined the group. Ransom explained.

"Sure," said Kohen. "I hear about those saples dat vas stole. You say you have dem here?"

Policeman Kohen took the end of Molly's late scarf in his hands and looked at it closely.

"Once," he said, "I sold furs in Sixth Avenue. Yes, dese are saples. Dey come from Alaska. Dis scarf is vort $12 and dis muff——"

"Biff!" came the palm of the Kid's powerful hand upon the policeman's mouth. Kohen staggered and rallied. Molly screamed. The detective threw himself upon Brady and with Kohen's aid got the nippers on his wrist.

"The scarf is vort $12 and the muff is vort $9," persisted the policeman. "Vot is dis talk about $1,000 saples?"

The Kid sat upon a pile of lumber and his face turned dark red.

"Correct, Solomonski!" he declared viciously. "I paid $21.50 for the set. I'd rather have got six months and not have told it. Me, the swell guy that wouldn't look at anything cheap! I'm a plain bluffer. Moll—my salary couldn't spell sables in Russian."

Molly cast herself upon his neck.

"What do I care for all the sables and money in the world," she cried. "It's my Kiddy I want. Oh, you dear, stuck-up, crazy blockhead!"

"You can take dose nippers off," said Kohen to the detective. "Before I leaf de station de report come in dat de lady vind her saples—hanging in her wardrobe. Young man, I excuse you dat punch in my face—dis von time."

Ransom handed Molly her furs. Her eyes were smiling upon the Kid. She wound the scarf and threw the end over her left shoulder with a duchess's grace.

"A gouple of young vools," said Policeman Kohen to Ransom: "come on away."

11

Jeff Peters as a Personal Magnet

JEFF PETERS has been engaged in as many schemes for making money as there are recipes for cooking rice in Charleston, S.C.

Best of all I like to hear him tell of his earlier days when he sold liniments and cough cures on street corners, living hand to mouth, heart to heart, with the people, throwing heads or tails with fortune for his last coin.

"I stuck Fisher Hill, Arkansaw," said he, "in a buckskin suit, moccasins, long hair and a thirty-carat diamond ring that I got from an actor in Texarkana. I don't know what he ever did with the pocket-knife I swapped him for it.

"I was Dr. Waugh-hoo, the celebrated Indian medicine man. I carried only one best bet just then, and that was Resurrection Bitters. It was made of life-giving plants and herbs accidentally discovered by Ta-qua-la, the beautiful wife of the chief of the Choctaw Nation, while gathering truck to garnish a platter of boiled dog for the annual corn dance.

"Business hadn't been good at the last town, so I only had five dollars. I went to the Fisher Hill druggist and he credited me for half a gross of eight-ounce bottles and corks. I had the labels and ingredients in my valise, left over from the last town. Life began to look rosy again after I got in my hotel room with the water running from the tap, and the Resurrection Bitters lining up on the table by the dozen.

"Fake? No, sir. There was two dollars' worth of fluid extract of cinchona and a dime's worth of aniline in that half-gross of bitters. I've gone through towns years afterwards and had folks ask for 'em again.

"I hired a wagon that night and commenced selling the bitters on Main Street. Fisher Hill was a low, malarial town; and a compound hypothetical pneumocardiac anti-scorbutic tonic was just what I diagnosed the crowd as needing. The bitters started off like sweetbreads-on-toast at a vegetarian dinner. I had sold two dozen at fifty cents apiece when I felt somebody pull my coat tail. I knew what this meant; so I climbed down and sneaked a five-dollar bill into the hand of a man with a German silver star on his lapel.

" 'Constable,' says I, 'it's a fine night.'

" 'Have you got a city licence,' he asks, 'to sell this illegitimate essence of spooju that you flatter by the name of medicine?'

" 'I have not,' says I. 'I didn't know you had a city. If I can find it to-morrow I'll take one out if it's necessary.'

" 'I'll have to close you up till you do,' says the constable.

"I quit selling and went back to the hotel. I was talking to the landlord about it.

" 'Oh, you won't stand no show in Fisher Hill,' says he. 'Dr. Hoskins, the only doctor here, is a brother-in-law of the Mayor, and they won't allow no fake doctor to practise in town.'

" 'I don't practise medicine,' says I, 'I've got a State pedlar's licence, and I take out a city one wherever they demand it.'

"I went to the Mayor's office the next morning and they told me he hadn't showed up yet. They didn't know when he'd be down. So Doc Waugh-hoo hunches down again in a hotel chair and lights a jimpson-weed regalia, and waits.

"By and by a young man in a blue neck-tie slips into the chair next to me and asks the time.

" 'Half-past ten,' says I, 'and you are Andy Tucker. I've seen you work. Wasn't it you that put up the Great Cupid Combination package on the Southern States? Let's see, it was a Chilian diamond engagement ring, a wedding-ring, a potato masher, a bottle of soothing syrup and Dorothy Vernon—all for fifty cents.'

"Andy was pleased to hear that I remembered him. He was a good street man; and he was more than that—he respected his profession, and he was satisfied with 300 per cent profit. He had plenty of offers to go into the illegitimate drug and garden seed business; but he was never to be tempted off of the straight path.

"I wanted a partner; so Andy and me agreed to go out together. I told him about the situation in Fisher Hill and how finances was low on account of the local mixture of politics and jalap. Andy had just got in on the train that morning. He was pretty low himself, and was going to canvass the town for a few dollars to build a new battleship by popular subscription at Eureka Springs. So we went out and sat on the porch and talked it over.

"The next morning at eleven o'clock, when I was sitting there alone, an Uncle Tom shuffles into the hotel and asked for the doctor to come and see Judge Banks, who, it seems, was the Mayor and a mighty sick man.

"'I'm no doctor,' says I. 'Why don't you go and get the doctor?'

"'Boss,' says he, 'Doc Hoskins am done gone twenty miles in de country to see some sick persons. He's de only doctor in de town, and Massa Banks am powerful bad off. He sent me to ax you to please, suh, come.'

"'As man to man,' says I, 'I'll go and look him over.' So I put a bottle of Resurrection Bitters in my pocket and goes up on the hill to the Mayor's mansion, the finest house in town, with a mansard roof and two cast-iron dogs on the lawn.

"This Mayor Banks was in bed all but his whiskers and feet. He was making internal noises that would have had everybody in San Francisco hiking for the parks. A young man was standing by the bed holding a cup of water.

"'Doc,' says the Mayor, 'I'm awful sick. I'm about to die. Can't you do nothing for me?'

"'Mr. Mayor,' says I, 'I'm not a regular preordained disciple of S. Q. Lapius. I never took a course in a medical

98

college,' says I, 'I've come just as a fellow-man to see if I could be of assistance.'

"'I'm deeply obliged,' says he. 'Doc Waugh-hoo, this is my nephew, Mr. Biddle. He has tried to alleviate my distress, but without success. Oh, Lordy! Ow-ow-ow!!' he sings out.

"I nods at Mr. Biddle and sets down by the bed and feels the Mayor's pulse. 'Let me see your liver—your tongue, I mean,' says I. Then I turns up the lids of his eyes and looks close at the pupils of 'em.

"'How long have you been sick?' I asked.

"'I was taken down—ow-ouch—last night,' says the Mayor. 'Gimme something for it, doc, won't you?'

"'Mr. Fiddle,' says I, 'raise the window shade a bit, will you?'

"'Biddle,' says the young man. 'Do you feel like you could eat some ham and eggs, Uncle James?'

"'Mr. Mayor,' says I, after laying me ear to his right shoulder-blade and listening, 'you've got a bad attack of super-inflammation of the right clavicle of the harpsichord!'

"'Good Lord!' says he, with a groan. 'Can't you rub something on it, or set it or anything?'

"I picks up my hat and starts for the door.

"'You ain't going, doc?' says the Mayor with a howl. 'You ain't going away and leave me to die with this—super-fluity of the clapboards, are you?'

"'Common humanity, Dr. Whoa-ha,' says Mr. Biddle, 'ought to prevent your deserting a fellow-human in distress.'

"'Dr. Waugh-hoo, when you get through ploughing,' says I. And then I walks back to the bed and throws back my long hair.

"'Mr. Mayor,' says I, 'there is only one hope for you. Drugs will do you no good. But there is another power higher yet, although drugs are high enough,' says I.

"'And what is that?' says he.

"'Scientific demonstrations,' says I. 'The triumph of mind over sarsaparilla. The belief that there is no pain and sickness except what is produced when we ain't feeling well. Declare yourself in arrears. Demonstrate.'

"'What is this paraphernalia you speak of, doc?' says the Mayor. 'You ain't a Socialist, are you?'

"'I am speaking,' says I, 'of the great doctrine of psychic financiering—of the enlightened school of long-distance, subconscientious treatment of fallacies and meningitis—of that wonderful indoor sport known as personal magnetism.'

"'Can you work it, doc?' asks the Mayor.

"'I'm one of the Sole Sanhedrims and Ostensible Hooplas of the Inner Pulpit,' says I. 'The lame talk and the blind rubber whenever I make a pass at 'em. I am a medium, a coloratura hypnotist and a spirituous control. It was only through me at the recent séances at Ann Arbour that the late president of the Vinegar Bitters Company could revisit the earth to communicate with his sister Jane. You see me peddling medicine on the streets,' says I, 'to the poor. I don't practise personal magnetism on them. I do not drag it in the dust,' says I, 'because they haven't got the dust.'

"'Will you treat my case?' asks the Mayor.

"'Listen,' says I. 'I've had a good deal of trouble with medical societies everywhere I've been. I don't practise medicine. But, to save your life, I'll give you the psychic treatment if you'll agree as Mayor not to push the licence question.'

"'Of course I will,' says he. 'And now get to work, doc, for them pains are coming on again.'

"'My fee will be $250, cure guaranteed in two treatments,' says I.

"'All right,' says the Mayor. 'I'll pay it. I guess my life's worth that much.'

"I sat down by the bed and looked him straight in the eye.

"'Now,' says I, get your mind off the disease. You ain't sick. You haven't got a heart or a clavicle or a funny-bone or brains or anything. You haven't got any pain. Declare

100

error. Now you feel the pain that you didn't have leaving, don't you?'

"'I do feel some little better, doc,' says the Mayor, 'darned if I don't. Now state a few lies about my not having this swelling in my left side, and I think I could be propped up and have some sausage and buckwheat cakes.'

"I made a few passes with my hands.

"'Now,' says I, 'the inflammation's gone. The right lobe of the perihelion has subsided. You're getting sleepy. You can't hold your eyes open any longer. For the present the disease is checked. Now, you are asleep.'

"The Mayor shut his eyes slowly and began to snore.

"'You observe, Mr. Tiddle,' says I, 'the wonders of modern science.'

"'Biddle,' says he. 'When will you give uncle the rest of the treatment, Dr. Pooh-pooh?'

"'Waugh-hoo,' says I. 'I'll come back at eleven to-morrow. When he wakes up give him eight drops of turpentine and three pounds of steak. Good morning.'

"The next morning I went back on time. 'Well, Mr. Riddle,' says I, when he opened the bedroom door, 'and how is uncle this morning?'

"'He seems much better,' says the young man.

"The Mayor's colour and pulse was fine. I gave him another treatment, and he said the last of the pain left him.

"'Now,' says I, 'you'd better stay in bed for a day or two, and you'll be all right. It's a good thing I happened to be in Fisher Hill, Mr. Mayor,' says I, 'for all the remedies in the cornucopia that the regular schools of medicine use couldn't have saved you. And now that error has flew and pain proved a perjurer, let's allude to a cheerfuller subject— say the fee of $250. No cheques, please; I hate to write my name on the back of a cheque almost as bad as I do on the front.'

"'I've got the cash here,' says the Mayor, pulling a pocket-book from under his pillow.

"He counts out five fifty-dollar notes and holds 'em in his hand.

"'Bring the receipt,' he says to Biddle.

"I signed the receipt and the Mayor handed me the money. I put it in my inside pocket careful.

"'Now do your duty, officer,' says the Mayor, grinning much unlike a sick man.

"Mr. Biddle lays his hand on my arm.

"'You're under arrest, Dr. Waugh-hoo, alias Peters,' says he, 'for practising medicine without authority under the State law.'

"'Who are you?' I asks.

"'I'll tell you who he is,' says Mr. Mayor, sitting up in bed. 'He's a detective employed by the State Medical Society. He's been following you over five counties. He came to me yesterday and we fixed up this scheme to catch you. I guess you won't do any more doctoring around these parts, Mr. Faker. What was it you said I had, doc?' the Mayor laughs, 'compound—well it wasn't softening of the brain, I guess, anyway.'

"'A detective,' says I.

"'Correct,' says Biddle. 'I'll have to turn you over to the sheriff.'

"'Let's see you do it,' says I, and I grabs Biddle by the throat and half throws him out of the window, but he pulls a gun and sticks it under my chin, and I stand still. Then he puts handcuffs on me, and takes the money out of my pocket.

"'I witness,' says he, 'that they're the same bills that you and I marked, Judge Banks. I'll turn them over to the sheriff when we get to his office, and he'll send you a receipt. They'll have to be used as evidence in the case.'

"'All right, Mr. Biddle,' says the Mayor. 'And now, Doc Waugh-hoo,' he goes on, 'why don't you demonstrate? Can't you pull the cork out of your magnetism with your teeth and hocus-pocus them handcuffs off?'

"'Come on, officer,' says I, dignified. 'I may as well make the best of it.' And then I turns to old Banks and rattles my chains.

"'Mr. Mayor,' says I, 'the time will come soon when you'll believe that personal magnetism is a success. And you'll be sure that it succeeded in this case, too.'

"And I guess it did.

"When we got nearly to the gate, I says: 'We might meet somebody now, Andy. I reckon you better take 'em off, and ——' Hey? Why, of course, it was Andy Tucker. That was his scheme; and that's how we got the capital to go into business together."

12

The Hand that Riles the World

"MANY of our great men," said I (apropos of many things), "have declared that they owe their success to the aid and encouragement of some brilliant woman."

"I know," said Jeff Peters. "I've read in history and mythology about Joan of Arc and Mme. Yale and Mrs. Caudle and Eve and other noted females of the past. But, in my opinion, the woman of to-day is of little use in politics or business. What's she best in, anyway?—men make the best cooks, milliners, nurses, housekeepers, stenographers, clerks, hairdressers and launderers. About the only job left that a woman can beat a man in is female impersonator in vaudeville."

"I would have thought," said I, "that occasionally, any-how, you would have found the wit and intuition of woman invaluable to you in your lines of—er—business."

"Now, wouldn't you," said Jeff, with an emphatic nod—"wouldn't you have imagined that? But a woman is an absolutely unreliable partner in any straight swindle. She's liable to turn honest on you when you are depending upon her the most. I tried 'em once.

"Bill Humble, an old friend of mine in the Territories, conceived the illusion that he wanted to be appointed United States Marshal. At that time me and Andy was doing a square, legitimate business of selling walking-canes. If you unscrewed the head of one and turned it up to your mouth a half-pint of good rye whisky would go trickling down your throat to reward you for your act of intelligence. The deputies was annoying me and Andy some, and when Bill spoke to me about his officious aspirations, I saw how the appointment as Marshal might help along the firm of Peters & Tucker.

"'Jeff,' says Bill to me, 'you are a man of learning and education, besides having knowledge and information concerning not only rudiments but facts and attainments.

"'I do so,' says I, 'and I have never regretted it. I am not one,' says I, 'who would cheapen education by making it free. Tell me,' says I, 'which is of the most value to mankind, literature or horse-racing?'

"'Why—er—playing the po—— I mean, of course, the poets and the great writers have got the call, of course,' says Bill.

"'Exactly,' says I. 'Then why do the master minds of finance and philanthropy,' says I, 'charge us $2 to get into a race-track and let us into a library free? Is that distilling into the masses,' says I, 'a correct estimate of the relative value of the two means of self-culture and disorder?'

"'You are arguing outside of my faculties of sense and rhetoric,' says Bill. 'What I wanted you to do is to go to Washington and dig out this appointment for me. I haven't no ideas of cultivation and intrigue. I'm a plain citizen and I need the job. I've killed seven men,' says Bill; 'I've got nine children; I've been a good Republican ever since the first of May; I can't read nor write, and I see no reason why I ain't illegible for the office. And I think your partner, Mr. Tucker,' goes on Bill, 'is also a man of sufficient ingratiation and connected system of mental delinquency to assist you in securing the appointment. I will give you preliminary,' says Bill, '$1,000 for drinks, bribes and car-fares in Washington. If you land the job I will pay you $1,000 more, cash down, and guarantee you impunity in boot-legging whisky for twelve months. Are you patriotic to the West enough to help me put this thing through the Whitewashed Wigwam of the Great Father of the most eastern flag station of the Pennsylvania Railroad?' says Bill.

"Well, I talked to Andy about it, and he liked the idea immense. Andy was a man of an involved nature. He was never content to plod along, as I was, selling to the peasantry some little tool like a combination steak beater, shoe horn, marcel waver, monkey-wrench, nail file, potato masher and Multum in Parvo tuning-fork. Andy had the artistic temper, which is not to be judged as a preacher's or a moral man's is by purely commercial deflections. So we accepted Bill's offer, and strikes out for Washington.

"Says I to Andy, when we got located at a hotel on South Dakota Avenue, G. S. S. W., 'now, Andy, for the first time in our lives we've got to do a real dishonest act. Lobbying is something we've never been used to; but we've got to scandalize ourselves for Bill Humble's sake. In a straight and legitimate business,' says I, 'we could afford to introduce a little foul play and chicanery, but in a disorderly and heinous piece of malpractice like this it seems to me that the straightforward and above board way is the best. I propose,' says I, 'that we hand over $500 of this money to the chairman of the national campaign committee, get a receipt, lay the receipt on the President's desk and tell him about Bill. The President is a man who would appreciate a candidate who went about getting office that way instead of pulling wires.'

"Andy agreed with me, but after we talked the scheme over with the hotel clerk we give that plan up. He told us that there was only one way to get an appointment in Washington, and that was through a lady lobbyist. He gave us the address of one he recommended, a Mrs. Avery, who, he said, was high up in sociable and diplomatic rings and circles.

"The next morning at ten o'clock me and Andy called at her hotel, and was shown up to her reception room.

"This Mrs. Avery was a solace and a balm to the eyesight. She had hair the colour of the back of a twenty-dollar gold certificate, blue eyes and a system of beauty that would make the girl on the cover of a July magazine look like a cook on a Monongahela coal barge.

"She had on a low-necked dress covered with silver spangles, and diamond rings and ear-bobs. Her arms was bare; and she was using a desk telephone with one hand, and drinking tea with the other.

"'Well, boys,' says she after a bit, 'what is it?'

"I told her in as few words as possible what we wanted for Bill, and the price we could pay.

"'Those western appointments,' says she, 'are easy. Le'me see, now,' says she, 'who could put that through for us? No use fooling with Territorial delegates. I guess,' says she, 'that Senator Sniper would be about the man. He's from somewhere in the West. Let's see how he stands on my private menu card.' She takes some papers out of a pigeon-hole with the letter 'S' over it.

"'Yes,' says she, 'he's marked with a star; that means "ready to serve". Now, let's see. "Age 55; married twice; Presbyterian, likes blondes, Tolstoi, poker and stewed terrapin; sentimental at third bottle of wine." Yes,' she goes on, 'I am sure I can have your friend, Mr. Bummer, appointed Minister of Brazil.'

"'Humble,' says I. 'And United States Marshal was the berth.'

"'Oh, yes,' says Mrs. Avery. 'I have so many deals of this sort I sometimes get them confused. Give me all the memoranda you have of the case, Mr. Peters, and come back in four days. I think it can be arranged by then.'

"So me and Andy goes back to our hotel and waits. Andy walks up and down and chews the left end of his moustache.

"'A woman of high intellect and perfect beauty is a rare thing, Jeff,' says he.

"'As rare,' says I, 'as an omelet made from the eggs of the fabulous bird known as the epidermis,' says I.

"'A woman like that,' says Andy, 'ought to lead a man to the highest positions of opulence and fame.'

"'I misdoubt,' says I, 'if any woman ever helped a man to secure a job any more than to have his meals ready promptly and spread a report that the other candidate's wife had once been a shoplifter. They are no more adapted for business and politics,' says I, 'than Algernon Charles Swinburne is to be floor manager at one of Chuck Connor's annual balls. I know,' says I to Andy, 'that sometimes a woman seems to step out into the kalsomine light as the chargé d'affairs of her man's political job. But how does it come out? Say, they have a neat little berth somewhere as foreign consul of record to Afghanistan or lock-keeper on the Delaware and Raritan Canal. One day this man finds his wife putting on her overshoes and three months' supply of bird-seed into the canary's cage. "Sioux Falls?" he asks with a kind of hopeful light in his eye. "No, Arthur," says she, "Washington. We're wasted here," says she. "You ought to be Toady Extraordinary to the Court of St. Bridget or Head Porter of the Island of Porto Rico. I'm going to see about it."'

"'Then this lady,' I says to Andy, 'moves against the authorities at Washington with her baggage and munitions, consisting of five dozen indiscriminating letters written to her by a member of the Cabinet when she was 15; a letter of introduction from King Leopold to the Smithsonian Institution and a pink silk costume with canary-coloured spats.

"'Well, and then what?' I goes on. 'She has the letters printed in the evening papers that match her costume, she lectures at an informal tea given in the palm room of the B. & O. depot and then calls on the President. The ninth Assistant Secretary of Commerce and Labour, the first aide-de-camp of the Blue Room and an unidentified coloured man are waiting there to grasp her by the hands—and feet. They carry her out to S. W. B. street and leave her on a cellar door. That ends it. The next time we hear of her she is writing postal cards to the Chinese Minister asking him to get Arthur a job in a tea store.'

"'Then,' says Andy, 'you don't think Mrs. Avery will land the Marshalship for Bill?'

"'I do not,' says I. 'I do not wish to be a sceptic, but I doubt if she can do as well as you and me could have done.'

"'I don't agree with you,' says Andy; 'I'll bet you she does. I'm proud of having a higher opinion of the talent and the powers of negotiation of ladies.'

"We was back at Mrs. Avery's hotel at the time she appointed. She was looking pretty and fine enough, as far as that went, to make any man let her name every officer in the country. But I hadn't much faith in looks, so I was certainly surprised when she pulls out a document with the great seal of the United States on it, and 'William Henry Humble' in a fine, big hand on the back.

"'You might have had it the next day, boys,' says Mrs. Avery, smiling. 'I hadn't the slightest trouble in getting it,' says she. 'I just asked for it, that's all. Now, I'd like to talk to you a while,' she goes on, 'but I'm awfully busy, and I know you'll excuse me. I've got an Ambassadorship, two Consulates and a dozen other minor applications to look after. I can hardly find time to sleep at all. You'll give my compliments to Mr. Humble when you get home, of course.'

"Well, I handed her the $500, which she pitched into her desk drawer without counting. I put Bill's appointment in my pocket and me and Andy made our adieux.

"We started back for the Territory the same day. We wired Bill: 'Job landed; get the tall glasses ready,' and we felt pretty good.

"Andy joshed me all the way about how little I knew about women.

"'All right,' says I. 'I'll admit that she surprised me. But it's the first time I ever knew one of 'em to manipulate a piece of business on time without getting it bungled up in some way,' says I.

"Down about the edge of Arkansas I got out Bill's appointment and looked it over, and then I handed it to Andy to read. Andy read it, but didn't add any remarks to my silence.

"The paper was for bill, all right, and a genuine document, but it appointed him postmaster of Dade City, Fla.

"Me and Andy got off the train at Little Rock and sent Bill's appointment to him by mail. Then we struck northeast towards Lake Superior.

"I never saw Bill Humble after that."

13

The Exact Science of Matrimony

"A s I have told you before," said Jeff Peters, "I never had much confidence in the perfidiousness of woman. As partners or coeducators in the most innocent line of graft they are not trustworthy."

"They deserve the compliment," said I. "I think they are entitled to be called the honest sex."

"Why shouldn't they be?" said Jeff. "They've got the other sex either grafting or working overtime for 'em. They're all right in business until they get their emotions or their hair touched up too much. Then you want to have a flat-footed, heavy-breathing man with sandy whiskers, five kids and a building and loan mortgage ready as an understudy to take her desk. Now there was that widow lady that me and Andy Tucker engaged to help us in a little matrimonial agency scheme we floated out in Cairo.

"When you've got enough advertising capital—say a roll as big as the little end of a wagon tongue—there's money in matrimonial agencies. We had about $6,000 and we expected to double it in two months, which is about as long as a scheme like ours can be carried on without taking out a New Jersey charter.

"We fixed up an advertisement that read about like this:

Charming widow, beautiful, home loving, 32 years, possessing $3,000 cash and owning a valuable country property, would remarry. Would prefer a poor man with affectionate disposition to one with means, as she realizes that the solid virtues are oftenest to be found in the humble walks of life. No objection to elderly man or one of homely appearance if faithful and true and competent to manage property and invest money with judgment. Address, with particulars,

LONELY

Care of Peters & Tucker, agents, Cairo, Ill.

"'So far, so pernicious,' says I, when we had finished the literary concoction. 'And now,' says I, 'where is the lady?'"

"Andy gives me one of his looks of calm irritation."

"'Jeff,' says he, 'I thought you had lost them ideas of realism in your art. Why should there be a lady? When they sell a lot of watered stock on Wall Street would you expect to find a mermaid in it? What has a matrimonial ad got to do with a lady?'"

"'Now listen,' says I, 'You know my rule, Andy, that in all my illegitimate inroads against the legal letter of the law the article sold must be existent, visible, producible. In that way and by a careful study of city ordinances and train schedules I have kept out of all trouble with the police that a five-dollar bill and a cigar could not square. Now, to work this scheme we've got to be able to produce bodily a charming widow or its equivalent with or without the beauty, hereditaments and appurtenances set forth in the catalogue and writ of errors, or hereafter be held by a justice of the peace.'"

"'Well,' says Andy, reconstructing his mind, 'maybe it would be safer in case the post office or the peace commission should try to investigate our agency. But where,' he says, 'could you hope to find a widow who would waste time on a matrimonial scheme that had no matrimony in it?'"

"I told Andy that I thought I knew of the exact party. An old friend of mine, Zeke Trotter, who used to draw soda-water and teeth in a tent show, had made his wife a widow a year before by drinking some dyspepsia cure of the old doctor's instead of the liniment that he always got boozed up on. I used to stop at their house often, and I thought we could get her to work with us.

"''Twas only sixty miles to the little town where she lived,

111

so I jumped out on the I. C. and finds her in the same cottage with the same sunflowers and roosters standing on the wash-tub. Mrs. Trotter fitted our ad first-rate except, maybe, for beauty and age and property valuation. But she looked feasible and praiseworthy to the eye, and it was a kindness to Zeke's memory to give her the job.

"'Is this an honest deal you are putting on, Mr. Peters?' she asks me when I tell her what we want.

"'Mrs Trotter,' says I, 'Andy Tucker and me have computed the calculation that 3,000 men in this broad and unfair country will endeavour to secure your fair hand and ostensible money and property through our advertisement. Out of that number something like thirty hundred will expect to give you in exchange, if they should win you, the carcass of a lazy and mercenary loafer, a failure in life, a swindler and contemptible fortune-seeker.

"'Me and Andy,' says I, 'propose to teach these preyers upon society a lesson. It was with difficulty,' says I, 'that me and Andy could refrain from forming a corporation under the title of the Great Moral and Millennial Malevolent Matrimonial Agency. Does that satisfy you?'

"'It does, Mr. Peters,' says she. 'I might have known you wouldn't have gone into anything that wasn't opprobrious. But what will my duties be? Do I have to reject personally these 3,000 ram-scallions you speak of, or can I throw them out in bunches?'

"'Your job, Mrs. Trotter,' says I, 'will be practically a cynosure. You will live at a quiet hotel and will have no work to do. Andy and I will attend to all the correspondence and business end of it.

"'Of course,' says I, 'some of the more ardent and impetuous suitors who can raise the railroad fare may come to Cairo to personally press their suit or whatever fraction of a suit they may be wearing. In that case you will be probably put to the inconvenience of kicking them out face to face. We will pay you $25 per week and hotel expenses.'

"'Give me five minutes,' says Mrs. Trotter, 'to get my

powder rag and leave the front-door key with a neighbour and you can let my salary begin.'

"So I conveys Mrs. Trotter to Cairo and establishes her in a family hotel far enough away from mine and Andy's quarters to be unsuspicious and available, and I tell Andy.

"'Great,' says Andy. 'And now that your conscience is appeased as to the tangibility and proximity of the bait, and leaving mutton aside, suppose we revenoo a noo fish.'

"So, we began to insert our advertisement in newspapers covering the country far and wide. One ad was all we used. We couldn't have used more without hiring so many clerks and marcelled paraphernalia that the sound of the gum-chewing would have disturbed the Postmaster-General.

"We placed $2,000 in a bank to Mrs. Trotter's credit and gave her the book to show in case anybody might question the honesty and good faith of the agency. I knew Mrs. Trotter was square and reliable and it was safe to leave it in her name.

"With that one ad Andy and me put in twelve hours a day answering letters.

"About one hundred a day was what came in. I never knew that there was so many large-hearted but indigent men in the country who were willing to acquire a charming widow and assume the burden of investing her money.

"Most of them admitted that they ran principally to whiskers and lost jobs and were misunderstood by the world, but all of 'em were sure that they were so chock-full of affection and manly qualities that the widow would be making the bargain of her life to get 'em.

"Every applicant got a reply from Peters & Tucker informing them that the widow had been deeply impressed by his straightforward and interesting letter and requesting them to write again; stating more particulars; and enclosing photograph if convenient. Peters & Tucker also informed the applicant that their fee for handing over the second letter to their fair client would be $2, enclosed therewith.

"There you see the simple beauty of the scheme. About

90 per cent of them domestic foreign noblemen raised the price somehow and sent it in. That was all there was to it. Except that me and Andy complained an amount about being put to the trouble of slicing open them envelopes, and taking the money out.

"Some few clients called in person. We sent 'em to Mrs. Trotter and she did the rest; except for three or four who came back to strike us for car-fare. After the letters began to get in from the r.f.d. districts Andy and me were taking in about $200 a day.

"One afternoon when we were busiest and I was stuffing the two and ones into cigar boxes and Andy was whistling 'No Wedding Bells for Her', a small, slick man drops in and runs his eye over the walls like he was on the trail of a lost Gainsborough painting or two. As soon as I saw him I felt a glow of pride, because we were running our business on the level.

"'I see you have quite a large mail to-day,' says the man.

"I reached and got my hat.

"'Come on,' says I. 'We've been expecting you. I'll show you the goods. How was Teddy when you left Washington?'

"I took him down to the Riverview Hotel and had him shake hands with Mrs. Trotter. Then I showed him her bank book with the $2,000 to her credit.

"'It seems to be all right,' says the Secret Service.

"'It is,' says I. 'And if you're not a married man I'll leave you to talk a while with the lady. We won't mention the two dollars.'

"'Thanks,' says he. 'If I wasn't, I might. Good day, Mr. Peters.'

"Toward the end of three months we had taken in something over $5,000, and we saw it was time to quit. We had a good many complaints made to us; and Mrs. Trotter seemed to be tired of the job. A good many suitors had been calling to see her, and she didn't seem to like that.

"So we decides to pull out, and I goes down to Mrs.

Trotter's hotel to pay her last week's salary and say farewell and get her cheque for the $2,000.

"When I got there I found her crying like a kid that don't want to go to school.

"'Now, now,' says I, 'what's it all about? Somebody sassed you or you getting home-sick?'

"'No, Mr. Peters,' says she. 'I'll tell you. You was always a friend of Zeke's, and I don't mind. Mr. Peters, I'm in love. I just love a man so hard I can't bear not to get him. He's just the ideal I've always had in mind.'

"'Then take him,' says I. 'That is, if it's a mutual case. Does he return the sentiment according to the specifications and painfulness you have described?'

"'He does,' says she. 'But he's one of the gentlemen that's been coming to see me about the advertisement and he won't marry me unless I give him the $2,000. His name is William Wilkinson.' And then she goes off again in the agitations and hysterics of romance.

"'Mrs. Trotter,' says I, 'there's no man more sympathizing with a woman's affections than I am. Besides, you was once the life partner of one of my best friends. If it was left to me I'd say take this $2,000 and the man of your choice and be happy.

"'We could afford to do that, because we have cleaned up over $5,000 from these suckers that wanted to marry you. But,' says I, 'Andy Tucker is to be consulted.

"'He is a good man, but keen in business. He is my equal partner financially. I will talk to Andy,' says I, 'and see what can be done.'

"I goes back to our hotel and lays the case before Andy.

"'I was expecting something like this all the time,' says Andy. 'You can't trust a woman to stick by you in any scheme that involves her emotions and preferences.'

"'It's a sad thing, Andy,' says I, 'to think that we've been the cause of the breaking of a woman's heart.'

"'It is,' says Andy, 'and I tell you what I'm willing to do, Jeff. You've always been a man of a soft and generous heart and disposition. Perhaps I've been too hard and worldly and suspicious, for once I'll meet you half-way. Go to Mrs. Trotter and tell her to draw the $2,000 from the bank and give it to this man she's infatuated with and be happy.'

"I jumps up and shakes Andy's hand for five minutes, and then I goes back to Mrs. Trotter and tells her, and she cries as hard for joy as she did for sorrow.

"Two days afterward me and Andy packed up to go.

"'Wouldn't you like to go down and meet Mrs. Trotter once before we leave?' I asks him. 'She'd like mightily to know you and express her encomiums and gratitude.'

"'Why, I guess not,' says Andy. 'I guess we'd better hurry and catch that train.'

"I was strapping our capital around me in a memory belt like we always carried it, when Andy pulls a roll of large bills out of his pocket and asks me to put 'em with the rest.

"'What's this?' says I.

"'It's Mrs. Trotter's two thousand,' says Andy.

"'How do you come to have it?' I asks.

"'She gave it to me,' says Andy. 'I've been calling on her three evenings a week for more than a month.'

"'Then you are William Wilkinson?' says I.

"'I was,' says Andy.

14

Conscience in Art

"I NEVER could hold my partner, Andy Tucker, down to legitimate ethics of pure swindling," said Jeff Peters to me one day.

"Andy had too much imagination to be honest. He used to devise schemes of money-getting so fraudulent and high-financial that they wouldn't have been allowed in the by-laws of a railroad rebate system.

"Myself, I never believed in taking any man's dollars unless I gave him something for it—something in the way of rolled gold jewellery, garden seeds, lumbago lotion, stock certificates, stove polish or a crack on the head to show for his money. I guess I must have had New England ancestors away back and inherited some of their staunch and rugged fear of the police.

"But Andy's family tree was in different kind. I don't think he could have traced his descent any further back than a corporation.

"One summer while he was in the Middle West, working down the Ohio valley with a line of family albums, headache powders and roach destroyer, Andy takes one of his notions of high and actionable financiering.

"'Jeff,' says he, 'I've been thinking that we ought to drop these rutabaga fanciers and give our attention to something more nourishing and prolific. If we keep on snapshooting these hinds for their egg money we'll be classed as nature fakers. How about plunging into the fastnesses of the sky-scraper country and biting some big bull caribous in the chest?'

"'Well,' says I, 'you know my idiosyncrasies. I prefer a

square, non-illegal style of business such as we are carrying on now. When I take money I want to leave some tangible object in the other fellow's hands for him to gaze at and to distract his attention from my spoor, even if it's only a Komical Kuss Trick Finger Ring for Squirting Perfume in a Friend's Eye. But if you've got a fresh idea, Andy,' says I, 'let's have a look at it. I'm not so wedded to petty graft that I would refuse something better in the way of a subsidy.'

"'I was thinking,' says Andy, 'of a little hunt without horn, hound or camera among the great herd of the Midas Americanus, commonly known as the Pittsburg-millionaires.'

"'In New York?' I asks.

"'No, sir,' says Andy, 'in Pittsburg. That's their habitat. They don't like New York. They go there now and then just because it's expected of 'em.'

"'A Pittsburg millionaire in New York is like a fly in a cup of hot coffee—he attracts attention and comment, but he don't enjoy it. New York ridicules him for "blowing" so much money in that town of sneaks and snobs, and sneers. The truth is, he don't spend anything while he is there. I saw a memorandum of expenses for a ten-days' trip to Bunkum Town made by a Pittsburg man worth $15,000,000 once. Here's the way he set it down:

R. R. fare to and from	.	.	· $21 00
Cab fare to and from hotel	.	·	2 00
Hotel bill ... $5 per day	.	.	· 50 00
Tips .	.	.	. · 5,750 00
Total	.	.	. $5,823 00

"'That's the voice of New York,' goes on Andy. 'The town's nothing but a head waiter. If you tip it too much it'll go and stand by the door and make fun of you to the hat check boy. When a Pittsburger wants to spend money and have a good time he stays at home. That's where we'll go to catch him.'

118

"Well, to make a dense story more condensed, me and Andy cached our Paris green and anti-pyrine powders and albums in a friend's cellar, and took the trail to Pittsburg. Andy didn't have any especial prospectus of chicanery and violence drawn up, but he always had plenty of confidence that his immoral nature would rise to any occasion that presented itself.

"As a concession to my ideas of self-preservation and rectitude he promised that if I should take an active and incriminating part in any little business venture that we might work up there should be something actual and cognizant to the senses of touch, sight, taste or smell to transfer to the victim for the money so my conscience might rest easy. After that I felt better and entered more cheerfully into the foul play.

"'Andy,' says I, as we strayed through the smoke along the cinderpath they call Smithfield Street, 'had you figured out how we are going to get acquainted with these coke kings and pig-iron squeezers? Not that I would decry my own worth or system of drawing-room deportment, and work with the olive fork and pie knife,' says I, 'but isn't the entre nous into the salons of the stogie smokers going to be harder than you imagined?'

"'If there's any handicap at all,' says Andy, 'it's our own refinement and inherent culture. Pittsburg millionaires are a fine body of plain, whole-hearted, unassuming, democratic men.

"'They are rough but uncivil in their manners, and though their ways are boisterous and unpolished, under it all they have a great deal of impoliteness and discourtesy. Nearly every one of 'em rose from obscurity,' says Andy, 'and they'll live in it till the town gets to using smoke consumers. If we act simple and unaffected and don't go too far from the saloons and keep making a noise like an import duty on steel rails we won't have any trouble in meeting some of 'em socially.'

"Well, Andy and me drifted about town three or four days

119

getting our bearings. We got to knowing several millionaires by sight.

"One used to stop his automobile in front of our hotel and have a quart of champagne brought out to him. When the waiter opened it he'd turn it up to his mouth and drink it out of the bottle. That showed he used to be a glass-blower before he made his money.

"One evening Andy failed to come to the hotel for dinner. About eleven o'clock he came into my room.

"'Landed one, Jeff,' says he. 'Twelve millions. Oil, rolling mills, real estate and natural gas. He's a fine man; no airs about him. Made all his money in the last five years. He's got professors posting him up now in education—art and literature and haberdashery and such things.

"'When I saw him he'd just won a bet of $10,000 with a Steel Corporation man that there'd be four suicides in the Allegheny rolling mills to-day. So everybody in sight had to walk up and have drinks on him. He took a fancy to me and asked me to dinner with him. We went to a restaurant in Diamond Alley and sat on stools and had sparkling Moselle and clam chowder and apple fritters.

"'Then he wanted to show me his bachelor apartment on Liberty Street. He's got ten rooms over a fish market with privilege of the bath on the next floor above. He told me it cost him $18,000 to furnish his apartment, and I believe it.

"'He's got $40,000 worth of pictures in one room, and $20,000 worth of curios and antiques in another. His name's Scudder, and he's 45, and taking lessons on the piano and 15,000 barrels of oil a day out of his wells.'

"'All right,' says I. 'Preliminary canter satisfactory. But, kay vooly, voo? What good is the art junk to us? And the oil?'

"'Now, that man,' says Andy, sitting thoughtfully on the bed, 'ain't what you would call an ordinary scutt. When he was showing me his cabinet of art curios his face lighted up like the door of a coke oven. He says that if some of his big deals go through he'll make J. P. Morgan's collection of sweetshop tapestry and Augusta, Me., beadwork look like the contents of an ostrich's craw thrown on a screen by a magic lantern.

"'And then he showed me a little carving,' went on Andy, 'that anybody could see was a wonderful thing. It was something like 2,000 years old, he said. It was a lotus flower with a woman's face in it carved out of a solid piece of ivory.

"'Scudder looks it up in a catalogue and describes it. An Egyptian carver named Khafra made two of 'em for King Rameses II about the year B.C. The other one can't be found. The junkshops and antique bugs have rubbered all Europe for it, but it seems to be out of stock. Scudder paid $2,000 for the one he has.'

"'Oh, well,' says I, 'this sounds like the purling of a rill to me. I thought we came here to teach the millionaires business, instead of learning art from 'em?'

"'Be patient,' says Andy kindly. 'Maybe we will see a rift in the smoke ere long.'

"All the next morning Andy was out. I didn't see him until about noon. He came to the hotel and called me into his room across the hall. He pulled a roundish bundle about as big as a goose egg out of his pocket and unwrapped it. It was an ivory carving just as he had described the millionaire's to me.

"'I went in an old second-hand store and pawnshop a while ago,' says Andy, 'and I see this half hidden under a lot of old daggers and truck. The pawnbroker said he'd had it several years and thinks it was soaked by some Arabs or Turks or some foreign dubs that used to live down by the river.

"'I offered him $2 for it, and I must have looked like I wanted it, for he said it would be taking the pumpernickel out of his children's mouth to hold any conversation that did not lead up to a price of $35. I finally got it for $25.

"'Jeff,' goes on Andy, 'this is the exact counterpart of Scudder's carving. It's absolutely a dead ringer for it. He'll pay $2,000 for it as quick as he'd tuck a napkin under his

121

chin. And why shouldn't it be the genuine other one, anyhow, that the old gipsy whittled out?'

"'Why not, indeed?' says I. 'And how shall we go about compelling him to make a voluntary purchase of it?'

"Andy had his plan all ready, and I'll tell you how we carried it out.

"I got a pair of blue spectacles, put on my black frock-coat, rumpled my hair up and became Prof. Pickleman. I went on to another hotel, registered, and sent a telegram to Scudder to come to see me at once on important art business. The elevator dumped him on me in less than an hour. He was a foggy man with a clarion voice, smelling of Connecticut wrappers and naphtha.

"'Hello, Profess!' he shouts. 'How's your conduct?'

"I rumpled my hair some more and gave him a blue-glass stare.

"'Sir,' says I. 'Are you Cornelius T. Scudder? Of Pittsburg, Pennsylvania?'

"'I am,' says he. 'Come out and have a drink.'

"'I have neither the time nor the desire,' says I, 'for such harmful and deleterious amusements. I have come from New York,' says I, 'on a matter of busi—on a matter of art.

"'I learned there that you are the owner of an Egyptian ivory carving of the time of Rameses II, representing the head of Queen Isis in a lotus flower. There were only two of such carvings made. One has been lost for many years. I recently discovered and purchased the other in a pawn—in an obscure museum in Vienna. I wish to purchase yours. Name your price.'

"'Well, the great ice jams, Profess!' says Scudder. 'Have you found the other one? Me sell? No. I don't guess Cornelius Scudder needs to sell anything that he wants to keep. Have you got the carving with you, Profess?'

"I shows it to Scudder. He examines it careful all over.

"'It's the article,' says he. 'It's a duplicate of mine, every line and curve of it. Tell you what I'll do,' he says. 'I won't sell, but I'll buy. Give you $2,500 for yours.'

122

"'Since you won't sell, I will,' says I. 'Large bills, please· I'm a man of few words. I must return to New York to-night. I lecture tomorrow at the aquarium.'

"Scudder sends a cheque down and the hotel cashes it. He goes off with his piece of antiquity and I hurry back to Andy's hotel, according to arrangement.

"Andy is walking up and down the room looking at his watch.

"'Well?' he says.

"'Twenty-five hundred,' says I. 'Cash.'

"'We've got just eleven minutes,' says Andy, 'to catch the B. & O. west-bound. Grab your baggage.'

"'What's the hurry?' says I. 'It was a square deal. And even if it was only an imitation of the original carving it'll take him some time to find it out. He seemed to be sure it was the genuine article.'

"'It was,' says Andy. 'It was his own. When I was looking at his curios yesterday he stepped out of the room for a moment and I pocketed it. Now, will you pick up your suit-case and hurry!'

"'Then,' says I, 'why was that story about finding another one in the pawn——"

"'Oh,' says Andy, 'out of respect for that conscience of yours. Come on.'"

15

The Man Higher Up

ACROSS our two dishes of spaghetti, in a corner of Provenzano's restaurant, Jeff Peters was explaining to me three kinds of graft.

Every winter Jeff comes to New York to eat spaghetti, to watch the shipping in East River from the depths of his chinchilla overcoat, and to lay in a supply of Chicago-made clothing at one of the Fulton Street stores. During the other three seasons he may be found further west—his range is from Spokane to Tampa. In his profession he takes a pride which he supports and defends with a serious and unique philosophy of ethics. His profession is no new one. He is an incorporated, uncapitalized, unlimited asylum for the reception of the restless and unwise dollars of his fellow-men.

In the wilderness of stone in which Jeff seeks his annual lonely holiday he is glad to palaver of his many adventures, as a boy will whistle after sundown in a wood. Wherefore, I mark on my calendar the time of his coming, and open a question of privilege at Provenzano's concerning the little wine-stained table in the corner between the rakish rubber plant and the framed palazzio della something on the wall.

"There are two kinds of grafts," said Jeff, "that ought to be wiped out by law. I mean Wall Street speculation, and burglary."

"Nearly everybody will agree with you as to one of them," said I, with a laugh.

"Well, burglary ought to be wiped out too," said Jeff; and I wondered whether the laugh had been redundant.

"About three months ago," said Jeff, "it was my privilege to become familiar with a sample of each of the aforesaid

branches of illegitimate art. I was *sine qua grata* with a member
of the housebreakers' union and one of the John D. Napoleons
of finance at the same time."

"Interesting combination," said I, with a yawn. "Did I
tell you I bagged a duck and a ground-squirrel at one shot
last week over in the Ramapos?" I knew well how to draw
Jeff's stories.

"Let me tell you first about these barnacles that clog the
wheels of society by poisoning the springs of rectitude with
their upas-like eye," said Jeff, with the pure gleam of the
muck-raker in his own.

"As I said, three months ago I got into bad company.
There are two times in a man's life when he does this—when
he's dead broke, and when he's rich.

"Now and then the most legitimate business runs out of
luck. It was out in Arkansas I made the wrong turn at a
cross-road, and drives into this town of Peavine by mistake.
It seems I had already assaulted and disfigured Peavine the
spring of the year before. I had sold $600 worth of young
fruit trees there—plums, cherries, peaches and pears. The
Peaviners were keeping an eye on the country road and hoping I might pass that way again. I drove down Main Street
as far as the Crystal Palace drug-store before I realized I had
committed ambush upon myself and my white horse Bill.

"The Peaviners took me by surprise and Bill by the bridle
and began a conversation that wasn't entirely dissociated
with the subject of fruit trees. A committee of 'em ran some
trace-chains through the armholes of my vest, and escorted
me through their gardens and orchards.

"Their fruit trees hadn't lived up to their labels. Most of
'em had turned out to be persimmons and dogwoods, with a
grove or two of blackjacks and poplars. The only one that
showed any signs of bearing anything was a fine young
cottonwood that had put forth a hornet's nest and half of an
old corset-cover.

"The Peaviners protracted our fruitless stroll to the edge
of town. They took my watch and money on account; and

they kept Bill and the wagon as hostages. They said the first time one of them dogwood trees put forth an Amsden's June peach I might come back and get my things. Then they took off the trace-chains and jerked their thumbs in the direction of the Rocky Mountains; and I struck a Lewis and Clark lope for the swollen rivers and impenetrable forests.

"When I regained intellectualness I found myself walking into an unidentified town on the A., T. & S. F. railroad. The Peaviners hadn't left anything in my pockets except a plug of chewing—they wasn't after my life—and that saved it. I bit off a chunk and sits down on a pile of ties by the track to recogitate my sensations of thought and perspicacity.

"And then along comes a fast freight which slows up a little at the town; and off of it drops a black bundle that rolls for twenty yards in a cloud of dust and then gets up and begins to spit soft coal and interjections. I see it is a young man broad across the face, dressed more for Pullmans than freights, and with a cheerful kind of smile in spite of it all that made Phœbe Snow's job look like a chimney-sweep's.

"'Fall off?' says I.

"'Nunk,' says he. 'Got off. Arrived at my destination. What town is this?'

"'Haven't looked it up on the map yet,' says I. 'I got in about five minutes before you did. How does it strike you?'

"'Hard,' says he, twisting one of his arms around. 'I believe that shoulder—no, it's all right.'

"He stoops over to brush the dust off his clothes, when out of his pocket drops a fine, nine-inch burglar's steel jimmy. He picks it up and looks at me sharp, and then grins and holds out his hand.

"'Brother,' says he, 'greetings. Didn't I see you in Southern Missouri last summer selling coloured sand at half a dollar a teaspoonful to put into lamps to keep the oil from exploding?'

"'Oil,' says I, 'never explodes. It's the gas that forms that explodes.' But I shake hands with him, anyway.

"'My name's Bill Bassett,' says he to me, 'and if you'll call it professional pride instead of conceit, I'll inform you that

126

you have the pleasure of meeting the best burglar that ever set a gum-shoe on ground drained by the Mississippi River.'

"Well, me and this Bill Bassett sits on the tie and exchanges brags as artists in kindred lines will do. It seems he didn't have a cent, either, and we went into close caucus. He explained why an able burglar sometimes had to travel on freights by telling me that a servant girl had played him false in Little Rock, and he was making a quick get-away.

"'It's part of my business,' says Bill Bassett, 'to play up the ruffles when I want to make a riffle as Raffles. 'Tis loves that makes the bit go 'round. Show me a house with the swag in it and a pretty parlourmaid, and you might as well call the silver melted down and sold, and me spilling truffles and that Château stuff on the napkin under my chin, while the police are calling it an inside job just because the old lady's nephew teaches a Bible class. I first make an impression on the girl,' says Bill, 'and when she lets me inside I make an impression on the locks. But this one in Little Rock done me,' says he. 'She saw me taking a trolley ride with another girl, and when I came round on the night she was to leave the door open for me it was fast. And I had keys made for the doors upstairs. But, no, sir. She had sure cut off my locks. She was a Delilah,' says Bill Bassett.

"It seems that Bill tried to break in anyhow with his jimmy, but the girl emitted a succession of bravura noises like the top-riders of a tally-ho, and Bill had to take all the hurdles between there and the depot. As he had no baggage they tried hard to check his departure, but he made a train that was just pulling out.

"'Well,' says Bill Bassett, when we had exchanged memoirs of our dead lives, 'I could eat. This town don't look like it was kept under a Yale lock. Suppose we commit some mild atrocity that will bring in temporary expense money. I don't suppose you've brought along any hair tonic or rolled-gold watch-chains, or similar law-defying swindles that you could sell on the plaza to the pikers of the paretic populace, have you?'

"'No,' says I, 'I left an elegant line of Patagonian diamond earrings and rainy-day sunbursts in my valise at Peavine. But they're to stay there till some of them black-gum trees begin to glut the market with yellow clings and Japanese plums. I reckon we can't count on them unless we take Luther Burbank in for a partner.'

"'Very well,' says Bassett, 'we'll do the best we can. Maybe after dark I'll borrow a hairpin from some lady, and open the Farmers' and Drovers' Marine Bank with it.'

"While we were talking, up pulls a passenger train to the depot near by. A person in a high hat gets off on the wrong side of the train and comes tripping down the track towards us. He was a little, fat man with a big nose and rat's eyes, but dressed expensive, and carrying a hand-satchel careful, as if it had eggs or railroad bonds in it. He passes by us and keeps on down the track, not appearing to notice the town.

"'Come on,' says Bill Bassett to me, starting after him.

"'Where?' I asks.

"'Lordy!' says Bill, 'had you forgot you was in the desert? Didn't you see Colonel Manna drop down right before your eyes? Don't you hear the rustling of General Raven's wings? I'm surprised at you, Elijah.'

"We overtook the stranger in the edge of some woods, and, as it was after sundown and in a quiet place, nobody saw us stop him. Bill takes the silk hat off the man's head and brushes it with his sleeve and puts it back.

"'What does this mean, sir?' says the man.

"'When I wore one of these,' says Bill, 'and felt embarrassed, I always done that. Not having one now, I had to use yours. I hardly know how to begin, sir, in explaining our business with you, but I guess we'll try your pockets first.'

"Bill Bassett felt in all of them, and looked disgusted.

"'Not even a watch,' he says. 'Ain't you ashamed of yourself, you whited sculpture? Going about dressed like a head-waiter, and financed like a Count! You haven't even got car-fare. What did you do with your transfer?'

"The man speaks up and says he has no assets or valuables of any sort. But Bassett takes his hand-satchel and opens it. Out comes some collars and socks and a half a page of a newspaper clipped out. Bill reads the clipping careful, and holds out his hand to the held-up party.

"'Brother,' says he, 'greetings! Accept the apologies of friends. I am Bill Bassett, the burglar. Mr. Peters, you must make the acquaintance of Mr. Alfred E. Ricks. Shake hands. Mr. Peters,' says Bill, 'stands about half-way between me and you, Mr. Ricks, in the line of havoc and corruption. He always gives something for the money he gets. I'm glad to meet you, Mr. Ricks—you and Mr. Peters. This is the first time I ever attended a full gathering of the National Synod of Sharks—housebreaking, swindling, and financiering all represented. Please examine Mr. Ricks's credentials, Mr. Peters.'

"The piece of newspaper that Bill Bassett handed me had a good picture of this Ricks on it. It was a Chicago paper, and it had obloquies of Ricks in every paragraph. By reading it over I harvested the intelligence that said alleged Ricks had laid off all that portion of the State of Florida that lies under water into town lots and sold 'em to alleged innocent investors from his magnificently furnished offices in Chicago. After he had taken in a hundred thousand or so dollars one of these fussy purchasers that are always making trouble—(I've had 'em actually try gold watches I've sold 'em with acid)—took a cheap excursion down to the land where it is always just before supper to look at his lot and see if it didn't need a new paling or two on the fence, and market a few lemons in time for the Christmas present trade. He hires a surveyor to find his lot for him. They run the line out and find the flourishing town of Paradise Hollow, so advertised, to be about 40 rods and 16 poles S., 27° E., of the middle of Lake Okeechobee. This man's lot was under thirty-six feet of water, and, besides, had been pre-empted so long by the alligators and gars that his title looked fishy.

"Naturally, the man goes back to Chicago and makes it

as hot for Alfred E. Ricks as the morning after a prediction of snow by the weather bureau. Ricks defied the allegation, but he couldn't deny the alligators. One morning the papers came out with a column about it, and Ricks came out by the fire-escape. It seems the alleged authorities had beat him to the safe-deposit box where he kept his winnings, and Ricks has to westward ho! with only feet-wear and a dozen 15½ English pokes in his shopping bag. He happened to have some mileage left in his book, and that took him as far as the town in the wilderness where he was spilled out on me and Bill Bassett as Elijah III with not a raven in sight for any of us.

"Then this Alfred E. Ricks lets out a squeak that he is hungry, too, and denies the hypothesis that he is good for the value, let alone the price, of a meal. And so, there was the three of us, representing, if we had a mind to draw syllogisms and parabolas, labour and trade and capital. Now, when trade has no capital there isn't a dicker to be made. And when capital has no money there's a stagnation in steak and onions. That put it up to the man with the jimmy.

"'Brother bushrangers,' says Bill Bassett, 'never yet, in trouble, did I desert a pal. Hard by, in yon wood, I seem to see unfurnished lodgings. Let us go there and wait till dark.'

"There was an old, deserted cabin in the grove, and we three took possession of it. After dark Bill Bassett tells us to wait, and goes out for half an hour. He comes back with a armful of bread and spareribs and pies.

"'Panhandled 'em at a farm-house on Washita Avenue,' says he. 'Eat, drink and be leary.'

"The full moon was coming up bright, so we sat on the floor of the cabin and ate in the light of it. And this Bill Bassett begins to brag.

"'Sometimes,' says he, with his mouth full of country produce, 'I lose all patience with you people that think you are higher up in the profession than I am. Now, what could either of you have done in the present emergency to set us on our feet again? Could you do it, Ricksy?'

"'I must confess, Mr. Bassett,' says Ricks, speaking nearly inaudible out of a slice of pie, 'that at this immediate juncture I could not, perhaps, promote an enterprise to relieve the situation. Large operations, such as I direct, naturally require careful preparations in advance. I——'

"'I know, Ricksy,' breaks in Bill Bassett. 'You needn't finish. You need $500 to make the first payment on a blonde typewriter, and four roomsful of quartered oak furniture. And you need $500 more for advertising contracts. And you need two weeks' time for the fish to begin to bite. Your line of relief would be about as useful in an emergency as advocating municipal ownership to cure a man suffocated by eighty-cent gas. And your graft ain't much swifter, Brother Peters,' he winds up.

"'Oh,' says I, 'I haven't seen you turn anything into gold with your wand yet, Mr. Good Fairy. Most anybody could rub the magic ring for a little left-over victuals.'

"'That was only getting the pumpkin ready,' says Bassett, braggy and cheerful. 'The coach and six'll drive up to the door before you know it, Miss Cinderella. Maybe you've got some scheme under your sleeve-holders that will give us a start.'

"'Son,' says I, 'I'm fifteen years older than you are, and young enough yet to take out an endowment policy. I've been broke before. We can see the lights of that town not half a smile away. I learned under Montague Silver, the greatest street man that ever spoke from a wagon. There are hundreds of men walking those streets this moment with grease-spots on their clothes. Give me a gasoline lamp, a dry-goods box and a two-dollar bar of white castile soap, cut into little——'

"'Where's your two dollars?' snickered Bill Bassett into my discourse. There was no use arguing with that burglar.

"'No,' he goes on; 'you're both babes-in-the-wood. Finance has closed the mahogany desk, and trade has put the shutters up. Both of you look to labour to start the wheels going. All right. You admit it. To-night I'll show you what Bill Bassett can do.'

"Bassett tells me and Ricks not to leave the cabin till he comes back, even if it's daylight, and then he starts off toward town, whistling gay.

"This Alfred E. Ricks pulls off his shoes and his coat, lays a silk handkerchief over his hat, and lays down on the floor.

"'I think I will endeavour to secure a little slumber,' he squeaks. 'The day has been fatiguing. Good night, my dear Mr. Peters.'

"'My regards to Morpheus,' says I. 'I think I'll sit up a while.'

"About two o'clock, as near as I could guess by my watch in Peavine, home comes our labouring man and kicks up Ricks, and calls us to the streak of bright moonlight shining in the cabin door. Then he spreads out five packages of one thousand dollars each on the floor, and begins to cackle over the nest-egg like a hen.

"'I'll tell you a few things about that town,' says he. 'It's named Rocky Springs, and they're building a Masonic temple, and it looks like the Democratic candidate for mayor is going to get soaked by a Pop, and Judge Tucker's wife, who has been down with pleurisy, is some better. I had a talk on these lilliputian thesises before I could get a siphon in the fountain of knowledge that I was after. And there's a bank there called the Lumberman's Fidelity and Ploughman's Savings Institution. It closed for business yesterday with $23,000 cash on hand. It will open this morning with $18,000 —all silver—that's the reason I didn't bring more. There you are, trade and capital. Now, will you be bad?'

"'My young friend,' says Alfred E. Ricks, holding up his hands, 'have you robbed this bank? Dear me, dear me!'

"'You couldn't call it that,' says Bassett. '"Robbing" sounds harsh. All I had to do was to find out what street it was on. That town is so quiet that I could stand on the corner and hear the tumblers clicking in that safe lock— "right to 45; left twice to 80; right once to 60; left to 15"— as plain as the Yale captain giving orders in the football dialect. New, boys,' says Bassett, 'this is an early rising town.

They tell me the citizens are all up and stirring before daylight. I asked what for, and they said because breakfast was ready at that time. And what of merry Robin Hood? It must be Yoicks! and away with the tinkers' chorus. I'll stake you. How much do you want? Speak up, Capital.'

"'My dear young friend,' says this ground squirrel of a Ricks, standing on his hind legs and juggling nuts in his paws, 'I have friends in Denver who would assist me. If I had a hundred dollars I——'

"Bassett unpins a package of the currency and throws five twenties to Ricks.

"'Trade, how much?' he says to me.

"'Put your money up, Labour,' says I. 'I never yet drew upon honest toil for its hard-earned pittance. The dollars I get are surplus ones that are burning the pockets of damfools and greenhorns. When I stand on a street corner and sell a solid gold diamond ring to a yap for $3.00, I make just $2.60. And I know he's going to give it to a girl in return for all the benefits accruing from a $125.00 ring. His profits are $122.00. Which of us is the biggest faker?'

"'And when you sell a poor woman a pinch of sand for fifty cents to keep her lamp from exploding,' says Bassett, 'what do you figure her gross earnings to be, with sand at forty cents a ton?'

"'Listen,' says I, 'I instruct her to keep her lamp clean and well filled. If she does that it can't burst. And with the sand in it she knows it can't, and she don't worry. It's a kind of Industrial Christian Science. She pays fifty cents, and gets both Rockefeller and Mrs. Eddy on the job. It ain't everybody that can let the gold-dust twins do their work.'

"Alfred E. Ricks all but licks the dust off of Bill Bassett's shoes.

"'My dear young friend,' says he, 'I will never forget your generosity. Heaven will reward you. But let me implore you to turn from your ways of violence and crime.'

"'Mousie,' says Bill, 'the hole in the wainscoting for yours. Your dogmas and inculcations sound to me like the last

133

words of a bicycle pump. What has your high moral, elevator-service system of pillage brought you to? Penuriousness and want. Even Brother Peters, who insists upon contaminating the art of robbery with theories of commerce and trade, admitted he was on the lift. Both of you live by the gilded rule. Brother Peters,' says Bill, 'you'd better choose a slice of this embalmed currency. You're welcome.'

"I told Bill Bassett once more to put his money in his pocket. I had never had the respect for burglary that some people have. I always gave something for the money I took, even if it was only some little trifle for a souvenir to remind 'em not to get caught again.

"And then Alfred E. Ricks grovels at Bill's feet again, and bids us adieu. He says he will have a team at a farm-house, and drive to the station below, and take the train for Denver. It salubrified the atmosphere when that lamentable bollworm took his departure. He was a disgrace to every non-industrial profession in the country. With all his big schemes and fine offices he had wound up unable even to get an honest meal except by the kindness of a strange and maybe unscrupulous burglar. I was glad to see him go, though I felt a little sorry for him, now that he was ruined for ever. What could such a man do without a big capital to work with? Why, Alfred E. Ricks, as we left him, was as helpless as a turtle on its back. He couldn't have worked a scheme to beat a little girl out of a penny slate-pencil.

"When me and Bill Bassett was left alone I did a little sleight-of-mind turn in my head with a trade secret at the end of it. Thinks I, I'll show this Mr. Burglar Man the difference between business and labour. He had hurt some of my professional self-adulation by casting his Persians upon commerce and trade.

"'I won't take any of your money as a gift, Mr. Bassett,' says I to him, 'but if you'll pay my expenses as a travelling companion until we get out of the danger zone of the immoral deficit you have caused in this town's finances to-night, I'll be obliged.'

"Bill Basset agreed to that, and we hiked westward as soon as we could catch a safe train.

"When we got to a town in Arizona called Los Perros I suggested that we once more try our luck on terra-cotta. That was the home of Montague Silver, my old instructor, now retired from business. I knew Monty would stake me to web money if I could show him a fly buzzing 'round in the locality. Bill Bassett said all towns looked alike to him as he worked mainly in the dark. So we got off the train in Los Perros, a fine little town in the silver region.

"I had an elegant little sure thing in the way of a commercial slungshot that I intended to hit Bassett behind the ear with. I wasn't going to take his money while he was asleep, but I was going to leave him with a lottery ticket that would represent in experience to him $4,755—I think that was the amount he had when we got off the train. But the first time I hinted to him about an investment, he turns on me and disencumbers himself of the following terms and expressions.

"'Brother Peters,' says he, 'it ain't a bad idea to go into an enterprise of some kind, as you suggest. I think I will. But if I do it will be such a cold proposition that nobody but Robert E. Peary and Charlie Fairbanks will be able to sit on the board of directors.'

"'I thought you might want to turn your money over,' says I.

"'I do,' says he, 'frequently. I can't sleep on one side all night. I'll tell you, Brother Peters,' says he, 'I'm going to start a poker room. I don't seem to care for the humdrum in swindling, such as peddling egg-beaters and working off breakfast food on Barnum and Bailey for sawdust to strew in their circus rings. But the gambling business,' says he, 'from the profitable side of the table is a good compromise between swiping silver spoons and selling penwipers at a Waldorf-Astoria charity bazaar.'

"'Then,' says I, 'Mr. Bassett, you don't care to talk over my little business proposition?'

"'Why,' says he, 'do you know, you can't get a Pasteur

institute to start up within fifty miles of where I live. I bite so seldom.'

"So, Bassett rents a room over a saloon and looks around for some furniture and chromos. The same night I went to Monty Silver's house, and he let me have $200 on my prospects. Then I went to the only store in Los Perros that sold playing cards and bought every deck in the house. The next morning when the store opened I was there bringing all the cards back with me. I said that my partner that was going to back me in the game had changed his mind; and I wanted to sell the cards back again. The storekeeper took 'em at half price.

"Yes, I was seventy-five dollars loser up to that time. But while I had the cards that night I marked every one in every deck. That was labour. And then trade and commerce had their innings, and the bread I had cast upon the waters began to come back in the form of cottage pudding with wine sauce.

"Of course I was among the first to buy chips at Bill Bassett's game. He had bought the only cards there was to be had in town, and I knew the back of every one of them better than I know the back of my head when the barber shows me my haircut in the two mirrors.

"When the game closed I had the five thousand and a few odd dollars, and all Bill Bassett had was the wanderlust and a black cat he had bought for a mascot. Bill shook hands with me when I left.

"'Brother Peters,' says he, 'I have no business being in business. I was preordained to labour. When a No. 1 burglar tries to make a James out of his jimmy he perpetrates an improfundity. You have a well-oiled and efficacious system of luck at cards,' says he. 'Peace go with you.' And I never afterwards sees Bill Bassett again."

"Well, Jeff," said I, when the Autolycan adventurer seemed to have divulged the gist of his tale, "I hope you took care of the money. That would be a respecta—that is a considerable working capital if you should choose some day to settle down to some sort of regular business."

"Me?" said Jeff virtuously. "You can bet I've taken care of that five thousand."

He tapped his coat over the region of his chest exultantly.

"Gold mining stock," he explained, "every cent of it. Shares par value one dollar. Bound to go up 500 per cent. within a year. Non-assessable. The Blue Gopher Mine. Just discovered a month ago. Better get in yourself if you've any spare dollars on hand."

"Sometimes," said I, "these mines are not——"

"Oh, this one's solid as an old goose," said Jeff. "Fifty thousand dollars' worth of ore in sight, and 10 per cent monthly earnings guaranteed."

He drew a long envelope from his pocket and cast it on the table.

"Always carry it with me," said he. "So the burglar can't corrupt or the capitalist break in and water it."

"I looked at the beautifully engraved certificate of stock.

"In Colorado, I see," said I. "And, by the way, Jeff, what was the name of the little man who went to Denver—the one you and Bill met at the station?"

"Alfred E. Ricks," said Jeff, "was the toad's designation."

"I see," said I, "the president of this mining company signs himself A. L. Fredericks. I was wondering——"

"Let me see that stock," said Jeff quickly, almost snatching it from me.

To mitigate, even though slightly, the embarrassment, I summoned the waiter and ordered another bottle of the Barbera. I thought it was the least I could do.

16

A Tempered Wind

THE first time my optical nerves was disturbed by the sight of Buckingham Skinner was in Kansas City. I was standing on a corner when I see Buck stick his straw-coloured head out of a third-storey window of a business block and holler, "Whoa, there! Whoa!" like you would in endeavouring to assuage a team of runaway mules.

I looked around; but all the animals I see in sight is a policeman, having his shoes shined, and a couple of delivery wagons hitched to posts. Then in a minute downstairs tumbles this Buckingham Skinner, and runs to the corner, and stands and gazes down the other street at the imaginary dust kicked up by the fabulous hoofs of the fictitious team of chimerical quadrupeds. And then B. Skinner goes back up to the third-storey room again, and I see that the lettering on the window is "The Farmers' Friend Loan Company".

By and by Straw-top comes down again, and I crossed the street to meet him, for I had my ideas. Yes, sir, when I got close I could see where he overdone it. He was Reub all right as far as his blue jeans and cowhide boots went, but he had a matinée actor's hands, and the rye straw stuck over his ear looked like it belonged to the property man of the Old Homestead Co. Curiosity to know what his graft was got the best of me.

"Was that your team broke away and run just now?" I asks him, polite. "I tried to stop 'em," says I, "but I couldn't. I guess they're half-way back to the farm by now."

"Gosh blame them darned mules," says Straw-top, in a voice so good that I nearly apologized; "they're a'lus bustin' loose." And then he looks at me close, and then he takes off

138

his hayseed hat, and says, in a different voice: "I'd like to shake hands with Parleyvoo Pickens, the greatest street man in the West, barring only Montague Silver, which you can no more than allow."

I let him shake hands with me.

"I learned under Silver," I said; "I don't begrudge him the lead. But what's your graft, son? I admit that the phantom flight of the non-existing animals at which you remarked 'Whoa!' has puzzled me somewhat. How do you win out on the trick?"

Buckingham Skinner blushed.

"Pocket money," says he; "that's all. I am temporarily unfinanced. This little coup de rye straw is good for forty dollars in a town of this size. How do I work it? Why, I involve myself, as you perceive, in the loathsome apparel of the rural dub. Thus embalmed I am Jonas Stubblefield—a name impossible to improve upon. I repair noisily to the office of some loan company conveniently located in the third floor front. There I lay my hat and yarn gloves on the floor and ask to mortgage my farm for $2,000 to pay for my sister's musical education in Europe. Loans like that always suit the loan companies. It's ten to one that when the note falls due the foreclosure will be leading the semiquavers by a couple of lengths.

"Well, sir, I reach in my pocket for the abstract of title; but I suddenly hear my team running away. I run to the window and emit the word—or exclamation, whichever it may be—viz. 'Whoa!' Then I rush downstairs and down the street, returning in a few minutes. 'Dang them mules,' I says; 'they done run away and busted the doubletree and two traces. Now I got to hoof it home, for I never brought no money along. Reckon we'll talk about that loan some other time, gen'lemen.'

"Then I spreads out my tarpaulin, like the Israelites, and waits for the manna to drop.

"'Why, no, Mr. Stubblefield,' says the lobster-coloured

party in the specs and dotted piqué vest; 'oblige us by accepting this ten-dollar bill until to-morrow. Get your harness repaired and call in at ten. We'll be pleased to accommodate you in the matter of this loan.'

"It's a slight thing," says Buckingham Skinner, modest, "but, as I said, only for temporary loose change."

"It's nothing to be ashamed of," says I, in respect for his mortification; "in case of an emergency. of course, it's small compared to organizing a trust or bridge whist, but even the Chicago University had to be started in a small way."

"What's your graft these days?" Buckingham Skinner asks me.

"The legitimate," says I. "I'm handling rhinestones and Dr. Oleum Sinapi's Electric Headache Battery and the Swiss Warbler's Bird Call, a small lot of the new queer ones and twos, and the Bonanza Budget, consisting of a rolled-gold wedding and engagement ring, six Egyptian lily bulbs, a combination pickle fork and nail-clipper, and fifty engraved visiting cards—no two names alike—all for the sum of thirty-eight cents."

"Two months ago," says Buckingham Skinner, "I was doing well down in Texas with a patent instantaneous fire kindler, made of compressed wood ashes and benzine. I sold loads of 'em in towns where they like to burn niggers quick, without having to ask somebody for a light. And just when I was doing the best they strikes oil down there and puts me out of business. 'Your machine's too slow, now, pardner,' they tells me. 'We can have a coon in hell with this here petroleum before your old flint-and-tinder truck can get him warm enough to perfess religion.' And so I gives up the kindler and drifts up here to K.C. This little curtain-raiser you seen me doing, Mr. Pickens, with the simulated farm and the hypothetical team, ain't in my line at all, and I'm ashamed you found me working it."

"No man," says I kindly, "need to be ashamed of putting the skibunk on a loan corporation for even so small a sum as ten dollars, when he is financially abashed. Still, it wasn't quite the proper thing. It's too much like borrowing money without paying it back."

I liked Buckingham Skinner from the start, for as good a man as ever stood over the axles and breathed gasoline smoke. And pretty soon we gets thick, and I lets him in on a scheme I'd had in mind for some time, and offers to go partners.

"Anything," says Buck, "that is not actually dishonest will find me willing and ready. Let us perforate into the inwardness of your proposition. I feel degraded when I am forced to wear property straw in my hair and assume a bucolic air for the small sum of ten dollars. Actually, Mr. Pickens, it makes me feel like the Ophelia of the Great Occidental All-Star One-Night Consolidated Theatrical Aggregation."

This scheme of mine was one that suited my proclivities. By nature I am some sentimental, and have always felt gentle toward the mollifying elements of existence. I am disposed to be lenient with the arts and sciences, and I find time to instigate a cordiality for the more human works of nature, such as romance and the atmosphere and grass and poetry and the seasons. I never skin a sucker without admiring the prismatic beauty of his scales. I never sell a little auriferous trifle to the man with the hoe without noticing the beautiful harmony there is between gold and green. And that's why I liked this scheme; it was so full of outdoor air and landscapes and easy money.

We had to have a young lady assistant to help us work this graft; and I asked Buck if he knew of one to fill the bill.

"One," says I, "that is cool and wise and strictly business from her pompadour to her Oxfords. No ex-toe-dancers or gum-chewers or crayon portrait canvassers for this."

Buck claimed he knew a suitable feminine and he takes me around to see Miss Sarah Malloy. The minute I see her I am pleased. She looked to be the goods as ordered. No sign of the three p's about her—no peroxide, patchouli, nor peau

141

de soie; about twenty-two, brown hair, pleasant ways—the kind of a lady for the place.

"A description of the sandbag, if you please," she begins.

"Why, ma'am," says I, "this graft of ours is so nice and refined and romantic, it would make the balcony scene in 'Romeo and Juliet' look like second-storey work."

We talked it over, and Miss Malloy agreed to come in as a business partner. She said she was glad to get a chance to give up her place as stenographer and secretary to a suburban lot company, and go into something respectable.

This is the way we worked our scheme. First, I figured it out by a kind of a proverb. The best grafts in the world are built up on copy-book maxims and psalms and proverbs and Esau's fables. They seem to kind of hit off human nature. Our peaceful little swindle was constructed on the old saying: "The whole push loves a lover."

One evening Buck and Miss Malloy drives up like blazes in a buggy to a farmer's door. She is pale but affectionate, clinging to his arm—always clinging to his arm. And one can see that she is a peach and of the cling variety. They claim they are eloping for to be married on account of cruel parents. They ask where they can find a preacher. Farmer says, "B'gum there ain't any preacher nigher than Reverend Abels, four miles over on Caney Creek." Farmeress wipes her hands on her apron and rubbers through her specs.

Then, lo and look ye! Up the road from the other way jogs Parleyvoo Pickens in a gig, dressed in black, white necktie, long face, sniffing his nose, emitting a spurious kind of noise resembling the long metre doxology.

"B'jinks!" says farmer, "if thar ain't a preacher now!"

It transpires that I am Rev. Abijah Green, travelling over to Little Bethel school-house for to preach next Sunday.

The young folks will have it they must be married, for pa is pursuing them with the plough mules and the buckboard. So the Reverend Green, after hesitation, marries 'em in farmer's parlour. And farmer grins, and has in cider, and says, "B'gum!" and farmeress sniffles a bit and pats the

bride on the shoulder. And Parleyvoo Pickens, the wrong
reverend, writes out a marriage certificate, and farmer and
farmeress sign it as witnesses. And the parties of the first,
second, and third part gets in their vehicles and rides away.
Oh, that was an idyllic graft! True love and the lowing kine
and the sun shining on the red barns—it certainly had all
other impostures I know about beat to a batter.

I suppose I happened along in time to marry Buck and
Miss Malloy at about twenty farmhouses. I hated to think
how the romance was going to fade later on when all them
marriage certificates turned up in banks where we'd dis-
counted 'em, and the farmers had to pay them notes of hand
they'd signed, running from $300 to $500.

On the 15th day of May us three divided about $6,000.
Miss Malloy nearly cried with joy. You don't often see a
tender-hearted girl or one that was so bent on doing right.

"Boys," says she, dabbing her eyes with a little handkerchief, "this stake comes in handier than a powder rag at a
fat man's ball. It gives me a chance to reform. I was trying
to get out of the real estate business when you fellows came
along. But if you hadn't taken me in on this neat little proposition for removing the cuticle of the rutabaga propagators
I'm afraid I'd have got into something worse. I was about
to accept a place in one of these Women's Auxiliary Bazaars,
where they build a parsonage by selling a spoonful of chicken
salad and a cream-puff for seventy-five cents and calling it
a Business Men's Lunch.

"Now I can go into a square, honest business, and give all
them queer jobs the shake. I'm going to Cincinnati and
start a palm reading and clairvoyant joint. As Madame
Saramaloi, the Egyptian Sorceress, I shall give everybody a
dollar's worth of good honest prognostication. Good-bye,
boys. Take my advice and go into some decent fake. Get
friendly with the police and newspapers and you'll be all
right."

So then we all shook hands, and Miss Malloy left us. Me
and Buck also rose up and sauntered off a few hundred

miles; for we didn't care to be around when them marriage certificates fell due.

With about $4,000 between us we hit that bumptious little town off the New Jersey coast they call New York.

If there ever was an aviary overstocked with jays it is that Yaptown-on-the-Hudson. Cosmopolitan they call it. You bet. So's a piece of fly-paper. You listen close when they're buzzing and trying to pull their feet out of the sticky stuff. "Little old New York's good enough for us"—that's what they sing.

There's enough Reubs walk down Broadway in one hour to buy up a week's output of the factory in Augusta, Maine, that makes Knaughty Knovelties and the little Phine Phun oroide gold finger ring that sticks a needle in your friend's hand.

You'd think New York people was all wise; but no. They don't get a chance to learn. Everything's too compressed. Even the hayseeds are baled hayseeds. But what else can you expect from a town that's shut off from the world by the ocean on one side and New Jersey on the other?

It's no place for an honest grafter with a small capital. There's too big a protective tariff on bunco. Even when Giovanni sells a quart of warm worms and chestnut hulls he has to hand out a pint to an insectivorous cop. And the hotel man charges double for everything in the bill that he sends by the patrol wagon to the altar where the duke is about to marry the heiress.

But old Badville-near-Coney is the ideal burg for a refined piece of piracy if you can pay the bunco duty. Imported grafts come pretty high. The custom-house officers that look after it carry clubs, and it's hard to smuggle in even a bib-and-tucker swindle to work Brooklyn with unless you can pay the toll. But now, me and Buck, having capital, descends upon New York to try and trade the metropolitan backwoodsmen a few glass beads for real estate just as the Vans did a hundred or two years ago.

At an East Side hotel we gets acquainted with Romulus G.

Atterbury, a man with the finest head for financial operations I ever saw. It was all bald and glossy except for grey side whiskers. Seeing that head behind an office railing, you'd deposit a million with it without a receipt. This Atterbury was well dressed, though he ate seldom; and the synopsis of his talk would make the conversation of a siren sound like a cab-driver's kick. He said he used to be a member of the Stock Exchange, but some of the big capitalists got jealous and formed a ring that forced him to sell his seat.

Atterbury got to liking me and Buck and he begun to throw on the canvas for us some of the schemes that had caused his hair to evacuate. He had one scheme for starting a National Bank on $45 that made the Mississippi Bubble look as solid as a glass marble. He talked this to us for three days, and when his throat was good and sore we told him about the roll we had. Atterbury borrowed a quarter from us and went out and got a box of throat lozenges and started all over again. This time he talked bigger things, and we got to see 'em as he did. The scheme he laid out looked like a sure winner, and he talked me and Buck into putting our capital against his burnished dome of thought. It looked all right for a kid-gloved graft. It seemed to be just about an inch and a half outside of the reach of the police, and as money-making as a mint. It was just what me and Buck wanted—a regular business at a permanent stand, with no open-air spieling with tonsillitis on the street corners every evening.

So, in six weeks you see a handsome furnished set of offices down in the Wall Street neighbourhood, with "The Golconda Gold Bond and Investment Company" in gilt letters on the door. And you see in his private room, with the door open, the secretary and treasurer, Mr. Buckingham Skinner, costumed like the lilies of the conservatory, with his high silk hat close to his hand. Nobody yet ever saw Buck outside of an instantaneous reach for his hat.

And you might perceive the president and general

145

manager, Mr. R. G. Atterbury, with his priceless polished poll, busy in the main office room dictating letters to a shorthand contess, who has got pomp and a pompadour that is no less than a guarantee to investors.

There is a book-keeper and an assistant, and a general atmosphere of varnish and culpability.

At another desk the eye is relieved by the sight of an ordinary man, attired with unscrupulous plainness, sitting with his feet up, eating apples, with his obnoxious hat on the back of his head. That man is no other than Colonel Tecumseh (once "Parleyvoo") Pickens, the vice-president of the company.

"No recherché rags for me," I says to Atterbury, when we was organizing the stage properties of the robbery. "I'm a plain man," says I, "and I do not use pajamas, French, or military hair-brushes. Cast me for the rôle of the rhinestone-in-the-rough or I don't go on exhibition. If you can use me in my natural, though displeasing form, do so."

"Dress you up?" says Atterbury. "I should say not! Just as you are you're worth more to the business than a whole roomful of the things they pin chrysanthemums on. You're to play the part of the solid but dishevelled capitalist from the Far West. You despise the conventions. You've got so many stocks you can afford to shake socks. Conservative, homely, rough, shrewd, saving—that's your pose. It's a winner in New York. Keep your feet on the desk and eat apples. Whenever anybody comes in eat an apple. Let 'em see you stuff the peelings in a drawer of your desk. Look as economical and rich and rugged as you can."

I followed out Atterbury's instructions. I played the Rocky Mountain capitalist without ruching or frills. The way I deposited apple peelings to my credit in a drawer when any customers came in made Hetty Green look like a spendthrift. I could hear Atterbury saying to victims, as he smiled at me, indulgent and venerating, "That's our vice-president, Colonel Pickens . . . fortune in Western investments . . . delightfully plain manners, but . . . could sign his cheque for

146

half a million . . . simple as a child . . . wonderful head . . . conservative and careful almost to a fault."

Atterbury managed the business. Me and Buck never quite understood all of it, though he explained it to us in full. It seems the company was a kind of co-operative one, and everybody that bought stock shared in the profits. First, we officers bought up a controlling interest—we had to have that—of the shares at fifty cents a hundred—just what the printer charged us—and the rest went to the public at a dollar each. The company guaranteed the stockholders a profit of ten per cent each month, payable on the last day thereof.

When any stockholder had paid in as much as $100, the company issued him a Gold Bond and he became a bond-holder. I asked Atterbury one day what benefits and appur-tenances these Gold Bonds was to an investor more so than the immunities and privileges enjoyed by the common sucker who only owned stock. Atterbury picked up one of them Gold Bonds, all gilt and lettered up with flourishes and a big red seal tied with a blue ribbon in a bow-knot, and he looked at me like his feelings was hurt.

"My dear Colonel Pickens," says he, "you have no soul for Art. Think of a thousand homes made happy by possessing one of these beautiful gems of the lithographer's skill! Think of the joy in the household where one of these Gold Bonds hangs by a pink cord to the whatnot, or is chewed by the baby, carolling gleefully upon the floor! Ah, I see your eye growing moist, Colonel—I have touched you, have I not?"

"You have not," says I, "for I've been watching you. The moisture you see is apple juice. You can't expect one man to act as a human cider-press and an art connoisseur too."

Atterbury attended to the details of the concern. As I understand it, they were simple. The investors in stock paid in their money, and—well, I guess that's all they had to do. The company received it, and—I don't call to mind anything else. Me and Buck knew more about selling corn salve than we did about Wall Street, but even we could see how the

Golconda Gold Bond Investment Company was making money. You take in money and pay back 10 per cent of it; it's plain enough that you make a clean, legitimate profit of 90 per cent, less expenses, as long as the fish bite.

Atterbury wanted to be president and treasurer too, but Buck winks an eye at him and says: "You was to furnish the brains. Do you call it good brain-work when you propose to take in money at the door too? Think again. I hereby nominate myself treasurer *ad valorem*, *sine die*, and by acclamation. I chip in that much brain-work free. Me and Pickens, we furnished the capital, and we'll handle the unearned increment as it incremates."

It cost us $500 for office rent and first payment on furniture; $1,500 more went for printing and advertising. Atterbury knew his business. "Three months to a minute we'll last," says he. "A day longer than that and we'll have to either go under or go under an alias. By that time we ought to clean up $60,000. And then a money belt and a lower berth for me, and the yellow journals and the furniture men can pick the bones."

Our ads. done the work. "Country weeklies and Washington hand-press dailies, of course," says I when we was ready to make contracts.

"Man," says Atterbury, "as its advertising manager you would cause a Limburger cheese factory to remain undiscovered during a hot summer. The game we're after is right here in New York and Brooklyn and the Harlem reading-rooms. They're the people that the street-car fenders and the Answers to Correspondents columns and the pickpocket notices are made for. We want our ads. in the biggest city dailies, top of column, next to editorials on radium and pictures of the girl doing health exercises."

Pretty soon the money begins to roll in. Buck didn't have to pretend to be busy; his desk was piled high up with money orders and cheques and green-backs. People began to drop in the office and buy stock every day.

Most of the shares went in small amounts—$10 and $25

and $50, and a good many $2 and $3 lots. And the bald and inviolate cranium of President Atterbury shines with enthusiasm and demerit, while Colonel Tecumseh Pickens, the rude but reputable Crœsus of the West, consumes so many apples that the peelings hang to the floor from the mahogany garbage chest that he calls his desk.

Just as Atterbury said, we ran along about three months without being troubled. Buck cashed the paper as fast as it came in and kept the money in a safe deposit vault a block or so away. Buck never thought much of banks for such purposes. We paid the interest regular on the stock we'd sold, so there was nothing for anybody to squeal about. We had nearly $50,000 on hand and all three of us had been living as high as prize-fighters out of training.

One morning, as me and Buck sauntered into the office, fat and flippant, from our noon grub, we met an easy-looking fellow, with a bright eye and a pipe in his mouth, coming out. We found Atterbury looking like he'd been caught a mile from home in a wet shower.

"Know that man?" he asked us.

We said we didn't.

"I don't either," says Atterbury, wiping off his head; "but I'll bet enough Gold Bonds to paper a cell in the Tombs that he's a newspaper reporter."

"What did he want?" asks Buck.

"Information," says our president. "He said he was thinking of buying some stock and asked me about nine hundred questions, and every one of 'em hit some sore place in the business. I know he's on a paper. You can't fool me. You see a man about half shabby, with an eye like a gimlet, smoking cut plug, with dandruff on his coat collar, and knowing more than J. P. Morgan and Shakespeare put together—if that ain't a reporter I never saw one. I was afraid of this. I don't mind detectives and post-office inspectors—I talk to 'em eight minutes and then sell 'em stock—but them reporters take the starch out of my collar. Boys, I recommend that we declare a dividend and fade away. The signs point that way."

Me and Buck talked to Atterbury and got him to stop sweating and stand still. That fellow didn't look like a reporter to us. Reporters always pull out a pencil and tablet on you, and tell you a story you've heard, and strike you for the drinks. But Atterbury was shaky and nervous all day.

The next day me and Buck comes down from the hotel about ten-thirty. On the way we buys the papers, and the first thing we see is a column on the front page about our little imposition. It was a shame the way that reporter intimated that we were no blood relatives of the late George W. Childs. He tells all about the scheme as he sees it, in a rich, racy kind of a guying style that might amuse most anybody except a stockholder. Atterbury was right; it behooveth the gaily clad treasurer and the pearly pated president and the rugged vice-president of Golconda Gold Bond and Investment Company to go away real sudden and quick that their days might be longer upon the land.

Me and Buck hurries down to the office. We finds on the stairs and in the hall a crowd of people trying to squeeze into our office, which is already jammed full inside to the railing. They've nearly all got Golconda stock and Gold Bonds in their hands. Me and Buck judged they'd been reading the papers, too.

We stopped and looked at our stockholders, some surprised. It wasn't quite the kind of a gang we supposed had been investing. They all looked like poor people; there was plenty of old women and lots of young girls that you'd say worked in factories and mills. Some was old men that looked like war veterans, and some was crippled, and a good many was just kids—bootblacks and newsboys and messengers. Some was working-men in overalls, with their sleeves rolled up. Not one of the gang looked like a stockholder in anything unless it was a peanut stand. But they all had Golconda stock and looked as sick as you please.

I saw a queer kind of a pale look come on Buck's face when he sized up the crowd. He stepped up to a sickly looking woman and says: "Madam, do you own any of this stock?"

"I put in a hundred dollars," says the woman, faint like. "It was all I had saved in a year. One of my children is dying at home now and I haven't a cent in the house. I came to see if I could draw out some. The circulars said you could draw it at any time. But they say now I will lose it all."

There was a smart kind of a kid in the gang—I guess he was a newsboy. "I got in twenty-fi', mister," he says, looking hopeful at Buck's silk hat and clothes. "Dey paid me two-fifty a mont' on it. Say, a man tells me dey can't do dat and be on the square. Is dat straight? Do you guess I can get out my twenty-fi'?"

Some of the old women was crying. The factory girls was plumb distracted. They'd lost all their savings and they'd be docked for the time they lost coming to see about it.

There was one girl—a pretty one in a red shawl, crying in a corner like her heart would dissolve. Buck goes over and asks her about it.

"It ain't so much losing the money, mister," says she, shaking all over, "though I've been two years saving it up; but Jakey won't marry me now. He'll take Rosa Steinfeld. I know J—J—Jakey. She's got $400 in the savings bank. Ai, ai, ai——" she sings out.

Buck looks all around with that same funny look on his face. And then we see leaning against the wall, puffing at his pipe, with his eye shining at us, this newspaper reporter. Buck and me walks over to him.

"You're a real interesting writer," says Buck. "How far do you mean to carry it? Anything more up your sleeve?"

"Oh, I'm just waiting around," says the reporter, smoking away, "in case any news turns up. It's up to your stockholders now. Some of them might complain, you know. Isn't that the patrol wagon now?" he says, listening to a sound outside. "No," he goes on, "that's Doc. Whittleford's old cadaver coupé from the Roosevelt. I ought to know that gong. Yes, I suppose I've written some interesting stuff at times."

"You wait," says Buck; "I'm going to throw an item of news in your way."

Buck reaches in his pocket and hands me a key. I knew what he meant before he spoke. Confounded old buccaneer—I knew what he meant. They don't make them any better than Buck.

"Pick," says he, looking at me hard, "ain't this graft a little out of our line? Do we want Jakey to marry Rosa Steinfeld?"

"You've got my vote," says I. "I'll have it here in ten minutes." And I starts for the safe deposit vaults.

I comes back with the money done up in a big bundle, and then Buck and me takes the journalist reporter around to another door and we let ourselves into one of the office rooms.

"Now, my literary friend," says Buck, "take a chair, and keep still, and I'll give you an interview. You see before you two grafters from Graftersville, Grafter County, Arkansas. Me and Pick have sold brass jewellery, hair tonic, song books, marked cards, patent medicines, Connecticut Smyrna rugs, furniture polish, and albums in every town from Old Point Comfort to the Golden Gate. We've grafted a dollar whenever we saw one that had a surplus look to it. But we never went after the simoleon in the toe of the sock under the loose brick in the corner of the kitchen hearth. There's an old saying you may have heard—'fussily decency averni'—which means it's an easy slide from the street-faker's dry-goods box to a desk in Wall Street. We've took that slide, but we didn't know exactly what was at the bottom of it. Now, you ought to be wise, but you ain't. You've got New York wiseness, which means that you judge a man by the outside of his clothes. That ain't right. You ought to look at the lining and seams and the button-holes. While we are waiting for the patrol wagon you might get out your little stub pencil and take notes for another funny piece in the paper."

And then Buck turns to me and says: "I don't care what Atterbury thinks. He only put in brains, and if he gets his capital out he's lucky. But what do you say, Pick?"

"Me?" said I. "You ought to know me, Buck. I didn't know who was buying the stock."

152

"All right," says Buck. And then he goes through the inside door into the main office and looks at the gang trying to squeeze through the railing. Atterbury and his hat was gone. And Buck makes 'em a short speech.

"All you lambs get in line. You're going to get your wool back. Don't shove so. Get in a line—a *line*—not in a pile. Lady, will you please stop bleating? Your money's waiting for you. Here, sonny, don't climb over that railing; your dimes are safe. Don't cry, sis; you ain't out a cent. Get in *line*, I say. Here, Pick, come and straighten 'em out and let 'em through and out by the other door."

Buck takes off his coat, pushes his silk hat on the back of his head, and lights up a reina victoria. He sets at the table with the boodle before him, all done up in neat packages. I gets the stockholders strung out and marches 'em, single file, through from the main room; and the reporter man passes 'em out of the side door into the hall again. As they go by, Buck takes up the stock and the Gold Bonds, paying 'em cash, dollar for dollar, the same as they paid in.

The shareholders of the Golconda Gold Bond and Investment Company can't hardly believe it. They almost grabs the money out of Buck's hands. Some of the women keep on crying, for it's a custom of the sex to cry when they have sorrow, to weep when they have joy, and to shed tears whenever they find themselves without either.

The old women's fingers shake when they stuff the skads in the bosom of their rusty dresses. The factory girls just stoop over and flap their dry goods a second, and you hear the elastic go "pop" as the currency goes down in the ladies' department of the "Old Domestic Lisle-Thread Bank".

Some of the stockholders that had been doing the Jeremiah act the loudest outside had spasms of restored confidence and wanted to leave the money invested. "Salt away that chicken feed in your duds, and skip along," says Buck. "What business have you got investing in bonds? The teapot or the crack in the wall behind the clock for your hoard of pennies."

153

When the pretty girl in the red shawl cashes in Buck hands her an extra twenty.

"A wedding present," says our treasurer, "from the Golconda Company. And say—if Jakey ever follows his nose even at a respectful distance, around the corner where Rosa Steinfeld lives, you are hereby authorized to knock a couple of inches of it off."

When they was all paid off and gone, Buck calls the newspaper reporter and shoves the rest of the money over to him.

"You begun this," says Buck; "now finish it. Over there are the books, showing every share and bond issued. Here's the money to cover, except what we've spent to live on. You'll have to act as receiver. I guess you'll do the square thing on account of your paper. This is the best way we know how to settle it. Me and our substantial but apple-weary vice-president are going to follow the example of our revered president, and skip. Now, have you got enough news for to-day, or do you want to interview us on etiquette and the best way to make over an old taffeta skirt?"

"News!" says the newspaper man, taking his pipe out; "do you think I could use this? I don't want to lose my job. Suppose I go around to the office and tell 'em this happened. What'll the managing editor say? He'll just hand me a pass to Bellevue and tell me to come back when I got cured. I might turn in a story about a sea serpent wiggling up Broadway, but I haven't got the nerve to try 'em with a pipe like this. A get-rich-quick—excuse me—gang giving back the boodle! Oh, no. I'm not on the comic supplement."

"You can't understand it, of course," says Buck, with his hand on the door-knob. "Me and Pick ain't Wall Streeters like you know 'em. We never allowed to swindle sick old women and working girls and take nickels off of kids. In the lines of graft we've worked we took money from the people the Lord made to be buncoed—sports and rounders and smart Aleks and street crowds, that always have a few dollars to throw away, and farmers that wouldn't ever be happy if the grafters didn't come around and play with 'em when they sold their crops. We never cared to fish for the kind of suckers that bite here. No, sir. We got too much respect for the profession and for ourselves. Good-bye to you, Mr. Receiver."

"Here!" says the journalist reporter; "wait a minute. There's a broker I know on the next floor. Wait till I put this truck in his safe. I want you fellows to take a drink on me before you go."

"On you?" says Buck, winking solemn. "Don't you go and try to make 'em believe at the office you said that. Thanks. We can't spare the time, I reckon. So long."

And me and Buck slides out the door; and that's the way the Colconda Company went into involuntary liquefaction.

*   *   *

If you had seen me and Buck the next night you'd have had to go to a little bum hotel over near the West Side ferry landings. We was in a little back room, and I was filling up a gross of six-ounce bottles with hydrant water coloured red with aniline and flavoured with cinnamon. Buck was smoking, contented, and he wore a decent brown derby in place of his silk hat.

"It's a good thing, Pick," says he, as he drove in the corks, "that we got Brady to loan us his horse and wagon for a week. We'll rustle up a stake by then. This hair tonic'll sell right along over in Jersey. Bald heads ain't popular over there on account of the mosquitoes."

Directly I dragged out my valise and went down in it for labels.

"Hair tonic labels are out," says I. "Only about a dozen on hand."

"Buy some more," says Buck.

We investigated our pockets and found we had just enough money to settle our hotel bill in the morning and pay our passage over the ferry.

"Plenty of the 'Shake-the-Shakes Chill Cure' labels," says I, after looking.

"What more do you want?" says Buck. "Slap 'em on. The chill season is just opening up in the Hackensack low grounds. What's hair, anyway, if you have to shake it off?"

We posted on the Chill Cure labels about half an hour and Buck says:

"Making an honest livin's better than that Wall Street, anyhow; ain't it, Pick?"

"You bet," says I.

17

Hostages to Momus

I NEVER got inside of the legitimate line of graft but once. But, one time, as I say, I reversed the decision of the revised statutes and undertook a thing that I'd have to apologize for even under the New Jersey trust laws.

Me and Caligula Polk, of Muskogee in the Creek Nation, was down in the Mexican State of Tamaulipas running a peripatetic lottery and monte game. Now, selling lottery tickets is a government graft in Mexico, just like selling forty-eight cents' worth of postage-stamps for forty-nine cents is over here. So Uncle Porfirio he instructs the *rurales* to attend to our case.

Rurales? They're a sort of country police; but don't draw any mental crayon portraits of the worthy constable with a tin star and a grey goatee. The *rurales*—well, if we'd mount our Supreme Court on broncos, arm 'em with Winchesters, and start 'em out after John Doe *et al.*, we'd have about the same thing.

When the *rurales* started for us we started for the States. They chased us as far as Matamoras. We hid in a brickyard; and that night we swum the Rio Grande, Caligula with a brick in each hand, absent-minded, which he drops upon the soil of Texas, forgetting he had 'em.

From there we emigrated to San Antone, and then over to New Orleans, where we took a rest. And in that town of cotton bales and other adjuncts to female beauty we made the acquaintance of drinks invented by the Creoles during the period of Louey Cans, in which they are still served at the side doors. The most I can remember of this town is that

157

me and Caligula and a Frenchman named McCarty—wait a minute; Adolph McCarty—was trying to make the French Quarter pay up the back trading-stamps due on the Louisiana Purchase, when somebody hollers that the johndarms are coming. I have an insufficient recollection of buying two yellow tickets through a window; and I seemed to see a man swing a lantern and say "All aboard!" I remembered no more, except that the train butcher was covering me and Caligula up with Augusta J. Evans' works and figs.

When we become revised, we find that we have collided up against the State of Georgia at a spot hitherto unaccounted for in time-tables except by an asterisk, which means that trains stop every other Thursday on signal by tearing up a rail. We was waked up in a yellow pine hotel by the noise of flowers and the smell of birds. Yes, sir, for the wind was banging sunflowers as big as buggy wheels against the weatherboarding and the chicken-coop was right under the window. Me and Caligula dressed and went downstairs. The landlord was shelling peas on the front porch. He was six feet of chills and fever, and Hong-Kong in complexion, though in other respects he seemed amenable in the exercise of his sentiments and features.

Caligula, who is a spokesman by birth, and a small man, though red-haired and impatient of painfulness of any kind, speaks up.

"Pardner," says he, "good morning, and be darned to you. Would you mind telling us why we are at? We know the reason we are where, but can't exactly figure out on account of at what place."

"Well, gentlemen," says the landlord, "I reckoned you-all would be inquiring this morning. You-all dropped off at the nine-thirty train here last night; and you was right tight. Yes, you were right smart in liquor. I can inform you that you are now in the town of Mountain Valley, in the State of Georgia."

"On top of that," says Caligula, "don't say that we can't have anything to eat."

"Sit down, gentlemen," says the landlord, "and in twenty minutes I'll call you to the best breakfast you can get anywhere in town."

That breakfast turned out to be composed of fried bacon and a yellowish edifice that proved up something between pound cake and flexible sandstone. The landlord calls it corn pone; and then he sets out a dish of the exaggerated breakfast food known as hominy; and so me and Caligula makes the acquaintance of the celebrated food that enabled every Johnny Reb to lick one and two-thirds Yankees for nearly four years at a stretch.

"The wonder to me is," says Caligula, "that Uncle Robert Lee's boys didn't chase the Grant and Sherman outfit clear up into Hudson's Bay. It would have made me that mad to eat this truck they call mahogany!"

"Hog and hominy," I explains, "is the staple food of this section."

"Then," says Caligula, "they ought to keep it where it belongs. I thought this was a hotel and not a stable. Now, if we was in Muskogee at the St. Lucifer House, I'd show you some breakfast grub. Antelope steaks and fried liver to begin on, and venison cutlets with *chili con carne* and pineapple fritters, and then some sardines and mixed pickles; and top it off with a can of yellow clings and a bottle of beer. You won't find a layout like that on the bill of affairs of any of your Eastern restauraws."

"Too lavish," say I. "I've travelled, and I'm unprejudiced. There'll never be a perfect breakfast eaten until some man grows arms long enough to stretch down to New Orleans for his coffee and over to Norfolk for his rolls, and reaches up to Vermont and digs a slice of butter out of a springhouse, and then turns over a beehive close to a white clover patch out in Indiana for the rest. Then he'd come pretty close to making a meal on the amber that the gods eat on Mount Olympia."

"Too ephemeral," says Caligula. "I'd want ham and eggs, or rabbit stew, anyhow, for a chaser. What do you consider the most edifying and casual in the way of a dinner?"

"I've been infatuated from time to time," I answers, "with fancy ramifications of grub such as terrapins, lobsters, reed birds, jambolaya, and canvas-covered ducks; but, after all, there's nothing less displeasing to me than a beefsteak smothered in mushrooms on a balcony in sound of the Broadway street-cars, with a hand-organ playing down below, and the boys hollering extras about the latest suicide. For the wine, give me a reasonable Ponty Cany. And that's all, except a *demi-tasse*."

"Well," says Caligula, "I reckon in New York you get to be a conniseer; and when you go around with the *demi-tasse* you are naturally bound to buy 'em stylish grub."

"It's a great town for epicures," says I. "You'd soon fall into their ways if you was there."

"I've heard it was," says Caligula. "But I reckon I wouldn't. I can polish my finger-nails all they need myself."

II

After breakfast we went out on the front porch, lighted up two of the landlord's *flor de upas* perfectos, and took a look at Georgie.

The instalment of scenery visible to the eye looked mighty poor. As far as we could see was red hills all washed down with gullies and scattered over with patches of piny woods. Blackberry bushes was all that kept the rail fences from falling down. About fifteen miles over to the north was a little range of well-timbered mountains.

That town of Mountain Valley wasn't going. About a dozen people permeated along the sidewalks; but what you saw mostly was rain-barrels and roosters, and boys poking around with sticks in piles of ashes made by burning the scenery of Uncle Tom shows.

And just then there passes down on the other side of the street a high man in a long black coat and a beaver hat. All the people in sight bowed, and some crossed the street to shake hands with him; folks came out of stores and houses to holler at him; women leaned out of windows and smiled; and all the kids stopped playing to look at him. Our landlord stepped out on the porch and bent himself double like a carpenter's rule, and sung out, "Good morning, Colonel," when he was a dozen yards gone by.

"And is that Alexander, pa?" says Caligula to the landlord; "and why is he called great?"

"That gentlemen," says the landlord, "is no less than Colonel Jackson T. Rockingham, the president of the Sunrise & Edenville Tap Railroad, mayor of Mountain Valley, and chairman of the Perry County board of immigration and public improvements."

"Been away a good many years, hasn't he?" I asked.

"No, sir; Colonel Rockingham is going down to the post office for his mail. His fellow-citizens take pleasure in greeting him thus every morning. The colonel is our most prominent citizen. Besides the height of the stock of the Sunrise & Edenville Tap Railroad, he owns a thousand acres of that land across the creek. Mountain Valley delights, sir, to honour a citizen of such worth and public spirit."

For an hour that afternoon Caligula sat on the back of his neck on the porch and studied a newspaper, which was unusual in a man who despised print. When he was through he took me to the end of the porch among the sunlight and drying dish-towels. I knew that Caligula had invented a new graft. For he chewed the ends of his moustache and ran the left catch of his suspenders up and down, which was his way.

"What is it now?" I asks. "Just so it ain't floating mining stocks or raising Pennsylvania pinks, we'll talk it over."

Pennsylvania pinks? Oh, that refers to a coin-raising scheme of the Keystoners. They burn the soles of old women's feet to make them tell where their money's hid.

Caligula's words in business was always few and bitter.

"You see them mountains," said he, pointing. "And you seen that colonel man that owns railroads and cuts more ice when he goes to the post office than Roosevelt does when he cleans 'em out. What we're going to do is to kidnap the latter into the former, and inflict a ransom of ten thousand dollars."

"Illegality," says I, shaking my head.

"I knew you'd say that," says Caligula. "At first sight it does seem to jar peace and dignity. But it don't. I got the idea out of that newspaper. Would you commit aspersions on a equitable graft that the United States itself has condoned and indorsed and ratified?"

"Kidnapping," says I, "is an immoral function in the derogatory list of the statutes. If the United States upholds it, it must be a recent enactment of ethics, along with race suicide and rural delivery."

"Listen," says Caligula, "and I'll explain the case set down in the papers. Here was a Greek citizen named Burdick Harris," says he, "captured for a graft by Africans; and the United States sends two gunboats to the State of Tangiers and makes the King of Morocco give up seventy thousand dollars to Raisuli."

"Go slow," says I. "That sounds too international to take in all at once. It's like 'thimble, thimble, who's got the naturalization papers?'"

"'Twas Press despatches from Constantinople," says Caligula. "You'll see, six months from now. They'll be confirmed by the monthly magazines; and then it won't be long till you'll notice 'em alongside of photos of the Mount Pelée eruption photos in the while-you-get-your-hair-cut weeklies. It's all right, Pick. This African man Raisuli hides Burdick Harris up in the mountains, and advertises his price to the governments of different nations. Now, you wouldn't think for a minute," goes on Caligula, "that John Hay would have chipped in and helped this graft along if it wasn't a square game, would you?"

"Why, no," says I. "I've always stood right in with Bryan's policies, and I couldn't consciously say a word against the Republican administration just now. But if

Harris was a Greek, on what system of international proto-
cols did Hay interfere?"

"It ain't exactly set forth in the papers," says Caligula.
"I suppose it's a matter of sentiment. You know he wrote this
poem, 'Little Breeches'; and them Greeks wear little or none.
But anyhow, John Hay sends the *Brooklyn* and the *Olympia*
over, and they cover Africa with thirty-inch guns. And then
Hay cables after the health of the *persona grata*. 'And how are
they this morning?' he wires. 'Is Burdick Harris alive yet, or
Mr. Raisuli dead?' And the King of Morocco sends up the
seventy thousand dollars, and they turn Burdick Harris loose.
And there's not half the hard feelings among the nations
about this little kidnapping matter as there was about the
peace congress. And Burdick Harris says to the reporters, in
the Greek language, that he's often heard about the United
States, and he admires Roosevelt next to Raisuli, who is one
of the whitest and most gentlemanly kidnappers that he ever
worked alongside of. So you see, Pick," winds up Caligula,
"we've got the law of nations on our side. We'll cut this
colonel man out of the herd, and corral him in them little
mountains, and stick up his heirs and assigns for ten thousand
dollars."

"Well, you seldom little red-headed territorial terror,"
I answers, "you can't bluff your uncle Tecumseh Pickens!
I'll be your company in this graft. But I misdoubt if you've
absorbed the inwardness of this Burdick Harris case, Calig;
and if on any morning we get a telegram from the Secretary
of State asking about the health of the scheme, I propose to
acquire the most propinquitous and celeritous mule in this
section and gallop diplomatically over into the neighbouring
and peaceful nation of Alabama."

III

Me and Caligula spent the next three days investigating
the bunch of mountains into which we proposed to kidnap
Colonel Jackson T. Rockingham. We finally selected an

upright slice of topography covered with bushes and trees that you could only reach by a secret path that we cut out up the side of it. And the only way to reach the mountain was to follow up the bend of a branch that wound among the elevations.

Then I took in hand an important sub-division of the proceedings. I went up to Atlanta on the train and laid in a two-hundred-and-fifty-dollar supply of the most gratifying and efficient lines of grub that money could buy. I always was an admirer of viands in their more palliative and revised stages. Hog and hominy are not only inartistic to my stomach, but they give indigestion to my moral sentiments. And I thought of Colonel Jackson T. Rockingham, president of the Sunrise & Edenville Tap Railroad, and how he would miss the luxury of his home fare as is so famous among wealthy Southerners. So I sunk half of mine and Caligula's capital in as elegant a layout of fresh and canned provisions as Burdick Harris or any other professional kidnappee ever saw in a camp.

I put another hundred in a couple of cases of Bordeaux, two quarts of cognac, two hundred Havana regalias with gold bands, and a camp-stove and stools and folding cots. I wanted Colonel Rockingham to be comfortable; and I hoped after he gave up the ten thousand dollars he would give me and Caligula as good a name for gentlemen and entertainers as the Greek man did the friend of his that made the United States his bill collector against Africa.

When the goods came down from Atlanta, we hired a wagon, moved them up on the little mountain, and established camp. And then we laid for the colonel.

We caught him one morning about two miles out from Mountain Valley, on his way to look after some of his burnt umber farm land. He was an elegant old gentleman, as thin and tall as a trout rod, with frazzled shirt-cuffs and specs on a black string. We explained to him, brief and easy, what we wanted; and Caligula showed him, careless, the handle of his forty-five under his coat.

"What?" says Colonel Rockingham. "Bandits in Perry County, Georgia! I shall see that the board of immigration and public improvements hears of this!"

"Be so unfoolhardly as to climb into that buggy," says Caligula, "by order of the board of perforation and public depravity. This is a business meeting, and we're anxious to adjourn *sine qua non*."

We drove Colonel Rockingham over the mountain and up the side of it as far as the buggy could go. Then we tied the horse, and took our prisoner on foot up to the camp.

"Now, colonel," I says to him, "we're after the ransom, me and my partner; and no harm will come to you if the King of Mor—if your friends send up the dust. In the meantime we are gentlemen the same as you. And if you give us your word not to try to escape, the freedom of the camp is yours."

"I give you my word," says the colonel.

"All right," says I; "and now it's eleven o'clock, and me and Mr. Polk will proceed to inoculate the occasion with a few well-timed trivialities in the line of grub."

"Thank you," says the colonel; "I believe I could relish a slice of bacon and a plate of hominy."

"But you won't," says I emphatic. "Not in this camp. We soar in higher regions than them occupied by your celebrated but repulsive dish."

While the colonel read his paper, me and Caligula took off our coats and went in for a little luncheon *de luxe* just to show him. Caligula was a fine cook of the Western brand. He could toast a buffalo or fricassee a couple of steers as easy as a woman could make a cup of tea. He was gifted in the way of knocking together edibles when haste and muscle and quantity was to be considered. He held the record west of the Arkansas River for frying pancakes with his left hand, broiling venison cutlets with his right, and skinning a rabbit with his teeth at the same time. But I could do things *en casserole* and *à la créole*, and handle the oil and tabasco as gently and nicely as a French *chef*.

So at twelve o'clock we had a hot lunch ready that looked like a banquet on a Mississippi River steamboat. We spread it on the tops of two or three big boxes, opened two quarts of the red wine, set the olives and a canned oyster cocktail and a ready-made Martini by the colonel's plate, and called him to grub.

Colonel Rockingham drew up his camp-stool, wiped off his specs, and looked at the things on the table. Then I thought he was swearing; and I felt mean because I hadn't taken more pains with the victuals. But he wasn't; he was asking a blessing; and me and Caligula hung our heads, and I saw a tear drop from the colonel's eye into his cocktail.

I never saw a man eat with so much earnestness and application—not hastily, like a grammarian, or one of the canal, but slow and appreciative, like a anaconda, or a real *vive bonjour*.

In an hour and a half the colonel leaned back. I brought him a pony of brandy and his black coffee, and set the box of Havana regalias on the table.

"Gentlemen," says he, blowing out the smoke and trying to breathe it back again, "when we view the eternal hills and the smiling and beneficient landscape, and reflect upon the goodness of the Creator who——"

"Excuse me, colonel," says I, "but there's some business to attend to now"; and I brought out paper and pen and ink and laid 'em before him. "Who do you want to send to for the money?" I asks.

"I reckon," says he, after thinking a bit, "to the vice-president of our railroad, at the general offices of the Company in Edenville."

"How far is it to Edenville from here?" I asked.

"About ten miles," says he.

Then I dictated these lines, and Colonel Rockingham wrote them out:

"I am kidnapped and held a prisoner by two desperate outlaws in a place which is useless to attempt to find. They demand ten thousand dollars at once for my release. The amount must be raised immediately, and these directions followed. Come alone with the money to Stony Creek, which runs out of Blacktop Mountains. Follow the bed of the creek till you come to a big flat rock on the left bank, on which is marked a cross in red chalk. Stand on the rock and wave a white flag. A guide will come to you and conduct you to where I am held. Lose no time."

After the colonel had finished this, he asked permission to tack on a postscript about how white he was being treated, so the railroad wouldn't feel uneasy in its bosom about him. We agreed to that. He wrote down that he had just had lunch with the two desperate ruffians; and then he set down the whole bill of fare, from cocktails to coffee. He wound up with the remark that dinner would be ready about six, and would probably be a more licentious and intemperate affair than lunch.

Me and Caligula read it, and decided to let it go; for we, being cooks, were amenable to praise, though it sounded out of place on a sight draft for ten thousand dollars.

I took the letter over to the Mountain Valley road and watched for a messenger. By and by a coloured equestrian came along on horseback, riding toward Edenville. I gave him a dollar to take the letter to the railroad offices; and then I went back to camp.

IV

About four o'clock in the afternoon, Caligula, who was acting as look-out, calls to me:

"I have to report a white shirt signalling on the starboard bow, sir."

I went down the mountain and brought back a fat, red man in an alpaca coat and no collar.

"Gentlemen," says Colonel Rockingham, "allow me to introduce my brother, Captain Duval C. Rockingham, vice-president of the Sunrise & Edenville Tap Railroad."

"Otherwise the King of Morocco," says I. "I reckon you

167

don't mind my counting the ransom, just as a business formality."

"Well, no, not exactly," says the fat man, "not when it comes. I turned the matter over to our second vice-president. I was anxious after Brother Jackson's safetiness. I reckon he'll be along right soon. What does that lobster salad you mentioned taste like, Brother Jackson?"

"Mr. Vice-President," says I, "you'll oblige us by remaining here till the second V.-P. arrives. This is a private rehearsal, and we don't want any roadside speculators selling tickets."

In half an hour Caligula sings out again:

"Sail ho! Looks like an apron on a broomstick."

I perambulated down the cliff again, and escorted up a man six foot three, with a sandy beard and no other dimensions that you could notice. Thinks I to myself, if he's got ten thousand dollars on his person it's in one bill and folded lengthwise.

"Mr. Patterson G. Coble, our second vice-president," announces the colonel.

"Glad to know you, gentlemen," says this Coble. "I came up to disseminate the tidings that Major Tallahassee Tucker, our general passenger agent, is now negotiating a peach-crate full of our railroad bonds with the Perry County Bank for a loan. My dear Colonel Rockingham, was that chicken gumbo or cracked goobers on the bill of fare in your note? Me and the conductor of fifty-six was having a dispute about it."

"Another white wings on the rocks!" hollers Caligula. "If I see any more I'll fire on 'em and swear they was torpedo-boats!"

The guide goes down again, and convoys into the lair a person in blue overalls carrying an amount of inebriety and a lantern. I am so sure that this is Major Tucker that I don't even ask him until we are up above; and then I discover that it is Uncle Timothy, the yard switchman at Edenville, who is sent ahead to flag our understandings with the gossip that

Judge Pendergast, the railroad's attorney, is in the process of mortgaging Colonel Rockingham's farming lands to make up the ransom.

While he is talking, two men crawl from under the bushes into camp, and Caligula, with no white flag to disinter him from his plain duty, draws his gun. But again Colonel Rockingham intervenes and introduces Mr. Jones and Mr. Batts, engineer and fireman of train number forty-two.

"Excuse us," says Batts, "but me and Jim have hunted squirrels all over this mounting, and we don't need no white flag. Was that straight, colonel, about the plum pudding and pineapples and real store cigars?"

"Towel on a fishing-pole in the offing!" howls Caligula. "Suppose it's the firing-line of the freight conductors and brake-men."

"My last trip down," says I, wiping off my face. "If the S. & E. T. wants to run an excursion up here just because we kidnapped their president, let 'em. We'll put out our sign. 'The Kidnapper's Café and Trainmen's Home.'"

This time I caught Major Tallahassee Tucker by his own confession, and I felt easier. I asked him into the creek, so I could drown him if he happened to be a track-walker or caboose porter. All the way up the mountain he drivelled to me about asparagus on toast, a thing that his intelligence in life had skipped.

Up above I got his mind segregated from food and asked if he had raised the ransom.

"My dear sir," says he, "I succeeded in negotiating a loan on thirty thousand dollars' worth of the bonds of our railroad, and——"

"Never mind just now, major," says I. "It's all right, then. Wait till after dinner, and we'll settle the business. All of you gentlemen," I continues to the crowd, "are invited to stay to dinner. We have mutually trusted one another, and the white flag is supposed to wave over the proceedings."

"The correct idea," says Caligula, who was standing by me. "Two baggage-masters and a ticket-agent dropped out of a tree while you was below the last time. Did the major man bring the money?"

"He says," I answered, "that he succeeded in negotiating the loan."

If any cooks ever earned ten thousand dollars in twelve hours, me and Caligula did that day. At six o'clock we spread the top of the mountain with as fine a dinner as the personnel of any railroad ever engulfed. We opened all the wine, and we concocted entrées and *pièces de résistance*, and stirred up little savoury *chef de cuisines* and organized a mass of grub such as had been seldom instigated out of canned and bottled goods. The railroad gathered around it, and the wassail and diversions was intense.

After the feast, me and Caligula, in the line of business, takes Major Tucker to one side and talks ransom. The major pulls out an agglomeration of currency about the size of the price of a town lot in the suburbs of Rabbitville, Arizona, and makes this outcry:

"Gentlemen," says he, "the stock of the Sunrise & Edenville Railroad has depreciated some. The best I could do with thirty thousand dollars' worth of the bonds was to secure a loan of eighty-seven dollars and fifty cents. On the farming lands of Colonel Rockingham, Judge Pendergast was able to obtain, on a ninth mortgage, the sum of fifty dollars. You will find the amount, one hundred and thirty-seven fifty correct."

"A railroad president," said I, looking this Tucker in the eye, "and the owners of a thousand acres of land; and yet——"

"Gentlemen," says Tucker, "the railroad is ten miles long. There don't any train run on it except when the crew goes out in the pines and gathers enough light-wood knots to get up steam. A long time ago, when times was good, the net earnings used to run as high as eighteen dollars a week. Colonel Rockingham's land has been sold for taxes thirteen times. There hasn't been a peach crop in this part of Georgia for two years. The wet spring killed the water-melons.

Nobody around here has money enough to buy fertilizer; and land is so poor the corn crop failed, and there wasn't enough grass to support the rabbits. All the people have had to eat in this section for over a year is hog and hominy, and——"

"Pick," interrupts Caligula, mussing up his red hair, "what are you going to do with that chicken-feed?"

I hands the money back to Major Tucker; and then I goes over to Colonel Rockingham and slaps him on the back.

"Colonel," says I, "I hope you've enjoyed our little joke. We don't want to carry it too far. Kidnappers! Well, wouldn't it tickle your uncle? My name's Rhinegelder, and I'm a nephew of Chaucey Depew. My friend's a second cousin of the editor of *Puck*. So you can see. We are down South enjoying ourselves in our humorous way. Now, there's two quarts of cognac to open yet, and then the joke's over."

What's the use to go into details? One or two will be enough. I remember Major Tallahassee Tucker playing on a jews' harp, and Caligula waltzing with his head on the watch-pocket of a tall baggage-master. I hesitate to refer to the cake-walk done by me and Mr. Patterson G. Coble with Colonel Jackson T. Rockingham between us.

And even on the next morning, when you wouldn't think it possible, there was a consolation for me and Caligula. We knew that Raisuli himself never made half the hit with Burdick Harris that we did with the Sunrise & Edenville Tap Railroad.

18

The Ethics of Pig

ON an east-bound train I went into the smoker and found
Jefferson Peters, the only man with a brain west of the
Wabash River who can use his cerebrum cerebellum and
medulla oblongata at the same time.

Jeff is in the line of unillegal graft. He is not to be dreaded
by widows and orphans; he is a reducer of surplusage. His
favourite disguise is that of the target-bird at which the
spendthrift or the reckless investor may shy a few incon-
sequential dollars. He is readily vocalized by tobacco; so,
with the aid of two thick and easy-burning brevas, I got the
story of his latest Autolycan adventure.

"In my line of business," said Jeff, "the hardest thing is to
find an upright, trustworthy, strictly honourable partner to
graft with. Some of the best men I ever worked with in a
swindle would resort to trickery at times.

"So, last summer, I thinks I will go over into this section
of country where I hear the serpent has not yet entered, and
see if I can find a partner naturally gifted with a talent from
crime, but not yet contaminated by success.

"I found a village that seemed to show the right kind of
a layout. The inhabitants hadn't found out that Adam had
been dispossessed, and were going right along naming the
animals and killing snakes just as if they were in the Garden
of Eden. They call this town Mount Nebo, and it's up near
the spot where Kentucky and West Virginia and North
Carolina corner together. Them States don't meet? Well, it
was in that neighbourhood, anyway.

"After putting in a week proving I wasn't a revenue
officer, I went over to the store where the rude fourflushers

172

of the hamlet lied, to see if I could get a line on the kind of man I wanted.

"'Gentlemen,' says I, after we had rubbed noses and gathered around the dried-apple barrel. 'I don't suppose there's another community in the whole world into which sin and chicanery has less extensively permeated than this. Life here, where all the women are brave and propitious and all the men honest and expedient, must, indeed, be an idol. It reminds me,' says I, 'of Goldstein's beautiful ballad entitled "The Deserted Village", which says:

Ill fares the land, to hastening ills a prey;
    What art can drive its charms away?
The judge rode slowly down the lane, mother,
    For I'm to be Queen of the May.

"'Why, yes, Mr. Peters," says the storekeeper. 'I reckon we air about as moral and torpid a community as there be on the mounting, according to censuses of opinion; but I reckon you ain't ever met Rufe Tatum.'

"'Why, no,' says the town constable, 'he can't hardly have ever. That air Rufe is shore the monstrousest scalawag that has escaped hangin' on the galluses. And that puts me in mind that I ought to have turned Rufe out of the lock-up day before yesterday. The thirty days he got for killin' Yance Goodloe was up then. A day or two more won't hurt Rufe any, though.'

"'Shucks, now,' says I, in the mountain idiom, 'don't tell me there's a man in Mount Nebo as bad as that.'

"'Worse,' says the storekeeper. 'He steals hogs.'

"I think I will look up this Mr. Tatum; so a day or two after the constable turned him out I got acquainted with him and invited him out on the edge of town to sit on a log and talk business.

"What I wanted was a partner with a natural rural make-up to play a part in some little one-act outrages that I was going to book with the Pitfall & Gin circuit in some of the

Western towns; and this R. Tatum was born for the rôle as sure as nature cast Fairbanks for the stuff that kept *Eliza* from sinking into the river.

"He was about the size of a first base-man; and he had ambiguous blue eyes like the china dog on the mantelpiece that Aunt Harriet used to play with when she was a child. His hair waved a little bit like the statue of the dinkus-thrower in the Vacation at Rome, but the colour of it reminded you of the 'Sunset in the Grand Cañon, by an American Artist', that they hang over the stovepipe holes in the salongs. He was the Reub, without needing a touch. You'd have known him for one, even if you'd seen him on the vaudeville stage with one cotton suspender and a straw over his ear.

"I told him what I wanted, and found him ready to jump at the job.

"'Overlooking such a trivial little peccadillo as the habit of manslaughter,' says I, 'what have you accomplished in the way of indirect brigandage or non-actionable thriftiness that you could point to, with or without pride, as an evidence of your qualifications for the position?'

"'Why,' says he, in his kind of Southern system of pro-crastinated accents, 'hain't you heard tell? There ain't any man, black or white, in the Blue Ridge that can tote off a shoat as easy as I can without bein' heard, seen, or cotched. I can lift a shoat,' he goes on, 'out of a pen, from under a porch, at the trough, in the woods, day or night, anywhere or anyhow, and I guarantee nobody won't hear a squeal. It's all in the way you grab hold of 'em and carry 'em after-wards. Some day,' goes on this gentle despoiler of pig-pens, 'I hope to become reckernized as the champion shoat-stealer of the world.'

"'It's proper to be ambitious,' says I; 'and hog-stealing will do very well for Mount Nebo; but in the outside world, Mr. Tatum, it would be considered as crude a piece of business as a bear raid on Bay State Gas. However, it will do as a guarantee of good faith. We'll go into partnership.

I've got a thousand dollars cash capital; and with that home-ward-plods atmosphere of yours we ought to be able to win out a few shares of Soon Parted, preferred, in the money market.'

"So I attaches Rufe, and we go away from Mount Nebo down into the lowlands. And all the way I coach him for his part in the grafts I had in mind. I had idled away two months on the Florida coast, and was feeling all to the Ponce de Leon, besides having so many new schemes up my sleeve that I had to wear kimonos to hold 'em.

"I intended to assume a funnel shape and mow a path nine miles wide through the farming belt of the Middle West; so we headed in that direction. But when we got as far as Lexington we found Binkley Brothers' circus there, and the blue-grass peasantry romping into town and pounding the Belgian blocks with their hand-pegged sabots as artless and arbitrary as an extra session of a Datto Bryan duma. I never pass a circus without pulling the valve-cord and coming down for a little Key West money; so I engaged a couple of rooms and board for Rufe and me at a house near the circus grounds run by a widow lady named Peevy. Then I took Rufe to a clothing store and gent's-outfitted him. He showed up strong, as I knew he would, after he was rigged up in the ready-made rutabaga regalia. Me and old Misfitzky stuffed him into a bright blue suit with a Nile green visible plaid effect, and riveted on a fancy vest of a light Tuskegee Normal tan colour, a red neck-tie, and the yellowest pair of shoes in town.

"They were the first clothes Rufe had ever worn except the gingham layette and the butternut top-dressing of his native kraal, and he looked as self-conscious as an Igorrote with a new nose-ring.

"That night I went down to the circus tents and opened a small shell game. Rufe was to be the capper. I gave him a roll of phony currency to bet with and kept a bunch of it in a special pocket to pay his winnings out of. No; I didn't mistrust him; but I simply can't manipulate the ball to lose when I see real money bet. My fingers go on a strike every time I try it.

"I set up my little table and began to show them how easy it was to guess which shell the little pea was under. The unlettered hinds gathered in a thick semicircle and began to nudge elbows and banter one another to bet. Then was when Rufe ought to have single-footed up and called the turn on the little joker for a few tens and fives to get them started. But, not Rufe. I'd seen him two or three times walking about and looking at the sideshow pictures with his mouth full of peanut candy; but he never came nigh.

"The crowd piked a little; but trying to work the shells without a capper is like fishing without bait. I closed the game with only forty-two dollars of the unearned increment, while I had been counting on yanking the yeomen for two hundred at least. I went home at eleven and went to bed. I supposed that the circus had proved too alluring for Rufe, and that he had succumbed to it, concert and all; but I meant to give him a lecture on general business principles in the morning.

"Just after Morpheus had got both my shoulders to the shuck mattress I hears a houseful of unbecoming and ribald noises like a youngster screeching with green-apple colic. I opens my door and calls out in the hall for the widow lady, and when she sticks her head out, I says: 'Mrs. Peevy, ma'am, would you mind choking off that kid of yours so that honest people can get their rest?'

"'Sir,' says she, 'it's no child of mine. It's the pig squealing that your friend Mr. Tatum brought home to his room a couple of hours ago. And if you are uncle or second cousin or brother to it, I'd appreciate your stopping its mouth, sir, yourself, if you please.'

"I put on some of the polite outside habiliments of external society and went into Rufe's room. He had gotten up and lit his lamp, and was pouring some milk into a tin pan on the floor for a dingy-white, half-grown, squealing pig.

"'How is this, Rufe?' says I. 'You flimflammed in your part of the work to-night and put the game on crutches. And how do you explain the pig? It looks like backsliding to me.'

"'Now, don't be too hard on me, Jeff,' says he. 'You know how long I've been used to stealing shoats. It's got to be a habit with me. And to-night, when I see such a fine chance, I couldn't help takin' it.'

"'Well,' says I, 'maybe you've really got kleptopigia. And maybe when we get out of the pig belt you'll turn your mind to higher and more remunerative misconduct. Why you should want to stain your soul with such a distasteful, feeble-minded, perverted, roaring beast as that I can't understand.'

"'Why, Jeff,' says he, 'you wain't in sympathy with shoats. You don't understand 'em like I do. This here seems to me to be an animal of more than common powers of ration and intelligence. He walked half across the room on his hind legs a while ago.'

"'Well, I'm going back to bed,' says I. 'See if you can impress it upon your friend's ideas of intelligence that he's not to make so much noise.'

"'He was hungry,' says Rufe. 'He'll go to sleep and keep quiet now.'

"I always get up before breakfast and read the morning paper whenever I happen to be within the radius of a Hoe cylinder or a Washington hand-press. The next morning I got up early and found a Lexington daily on the front porch where the carrier had thrown it. The first thing I saw in it was a double-column ad. on the front page that read like this:

FIVE THOUSAND DOLLARS REWARD

The above amount will be paid, and no questions asked, for the return, alive and uninjured, of Beppo, the famous European educated pig, that strayed or was stolen from the side-show tents of Binkley Bros.' circus last night.

GEO. B. TAPLEY, Business Manager.

At the Circus Grounds.

"I folded up the paper flat, put it into my inside pocket, and went to Rufe's room. He was nearly dressed, and was feeding the pig with the rest of the milk and some apple-peelings.

"'Well, well, well, good morning all,' I says, hearty and amiable. 'So we are up? And piggy is having his breakfast. What had you intended doing with that pig, Rufe?'

"'I'm going to crate him up,' says Rufe, 'and express him to ma in Mount Nebo. He'll be company for her while I am away.'

"'He's a mighty fine pig,' says I, scratching him on the back.

"'You called him a lot of names last night,' says Rufe.

"'Oh, well,' says I, 'he looks better to me this morning. I was raised on a farm, and I'm very fond of pigs. I used to go to bed at sundown, so I never saw one by lamplight before. Tell you what I'll do, Rufe,' I says. 'I'll give you ten dollars for that pig.'

"'I reckon I wouldn't sell this shoat,' says he. 'If it was any other one I might.'

"'Why not this one?' I asked, fearful that he might know something.

"'Why, because,' says he, 'it was the grandest achievement of my life. There ain't any other man that could have done it. If I ever have a fireside and children, I'll sit beside it and tell 'em how their daddy toted off a shoat from a whole circus full of people. And maybe my grandchildren, too. They'll certainly be proud a whole passel. Why,' says he, 'there was two tents, one openin' into the other. This shoat was on a platform, tied with a little chain. I seen a giant and a lady with a fine chance of bushy white hair in the other tent. I got the shoat and crawled out from under the canvas again without him squeakin' as loud as a mouse. I put him under my coat, and I must have passed a hundred folks before I got out where the streets was dark. I reckon I wouldn't sell that shoat, Jeff. I'd want ma to keep it, so there'd be a witness to what I done.'

" 'The pig won't live long enough,' I says, 'to use as an exhibit in your senile fireside mendacity. Your grandchildren will have to take your word for it. I'll give you one hundred dollars for the animal.'

"Rufe looked at me astonished.

" 'The shoat can't be worth anything like that to you,' he says. 'What do you want him for?'

" 'Viewing me casuistically,' says I, with a rare smile, 'you wouldn't think that I've got an artistic side to my temper. But I have. I'm a collector of pigs. I've scoured the world for unusual pigs. Over in the Wabash Valley I've got a hog ranch with most every specimen on it, from a Merino to a Poland China. This looks like a blooded pig to me, Rufe,' says I. 'I believe it's a genuine Berkshire. That's why I'd like to have it.'

" 'I'd shore like to accommodate you,' says he, 'but I've got the artistic tenement, too. I don't see why it ain't art when you can steal a shoat better than anybody else can. Shoats is a kind of inspiration and genius with me. Specially this one. I wouldn't take two hundred and fifty for that animal.'

" 'Now, listen,' says I, wiping off my forehead. 'It's not so much a matter of business with me as it is art; and not so much art as it is philosophy. Being a connoisseur and disseminator of pigs, I wouldn't feel like I'd done my duty to the world unless I added that Berkshire to my collection. Not intrinsically, but according to the ethics of pigs as friends and coadjutors of mankinds, I offer you five hundred dollars for the animal.'

" 'Jeff,' says this pork esthete, 'it ain't money; it's sentiment with me.'

" 'Seven hundred,' says I.

" 'Make it eight hundred,' says Rufe, 'and I'll crush the sentiment out of my heart.'

"I went under my clothes for my money-belt, and counted him out forty twenty-dollar gold certificates.

"'I'll just take him into my own room,' says I, 'and lock him up till after breakfast.'

"I took the pig by the hind leg. He turned on a squeal like the steam calliope at the circus.

"'Let me tote him in for you,' says Rufe; and he picks up the beast under one arm, holding his snout with the other hand, and packs him into my room like a sleeping baby.

"After breakfast Rufe, who had a chronic case of haberdashery ever since I got his trousseau, says he believes he will amble down to Misfitzky's and look over some royal-purple socks. And then I got as busy as a one-armed man with the nettle-rash pasting on wallpaper. I found an old negro man with an express wagon to hire; and we tied the pig in a sack and drove down to the circus grounds.

"I found George B. Tapley in a little tent with a window flap open. He was a fattish man with an immediate eye, in a black skull-cap, with a four-ounce diamond screwed into the bosom of his red sweater.

"'Are you George B. Tapley?' I asks.

"'I swear it,' says he.

"'Well, I've got it,' says I.

"'Designate,' says he. 'Are you the guinea pigs for the Asiatic python or the alfalfa for the sacred buffalo?'

"'Neither,' says I. 'I've got Beppo, the educated hog, in a sack in that wagon. I found him rooting up the flowers in my front yard this morning. I'll take the five thousand dollars in large bills, if it's handy.'

"George B. hustles out of his tent, and asks me to follow. We went into one of the side-shows. In there was a jet-black pig with a pink ribbon around his neck lying on some hay and eating carrots that a man was feeding to him.

"'Hey, Mac,' calls G. B. 'Nothing wrong with the world-wide this morning, is there?'

"'Him? No,' says the man. 'He's got an appetite like a chorus girl at 1 a.m.'

"'How'd you get this pipe?' says Tapley to me. 'Eating too many pork chops last night?'

"I pulls out the paper and shows him the ad.

"'Fake,' says he. 'Don't know anything about it. You've beheld with your own eyes the marvellous, world-wide porcine wonder of the four-footed kingdom eating with preternatural sagacity his matutinal meal, unstrayed and unstole. Good morning.'

"I was beginning to see. I got in the wagon and told Uncle Ned to drive to the most adjacent orifice of the nearest alley. There I took out my pig, got the range carefully for the other opening, set his sights, and gave him such a kick that he went out the other end of the alley twenty feet ahead of his squeal.

"Then I paid Uncle Ned his fifty cents, and walked down to the newspaper office. I wanted to hear it in cold syllables. I got the advertising man to his window.

"'To decide a bet,' says I, 'wasn't the man who had this ad. put in last night short and fat, with long, black whiskers and a club-foot?'

"'He was not,' says the man. 'He would measure about six feet by four and a half inches, with corn-silk hair, and dressed like the pansies of the conservatory.'

"At dinner-time I went back to Mrs. Peevy's.

"'Shall I keep some soup hot for Mr. Tatum till he comes back?' she asks.

"'If you do, ma'am,' says I, 'you'll more than exhaust for firewood all the coal in the bosom of the earth and all the forests on the outside of it.'

"So there, you see," said Jefferson Peters, in conclusion, "how hard it is ever to find a fair-minded and honest business-partner."

"But," I began, with the freedom of long acquaintance, "the rule should work both ways. If you had offered to divide the reward you would not have lost——"

Jeff's look of dignified reproach stopped me.

181

"That don't involve the same principles at all," said he. "Mine was a legitimate and moral attempt at speculation. Buy low and sell high—don't Wall Street endorse it? Bulls and bears and pigs—what's the difference? Why not bristles as well as horns and fur?"

19

The Atavism of John Tom Little Bear

[O. Henry thought this the best of the Jeff Peters stories, all the rest of which are included in *The Gentle Grafter*, except "Cupid à la Carte" in the *Heart of the West*.]

I saw a light in Jeff Peters's room over the Red Front Drug Store. I hastened toward it, for I had not known that Jeff was in town. He is a man of the Hadji breed, of a hundred occupations, with a story to tell (when he will) of each one.

I found Jeff re-packing his grip for a run down to Florida to look at an orange grove for which he had traded, a month before, his mining claim on the Yukon. He kicked me a chair, with the same old humorous, profound smile on his seasoned countenance. It had been eight months since we had met, but his greeting was such as men pass from day to day. Time is Jeff's servant, and the continent is a big lot across which cuts to his many roads.

For a while we skirmished along the edges of unprofitable talk which culminated in that unquiet problem of the Philippines.

"All them tropical races," said Jeff, "could be run out better with their own jockeys up. The tropical man knows what he wants. All he wants is a season ticket to the cock-fights and a pair of Western Union climbers to go up the bread-fruit tree. The Anglo-Saxon man wants him to learn to conjugate and wear suspenders. He'll be happiest in his own way."

I was shocked.

"Education, man," I said, "is the watchword. In time

they will rise to our standard of civilization. Look at what education has done for the Indian."

"O-ho!" sang Jeff, lighting his pipe (which was a good sign). "Yes, the Indian! I'm looking. I hasten to contemplate the redman as a standard-bearer of progress. He's the same as the other brown boys. You can't make an Anglo-Saxon of him. Did I ever tell you about the time my friend John Tom Little Bear bit off the right ear of the arts of culture and education and spun the teetotum back round to where it was when Columbus was a little boy? I did not?

"John Tom Little Bear was an educated Cherokee Indian and an old friend of mine when I was in the Territories. He was a graduate of one of them Eastern football colleges that have been so successful in teaching the Indian to use the gridiron instead of burning his victims at the stake. As an Anglo-Saxon, John Tom was copper-coloured in spots. As an Indian, he was one of the whitest men I ever knew. As a Cherokee, he was a gentleman, on the first ballot. As a ward of the nation he was mighty hard to carry at the primaries.

"John Tom and me got together and began to make medicine—how to get up some lawful, genteel swindle which we might work in a quiet way so as not to excite the stupidity of the police or the cupidity of the larger corporations. We had close upon $500 between us, and we pined to make it grow, as all respectable capitalists do.

"So we figured out a proposition which seems to be as honourable as a gold mine prospectus and as profitable as a church raffle. And inside of thirty days you find us swarming into Kansas with a pair of fluent horses and a red camping-wagon on the European plan. John Tom is Chief Wish-Heap-Dough, the famous Indian medicine man and Samaritan Sachem of the Seven Tribes. Mr. Peters is business manager and half owner. We needed a third man, so we looked around and found J. Conyngham Binkly leaning against the want column of a newspaper. This Binkly has a disease for Shakespearean rôles, and an hallucination about

a 200 nights' run on the New York stage. But he confesses
that he never could earn the butter to spread on his William
S. rôles, so he is willing to drop to the ordinary baker's kind,
and be satisfied with a 200-mile run behind the medicine
ponies. Besides Richard III, he could do twenty-seven coon
songs and banjo specialties, and was willing to cook, and
curry the horses. We carried a fine line of excuses for taking
money. One was a magic soap for removing grease spots and
quarters from clothes. One was a Sum-wah-tah, the great
Indian Remedy made from a prairie herb revealed by the
Great Spirit in a dream to his favourite medicine men, the
great chiefs MacGarrity and Silberstein, bottlers, Chicago.
And the other was a frivolous system of pick-pocketing the
Kansasters that had the department stores reduced to a
decimal fraction. Look ye! A pair of silk garters, a dream
book, one dozen clothes-pins, a gold tooth, and 'When
Knighthood Was in Flower' all wrapped up in a genuine
Japanese silkarina handkerchief and handed to the handsome
lady by Mr. Peters for the trivial sum of fifty cents, while
Professor Binkly entertains us in a three-minute round with
the banjo.

"'Twas an eminent graft we had. We ravaged peacefully
through the State, determined to remove all doubt as to why
'twas called bleeding Kansas. John Tom Little Bear, in full
Indian chief's costume, drew crowds away from the parchesi
sociables and government ownership conversaziones. While
at the football college in the East he had acquired quantities
of rhetoric and the art of calisthenics and sophistry in his
classes, and when he stood up in the red wagon and explained
to the farmers, eloquent, about chilblains and hyperæsthesia
of the cranium, Jeff couldn't hand out the Indian Remedy
fast enough for 'em.

"One night we was camped on the edge of a little town out
west of Salina. We always camped near a stream, and put up
a little tent. Sometimes we sold out of the Remedy unexpected, and then Chief Wish-Heap-Dough would have a
dream in which the Manitou commanded him to fill up a few

bottles of Sum-wah-tah at the most convenient place. 'Twas about ten o'clock, and we'd just got in from a street performance. I was in the tent with the lantern, figuring up the day's profits. John Tom hadn't taken off his Indian make-up, and was sitting by the camp-fire minding a fine sirloin steak in the pan for the Professor till he finished his hair-raising scene with the trained horses.

"All at once out of dark bushes comes a pop like a fire-cracker, and John Tom gives a grunt and digs out of his bosom a little bullet that has dented itself against his collar-bone. John Tom makes a dive in the direction of the fire-works and comes back dragging by the collar a kid about nine or ten years young, in a velveteen suit, with a little nickel-mounted rifle in his hand about as big as a fountain-pen.

"'Here, you pappoose,' says John Tom, 'what are you gunning for with that howitzer? You might hit somebody in the eye. Come out, Jeff, and mind the steak. Don't let it burn, while I investigate this demon with the pea-shooter.'

"'Cowardly redskin,' says the kid like he was quoting from a favourite author. 'Dare to burn me at the stake and the paleface will sweep you from the prairies like—like everything. Now, you lemme go, or I'll tell mamma.'

"John Tom plants the kid on a camp-stool, and sits down by him. 'Now, tell the big chief,' he says, 'why you try to shoot pellets into your Uncle John's system. Didn't you know it was loaded?'

"'Are you a Indian?' asks the kid, looking up, cute as you please, at John Tom's buckskin and eagle feathers. 'I am,' says John Tom.

"'Well, then, that's why,' answers the boy, swinging his feet. I nearly let the steak burn watching the nerve of that youngster.

"'Oh-ho!' says John Tom, 'I see. You're the Boy Avenger. And you've sworn to rid the continent of the savage redman. Is that about the way of it, son?'

"The kid half-way nodded his head. And then he looked

186

glum. 'Twas indecent to wring his secret from his bosom before a single brave had fallen before his parlour-rifle.

"'Now, tell us where your wigwam is, pappoose,' says John Tom—'where you live? Your mamma will be worrying about you being out so late. Tell me, and I'll take you home.'

"The kid grins. 'I guess not,' he says. 'I live thousands and thousands of miles over there.' He gyrated his hand toward the horizon. 'I come on the train,' he says, 'by myself. I got off here because the conductor said my ticket had ex-pirated.' He looks at John Tom with sudden suspicion. I bet you ain't a Indian,' he says. 'You don't talk like a Indian. You look like one, but all a Indian can say is "heap good" and "pale-face die." Say, I bet you are one of them make-believe Indians that sell medicine on the streets. I saw one once in Quincy.'

"'You never mind,' says John Tom, 'whether I'm a cigar-sign or a Tammany cartoon. The question before the council is what's to be done with you. You've run away from home. You've been reading Howells. You've disgraced the profession of boy avengers by trying to shoot a tame Indian, and never saying: "Die, dog of a redskin! You have crossed the path of the Boy Avenger nineteen times too often." What do you mean by it?'

"The kid thought for a minute. 'I guess I made a mistake,' he says. 'I ought to have gone farther west. They find 'em wild out there in the cañons.' He holds out his hand to John Tom, the little rascal. 'Please excuse me, sir,' says he, 'for shooting at you. I hope it didn't hurt you. But you ought to be more careful. When a scout sees a Indian in his war-dress, his rifle must speak.' Little Bear give a big laugh with a whoop at the end of it, and swings the kid ten feet high and sets him on his shoulder, and the runaway fingers the fringe and the eagle feathers and is full of the joy the white man knows when he dangles his heels against an inferior race. It is plain that Little Bear and that kid are chums from that on. The little renegade has already smoked the pipe of peace with the savage; and you can see in his eye that he is figuring on a tomahawk and a pair of moccasins, children's size.

"We have supper in the tent. The youngster looks upon me and the Professor as ordinary braves, only intended as a background to the camp scene. When he is seated on a box of Sum-wah-tah, with the edge of the table sawing his neck, and his mouth full of beefsteak, Little Bear calls for his name. 'Roy,' says the kid, with a sirloiny sound to it. But when the rest of it and his post-office address is referred to, he shakes his head. 'I guess not,' he says. 'You'll send me back. I want to stay with you. I like this camping out. At home, we fellows had a camp in our back yard. They called me Roy, the Red Wolf. I guess that'll do for a name. Gimme another piece of beefsteak, please.'

"We had to keep that kid. We knew there was a hullabaloo about him somewheres, and that Mamma, and Uncle Harry, and Aunt Jane, and the Chief of Police were hot after finding his trail, but not another word would he tell us. In two days he was the mascot of Big Medicine outfit, and all of us had a sneaking hope that his owners wouldn't turn up. When the red wagon was doing business he was in it, and passed up the bottles to Mr. Peters as proud and satisfied as a prince that's abjured a two-hundred-dollar crown for a million-dollar parvenuess. Once John Tom asked him something about his papa. 'I ain't got any papa,' he says. 'He runned away and left us. He made my mamma cry. Aunt Lucy says he's a shape.' 'A what?' somebody asks him. 'A shape,' says the kid: 'some kind of a shape—lemme see—oh, yes, a feendenuman shape. I don't know what it means.' John Tom was for putting our brand on him, and dressing him up like a little chief, with wampun and beads, but I vetoes it. 'Somebody's lost that kid, is my view of it, and they may want him. You let me try him with a few strategems, and see if I can't get a look at his visiting-card.'

"So that night I goes up to Mr. Roy Blank by the camp-fire, and looks at him contemptuous and scornful. 'Snickenwitzel!' says I, like the word made me sick; 'Snickenwitzel! Bah! Before I'd be named Snickenwitzel!'

"'What's the matter with you, Jeff?' says the kid, opening his eyes wide.

"Snickenwitzel!' I repeats, and I spat the word out. 'I saw a man to-day from your town, and he told me your name. I'm not surprised you was ashamed to tell it. Snickenwitzel! Whew!'

"'Ah, here, now,' says the boy, indignant and wriggling all over, 'what's the matter with you? That ain't my name. It's Conyers. What's the matter with you?'

"'And that's not the worst of it,' I went on quick, keeping him hot and not giving him time to think. 'We thought you was from a nice, well-to-do family. Here's Mr. Little Bear, a chief of the Cherokees, entitled to wear nine otter tails on his Sunday blanket, and Professor Binkly, who plays Shakespeare and the banjo, and me, that's got hundreds of dollars in that black tin box in the wagon, and we've got to be careful about the company we keep. That man tells me your folks live way down in little Hencoop Alley, where there are no sidewalks, and the goats eat off the table with you.'

"That kid was almost crying now. "Tain't so,' he splutters. 'He—he don't know what he's talking about. We live on Poplar Av'noo. I don't 'sociate with goats. What's the matter with you?'

"'Poplar Avenue,' says I, sarcastic. 'Poplar Avenue! That's a street to live on! It only runs two blocks and then falls off a bluff. You can throw a keg of nails the whole length of it. Don't talk to me about Poplar Avenue.'

"'It's—it's miles long,' says the kid. 'Our number's 862 and there's lots of houses after that. What's the matter with —aw, you make me tired, Jeff.'

"'Well, well, now,' says I. 'I guess that man made a mistake. Maybe it was some other boy he was talking about. If I catch him I'll teach him to go around slandering people.' And after supper I goes up-town and telegraphs to Mrs Conyers, 862 Poplar Avenue, Quincy, Ill., that the kid is safe and sassy with us, and will be held for further orders.

In two hours an answer comes to hold him tight, and she'll start for him by next train.

"The next train was due at 6 p.m. the next day, and me and John Tom was at the depot with the kid. You might scour the plains in vain for the big Chief Wish-Heap-Dough. In his place is Mr. Little Bear in the human habiliments of the Anglo-Saxon sect; and the leather of his shoes is patented and the loop of his necktie is copyrighted. For these things John Tom had grafted on him at college along with metaphysics and the knock-out guard for the low tackle. But for his complexion, which is some yellowish, and the black mop of his straight hair, you might have thought here was an ordinary man out of the city directly that subscribes for magazines and pushes the lawn-mower in his shirt-sleeves of evenings.

"Then the train rolled in, and a little woman in a grey dress, with a sort of illuminating hair, slides off and looks around quick. And the Boy Avenger sees her, and yells 'Mamma,' and she cries 'Oh!' and they meet in a clinch, and now the pesky redskins can come forth from their caves on the plains without fear any more of the rifle of Roy, the Red Wolf. Mrs. Conyers comes up and thanks me an' John Tom without the usual extremities you always look for in a woman. She says just enough, in a way to convince, and there is no incidental music by the orchestra. I made a few illiterate requisitions upon the art of conversation, at which the lady smiles friendly, as if she had known me a week. And then Mr. Little Bear adorns the atmosphere with the various idioms into which education can fracture the wind of speech. I could see the kid's mother didn't quite place John Tom; but it seemed she was apprised in his dialects, and she played up to his lead in the science of making three words do the work of one.

"That kid introduced us, with some footnotes and explanations that made things plainer than a week of rhetoric. He danced around, and punched us in the back, and tried to climb John Tom's leg. 'This is John Tom, mamma,'

190

says he. 'He's a Indian. He sells medicine in a red wagon.
I shot him, but he wasn't wild. The other one's Jeff. He's a
fakir, too. Come and see the camp where we live, won't you,
mamma?'

"It is plain to see that the life of the woman is in that boy.
She has got him again where her arms can gather him, and
that's enough. She's ready to do anything to please him. She
hesitates the eighth of a second and takes another look at
these men. I imagine she says to herself about John Tom,
'Seems to be a gentleman, if his hair don't curl.' And Mr.
Peters she disposes of as follows: 'No ladies' man, but a man
who knows a lady.'

"So we all rambled down to the camp as neighbourly as
coming from a wake. And there she inspects the wagon,
and pats the place with her hand where the kid used to sleep,
and dabs around her eyewinkers with her handkerchief.
And Professor Binkly gives us 'Trovatore' on one string of
the banjo, and is about to slide off into Hamlet's monologue
when one of the horses gets tangled in his rope and he must go
look after him, and says something about 'foiled again'.

"When it got dark me and John Tom walked back up to
the Corn Exchange Hotel, and the four of us had supper
there. I think the trouble started at that supper, for then was
when Mr. Little Bear made an intellectual balloon ascen-
sion. I held on to the tablecloth, and listened to him soar. That
redman, if I could judge, had the gift of information. He
took language, and did with it all a Roman can do with
macaroni. His vocal remarks was all embroidered over
with the most scholarly verbs and prefixes. And his syllables
was smooth, and fitted nicely to the joints of his idea. I
thought I'd heard him talk before, but I hadn't. And it
wasn't the size of his words, but the way they come; and
'twasn't his subjects, for he spoke of common things like
cathedrals and footballs and poems and catarrh and souls
and freight rates and sculpture. Mrs. Conyers understood his
accents, and the elegant sounds went back and forth between
'em. And now and then Jefferson D. Peters would intervene

a few shop-worn, senseless words to have the butter passed or another leg of the chicken.

"Yes, John Tom Little Bear appeared to be inveigled some in his bosom about that Mrs. Conyers. She was of the kind that pleases. She had the good looks and more, I'll tell you. You take one of these cloak models in a big store. They strike you as being on the impersonal system. They are adapted for the eye. What they run to is inches around and complexion, and the art of fanning the delusion that the sealskin would look just as well on the lady with the warts and the pocket-book. Now, if one of them models was off duty, and you took it, and it would say 'Charlie' when you pressed it, and sit up at the table, why, then you would have something similar to Mrs. Conyers. I could see how John Tom could resist any inclination to hate that white squaw.

"The lady and the kid stayed at the hotel. In the morning, they say, they will start for home. Me and Little Bear left at eight o'clock, and sold Indian Remedy on the courthouse square till nine. He leaves me and the Professor to drive down to camp, while he stays up town. I am not enamoured with that plan, for it shows John Tom is uneasy in his composures, and that leads to fire-water, and sometimes to the green corn dance and costs. Not often does Chief Wish-Heap-Dough get busy with the fire-water, but whenever he does there is heap much doing in the lodges of the palefaces who wear blue and carry the club.

"At half-past nine Professor Binkly is rolled in his quilt snoring in blank verse, and I am sitting by the fire listening to the frogs. Mr. Little Bear slides into camp, and sits down against a tree. There is no symptoms of fire-water.

"'Jeff,' says he, after a long time, 'a little boy came West to hunt Indians.'

"'Well, then?' says I, for I wasn't thinking as he was.

"'And he bagged one,' says John Tom, 'and 'twas not with a gun, and he never had on a velveteen suit of clothes in his life.' And then, I began to catch his smoke.

"'I know it,' says I. 'And I'll bet you his pictures are on valentines, and fool men are his game, red and white.'

"'You win on the red,' says John Tom, calm. 'Jeff, for how many ponies do you think I could buy Mrs. Conyers?'

"'Scandalous talk!' I replies. ''Twas not a paleface custom.' John Tom laughs loud and bites into a cigar. 'No,' he answers; ''tis the savage equivalent for the dollars of the white man's marriage settlement. Oh, I know. There's an eternal wall between the races. If I could do it, Jeff, I'd put a torch to every white college that a redman has ever set foot inside. Why don't you leave us alone,' says he, 'to our own ghost-dances and dog-feasts, and our dingy squaws to cook our grasshopper soup and darn our moccasins?'

"'Now, you sure don't mean disrespect to the perennial blossom entitled education?' says I, scandalized, 'because I wear it in the bosom of my own intellectual shirt-waist. I've had education,' says I, 'and never took any harm from it.'

"'You lasso us,' goes on Little Bear, not noticing my prose insertions, 'and teach us what is beautiful in literature and in life, and how to appreciate what is fine in men and women. What have you done to me?' says he. 'You've made me a Cherokee Moses. You've taught me to hate the wigwams and love the white man's ways. I can look over into the promised land and see Mrs. Conyers, but my place is—on the reservation.'

"Little Bear stands up in his chief's dress, and laughs again. 'But, white man Jeff,' he goes on, 'the paleface provides a recourse. 'Tis a temporary one, but it gives a respite and the name of it is whisky.'

"And straight off he walks up the path to town again. 'Now,' says I in my mind, 'may the Manitou move him to do only bailable things this night!' For I perceive that John Tom is about to avail himself of the white man's solace.

"Maybe it was 10.30, as I sat smoking, when I hear pit-a-pats on the path, and here comes Mrs. Conyers running, her hair twisted up any way, and a look on her face that says burglars and mice and the flour's all-out rolled in one. 'Oh, Mr. Peters,' she calls out, as they will, 'oh, oh!' I made a quick think, and I spoke the gist of it out loud. 'Now,' says I, 'we've been brothers, me and that Indian, but I'll make a good one of him in two minutes if——'

"'No, no,' she says, wild and cracking her knuckles. 'I haven't seen Mr. Little Bear. 'Tis my—husband. He's stolen my boy. Oh,' she says, 'just when I had him back in my arms again! That heartless villain! Every bitterness life knows,' she says, 'he's made me drink. My poor little lamb, that ought to be warm in his bed, carried off by that fiend!'

"'How did all this happen?' I ask. 'Let's have the facts.'

"'I was fixing his bed,' she explains, 'and Roy was playing on the hotel porch and he drives up to the steps. I heard Roy scream and ran out. My husband had him in the buggy then. I begged him for my child. This is what he gave me.' She turns her face to the light. There is a crimson streak running across her cheek and mouth. 'He did that with his whip,' she says.

"'Come back to the hotel,' says I, 'and we'll see what can be done.'

"On the way she tells me some of the wherefores. When he slashed her with the whip he told her he found out she was coming for the kid, and he was on the same train. Mrs. Conyers had been living with her brother, and they'd watched the boy always, as her husband had tried to steal him before. I judge that man was worse than a street railway promoter. It seems he had spent her money and slugged her and killed her canary bird, and told it around that she had cold feet.

"At the hotel we found a mass meeting of five infuriated citizens chewing tobacco and denouncing the outrage. Most of the town was asleep by ten o'clock. I talks the lady some quiet, and tells her I will take the one o'clock train for the next town, forty miles east, for it is likely that the esteemed

Mr. Conyers will drive there to take the cars. 'I don't know,' I tells her, 'but what he has legal rights; but if I find him I can give him an illegal left in the eye, and tie him up for a day or two, anyhow, on a disturbal of the peace proposition.'

"Mrs. Conyers goes inside and cries with the landlord's wife, who is fixing some catnip tea that will make everything all right for the poor dear. The landlord comes out on the porch, thumbing his one suspender, and says to me:

"'Ain't had so much excitements in town since Bedford Steegall's wife swallered a spring lizard. I seen him through the winder hit her with the buggy whip, and everything. What's that suit of clothes cost you you got on? 'Pears like we'd have some rain, don't it? Say, doc, that Indian of yorn's on a kind of a whizz to-night, ain't he? He comes along just before you did, and I told him about this here occurrence. He gives a cur'us kind of a hoot, and trotted off. I guess our constable 'll have him in the lock up 'fore morning.'

"I thought I'd sit on the porch and wait for the one o'clock train. I wasn't feeling saturated with mirth. Here was John Tom on one of his sprees, and this kidnapping business losing sleep for me. But then, I'm always having trouble with other people's troubles. Every few minutes Mrs. Conyers would come out on the porch and look down the road the way the buggy went, like she expected to see that kid coming back on a white pony with a red apple in his hand. Now, wasn't that like a woman? And that brings up cats. 'I saw a mouse go in this hole,' says Mrs. Cat; 'you can go prise up a plank over there if you like; I'll watch this hole.'

"About a quarter to one o'clock the lady comes out again, restless, crying easy, as females do for their own amusement, and she looks down that road again and listens. 'Now, ma'am,' says I, 'there's no use watching cold wheel-tracks. By this time they're half-way to——' 'Hush,' she says, holding up her hand. And I do hear something coming 'flip-flap' in the dark; and then there is the awfulest war-whoop ever heard outside of Madison Square Garden at a Buffalo Bill matinée. And up the steps and on to the porch jumps the disrespectable Indian. The lamp in the hall shines on him, and I fail to recognize Mr. J. T. Little Bear, alumnus of the class of '91. What I see is a Cherokee brave, and the warpath is what he has been travelling. Fire-water and other things have got him going. His buckskin is hanging in strings, and his feathers are mixed up like a frizzly hen's. The dust of miles is on his moccasins, and the light in his eye is the kind the aborigines wear. But in his arms he brings that kid, his eyes half closed, with his little shoes dangling and one hand fast around the Indian's collar.

"'Pappoose!' says John Tom, and I notice that the flowers of the white Man's syntax have left his tongue. He is the original proposition in bear's claws and copper colour. 'Me bring,' says he, and he lays the kid in his mother's arms. 'Run fifteen mile,' says John Tom—'Ugh! Catch white man. Bring pappoose.'

"The little woman is in extremities of gladness. She must wake up that stir-up trouble youngster and hug him and make proclamation that he is his mamma's own precious treasure. I was about to ask questions, but I looked at Mr. Little Bear, and my eye caught the sight of something in his belt. 'Now go to bed, ma'am,' says I, 'and this gadabout youngster likewise, for there's no more danger, and the kidnapping business is not what it was earlier in the night.'

"I inveigled John Tom down to camp quick, and when he tumbled over asleep I got that thing out of his belt and disposed of it where the eye of education can't see it. For even the football colleges disapprove of the art of scalp-taking in their curriculums.

"It is ten o'clock next day when John Tom wakes up and looks around. I am glad to see the nineteenth century in his eye again.

"'What was it, Jeff?' he asks.

"'Heap fire-water,' says I.

"John Tom frowns, and thinks a little. 'Combined,' says he directly, 'with the interesting little physiological shake-up known as reversion to type. I remember now. Have they gone yet?'

"'On the 7.30 train,' I answers.

"'Ugh!' says John Tom; 'better so. Paleface, bring big Chief Wish-Heap-Dough a little bromoseltzer, and then he'll take up the redman's burden again.'"

20

The Chair of Philanthromathematics

"I SEE that the cause of Education has received the princely gift of more than fifty millions of dollars," said I.

I was gleaning the stray items from the evening papers while Jeff Peters packed his briar pipe with plug cut.

"Which same," said Jeff, "calls for a new deck, and a recitation by the entire class in philanthromathematics."

"Is that an allusion?" I asked.

"It is," said Jeff. "I never told you about the time when me and Andy Tucker was philanthropists, did I? It was eight years ago in Arizona. Andy and me was out in the Gila mountains with a two-horse wagon prospecting for silver. We struck it, and sold out to parties in Tucson for $25,000. They paid our cheque at the bank in silver—a thousand dollars in a sack. We loaded it in our wagon and drove east a hundred miles before we recovered our presence of intellect. Twenty-five thousand dollars don't sound like so much when you're reading the annual report of the Pennsylvania Railroad or listening to an actor talking about his salary; but when you can raise up a wagon sheet and kick around with your boot-heel and hear every one of 'em ring against another it makes you feel like you was a night-and-day bank with the clock striking twelve.

"The third day out we drove into one of the most specious and tidy little towns that Nature or Rand and McNally ever turned out. It was in the foothills, and mitigated with trees and flowers and about 2,000 head of cordial and dilatory inhabitants. The town seemed to be called Floresville, and Nature had not contaminated it with many railroads, fleas or Eastern tourists.

"Me and Andy deposited our money to the credit of Peters and Tucker in the Esperanza Savings Bank, and got rooms at the Skyview Hotel. After supper we lit up, and sat out on the gallery and smoked. Then was when the philanthropy idea struck me. I suppose every grafter gets it some time.

"When a man swindles the public out of a certain amount he begins to get scared and wants to return part of it. And if you'll watch close and notice the way his charity runs you'll see that he tries to restore it to the same people he got it from. As a hydrostatical case, take, let's say, A. A made his millions selling oil to poor students who sit up nights studying political economy and methods for regulating the trusts. So, back to the universities and colleges goes his conscience dollars.

"There's B got his from the common labouring man that works with his hands and tools. How's he to get some of the remorse fund back into their overalls?

"'Aha!' says B, 'I'll do it in the name of Education. I've skinned the labouring man,' says he to himself, 'but, according to the old proverb, "Charity covers a multitude of skins."'

"So he puts up eighty million dollars' worth of libraries; and the boys with the dinner pail that builds 'em gets the benefit.

"'Where's the books?' asks the reading public.

"'I dinna ken,' says B. 'I offered ye libraries; and there they are. I suppose if I'd given ye preferred steel trust stock instead ye'd have wanted the water in it set out in cut-glass decanters. Hoot, for ye!'

"But, as I said, the owning of so much money was beginning to give me philanthropitis. It was the first time me and Andy had ever made a pile big enough to make us stop and think how we got it.

"'Andy,' says I, 'we're wealthy—not beyond the dreams of average; but in our humble way we are comparatively as rich as Greasers. I feel as if I'd like to do something for as well as to humanity.'

199

"'I was thinking the same thing, Jeff,' says he. 'We've been gouging the public for a long time with all kinds of little schemes from selling self-igniting celluloid collars to flooding Georgia with Hoke Smith presidential campaign buttons. I'd like, myself, to hedge a bet or two in the graft game if I could do it without actually banging the cymbalines in the Salvation Army or teaching a Bible class by the Bertillon system.'

"'What'll we do?' says Andy. 'Give free grub to the poor or send a couple of thousand to George Cortelyou?'

"'Neither,' says I, 'We've got too much money to be implicated in plain charity; and we haven't got enough to make restitution. So, we'll look about for something that's about half-way between the two.'

"The next day in walking around Floresville we see on a hill a big red-brick building that appears to be disinhabited. The citizens speak up and tell us that it was begun for a residence several years before by a mine-owner. After running up the house he finds he only had $2.80 left to furnish it with, so he invests that in whisky and jumps off the roof on a spot where he now requiescats in pieces.

"As soon as me and Andy saw that building the same idea struck both of us. We would fix it up with lights and pen-wipers and professors, and put an iron dog and statues of Hercules and Father John on the lawn, and start one of the finest free educational institutions in the world right there.

"So we talks it over to the prominent citizens of Floresville, who falls in with the idea. They give a banquet in the engine-house to us, and we make our bow for the first time as bene-factors to the cause of progress and enlightenment. Andy makes an hour-and-a-half speech on the subject of irrigation in Lower Egypt, and we have a moral tune on the phono-graph and pineapple sherbet.

"Andy and me didn't lose any time in philanthropping. We put every man in town that could tell a hammer from a step-ladder to work on the building, dividing it up into classrooms and lecture halls. We wire to 'Frisco for a car-load of desks, footballs, arithmetic, penholders, dictionaries, chairs for the professors, slates, skeletons, sponges, twenty-seven cravenetted gowns and caps for the senior class, and an open order for all the truck that goes with a first-class university. I took it on myself to put up a campus and a curriculum on the list; but the telegraph operator must have got the words wrong, being an ignorant man, for when the goods come we found a can of peas and a currycomb among 'em.

"While the weekly paper was having chalk-plate cuts of me and Andy we wired an employment agency in Chicago to express us f.o.b. six professors immediately—one English literature, one up-to-date dead languages, one chemistry, one political economy—democrat preferred—one logic, and one wise to painting, Italian and music, with union card. The Esperanza bank guaranteed salaries, which was to run between $800 and $800.50

"Well, sir, we finally got in shape. Over the front door was carved the words: 'The World's University; Peters & Tucker, Patrons and Proprietors.' And when September the first got a cross-mark on the calendar, the come-ons begun to roll in. First the faculty got off the tri-weekly express from Tucson. They was mostly young, spectacles and red-headed, with sentiments divided between ambition and food. Andy and me got 'em billeted on the Floresvillains and then laid for the students.

"They came in bunches. We had advertised the University in all the State papers, and it did us good to see how quick the country responded. Two hundred and nineteen husky lads ageing along from 18 up to chin-whiskers answered the clarion call of free education. They ripped open that town, sponged the seams, turned it, lined it with new mohair; and you couldn't have told it from Harvard or Goldfields at the March term of court.

"They marched up and down the streets waving flags with the World's University colours—ultramarine and blue —and they certainly made a lively place of Floresville. Andy

201

made 'em a speech from the balcony of the Skyview Hotel, and the whole town was out celebrating.

"In about two weeks the professors got the students disarmed and herded into classes. I don't believe there's any pleasure equal to being a philanthropist. Me and Andy bought high silk hats and pretended to dodge the two reporters of the *Floresville Gazette*. The paper had a man to kodak us whenever we appeared on the street, and ran our pictures every week over the column headed 'Educational Notes'. Andy lectured twice a week at the University; and afterwards I would rise and tell a humorous story. Once the *Gazette* printed my pictures with Abe Lincoln on one side and Marshall P. Wilder on the other.

"Andy was as interested in philanthropy as I was. We used to wake up of nights and tell each other new ideas for booming the University.

"'Andy,' says I to him one day, 'there's something we overlooked. The boys ought to have dromedaries.'

"'What's that?' Andy asks.

"'Why, something to sleep in, of course,' says I. 'All colleges have 'em.'

"'Oh, you mean pajamas,' says Andy.

"'I do not,' says I. 'I mean dromedaries.' But I never could make Andy understand; so we never ordered 'em. Of course, I meant them long bedrooms in colleges where the scholars sleep in a row.

"Well, sir, the World's University was a success. We had scholars from five States and territories, and Floresville had a boom. A new shooting gallery and a pawnshop and two more saloons started; and the boys got up a college yell that went this way:

> Raw, raw, raw,
> Done, done, done,
> Peters, Tucker,
> Lots of fun.
> Bow-wow-wow,

Haw-hee-haw,
World University,
Hip, hurrah!

"The scholars was a fine lot of young men, and me and Andy was as proud of 'em as if they belonged to our own family.

"But one day about the last of October Andy comes to me and asks if I have any idea how much money we had left in the bank. I guesses about sixteen thousand. 'Our balance,' says Andy, 'is $821.62.'

"'What!' says I, with a kind of a yell. 'Do you mean to tell me that them infernal, clod-hopping, dough-headed, pup-faced, goose-brained, gate-stealing, rabbit-eared sons of horse thieves have soaked us for that much?'

"'No less,' says Andy.

"'Then, to Helvetia with philanthropy,' says I.

"'Not necessarily,' says Andy. 'Philanthropy,' says he, 'when run on a good business basis is one of the best grafts going. I'll look into the matter and see if it can't be straightened out.'

"The next week I am looking over the pay-roll of our faculty when I run across a new name—Professor James Darnley McCorkle, chair of mathematics; salary $100 per week. I yells so loud that Andy runs in quick.

"'What's this?' says I. 'A professor of mathematics at more than $5,000 a year? How did this happen? Did he get in through the window and appoint himself?'

"'I wired to 'Frisco for him a week ago,' says Andy. 'In ordering the faculty we seemed to have overlooked the chair of mathematics.'

"'A good thing we did,' says I. 'We can pay his salary two weeks, and then our philanthropy will look like the ninth hole on the Skibo golf links.'

"'Wait a while,' says Andy, 'and see how things turn out. We have taken up too noble a cause to draw out now. Besides, the further I gaze into the retail philanthropy business the better it looks to me. I never thought about investigating it before. Come to think of it now,' goes on Andy, 'all the philanthropists I ever knew had plenty of money. I ought to have looked into that matter long ago, and located which was the cause and which was the effect.'

"I had confidence in Andy's chicanery in financial affairs, so I left the whole thing in his hands. The University was flourishing fine, and me and Andy kept our silk hats shined up, and Floresville kept on heaping honours on us like we was millionaires instead of almost busted philanthropists.

"The students kept the town lively and prosperous. Some stranger came to town and started a faro bank over the Red Front livery stable, and began to amass money in quantities. Me and Andy strolled up one night and piked a dollar or two for sociability There were about fifty of our students there drinking rum punches and shoving high stacks of blues and reds about the table as the dealer turned the cards up.

"'Why, dang it, Andy,' says I, 'these free-school-hunting, gander-headed, silk-socked little sons of sap-suckers have got more money than you and me ever had. Look at the rolls they're pulling out of their pistol pockets!'

"'Yes,' says Andy, 'a good many of them are sons of wealthy miners and stockmen. It's very sad to see 'em wasting their opportunities this way.'

"At Christmas all the students went home to spend the holidays. We had a farewell blow-out at the University, and Andy lectured on 'Modern Music and Prehistoric Literature of the Archipelagos'. Each one of the faculty answered to toasts, and compared me and Andy to Rockefeller and the Emperor Marcus Autolycus. I pounded on the table and yelled for Professor McCorkle; but it seems he wasn't present on the occasion. I wanted a look at the man that Andy thought could earn $100 a week in philanthropy that was on the point of making an assignment.

"The students all left on the night train; and the town

204

sounded as quiet as the campus of a correspondence school at midnight. When I went to the hotel I saw a light in Andy's room, and I opened the door and walked in.

"There sat Andy and the faro dealer at a table dividing a two-foot high stack of currency in thousand-dollar packages.

"'Correct,' says Andy. 'Thirty-one thousand apiece. Come in, Jeff,' says he. 'This is our share of the profits of the first half of the scholastic term of the World's University, incorporated and philanthropated. Are you convinced now,' says Andy, 'that philanthropy when practised in a business way is an art that blesses him who gives as well as him who receives?'

"'Great!' says I, feeling fine. 'I'll admit you are the doctor this time.'

"'We'll be leaving on the morning train,' says Andy. 'You'd better get your collars and cuffs and Press clippings together.'

"'Great!' says I. 'I'll be ready. But, Andy,' says I, 'I wish I could have met that Professor James Darnley McCorkle before we went. I had a curiosity to know that man.'

"'That'll be easy,' says Andy, turning around to the faro dealer.

"'Jim,' says Andy, 'shake hands with Mr. Peters.'"

21

Innocents of Broadway

"I HOPE some day to retire from business," said Jeff Peters; "and when I do I don't want anybody to be able to say that I ever got a dollar of any man's money without giving him a *quid pro rata* for it. I've always managed to leave a customer some little gewgaw to paste in his scrapbook or stick between his Seth Thomas clock and the wall after we are through trading.

"There was one time I came near having to break this rule of mine and do a profligate and illaudable action, but I was saved from it by the laws and statutes of our great and profitable country.

"One summer me and Andy Tucker, my partner, went to New York to lay in our annual assortment of clothes and gents' furnishings. We was always pompous and regardless dressers, finding that looks went further than anything else in our business, except maybe our knowledge of railroad schedules and an autograph photo of the President that Loeb sent us, probably by mistake. Andy wrote a nature letter once and sent it in about animals that he had seen caught in a trap lots of times. Loeb must have read it 'triplets', instead of 'trap lots', and sent the photo. Anyhow, it was useful to us to show people as a guarantee of good faith.

"Me and Andy never cared much to do business in New York. It was too much like pot-hunting. Catching suckers in that town, is like dynamiting a Texas lake for brass. All you have to do anywhere between the North and East rivers is to stand in the street with an open bag marked, 'Drop packages of money here. No cheques or loose bills taken.' You have a cop handy to club pikers who try to chip in post-office orders and Canadian money, and that's all there is to New York for a hunter who loves his profession. So me and Andy used to just nature fake the town. We'd get our spy-glass and watch the woodcocks along the Broadway swamps putting plaster casts on their broken legs, and then we'd sneak away without firing a shot.

"One day in the papier-mâché palm-room of a chloral hydrate and hops agency in a side street about eight inches off Broadway me and Andy had thrust upon us the acquaintance of a New Yorker. We had been together until we discovered that each of us knew a man named Hellsmith, travelling for a stove factory in Duluth. This caused us to remark that the world was a very small place, and then this New Yorker busts his string and takes off his tinfoil and excelsior packing and starts in giving us his Ellen Terris, beginning with the time he used to sell shoe-laces to the Indians on the spot where Tammany Hall now stands.

"This New Yorker had made his money keeping a cigar store in Beekman Street, and he hadn't been above Fourteenth Street in ten years. Moreover, he had whiskers, and the time has gone by when a true sport will do anything to a man with whiskers. No grafter except a boy who is soliciting subscribers to an illustrated weekly to win the prize air rifle, or a widow, would have the heart to tamper with the man behind with the razor. He was a typical city Reub—I'd bet the man hadn't been out of sight of a sky-scraper in twenty-five years.

"Well, presently this metropolitan backwoodsman pulls out a roll of bills with an old blue sleeve elastic fitting tight around it and opens it up.

"'There's $5,000, Mr. Peters,' says he, shoving it over the table to me, 'saved during my fifteen years of business. Put that in your pocket and keep it for me, Mr. Peters. I'm glad to meet you gentlemen from the West, and I may take a drop too much. I want you to take care of my money for me. Now, let's have another beer.'

"'You'd better keep this yourself,' says I. 'We are strangers to you, and you can't trust everybody you meet. Put your roll back in your pocket,' says I. 'And you'd better run along home before some farm-hand from the Kaw River bottoms strolls in here and sells you a copper mine.'

"'Oh, I don't know,' says Whiskers. 'I guess Little Old New York can take care of herself. I guess I know a man that's on the square when I see him. I've always found the Western people all right. I ask you as a favour, Mr. Peters,' says he, 'to keep that roll in your pocket for me. I know a gentleman when I see him. And now let's have some more beer.'

"In about ten minutes this fall of manna leans back in his chair and snores. Andy looks at me and says: 'I reckon I'd better stay with him for five minutes or so, in case the waiter comes in.'

"I went out the side door and walked half a block up the street. And then I came back and sat down at the table.

"'Andy,' says I, 'I can't do it. It's too much like swearing off taxes. I can't go off with this man's money without doing something to earn it, like taking advantage of the Bankrupt Act or leaving a bottle of eczema lotion in his pocket to make it look more like a square deal.'

"'Well,' says Andy, 'it does seem kind of hard on one's professional pride to lope off with a bearded pard's competency, especially after he has nominated you custodian of his bundle in the sappy insouciance of his urban indiscrimination. Suppose we wake him up and see if we can formulate some commercial sophistry by which he will be enabled to give us both his money and a good excuse.'

"We wakes up Whiskers. He stretches himself and yawns out the hypothesis that he must have dropped off for a minute. And then he says he wouldn't mind sitting in at a little gentleman's game of poker. He used to play some when he attended high school in Brooklyn; and as he was out for a good time, why—and so forth.

"Andy brightens up a little at that, for it looks like it might be a solution to our financial troubles. So we all three go to our hotel further down Broadway and have the cards and chips brought up to Andy's room. I tried once more to make this Babe in the Horticultural Gardens take his five thousand. But no.

"'Keep that little roll for me, Mr. Peters,' says he, 'and oblige. I'll ask you for it when I want it. I guess I know when I'm among friends. A man that's done business on Beekman Street for twenty years, right in the heart of the wisest little old village on earth, ought to know what he's about. I guess I can tell a gentleman from a con man or a flimflammer when I meet him. I've got some odd change in my clothes— enough to start the game with, I guess.'

"He goes through his pockets and rains $20 gold certificates on the table till it looked like a $10,000 'Autumn Day in a Lemon Grove' picture by Turner in the salons. Andy almost smiled.

"The first round that was dealt, this boulevardier slaps down his hand, claims low and jack and big casino and rakes in the pot.

"Andy always took a pride in his poker playing. He got up from the table and looked sadly out of the window at the street doors.

"'Well, gentlemen,' says the cigar man, 'I don't blame you for not wanting to play. I've forgotten the fine points of the game, I guess, it's been so long since I indulged. Now, how long are you gentlemen going to be in the city?'

"I told him about a week longer. He says that'll suit him fine. His cousin is coming over from Brooklyn that evening and they are going to see the sights of New York. His cousin, he says, is in the artificial limb and lead casket business, and hasn't crossed the bridge in eight years. They expect to have the time of their lives, and he winds up by asking me to keep his roll of money for him till next day. I tried to make him take it, but it only insulted him to mention it.

"'I'll use what I've got in loose change,' says he. 'You keep the rest for me. I'll drop in on you and Mr. Tucker to-morrow afternoon about six or seven,' says he, 'and we'll have dinner together. Be good.'

"After Whiskers had gone Andy looked at me curious and doubtful.

"'Well, Jeff,' says he, 'it looks like the ravens are trying to feed us two Elijahs so hard that if we turned 'em down again we ought to have the Audubon Society after us. It won't do to put the crown aside too often. I know this is something like paternalism, but don't you think Opportunity has skinned its knuckles about enough knocking at our door?'

"I put my feet on the table and my hands in my pockets, which is an attitude unfavourable to frivolous thoughts.

"'Andy,' says I, 'this man with the hirsute whiskers has got us in a predicament. We can't move hand or foot with his money. You and me have got a gentleman's agreement with Fortune that we can't break. We've done business in the West where it's more of a fair game. Out there the people we skin are trying to skin us, even the farmers and the remittance men that the magazines send out to write up Goldfields. But there's little sport in New York city for rod, reel or gun. They hunt here with either one of two things— a slungshot or a letter of introduction. The town has been stocked so full of carp that the game fish are all gone. If you spread a net here, do you catch legitimate suckers in it, such as the Lord intended to be caught—fresh guys who know it all, sports with a little coin and the nerve to play another man's game, street crowds out for the fun of dropping a dollar or two and village smarties who know just where the little pea is? No, sir,' says I. 'What the grafters live on here is widows and orphans, and foreigners who save up a bag of money and hand it out over the first counter they see with an iron railing to it, and factory girls and little shopkeepers that never leave the block they do business on. That's what they ca l suckers here. They're nothing but canned sardines, and all the bait you need to catch 'em is a pocket-knife and a soda cracker.

"'Now, this cigar man,' I went on, 'is one of the types. He's lived twenty years on one street without learning as much as you would in getting a once-over shave from a lock-jawed barber in a Kansas cross-roads town. But he's a New Yorker, and he'll brag about that all the time when he isn't picking up live wires or getting in front of street cars or paying out money to wire-tappers or standing under a safe that's being hoisted into a sky-scraper. When a New Yorker does loosen up,' says I, 'it's like the spring decomposition of the ice jam in the Allegheny River. He'll swamp you with cracked ice and backwater if you don't get out of the way.'

"'It's mighty lucky for us, Andy,' says I, 'that this cigar exponent with the parsley dressing saw fit to bedeck us with his childlike trust and altruism. For,' says I, 'this money of his is an eyesore to my sense of rectitude and ethics. We can't take it, Andy; you know we can't,' says I, 'for we haven't a shadow of a title to it—not a shadow. If there was the least bit of a way we could put in a claim to it I'd be willing to see him start in for another twenty years and make another $5,000 for himself, but we haven't sold him anything, we haven't been embroiled in a trade or anything commercial. He approached us friendly,' says I, 'and with blind and beautiful idiocy laid the stuff in our hands. We'll have to give it back to him when he wants it.'

"'Your arguments,' says Andy, 'are past criticism or comprehension. No, we can't walk off with the money—as things now stand. I admire your conscious way of doing business, Jeff,' says Andy, 'and I wouldn't propose anything that wasn't square in line with your theories of morality and initiative.'

"'But I'll be away to-night and most of to-morrow, Jeff,' says Andy. 'I've got some business affairs that I want to attend to. When this free greenbacks party comes in to-morrow afternoon hold him here till I arrive. We've all got an engagement for dinner, you know.'

"Well, sir, about five the next afternoon in trips the cigar man, with his eyes half open.

"'Been having a glorious time, Mr. Peters.' says he. 'Took in all the sights. I tell you New York is the onliest only. Now if you don't mind,' says he, 'I'll lie down on the couch and

doze off for about nine minutes before Mr. Tucker comes.
I'm not used to being up all night. And to-morrow, if you
don't mind, Mr. Peters. I'll take that five thousand. I met
a man last night that's got a sure winner at the race-track
to-morrow. Excuse me for being so impolite as to go to
sleep, Mr. Peters.'

"And so this inhabitant of the second city in the world
reposes himself and begins to snore, while I sit there musing
over things and wishing I was back in the West, where you
could always depend on a customer fighting to keep his
money hard enough to let your conscience take it from him.

"At half-past five Andy comes in and sees the sleeping
form.

"'I've been over to Trenton,' says Andy, pulling a
document out of his pocket. 'I think I've got this matter
fixed up all right, Jeff. Look at that.'

"I open the paper and see that it is a corporation charter
issued by the State of New Jersey to 'The Peters & Tucker
Consolidated and Amalgamated Aerial Franchise Develop-
ment Company, Limited.'

"'It's to buy up rights of way for airship lines,' explained
Andy. 'The Legislature wasn't in session, but I found a man
at a post-card stand in the lobby that kept a stock of charters
on hand. There are 100,000 shares,' says Andy, 'expect to
reach a par value of $1. I had one blank certificate of stock
printed.'

"Andy takes out the blank and begins to fill it in with a
fountain-pen.

"'The whole bunch,' says he, 'goes to our friend in dream-
land for $5,000. Did you learn his name?'

"'Make it out to bearer,' says I.

"We put the certificate of stock in the cigar man's hand
and went out to pack our suit-cases.

"On the ferry-boat Andy says to me: 'Is your conscience
easy about taking the money now, Jeff?'

"'Why shouldn't it be?' says I. 'Are we any better than
any other Holding Corporation?'"

22

Shearing the Wolf

JEFF PETERS was always eloquent when the ethics of his profession was under discussion.

"The only times," said he, "that me and Andy Tucker ever had any hiatuses in our cordial intents was when we differed on the moral aspects of grafting. Andy had his standards and I had mine. I didn't approve of all of Andy's schemes for levying contributions from the public, and he thought I allowed my conscience to interfere too often for the financial good of the firm. We had high arguments sometimes. Once one word led on to another till he said I reminded him of Rockefeller.

"'I know how you mean that, Andy,' says I, 'but we have been friends too long for me to take offence at a taunt that you will regret when you cool off. I have yet,' says I, 'to shake hands with a subpœna server.'

"One summer me and Andy decided to rest up a spell in a fine little town in the mountains of Kentucky called Grassdale. We was supposed to be horse drovers, and good decent citizens besides, taking a summer vacation. The Grassdale people liked us, and me and Andy declared a secession of hostilities, never so much as floating the fly-leaf of a rubber concession prospectus or flashing a Brazilian diamond while we was there.

"One day the leading hardware merchant of Grassdale drops around to the hotel where me and Andy stopped, and smokes with us, sociable, on the side porch. We knew him pretty well from pitching quoits in the afternoons in the court-house yard. He was a loud, red man, breathing hard, but fat and respectable beyond all reason.

213

"After we talk on all the notorious themes of the day, this Murkison—for such was his entitlements—takes a letter out of his coat pocket in a careful, careless way and hands it to us to read.

"'Now, what do you think of that?' says he, laughing—'a letter like that to ME!'

"Me and Andy sees at a glance what it is; but we pretend to read it through. It was one of them old-time typewritten green goods letters explaining how for $1,000 you could get $5,000 in bills that an expert couldn't tell from the genuine; and going on to tell how they were made from plates stolen by an employee of the Treasury at Washington.

"'Think of 'em sending a letter like that to ME!' says Murkison again.

"'Lots of good men get 'em,' says Andy. 'If you don't answer the first letter they let you drop. If you answer it they write again asking you to come on with your money and do business.'

"'But think of 'em writing to ME!' says Murkison.

"A few days later he drops around again.

"'Boys,' says he, 'I know you are all right or I wouldn't confide in you. I wrote to them rascals again just for fun. They answered and told me to come on to Chicago. They said telegraph to J. Smith when I would start. When I get there I'm to wait on a certain street corner till a man in a grey suit comes along and drops a newspaper in front of me. Then I am to ask him how the water is, and he knows it's me and I know it's him.'

"'Ah, yes,' says Andy, gaping, 'it's the same old game. I've often read about it in the papers. Then he conducts you to the private abattoir in the hotel, where Mr. Jones is already waiting. They show you brand-new real money and sell you all you want at five for one. You see 'em put it in a satchel for you and know it's there. Of course it's brown paper when you come to look at it afterward.'

"'Oh, they couldn't switch it on me,' says Murkison. 'I haven't built up the best paying business in Grassdale with-

214

out having witticisms about me. You say it's real money they
show you, Mr. Tucker?'

"'I've always—I see by the papers that it always is,' says
Andy.

"'Boys,' says Murkison, 'I've got it in my mind that them
fellows can't fool me. I think I'll put a couple of thousand in
my jeans and go up there and put it all over 'em. If Bill
Murkison gets his eyes once on them bills they show him he'll
never take 'em off of 'em. They offer $5 for $1, and they'll
have to stick to the bargain if I tackle 'em. That's the kind of
trader Bill Murkison is. Yes, I jist believe I'll drop up
Chicago way and take a 5 to 1 shot on J. Smith, I guess the
water'll be fine enough.'

"Me and Andy tries to get this financial misquotation out
of Murkison's head, but we might as well have tried to keep
the man who rolls peanuts with a toothpick from betting on
Bryan's election. No, sir; he was going to perform a public
duty by catching these green goods swindlers at their own
game. Maybe it would teach 'em a lesson.

"After Murkison left us me and Andy sat a while pre-
pondering over our silent meditations and heresies of reason.
In our idle hours we always improved our higher selves by
ratiocination and mental thought.

"'Jeff,' says Andy after a long time, 'quite unseldom I
have seen fit to impugn your molars when you have been
chewing the rag with me about your conscientious way of
doing business. I may have been often wrong. But here is a
case where I think we can agree. I feel that it would be wrong
for us to allow Mr. Murkison to go alone to meet those
Chicago green goods men. There is but one way it can end.
Don't you think we would both feel better if we was to
intervene in some way and prevent the doing of this deed?'

"I got up and shook Andy Tucker's hand hard and long.

"'Andy,' says I, 'I may have had one or two hard thoughts
about the heartlessness of your corporation, but I retract
'em now. You have a kind nucleus at the interior of your
exterior after all. It does you credit. I was just thinking

215

the same thing that you have expressed. It would not be honourable or praiseworthy,' says I, 'for us to let Murkison go on with this project he has taken up. If he is determined to go, let us go with him and prevent this swindle from coming off.'

"Andy agreed with me; and I was glad to see that he was in earnest about breaking up this green goods scheme.

"'I don't call myself a religious man,' says I, 'or a fanatic in moral bigotry, but I can't stand still and see a man who has built up a business by his own efforts and brains and risk be robbed by an unscrupulous trickster who is a menace to the public good.'

"'Right, Jeff,' says Andy. 'We'll stick right along with Murkison if he insists on going and block this funny business. I'd hate to see any money dropped in it as bad as you would.'

"Well, we went to see Murkison.

"'No, boys,' says he. 'I can't consent to let the song of this Chicago siren waft by men on the summer breeze. I'll fry some fat out of this ignis fatuus or burn a hole in the skillet. But I'd be plumb diverted to death to have you all go along with me. Maybe you could help some when it comes to cashing in the ticket to that 5 to 1 shot. Yes, I'd really take it as a pastime and regalement if you boys would go along too.'

"Murkison gives it out in Grassdale that he is going for a few days with Mr. Peters and Mr. Tucker to look over some iron ore property in West Virginia. He wires J. Smith that he will set foot in the spider web on a given date; and the three of us lights out for Chicago.

"On the way Murkison amuses himself with premonitions and advance pleasant recollections.

"'In a grey suit,' says he, 'on the south-west corner of Wabash Avenue and Lake Street. He drops the paper, and I ask how the water is. Oh, my, my, my!' And then he laughs all over for five minutes.

"Sometimes Murkison was serious and tried to talk himself out of his cogitations, whatever they was.

216

" 'Boys,' says he, 'I wouldn't have this to get out in Grass-dale for ten times a thousand dollars. It would ruin me there. But I know you all are all right. I think it's the duty of every citizen,' says he, 'to try to do up these robbers that prey upon the public. I'll show 'em whether the water's fine. Five dollars for one—that's what J. Smith offers, and he'll have to keep his contract if he does business with Bill Murkison.'

"We got into Chicago about 7 p.m. Murkison was to meet the grey man at half-past nine. We had dinner at a hotel and then went up to Murkison's room to wait for the time to come.

" 'Now, boys,' says Murkison, 'let's get our gumption together and inoculate a plan for defeating the enemy. Suppose while I'm exchanging airy badinage with the grey capper you gents come along, by accident, you know, and holler, "Hello, Murk!" and shake hands with symptoms of surprise and familiarity. Then I take the capper aside and tell him you all are Jenkins and Brown of Grassdale, groceries and feed, good men and maybe willing to take a chance while away from home.'

" ' "Bring 'em along," he'll say, of course, "if they care to invest." Now, how does that scheme strike you?'

" 'What do you say, Jeff?' says Andy, looking at me.

" 'Why, I'll tell you what I say,' says I. 'I say let's settle this thing right here now. I don't see any use of wasting any more time.' I took a nickel-plated .38 out of my pocket and clocked the cylinder around a few times.

" 'You undevout, sinful, insidious hog,' says I to Murkison, 'get out that two thousand and lay it on the table. Obey with velocity,' says I, 'for otherwise alternatives are impending. I am preferably a man of mildness, but now and then I find myself in the middle of extremities. Such men as you,' I went on after he had laid the money out, 'is what keeps the jails and court-houses going. You come up here to rob these men of their money. Does it excuse you,' I asks, 'that they were trying to skin you? No, sir; you was going to rob Peter to stand off Paul. You are ten times worse,' says I, 'than that green goods man. You go to church at home and pretend to be a decent citizen, but you'll come to Chicago and commit larceny from men that have built up a sound and profitable business by dealing with such contemptible scoundrels as you have tried to be to-day. How do you know,' says I, 'that that green goods man hasn't a large family dependent upon his extortions? It's you supposedly respectable citizens who are always on the look-out to get something for nothing,' says I, 'that support the lotteries and wild-cat mines and stock exchanges and wire-tappers of this country. If it wasn't for you they'd go out of business. The green goods man you was going to rob,' says I, 'studied maybe for years to learn his trade. Every turn he makes he risks his money and liberty and maybe his life. You come up here all sanctified and panoplied with respectability and a pleasing post-office address to swindle him. If he gets the money you can squeal to the police. If you get it he hocks the grey suit to buy supper and says nothing. Mr. Tucker and me sized you up,' says I, 'and came along to see that you got what you deserved. Hand over the money,' says I, 'you grass-fed hypocrite.'

"I put the two thousand, which was all in twenty-dollar bills, in my inside pocket.

"'Now get out your watch,' says I to Murkison. 'No, I don't want it,' says I. 'Lay it on the table and you sit in that chair till it ticks off an hour. Then you can go. If you make any noise or leave any sooner we'll handbill you all over Grassdale. I guess your high position there is worth more than $2,000 to you.'

"Then me and Andy left.

"On the train Andy was a long time silent. Then he says: 'Jeff, do you mind my asking you a question?'

"'Two,' says I, 'or forty.'

"'Was that the idea you had,' says he, 'when we started out with Murkison?'

"'Why, certainly,' says I. 'What else could it have been? Wasn't it yours too?'

"In about half an hour Andy spoke again. I think there

are times when Andy don't exactly understand my system of
ethics and moral hygiene.

"'Jeff,' says he, 'some time when you have the leisure I
wish you'd draw off a diagram and footnotes of that conscience of yours. I'd like to have it to refer to occasionally.'"

23

The Octopus Marooned

" A TRUST is its weakest point," said Jeff Peters.
"That," said I, "sounds like one of those unintelligible
remarks such as, 'Why is a policeman?'"

"It is not," said Jeff. "There are no relations between a
trust and a policeman. My remark was an epitogram—an
axis—a kind of mulct'em in parvo. What it means is that a
trust is like an egg, and it is not like an egg. If you want to
break an egg you have to do it from the outside. The only
way to break up a trust is from the inside. Keep sitting on it
until it hatches. Look at the brood of young colleges and
libraries that's chirping and peeping all over the country.
Yes, sir, every trust bears in its own bosom the seeds of its
destruction like a rooster that crows near a Georgia coloured
Methodist camp meeting, or a Republican announcing himself a candidate for governor of Texas."

I asked Jeff, jestingly, if he had ever, during his checkered,
plaided, mottled, pied and dappled career, conducted an
enterprise of the class to which the word "trust" has been
applied. Somewhat to my surprise he acknowledged the
corner.

"Once," said he. "And the state seal of New Jersey never
bit into a charter that opened up a solider and safer piece of
legitimate octopusing. We had everything in our favour—
wind, water, police, nerve, and a clean monopoly of an
article indispensable to the public. There wasn't a trust
buster on the globe that could have found a weak spot in our
scheme. It made Rockefeller's little kerosene speculation
look like a bucket-shop. But we lost out."

"Some unforeseen opposition came up, I suppose," I said.

"No, sir, it was just as I said. We were self-curbed. It was a case of auto-suppression. There was a rift within the loot, as Albert Tennyson says.

"You remember I told you that me and Andy Tucker was partners for some years. That man was the most talented conniver at stratagems I ever saw. Whenever he saw a dollar in another man's hands he took it as a personal grudge, if he couldn't take it any other way. Andy was educated, too, besides having a lot of useful information. He had acquired a big amount of experience out of books, and could talk for hours on any subject connected with ideas and discourse. He had been in every line of graft from lecturing on Palestine with a lot of magic-lantern pictures of the annual Custom-made Clothiers' Association Convention at Atlantic City to flooding Connecticut with bogus wood alcohol distilled from nutmegs.

"One Spring me and Andy had been over in Mexico on a flying trip during which a Philadelphia capitalist had paid us $2,500 for a half interest in a silver mine in Chihuahua. Oh, yes, the mine was all right. The other half interest must have been worth two or three hundred thousand. I often wondered who owned that mine.

"In coming back to the United States me and Andy stubbed our toes against a little town in Texas on the bank of the Rio Grande. The name of it was Bird City; but it wasn't. The town had about 2,000 inhabitants, mostly men. I figured out that their principal means of existence was in living close to tall chaparral. Some of 'em were stockmen and some gamblers and some horse speculators and plenty were in the smuggling line. Me and Andy put up at a hotel that was built like something between a roof-garden and a sectional bookcase. It began to rain the day we got there. As the saying is, Juniper Aquarius was sure turning on the water-plugs on Mount Amphibious.

"Now, there were three saloons in Bird City, though neither Andy nor me drank. But we could see the towns-people making a triangular procession from one to another all day and half the night. Everybody seemed to know what to do with as much money as they had.

"The third day of the rain it slacked up awhile in the afternoon, so me and Andy walked out to the edge of town to view the mudscape. Bird City was built between the Rio Grande and a deep wide arroyo that used to be the old bed of the river. The bank between the stream and its old bed was cracking and giving away, when we saw it, on account of the high water caused by the rain. Andy looks at it a long time. That man's intellects was never idle. And then he unfolds to me a instantaneous idea that has occurred to him. Right there was organized a trust; and we walked back into town and put it on the market.

"First we went to the main saloon in Bird City, called the Blue Snake, and bought it. It cost us $1.200. And then we dropped in, casual, at Mexican Joe's place, referred to the rain, and bought him out for $500. The other one came easy at $400.

"The next morning Bird City woke up and found itself an island. The river had busted through its old channel, and the town was surrounded by roaring torrents. The rain was still raining, and there was heavy clouds in the north-west that presaged about six more mean annual rainfalls during the next two weeks. But the worst was yet to come.

"Bird City hopped out of its nest, waggled its pin feathers and strolled out for its matutinal toot. Lo! Mexican Joe's place was closed and likewise the other little 'dobe lifesaving station. So, naturally, the body politics emits thirsty ejaculations of surprise and ports hellum for the Blue Snake. And what does it find there?

"Behind one end of the bar sits Jefferson Peters, octopus, with a sixshooter on each side of him, ready to make change or corpses as the case may be. There are three bartenders; and on the wall is a ten-foot sign reading: 'All Drinks One Dollar.' Andy sits on the safe in his neat blue suit and gold-banded cigar, on the look-out for emergencies. The town marshal is there with two deputies to keep order, having been promised free drinks by the trust.

"Well, sir, it took Bird City just ten minutes to realize that it was in a cage. We expected trouble; but there wasn't any. The citizens saw that we had 'em. The nearest railroad was thirty miles away; and it would be two weeks at least before the river would be fordable. So they began to cuss, amiable, and throw down dollars on the bar till it sounded like a selection on the xylophone.

"There was about 1,500 grown-up adults in Bird City that had arrived at years of indiscretion; and the majority of 'em required from three to twenty drinks a day to make life endurable. The Blue Snake was the only place where they could get 'em till the flood subsided. It was beautiful and simple as all truly great swindles are.

"About ten o'clock the silver dollars dropping on the bar slowed down to playing two-steps and marches instead of jigs. But I looked out the windows and saw a hundred or two of our customers standing in line at the Bird City Savings and Loan Co., and I knew they were borrowing more money to be sucked in by the clammy tendrils of the octopus.

"At the fashionable hour of noon everybody went home to dinner. We told the bartenders to take advantage of the lull, and do the same. Then me and Andy counted the receipts. We had taken in $1,300. We calculated that if Bird City would only remain an island for two weeks the trust would be able to endow the Chicago University with a new dormitory of padded cells for the faculty, and present every worthy poor man in Texas with a farm, provided he furnished the site for it.

"Andy was especial inroaded by self-esteem at our success, the rudiments of the scheme having originated in his own surmises and premonitions. He got off the safe and lit the biggest cigar in the house.

"'Jeff,' says he, 'I don't suppose that anywhere in the world you could find three cormorants with brighter ideas about down-treading the proletariat than the firm of Peters, Satan and Tucker, incorporated. We have sure handed the small consumer a giant blow in the sole apoplectic region. No?'

"'Well,' says I, 'it does look as if we would have to take up gastritis and golf or be measured for kilts in spite of ourselves. This little turn in bug juice is, verily, all to the Skibo. And I can stand it,' says I. 'I'd rather batten than bant any day.'

"Andy pours himself out four fingers of our best rye and does with it as was so intended. It was the first drink I had ever known him to take.

"'By way of liberation,' says he, 'to the gods.'

"And then after thus doing umbrage to the heathen diabetes he drinks another to our success. And then he begins to toast the trade, beginning with Raisuli and the Northern Pacific, and on down the line to the little ones like the school book combine and the oleomargarine outrages and the Lehigh Valley and Great Scott Coal Federation.

"'It's all right, Andy,' says I, 'to drink the health of our brother monopolists, but don't overdo the wassail. You know our most eminent and loathed multi-corruptionists live on weak tea and dog biscuits.'

"Andy went in the back room awhile and came out dressed in his best clothes. There was a kind of murderous and soulful look of gentle riotousness in his eye that I didn't like. I watched him to see what turn the whisky was going to take in him. There are two times when you never can tell what is going to happen. One is when a man takes his first drink: and the other is when a woman takes her latest.

"In less than an hour Andy's skate had turned to an ice yacht. He was outwardly decent and managed to preserve his aquarium, but inside he was impromptu and full of unexpectedness.

"'Jeff,' says he, 'do you know that I'm a crater—a living crater?'

"'That's a self-evident hypothesis,' says I. 'But you're not

224

Irish. Why don't you say "creature", according to the rules and syntax of America?'

"'I'm the crater of a volcano,' says he. 'I'm all aflame and crammed inside with an assortment of words and phrases that have got to have an exodus. I can feel millions of synonyms and parts of speech rising in me,' says he, 'and I've got to make a speech of some sort. Drink,' says Andy, 'always drives me to oratory.'

"'It could do no worse,' says I.

"'From my earliest recollections,' says he, 'alcohol seemed to stimulate my sense of recitation and rhetoric. Why, in Bryan's second campaign,' says Andy, 'they used to give me three gin rickeys and I'd speak two hours longer than Billy himself could on the silver question. Finally they persuaded me to take the gold cure.'

"'If you've got to get rid of your excess verbiage,' says I 'why not go out on the river bank and speak a piece? It seems to me there was an old spellbinder named Cantharides that used to go and disincorporate himself of his windy numbers along the seashore.'

"'No,' says Andy, 'I must have an audience. I feel like if I once turned loose people would begin to call Senator Beveridge the Grand Young Sphinx of the Wabash. I've got to get an audience together, Jeff, and get this oral distension assuaged or it may turn in on me and I'd go about feeling like a deckle-edge edition de luxe of Mrs. E. D. E. N. Southworth.'

"'On what special subject of the theorems and topics does your desire for vocality seem to be connected with?' I asks.

"'I ain't particular,' says Andy. 'I am equally good and varicose on all subjects. I can take up the matter of Russian immigration, or the poetry of John W. Keats, or the tariff, or Kabyle literature, or drainage, and make my audience weep, cry, sob and shed tears by turns.'

"'Well, Andy,' says I, 'if you are bound to get rid of this accumulation of vernacular, suppose you go out in town and work it on some indulgent citizen. Me and the boys will take care of the business. Everybody will be through dinner pretty soon, and salt pork and beans makes a man pretty thirsty. We ought to take in $1,500 more by midnight.'

"So Andy goes out of the Blue Snake, and I see him stopping men on the street and talking to 'em. By and by he has half a dozen in a bunch listening to him; and pretty soon I see him waving his arms and elocuting at a good-sized crowd on a corner. When he walks away they string out after him, talking all the time; and he leads 'em down the main street of Bird City with more men joining the procession as they go. It reminded me of the old legerdemain that I'd read in books about the Pied Piper of Heidsieck charming the children away from the town.

"One o'clock came; and then two; and three got under the wire for place; and not a Bird citizen came in for a drink. The streets were deserted except for some ducks and ladies going to the stores. There was only a light drizzle falling then.

"A lonesome man came along and stopped in front of the Blue Snake to scrape the mud off his boots.

"'Pardner,' says I, 'what has happened? This morning there was hectic gaiety afoot; and now it seems more like one of them ruined cities of Tyre and Siphon where the lone lizard crawls on the walls of the main portcullis.'

"'The whole town,' says the muddy man, 'is up in Sperry's wool warehouse listening to your side-kicker make a speech. He is some gravy on delivering himself of audible sounds relating to matters and conclusions,' says the man.

"'Well, I hope he'll adjourn, *sine qua non*, pretty soon,' says I, 'for trade languishes.'

"Not a customer did we have that afternoon. At six o'clock two Mexicans brought Andy to the saloon lying across the back of a burro. We put him to bed while he still muttered and gesticulated with his hands and feet.

"Then I locked up the cash and went out to see what had happened. I met a man who told me all about it. Andy had

226

made the finest two-hour speech that had ever been heard in Texas, he said, or anywhere else in the world.

"'What was it about?' I asked.

"'Temperance,' says he. 'And when he got through, every man in Bird City signed the pledge for a year.'"

24

Cupid à la Carte

"THE dispositions of woman," said Jeff Peters, after various opinions on the subject had been advanced, "run, regular, to diversions. What a woman wants is what you're out of. She wants more of a thing when it's scarce. She likes to have souvenirs of things that never happened. She likes to be reminded of things she never heard of. A one-sided view of objects is disjointing to the female composition.

"'Tis a misfortune of mine, begotten by nature and travel," continued Jeff, looking thoughtfully between his elevated feet at the grocery stove, "to look deeper into some subjects than most people do. I've breathed gasoline smoke talking to street crowds in nearly every town in the United States. I've held 'em spellbound with music, oratory, sleight of hand, and prevarications, while I've sold 'em jewellery, medicine, soap, hair tonic, and junk of other nominations. And during my travels, as a matter of recreation and expiation, I've taken cognisance some of women. It takes a man a lifetime to fall out about one particular woman; but if he puts in, say, ten years, industrious and curious, he can acquire the general rudiments of the sex. One lesson I picked up was when I was working the West with a line of Brazilian diamonds and a patent fire kindler just after my trip from Savannah down through the cotton belt with Dalby's Anti-Explosive Lamp Oil Powder. 'Twas when the Oklahoma country was in first bloom. Guthrie was rising in the middle of it like a lump of self-raising dough. It was a boom town of the regular kind— you stood in line to get a chance to wash your face; if you ate over ten minutes you had a lodging bill added on; if you slept on a plank at night they charged it to you as board the next morning.

"By nature and doctrines I am addicted to the habit of discovering choice places wherein to feed. So I looked around and found a proposition that exactly cut the mustard. I found a restaurant tent just opened up by an outfit that had drifted in on the tail of the boom. They had knocked together a box house, where they lived and did the cooking, and served the meals in a tent pitched against the side. That tent was joyful with placards on it calculated to redeem the world-worn pilgrim from the sinfulness of boarding-houses and pick-me-up hotels. 'Try Mother's Home-Made Biscuits', 'What's the Matter with Our Apple Dumplings and Hard Sauce?' 'Hot Cakes and Maple Syrup Like You Ate When a Boy', 'Our Fried Chicken Never Was Heard to Crow'— there was literature doomed to please the digestions of man! I said to myself that mother's wandering boy should munch there that night. And so it came to pass. And there is where I contracted my case of Mame Dugan.

"Old Man Dugan was six feet by one of Indiana loafer, and he spent his time sitting on his shoulderblades in a rocking-chair in the shanty memorializing the great corn-crop failure of '86. Ma Dugan did the cooking, and Mame waited on the table.

"As soon as I saw Mame I knew there was a mistake in the census reports. There wasn't but one girl in the United States. When you come to specifications it isn't easy. She was about the size of an angel, and she had eyes, and ways about her. When you come to the kind of a girl she was, you'll find a belt of 'em reaching from the Brooklyn Bridge west as far as the courthouse in Council Bluffs, Ia. They earn their own living in stores, restaurants, factories, and offices. They're descended straight from Eve, and they're the crowd that's got woman's rights, and if a man wants to dispute it he's in line to get one of them against his jaw. They're chummy and honest and free and tender and sassy, and they look life straight in the eye. They've met man face to face, and discovered that he's a poor creature. They've dropped to it that the reports in the Seaside Library about his being a fairy prince lack confirmation.

"Mame was that sort. She was full of life and fun, and breezy; she passed the repartee with the boarders quick as a wink; you'd have smothered laughing. I am disinclined to make excavations into the insides of a personal affection. I am glued to the theory that the diversions and discrepancies of the indisposition known as love should be as private a sentiment as a toothbrush. 'Tis my opinion that the biographies of the heart should be confined with the historical romances of the liver to the advertising pages of the magazines. So, you'll excuse the lack of an itemized bill of my feelings toward Mame.

"Pretty soon I got a regular habit of dropping into the tent to eat at irregular times when there wasn't so many around. Mame would sail in with a smile, in a black dress and white apron, and say: 'Hallo, Jeff—why don't you come at mealtime? Want to see how much trouble you can be, of course. Friedchickenbeefsteakporkpiechopshamandeggspotpie'—and so on. She called me Jeff, but there was no significations attached. Designations was all she meant. The front names of any of us she used as they came to hand. I'd eat about two meals before I left, and string 'em out like a society spread where they change plates and wives, and josh one another festively between bites. Mame stood for it, pleasant, for it wasn't up to her to take any canvas off the tent by declining dollars just because they were chipped in after meal-times.

"It wasn't long until there was another fellow named Ed Collier got the between-meals affliction, and him and me put in bridges between breakfast and dinner, and dinner and supper, that made a three-ringed circus of that tent, and Mame's turn as waiter a continuous performance. That Collier man was saturated with designs and contrivings. He was in well-boring or insurance or claim-jumping, or something—I've forgotten which. He was a man well lubricated with gentility, and his words were such as recommended you to his point of view. So, Collier and me infested the grub tent with care and activity. Mame was level full of impartiality. 'Twas like a casino hand the way she dealt out her favours—one to Collier and one to me and one to the board, and not a card up her sleeve.

"Me and Collier naturally got acquainted, and gravitated together some on the outside. Divested of his strategems, he seemed to be a pleasant chap, full of an amiable sort of hostility.

"'I notice you have an affinity for grubbing in the banquet hall after the guests have fled,' says I to him one day, to draw his conclusions.

"'Well, yes,' says Collier, reflecting; 'the tumult of a crowded board seems to harass my sensitive nerves.'

"'It exasperates mine some, too,' says I. 'Nice little girl, don't you think?'

"'I see,' says Collier, laughing. 'Well, now that you mention it, I have noticed that she doesn't seem to displease the optic nerve.'

"'She's a joy to mine,' says I, 'and I'm going after her. Notice is hereby served.'

"'I'll be as candid as you,' admits Collier, 'and if the drug stores don't run out of pepsin I'll give you a run for your money that'll leave you a dyspeptic at the wind-up.'

"So Collier and me begins the race; the grub department lays in new supplies; Mame waits on us, jolly and kind and agreeable, and it looks like an even break, with Cupid and the cook working overtime in Dugan's restaurant.

"'Twas one night in September when I got Mame to take a walk after supper when the things were all cleared away. We strolled out a distance and sat on a pile of lumber at the edge of town. Such opportunities was seldom, so I spoke my piece, explaining how the Brazilian diamonds and the fire kindler were laying up sufficient treasure to guarantee the happiness of two, and that both of 'em together couldn't

equal the light from somebody's eyes, and that the name of
Dugan should be changed to Peters, or reasons why not
would be in order.

"Mame didn't say anything right away. Directly she
gave a kind of shudder, and I began to learn something.

"'Jeff,' she says, 'I'm sorry you spoke. I like you as well
as any of them, but there isn't the man in the world I'd ever
marry, and there never will be. Do you know what a man is
in my eye? He's a tomb. He's a sarcophagus for the inter-
ment of Beefsteakporkchopsliver'nbaconhamandeggs. He's
that and nothing more. For two years I've watched men eat,
eat, eat, until they represent nothing on earth to me but
ruminant bipeds. They're absolutely nothing but something
that goes in front of a knife and fork and plate at the table.
They're fixed that way in my mind and memory. I've tried
to overcome it, but I can't. I've heard girls rave about their
sweethearts, but I never could understand it. A man and a
sausage grinder and a pantry awake in me exactly the same
sentiments. I went to a matinée once to see an actor the girls
were crazy about. I got interested enough to wonder whether
he liked his steak rare, medium, or well done, and his eggs
over or straight up. That was all. No, Jeff; I'll marry no man
and see him sit at the breakfast-table and eat, and come
back to dinner and eat, and happen in again at supper to eat,
eat, eat.'

"'But, Mame,' says I, 'it'll wear off. You've had too much
of it. You'll marry some time, of course. Men don't eat
always.'

"'As far as my observation goes, they do. No, I'll tell you
what I'm going to do.' Mame turns sudden, to animation
and bright eyes. 'There's a girl named Susie Foster in Terre
Haute, a chum of mine. She waits in the railroad eating-
house there. I worked two years in a restaurant in that town.
Susie has it worse than I do, because the men who eat at
railroad stations gobble. They try to flirt and gobble at the
same time. Whew! Susie and I have it all planned out.
We're saving our money, and when we get enough we're

going to buy a little cottage and five acres we know of, and live together, and grow violets for the Eastern market. A man better not bring his appetite within a mile of that ranch.'

"'Don't girls ever——' I commenced, but Mame heads me off, sharp.

"'No, they don't. They nibble a little bit sometimes; that's all.'

"'I thought the confect——'

"'For goodness' sake, change the subject,' says Mame.

"As I said before, that experience put me wise that the feminine arrangement ever struggles after deceptions and illusions. Take England—beef made her; wieners elevated Germany; Uncle Sam owes his greatness to fried chicken and pie, but the young ladies of the Shetalkyou schools, they'll never believe it. Shakespeare, they allow, and Rubinstein, and the Rough Riders is what did the trick.

"''Twas a situation calculated to disturb. I couldn't bear to give up Mame; and yet it pained me to think of abandoning the practice of eating. I had acquired the habit too early. For twenty-seven years I had been blindly rushing upon my fate, yielding to the insidious lures of that deadly monster, food. It was too late. I was a ruminant biped for keeps. It was lobster salad to a doughnut that my life was going to be blighted by it.

"I continued to board at the Dugan tent, hoping that Mame would relent. I had sufficient faith in true love to believe that since it has often outlived the absence of a square meal it might, in time, overcome the presence of one. I went on ministering to my fatal vice, although I felt that each time I shoved a potato into my mouth in Mame's presence I might be burying my fondest hopes.

"I think Collier must have spoken to Mame and got the same answer, for one day he orders a cup of coffee and a cracker, and sits nibbling the corner of it like a girl in the parlour, that's filled up in the kitchen, previous, on cold roast and fried cabbage. I caught on and did the same, and maybe we thought we'd made a hit! The next day we tried it again, and out comes old man Dugan fetching in his hands the fairy viands.

"'Kinder off yer feed, ain't ye, gents?' he asks, fatherly and some sardonic. 'Thought I'd spell Mame a bit, seein' the work was light, and my rheumatiz can stand the strain.'

"So back me and Collier had to drop to the heavy grub again. I noticed about that time that I was seized by a most uncommon and devastating appetite. I ate until Mame must have hated to see me darken the door. Afterward I found out that I had been made the victim of the first dark and irreligious trick played on me by Ed Collier. Him and me had been taking drinks together up town regular, trying to drown our thirst for food. That man had bribed about ten bar-tenders to always put a big slug of Appletree's Anaconda Appetite Bitters in every one of my drinks. But last trick he played me was hardest to forget.

"One day Collier failed to show up at the tent. A man told me he left town that morning. My only rival now was the bill of fare. A few days before he left Collier had presented me with a two-gallon jug of fine whisky which he said a cousin had sent him from Kentucky. I now have reason to believe that it contained Appletree's Anaconda Appetite Bitters almost exclusively. I continued to devour tons of provisions. In Mame's eyes I remained a mere biped, more ruminant than ever.

"About a week after Collier pulled his freight there came a kind of side-show to town, and hoisted a tent near the railroad. I judged it was a sort of fake museum and curiosity business. I called to see Mame one night, and Ma Dugan said she and Thomas, her younger brother, had gone to the show. That same thing happened for three nights that week. Saturday night I caught her on the way coming back, and got to sit on the steps a while and talk to her. I noticed she looked different. Her eyes were softer, and shiny like. Instead of a Mame Dugan to fly from the voracity of man and raise violets, she seemed to be a Mame more in line as God intended

her, approachable, and suited to bask in the light of the
Brazilians and the Kindler.

"'You seem to be right smart inveigled,' says I, 'with the
Unparalleled Exhibition of the World's Living Curiosities
and Wonders.'

"'It's a change,' says Mame.

"'You'll need another,' says I, 'if you keep on going every
night.'

"'Don't be cross, Jeff,' says she, 'it takes my mind off
business.'

"'Don't the curiosities eat?' I ask.

"'Not all of them. Some of them are wax.'

"'Look out, then, that you don't get stuck,' says I, kind
of flip and foolish.

"Mame blushed. I didn't know what to think about her.
My hopes raised some that perhaps my attentions had palli-
ated man's awful crime of visibly introducing nourishment
into his system. She talked some about the stars, referring to
them with respect and politeness, and I drivelled a quantity
about united hearts, homes made bright by true affection, and
the Kindler. Mame listened without scorn, and I says to
myself, 'Jeff, old man, you're removing the hoodoo that has
clung to the consumer of victuals; you're setting your heel
upon the serpent that lurks in the gravy bowl.'

"Monday night I drop around. Mame is at the Unparalleled Exhibition with Thomas.

"'Now, may the curse of the forty-one seven-sided sea
cooks,' says I, 'and the bad luck of the nine impenitent
grasshoppers rest upon this self-same side-show at once and
for ever more. Amen. I'll go to see it myself to-morrow night
and investigate its baleful charm. Shall man that was made
to inherit the earth be bereft of his sweetheart first by a
knife and fork and then by a ten-cent circus?'

"The next night before starting out for the exhibition tent
I inquire and find out that Mame is not at home. She is not
at the circus with Thomas this time, for Thomas waylays

me in the grass outside of the grub tent with a scheme of his own before I had time to eat supper.

"'What'll you give me, Jeff,' says he, 'if I tell you something?'

"'The value of it, son,' I says.

"'Sis is stuck on a freak,' says Thomas, 'one of the sideshow freaks. I don't like him. She does. I overheard 'em talking. Thought maybe you'd like to know. Say, Jeff, does it put you wise two dollars' worth? There's a target rifle up town that——'

"I frisked my pockets and commenced to dribble a stream of halves and quarters into Thomas's hat. The information was of the pile-driver system of news, and it telescoped my intellects for a while. While I was leaking small change and smiling foolish on the outside, and suffering disturbances internally, I was saying, idiotically and pleasantly—

"'Thank you, Thomas—thank you—er—a freak, you said, Thomas. Now, could you make out the monstrosity's entitlements a little clearer, if you please, Thomas?'

"'This is the fellow,' says Thomas, pulling out a yellow handbill from his pocket and shoving it under my nose. 'He's the Champion Faster of the Universe. I guess that's why Sis got soft on him. He don't eat nothing. He's going to fast forty-nine days. This is the sixth. That's him.'

"I looked at the name Thomas pointed out—'Professor Eduardo Collieri.' 'Ah!' says I, in admiration, 'that's not so bad, Ed Collier. I give you credit for the trick. But I don't give you the girl until she's Mrs. Freak.'

"I hit the sod in the direction of the show. I came up to the rear of the tent, and, as I did so, a man wiggled out like a snake from under the bottom of the canvas, scrambled to his feet, and ran into me like a locoed bronco, I gathered him by the neck and investigated him by the light of the stars. It is Professor Eduardo Collieri, in human habiliments, with a desperate look in one eye and impatience in the other.

"'Hallo, Curiosity,' says I. 'Get still a minute and let's

236

have a look at your freakship. How do you like being the willopus-wallopus or the bimbam from Borneo, or whatever name you are denounced by in the side-show business?'

"'Jeff Peters,' says Collier, in a weak voice. 'Turn me loose, or I'll slug you one. I'm in the extremest kind of a large hurry. Hands off!'

"'Tut, tut, Eddie,' I answers, holding him hard; let an old friend gaze on the exhibition of your curiousness. It's an eminent graft you fell onto, my son. But don't speak of assaults and battery, because you're not fit. The best you've got is a lot of nerve and a mighty empty stomach.' And so it was. The man was as weak as a vegetarian cat.

"'I'd argue this case with you, Jeff,' says he, regretful in his style, 'for an unlimited number of rounds if I had half an hour to train in and a slab of beefsteak two feet square to train with. Curse the man, I say, that invented the art of going foodless. May his soul in eternity be chained up within two feet of a bottomless pit of red-hot hash. I'm abandoning the conflict, Jeff; I'm deserting to the enemy. You'll find Miss Dugan inside contemplating the only living mummy and the informed hog. She's a fine girl, Jeff. I'd have beat you if I could have kept up the grubless habit a little while longer. You'll have to admit that the fasting dodge was aces up for a while. I figured it out that way. But, say, Jeff, it's said that love makes the world go around. Let me tell you, the announcement lacks verification. It's the wind from the dinner horn that does it. I love that Mame Dugan. I've gone six days without food in order to coincide with her sentiments. Only one bite did I have. That was when I knocked the tattooed man down with a war club and got a sandwich he was gobbling. The manager fined me all my salary; but salary wasn't what I was after. 'Twas that girl. I'd give my life for her, but I'd endanger my immortal soul for a beefstew. Hunger is a horrible thing, Jeff. Love and business and family and religion and art and patriotism are nothing but shadows of words when a man's starving!'

"In such language Ed Collier discoursed to me, pathetic.

237

I gathered the diagnosis that his affections and his digestions had been implicated in a scramble and the commissary had won out. I never disliked Ed Collier. I searched my internal admonitions of suitable etiquette to see if I could find a remark of a consoling nature, but there was none convenient.

"'I'd be glad, now,' says Ed, 'if you'll let me go. I've been hard hit, but I'll hit the ration supply harder. I'm going to clean out every restaurant in town. I'm going to wade waist deep in sirloins and swim in ham and eggs. It's an awful thing, Jeff Peters, for a man to come to this pass—to give up his girl for something to eat—it's worse than that man Esau, that swapped his copyright for a partridge—but then, hunger's a fierce thing. You'll excuse me, now, Jeff, for I smell a pervasion of ham frying in the distance, and my legs are crying out to stampede in that direction.'

"'A hearty meal to you, Ed Collier,' I says to him, 'and no hard feelings. For myself, I am projected to be an unseldom eater, and I have condolence for your predicaments.'

"There was a sudden big whiff of frying ham smell on the breeze; and the champion Faster gives a snort and gallops off in the dark toward fodder.

"I wish some of the cultured outfit that are always advertising the extenuating circumstances of love and romance had been there to see. There was Ed Collier, a fine man full of contrivances and flirtations, abandoning the girl of his heart and ripping out into the contiguous territory in the pursuit of sordid grub. 'Twas a rebuke to the poets and a slap at the best-paying element of fiction. An empty stomach is a sure antidote to an overfull heart.

"I was naturally anxious to know how far Mame was infatuated with Collier and his stratagems. I went inside the Unparalleled Exhibition, and there she was. She looked surprised to see me, but unguilty.

"'It's an elegant evening outside,' says I. 'The coolness is quite nice and gratifying, and the stars are lined out, first class, up where they belong. Wouldn't you shake these by-products of the animal kingdom long enough to take a walk with a common human who never was on a programme in his life?'

"Mame gave a sort of sly glance around, and I knew what that meant.

"'Oh, says I, 'I hate to tell you; but the curiosity that lives on wind has flew the coop. He just crawled out under the tent. By this time he has amalgamated himself with half the delicatessen truck in town.'

"'You mean Ed Collier?' says Mame.

"'I do,' I answers; 'and a pity it is that he has gone back to crime again. I met him outside the tent, and he exposed his intentions of devastating the food crop of the world. 'Tis enormously sad when one's ideal descends from his pedestal to make a seventeen-year locust of himself.'

"Mame looked me straight in the eye until she had cork-screwed my reflections.

"'Jeff,' says she, 'it isn't quite like you to talk that way. I don't care to hear Ed Collier ridiculed. A man may do ridiculous things, but they don't look ridiculous to the girl he does 'em for. That was one man in a hundred. He stopped eating just to please me. I'd be hardhearted and ungrateful if I didn't feel kindly toward him. Could you do what he did?'

"'I know,' says I, seeing the point, 'I'm condemned. I can't help it. The brand of the consumer is upon my brow. Mrs. Eve settled that business for me when she made the dicker with the snake. I fell from the fire into the frying-pan. I guess I'm the Champion Feaster of the Universe.' I spoke humble, and Mame mollified herself a little.

"'Ed Collier and I are good friends,' she said, 'the same as me and you. I gave him the same answer I did you—no marrying for me. I liked to be with Ed and talk with him. There was something mighty pleasant to me in the thought that here was a man who never used a knife and fork, and all for my sake.'

"'Wasn't you in love with him?' I asks, all injudicious. 'Wasn't there a deal on for you to become Mrs. Curiosity?'

"All of us do it sometimes. All of us get jostled out of the line of profitable talk now and then. Mame put on that little lemon *glacé* smile that runs between ice and sugar, and says, much too pleasant: 'You're short on credentials for asking that question, Mr. Peters. Suppose you do a forty-nine-day fast, just to give you ground to stand on, and then maybe I'll answer it.'

"So, even after Collier was kidnapped out of the way by the revolt of his appetite, my own prospects with Mame didn't seem to be improved. And then business played out in Guthrie.

"I had stayed too long there. The Brazilians I had sold commenced to show signs of wear, and the Kindler refused to light up right frequent on wet mornings. There is always a time, in my business, when the star of success says, 'Move on to the next town.' I was travelling by wagon at that time so as not to miss any of the small towns; so I hitched up a few days later and went down to tell Mame good-bye. I wasn't abandoning the game; I intended running over to Oklahoma City and work it for a week or two. Then I was coming back to institute fresh proceedings against Mame.

"What do I find at the Dugans' but Mame all conspicuous in a blue travelling dress, with her little trunk at the door. It seems that sister Lottie Bell, who is a typewriter in Terre Haute, is going to be married next Thursday, and Mame is off for a week's visit to be an accomplice at the ceremony. Mame is waiting for a freight wagon that is going to take her to Oklahoma, but I condemns the freight wagon with promptness and scorn, and offers to deliver the goods myself. Ma Dugan sees no reason why not, as Mr. Freighter wants pay for the job; so, thirty minutes later, Mame and I pull out in my light spring wagon with white canvas cover, and head due south.

"That morning was of a praiseworthy sort. The breeze was lively, and smelled excellent of flowers and grass, and the little cotton-tail rabbits entertained themselves with skylarking across the road. My two Kentucky bays went for the horizon until it come sailing in so fast you wanted to dodge it like a clothes-line. Mame was full of talk and rattled on like a kid about her old home and her school pranks and the things she liked and the hateful ways of those Johnson girls just across the street, 'way up in Indiana. Not a word was said about Ed Collier or victuals or such solemn subjects. About noon Mame looks and finds that the lunch she had put up in a basket had been left behind. I could have managed quite a coltation, but Mame didn't seem to be grieving over nothing to eat, so I made no lamentations. It was a sore subject with me, and I ruled provender in all its branches out of my conversation.

"I am minded to touch light on explanations how I came to lose the way. The road was dim and well grown with grass; and there was Mame by my side confiscating my intellects and attention. The excuses are good or they are not, as they may appear to you. But I lost it, and at dusk that afternoon, when we should have been in Oklahoma City, we were seesawing along the edge of nowhere in some undiscovered river bottom, and the rain was falling in large, wet bunches. Down there in the swamps we saw a little log house on a small knoll of high ground. The bottom grass and the chaparral and the lonesome timber crowded all around it. It seemed to be a melancholy little house, and you felt sorry for it. 'Twas that house for the night, the way I reasoned it. I explained to Mame, and she leaves it to me to decide. She doesn't become galvanic and prosecuting, as most women would, but she says it's all right; she knows I didn't mean to do it.

"We found the house was deserted. It had two empty rooms. There was a little shed in the yard where beasts had once been kept. In a loft of it was a lot of old hay. I put my horses in there and gave them some of it, for which they looked at me sorrowful, expecting apologies. The rest of the hay I carried into the house by armfuls, with a view to accommodations. I also brought in the patent kindler and the Brazilians, neither of which are guaranteed against the action of water.

"Mame and I sat on the wagon seats on the floor, and I lit a lot of the kindler on the hearth, for the night was chilly. If I was any judge, that girl enjoyed it. It was a change for her. It gave her a different point of view. She laughed and talked, and the kindler made a dim light compared to her eyes. I had a pocketful of cigars, and as far as I was concerned there had never been any fall of man. We were at the same old stand in the Garden of Eden. Out there somewhere in the rain and the dark was the river of Zion, and the angel with the flaming sword had not yet put up the keep-off-the-grass sign. I opened up a gross or two of the Brazilians and made Mame put them on—rings, brooches, necklaces, ear-drops, bracelets, girdles, and lockets. She flashed and sparkled like a million-dollar princess until she had pink spots in her cheeks and almost cried for a looking-glass.

"When it got late I made a fine bunk on the floor for Mame with the hay and my lap robes and blankets out of the wagon, and persuaded her to lie down. I sat in the other room burning tobacco and listening to the pouring rain and meditating on the many vicissitudes that come to a man during the seventy years or so immediately preceding his funeral.

"I must have dozed a little before morning, for my eyes were shut, and when I opened them it was daylight, and there stood Mame with her hair all done up neat and correct, and her eyes bright with admiration of existence.

"'Gee whiz, Jeff!' she exclaims, 'but I'm hungry. I could eat a——'

"I looked up and caught her eye. Her smile went back in and she gave me a cold look of suspicion. Then I laughed and laid down on the floor to laugh easier. It seemed funny to me. By nature and geniality I am a hearty laugher, and I went the limit. When I came to, Mame was sitting with her back to me, all contaminated with dignity.

"'Don't be angry, Mame,' I says, 'for I couldn't help it. It's the funny way you've done up your hair. If you could only see it!'

242

"'You needn't tell stories, sir,' said Mame, cool and advised. 'My hair is all right. I know what you were laughing about. Why, Jeff, look outside,' she winds up, peeping through a chink between the logs. I opened the little wooden window and looked out. The entire river bottom was flooded, and the knob of land on which the house stood was an island in the middle of a rushing stream of yellow water a hundred yards wide. And it was still raining hard. All we could do was to stay there till the dove brought in the olive branch.

"I am bound to admit that conversations and amusements languished during that day. I was aware that Mame was getting a too prolonged one-sided view of things again, but I had no way to change it. Personally, I was wrapped up in a desire to eat. I had hallucinations of hash and visions of ham, and I kept saying to myself all the time, 'What'll you have to eat, Jeff?—what'll you order, now, old man, when the waiter comes?' I picks out to myself all sorts of favourites from the bill of fare, and imagines them coming. I guess it's that way with all very hungry men. They can't get their cogitations trained on anything but something to eat. It shows that the little table with the broken-legged caster and the imitation Worcester sauce and the napkin covering up the coffee stains is the paramount issue after all, instead of the question of immortality or peace between nations.

"I sat there, musing along, arguing with myself quite heated as to how I'd have my steak—with mushrooms or *à la créole*. Mame was on the other seat, pensive, her head leaning on her hand. 'Let the potatoes come home-fried,' I states in my mind, 'and brown the hash in the pan, with nine poached eggs on the side.' I felt, careful, in my own pockets to see if I could find a peanut or a grain or two of pop-corn.

"Night came on again with the river still rising and the rain still falling. I looked at Mame and I noticed that desperate look on her face that a girl always wears when she passes an ice-cream lair. I knew that poor girl was hungry—maybe for the first time in her life. There was that anxious look in her eye that a woman has only when she has missed a meal or feels her skirt coming unfastened in the back.

"It was about eleven o'clock or so on the second night when we sat, gloomy, in our shipwrecked cabin. I kept jerking my mind away from the subject of food, but it kept flopping back again before I could fasten it. I thought of everything good to eat I had ever heard of. I went away back in my kidhood and remembered the hot biscuit sopped in sorghum and bacon gravy with partiality and respect. Then I trailed along up the years, pausing at green apples and salt, flapjacks and maple, lye hominy, fried chicken Old Virginia style, corn on the cob, spare-ribs and sweet potato pie, and wound up with Georgia Brunswick stew, which is the top notch of good things to eat, because it comprises 'em all.

"They say a drowning man sees a panorama of his whole life pass before him. Well, when a man's starving he sees the ghost of every meal he ever ate set out before him, and he invents new dishes that would make the fortune of a chef. If somebody would collect the last words of men who starved to death they'd have to sift 'em mighty fine to discover the sentiment, but they'd compile into a cook book that would sell into the millions.

"I guess I must have had my conscience pretty well inflicted with culinary meditations, for, without intending to do so, I says, out loud, to the imaginary waiter, 'Cut it thick, with the French fried, and six, soft-scrambled on toast.'

"Mame turned her head quick as a wink. Her eyes were sparkling and she smiled sudden.

"'Medium done for me,' she rattles out, 'with the Juliennes. Oh, Jeff, wouldn't it be glorious! And then I'd like to have a half fry, and a little chicken curried with rice, and a cup custard with ice cream, and——'

"'Go easy,' I interrupts; 'where's the chicken liver pie, and the kidney *sauté* on toast, and the roast lamb, and——'

"'Oh,' cuts in Mame, all excited, 'with mint sauce, and

244

the turkey salad, and stuffed olives, and raspberry tarts, and——'

"'Keep it going,' says I. 'Hurry up with the fried squash, and the hot corn pone with sweet milk, and don't forget the apple dumpling with hard sauce, and the cross-barred dewberry pie——'

"Yes, for ten minutes we kept up that kind of restaurant repartee. We ranges up and down and backward and forward over the main trunk lines and the branches of the victual subject, and Mame leads the game, for she is apprised in the ramifications of grub, and the dishes she nominates aggravates my yearnings. It seems that there is set up a feeling that Mame will line up friendly again with food. It seems that she looks upon the obnoxious science of eating with less contempt than before.

"The next morning we find that the flood has subsided. I geared up the bays, and we splashed out through the mud. some precarious, until we found the road again. We were only a few miles wrong, and in two hours we were in Oklahoma City. The first thing we saw was a big restaurant sign, and we piled into there in a hurry. Here I finds myself sitting with Mame at table, with knives and forks and plates between us, and she not scornful, but smiling with starvation and sweetness.

"'Twas a new restaurant and well stocked. I designated a list of quotations from the bill of fare that made the waiter look out toward the wagon to see how many more might be coming.

"There we were, and there was the order being served. 'Twas a banquet for a dozen, but we felt like a dozen. I looked across the table at Mame and smiled, for I had recollections. Mame was looking at the table like a boy looks at his first stem-winder. Then she looked at me, straight in the face, and two big tears came in her eyes. The waiter was gone after more grub.

"'Jeff,' she says, soft like, 'I've been a foolish girl. I've looked at things from the wrong side. I never felt this way before. Men get hungry every day like this, don't they? They're big and strong, and they do the hard work of the world, and they don't eat just to spite silly waiter girls in restaurants, do they, Jeff? You said once—that is, you asked me—you wanted me to—well, Jeff, if you still care—I'd be glad and willing to have you always sitting across the table from me. Now give me something to eat, quick please.'

"So, as I've said, a woman needs to change her point of view now and then. They get tired of the same old sights— the same old dinner-table, washtub, and sewing machine. Give 'em a touch of the various—a little travel and a little rest, a little tomfoolery along with the tragedies of keeping house, a little petting after the blowing-up, a little upsetting and jostling around—and everybody in the game will have chips added to their stack by the play."

25

The Plutonian Fire

THERE are a few editor men with whom I am privileged to come in contact. It has not been long since it was their habit to come in contact with me. There is a difference.

They tell me that with a large number of the manuscripts that are submitted to them come advices (in the way of a boost) from the author asseverating that the incidents in the story are true. The destination of such contributions depends wholly upon the question of the enclosure of stamps. Some are returned, the rest are thrown on the floor in a corner on top of a pair of gum shoes, an overturned statuette of the Winged Victory, and a pile of old magazines containing a picture of the editor in the act of reading the latest copy of *Le Petit Journal*, right side up—you can tell by the illustrations. It is only a legend that there are waste baskets in editors' offices.

Thus is truth held in disrepute. But in time truth and science and nature will adapt themselves to art. Things will happen logically, and the villain be discomfited instead of being elected to the board of directors. But in the meantime fiction must not only be divorced from fact, but must pay alimony and be awarded custody of the press dispatches.

This preamble is to warn you off the grade crossing of a true story. Being that, it shall be told simply, with conjunctions substituted for adjectives wherever possible, and whatever evidences of style may appear in it shall be due to the linotype man. It is a story of the literary life in a great city, and it should be of interest to every author within a 20-mile radius of Gosport, Ind., whose desk holds a MS. story beginning thus: "While the cheers following his nomination

247

were still ringing through the old court-house, Harwood broke away from the congratulating handclasps of his henchmen, and hurried to Judge Creswell's house to find Ida."

Pettit came up out of Alabama to write fiction. The Southern papers had printed eight of his stories under an editorial caption identifying the author as the son of "the gallant Major Pettingill Pettit, our former County Attorney, and hero of the Battle of Look-out Mountain."

Pettit was a rugged fellow, with a kind of shamefaced culture, and my good friend. His father kept a general store in a little town called Hosea. Pettit had been raised in the pine-woods and broom-sedge fields adjacent thereto. He had in his gripsack two manuscript novels of the adventures in Picardy of one Gaston Laboulaye, Vicompte de Montrepos, in the year 1329. That's nothing. We all do that. And some day, when we make a hit with the little sketch about a newsy and his lame dog, the editor prints the other one for us—or "on us", as the saying is—and then—and then we have to get a big valise and peddle those patent air-draft gas-burners. At $1.25 everybody should have 'em.

I took Pettit to the red-brick house which was to appear in an article entitled "Literary Landmarks of Old New York", some day when we got through with it. He engaged a room there, drawing on the general store for his expenses. I showed New York to him, and he did not mention how much narrower Broadway is than Lee Avenue in Hosea. This seemed a good sign, so I put the final test.

"Suppose you try your hand at a descriptive article," I suggested, "giving your impressions of New York as seen from the Brooklyn Bridge. The fresh point of view, the——"

"Don't be a fool," said Pettit. "Let's go have some beer. On the whole, I rather like the city."

We discovered and enjoyed the only true Bohemia. Every day and night we repaired to one of those palaces of marble and glass and tilework, where goes on a tremendous and sounding epic of life. Valhalla itself could not be more glorious and sonorous. The classic marble on which we ate, the great, light-flooded vitreous front, adorned with snow-white scrolls; the grand Wagnerian din of clanking cups and bowls, the flashing staccato of brandishing cutlery, the piercing recitative of the white-aproned grub-maidens at the morgue-like banquet tables; the recurrent lied-motif of the cash-register—it was a gigantic, triumphant welding of art and sound, a deafening, soul-uplifting pageant of heroic and emblematic life. And the beans were only ten cents. We wondered why our fellow-artists cared to dine at sad little tables in their so-called Bohemian restaurants; and we shuddered lest they should seek out our resorts and make them conspicuous with their presence.

Pettit wrote many stories, which the editors returned to him. He wrote love stories, a thing I have always kept free from, holding the belief that the well-known and popular sentiment is not properly a matter for publication, but something to be privately handled by the alienists and florists. But the editors had told him that they wanted love stories, because they said the women read them.

Now, the editors are wrong about that, of course. Women do not read the love stories in the magazines. They read the poker-game stories and the recipes for cucumber lotion. The love stories are read by fat cigar drummers and little ten-year-old girls. I am not criticizing the judgment of editors. They are mostly very fine men, but a man can be but one man, with individual opinions and tastes. I knew two associate editors of a magazine who were wonderfully alike in almost everything. And yet one of them was very fond of Flaubert, while the other preferred gin.

Pettit brought me his returned manuscripts, and we looked them over together to find out why they were not accepted. They seemed to me pretty fair stories, written in a good style, and ended, as they should, at the bottom of the last page.

They were well constructed, and the events were marshalled in orderly and logical sequence. But I thought I detected a lack of living substance—it was much as if I gazed at a symmetrical array of presentable clamshells from which the succulent and vital inhabitants had been removed. I intimated that the author might do well to get better acquainted with his theme.

"You sold a story last week," said Pettit, "about a gun fight in an Arizona mining town in which the hero drew his Colt's ·45 and shot seven bandits as fast as they came in the door. Now, if a six-shooter could——"

"Oh, well," said I, "that's different. Arizona is a long way from New York. I could have a man stabbed with a lariat or chased by a fair of chaparreras if I wanted to, and it wouldn't be noticed until the usual error-sharp from around McAdams Junction isolates the erratum and writes in to the papers about it. But you are up against another proposition. This thing they call love is as common around New York as it is in Sheboygan during the young onion season. It may be mixed here with a little commercialism—they read Byron, but they look up Bradstreet's, too, while they're among the B's, and Brigham also if they have time—but it's pretty much the same old internal disturbance everywhere. You can fool an editor with a fake picture of a cowboy mounting a pony with his left hand on the saddle-horn, but you can't put him up a tree with a love story. So you've got to fall in love and then write the real thing."

Pettit did. I never knew whether he was taking my advice or whether he fell an accidental victim.

There was a girl he had met at one of these studio contrivances—a glorious, impudent, lucid, openminded girl with hair the colour of Culmbacher, and a good-natured way of despising you. She was a New York girl.

Well (as the narrative style permits us to say infrequently), Pettit went to pieces. All those pains, those lover's doubts, those heart-burnings and tremors of which he had written so unconvincingly were his. Talk about Shylock's pound of flesh! Twenty-five pounds Cupid got from Pettit. Which is the usurer?

One night Pettit came to my room exalted. Pale and haggard, but exalted. She had given him a jonquil.

"Old Hoss," said he, with a new smile flickering around his mouth, "I believe I could write that story to-night—the one, you know, that is to win out. I can feel it. I don't know whether it will come out or not, but I can feel it."

I pushed him out of my door. "Go to your room and write it," I ordered. "Else I can see your finish. I told you this must come first. Write it to-night, and put it under my door when it is done. Put it under my door to-night when it is finished—don't keep it until to-morrow."

I was reading my bully old pal Montaigne at two o'clock, when I heard the sheets rustle under my door. I gathered them up and read the story.

The hissing of geese, the languishing cooing of doves, the braying of donkeys, the chatter of irresponsible sparrows—these were in my mind's ear as I read. "Suffering Sappho!" I exclaimed to myself. "Is this the divine fire that is supposed to ignite genius, and make it practicable and wage-earning?"

The story was sentimental drivel, full of whimpering soft-heartedness and gushing egoism. All the art that Pettit had acquired was gone. A perusal of its buttery phrases would have made a cynic of a sighing chamber-maid.

In the morning Pettit came to my room. I read him his doom mercilessly. He laughed idiotically.

"All right, Old Hoss," he said, cheerily, "make cigar-lighters of it. What's the difference? I'm going to take her to lunch at Claremont to-day."

There was about a month of it. And then Pettit came to me bearing an invisible mitten, with the fortitude of a dish-rag. He talked of the grave and South America and prussic acid; and I lost an afternoon getting him straight. I took him out, and saw that large and curative doses of whisky were administered to him. I warned you this was a true story—'ware your white ribbons if you follow this tale. For two weeks I fed him whisky and Omar, and read to him regularly every evening the column in the evening paper that reveals the secrets of female beauty. I recommend the treatment.

After Pettit was cured he wrote more stories. He recovered his old-time facility, and did work just short of good enough. Then the curtain rose on the third act.

A little, dark-eyed, silent girl from New Hampshire, who was studying applied design, fell deeply in love with him. She was the intense sort, but externally *glacé*, such as New England sometimes fools us with. Pettit liked her mildly, and took her about a good deal. She worshipped him, and now and then bored him.

There came a climax when she tried to jump out of a window, and he had to save her by some perfunctory, unmeant wooing. Even I was shaken by the depths of the absorbing affection she showed. Home, friends, traditions, creeds went up like thistle-down in the scale against her love. It was really discomposing.

One night again Pettit sauntered in, yawning. As he had told me before, he said he felt that he could do a great story, and as before I hunted him to his room and saw him open his inkstand. At one o'clock the sheets of paper slid under my door.

I read that story, and I jumped up, late as it was, with a whoop of joy. Old Pettit had done it. Just as though it lay there, red and bleeding, a woman's heart was written into the lines. You couldn't see the joining, but art, exquisite art, and pulsing nature had been combined into a love story that took you by the throat like the quinsy. I broke into Pettit's room and beat him on the back and called him names —names high up in the galaxy of the immortals that we admired. And Pettit yawned and begged to be allowed to sleep.

On the morrow I dragged him to an editor. The great man read, and, rising, gave Pettit his hand. That was a decoration, a wreath of bay, and a guarantee of rent.

And then old Pettit smiled slowly. I call him Gentleman

Pettit now to myself. It's a miserable name to give a man, but it sounds better than it looks in print.

"I see," said old Pettit, as he took up his story and began tearing it into small strips, "I see the game now. You can't write with ink, and you can't write with your own heart's blood, but you can write with the heart's blood of some one else. You have to be a cad before you can be an artist. Well, I am for old Alaham and the Major's store. Have you got a light, old Hoss?"

I went with Pettit to the depot and died hard.

"Shakespeare's sonnets?" I blurted, making a last stand. "How about him?"

"A cad," said Pettit. "They give it to you, and you sell it —love, you know. I'd rather sell ploughs for father."

"But," I protested, "you are reversing the decision of the world's greatest——"

"Goodbye, Old Hoss," said Pettit.

"Critics," I continued. "But—say—if the Major can use a fairly good salesman and bookkeeper down there in the store, let me know, will you?"

26

By Courier

A T was neither the season nor the hour when the park had frequenters; and it is likely that the young lady, who was seated on one of the benches at the side of the walk, had merely obeyed a sudden impulse to sit for awhile and enjoy a foretaste of coming spring.

She rested there, pensive and still. A certain melancholy that touched her countenance must have been of recent birth, for it had not yet altered the fine and youthful contours of her cheek, nor subdued the arch though resolute curve of her lips.

A tall young man came striding through the park along the path near which she sat. Behind him tagged a boy carrying a suit-case. At sight of the young lady, the man's face changed to red and back to pale again. He watched her countenance as he drew nearer, with hope and anxiety mingled on his own. He passed within a few yards of her, but he saw no evidence that she was aware of his presence or existence.

Some fifty yards further on he suddenly stopped and sat on a bench at one side. The boy dropped the suit-case and stared at him with wondering, shrewd eyes. The young man took out his handkerchief, and wiped his brow. It was a good handkerchief, a good brow, and the young man was good to look at. He said to the boy:

"I want you to take a message to that young lady on that bench. Tell her I am on my way to the station, to leave for San Francisco, where I shall join that Alaska moose-hunting expedition. Tell her that, since she had commanded me neither to speak nor to write to her, I take this means of

making one last appeal to her sense of justice, for the sake of
what has been. Tell her that to condemn and discard one
who has not deserved such treatment, without giving him
her reasons or a chance to explain, is contrary to her nature
as I believe it to be. Tell her that I have thus, to a certain
degree disobeyed her injunctions, in the hope that she
may yet be inclined to see justice done. Go, and tell her
that."

The young man dropped a half-dollar into the boy's hand.
The boy looked at him for a moment with bright, canny eyes
out of a dirty, intelligent face, and then set off at a run. He
approached the lady on the bench a little doubtfully, but
unembarrassed. He touched the brim of the old plaid bicycle
cap perched on the back of his head. The lady looked at him
coolly, without prejudice or favour.

"Lady," he said, "dat gent on de oder bench sent yer a
song and dance by me. If yer don't know de guy, and he's
tryin' to do de Johnny act, say de word, and I'll call a cop
in t'ree minutes. If yer does know him, and he's on de
square, w'y I'll spiel yer de bunch of hot air he sent yer."

The young lady betrayed a faint interest.

"A song and dance!" she said, in a deliberate, sweet
voice that seemed to clothe her words in a diaphanous
garment of impalpable irony. "A new idea—in the
troubadour line, I suppose. I—used to know the gentleman
who sent you, so I think it will hardly be necessary to call
the police. You may execute your song and dance, but do not
sing too loudly. It is a little early yet for open-air vaudeville,
and we might attract attention."

"Awe," said the boy, with a shrug down the length of
him. "yer know what I mean, lady. 'Tain't a turn, it's wind.
He told me to tell yer he's got his collars and cuffs in dat
grip for a scoot clean out to 'Frisco. Den he's goin' to shoot
snowbirds in de Klondike. He says yer told him not to send
'round no more pink notes nor come hangin' over de garden
gate, and he takes dis means of puttin' yer wise. He says yer
refereed him out like a has-been, and never gave him no

255

chance to kick at de decision. He says yer swiped him, and never said why."

The slightly awakened interest in the young lady's eyes did not abate. Perhaps it was caused by either the originality or the audacity of the snow-bird hunter, in thus circumventing her express commands against the ordinary modes of communication. She fixed her eye on a statue standing disconsolate in the dishevelled park, and spoke into the transmitter:

"Tell the gentleman that I need not repeat to him a description of my ideals. He knows what they have been and what they still are. So far as they touch on this case, absolute loyalty and truth are the ones paramount. Tell him that I have studied my own heart as well as one can, and I know its weakness as well as I do its needs. That is why I decline to hear his pleas, whatever they may be. I did not condemn him through hearsay or doubtful evidence, and that is why I make no charge. But, since he persists in hearing what he already well knows, you may convey the matter.

"Tell him that I entered the conservatory that evening from the rear, to cut a rose for my mother. Tell him I saw him and Miss Ashburton beneath the pink oleander. The tableau was pretty, but the pose and juxtaposition were too eloquent and evident to require explanation. I left the conservatory, and, at the same time, the rose and my ideal. You may carry that song and dance to your impresario."

"I'm shy on one word, lady. Jux—jux—put me wise on dat, will yer?"

"Juxtaposition—or you may call it propinquity—or, if you like, being rather too near for one maintaining the position of an ideal."

The gravel spun from beneath the boy's feet. He stood by the other bench. The man's eyes interrogated him, hungrily. The boy's were shining with the impersonal zeal of the translator.

"De lady says dat she's on to de fact dat gals is dead easy when a feller comes speilin' ghost stories and tryin' to make

256

up, and dat's why she won't listen to no soft-soap. She says she caught yer dead to rights, huggin' a bunch o' calico in de hothouse. She side-stepped in to pull some posies and yer was squeezin' the oder gal to beat the band. She says it looked cute, all right all right, but it made her sick. She says yer better git busy, and make a sneak for de train."

The young man gave a low whistle and his eyes flashed with a sudden thought. His hand flew to the inside pocket of his coat, and drew out a handful of letters. Selecting one, he handed it to the boy, following it with a silver dollar from his vest pocket.

"Give that letter to the lady," he said, "and ask her to read it. Tell her that it should explain the situation. Tell her that, if she had mingled a little trust with her conception of the ideal, much heartache might have been avoided. Tell her that the loyalty she prizes so much has never wavered. Tell her I am waiting for an answer."

The messenger stood before the lady.

"De gent says he's had de ski-bunk put on him widout no cause. He says he's no bum guy; and, lady, yer read dat letter, and I'll bet yer he's a white sport, all right."

The young lady unfolded the letter, somewhat doubtfully, and read it.

DEAR DR. ARNOLD: I want to thank you for your most kind and opportune aid to my daughter last Friday evening, when she was overcome by an attack of her old heart-trouble in the conservatory at Mrs. Waldron's reception. Had you not been near to catch her as she fell and to render proper attention, we might have lost her. I would be glad if you would call and undertake the treatment of her case.

Gratefully yours,
ROBERT ASHBURTON.

The young lady refolded the letter, and handed it to the boy.

"De gent wants an answer," said the messenger. "Wot's de word?"

The lady's eyes suddenly flashed on him, bright, smiling and wet.

"Tell that guy on the other bench," she said, with a happy tremulous laugh, "that his girl wants him."

27

The Bruised Reed

THE popular preacher sat in his study before a glowing
grate, and a satisfied smile stole over his features, as
he remembered his sermon of that morning. He had struck
strong blows at sin; relating to his breathless congregation,
in plain and burning words, tales of the wickedness, de-
bauchery, drunkenness and depravity that was going on in
their very midst.

Following the prominent example of a certain pure-minded
and original servant of the Lord, he had gone down himself
among the lowest haunts of vice and iniquity, and there
sketched in his mind those flaming and accusive portraits
that he had painted before the astonished eyes of his congregation, with a broad brush and vivid colours. He had
heard blasphemies from lips that were once as pure as his
sisters'; he had stood in the midst of unbridled vice, where
wine flowed like water and amidst songs, curses, laughing and
revelry, the chink of money, earned by dripping hearts' blood,
could be heard as it fell into the coffers of the devil. Oh, he
had astonished his flock! He had hurled at them fiery words
of blame that these things were allowed to exist. It had been
a new departure for him, but he expected grand results.
And now he sat by his anthracite fire, and thought over
the success of his labours, and smiled with satisfaction. The
latch of his study door clicked and a being entered. He was
grizzly, rum-soaked, dirty, ragged, disreputable, bleary-eyed
and of uncertain step. Once, he might have been a man.

Across his forehead stretched a long strip of dingy court
plaster; on the bridge of his nose an unhealed wound showed
scarlet against the milder red of his face. He brought with

him an odour of disrespectability, rum and unsanctification.

The preacher rose; a slight distension visible in his delicate nostril; a little shiver of repulsion rippling through his broadcloth-vestured figure.

"What is it, my good man?" he asked.

*   *   *

The being spoke, and the preacher, still standing, followed him through the husky labyrinth of his speech.

"Don't yer know me? I lives in 'Hell's Delight'. I knows you. You come down, you did, and wants ter take in ther sights. You asks Tony, the Dago, fer a guide and he sends yer to Creepy Jake. That's me. I takes yer through the dives, one and all. I knows yer a preacher from the way yer did. Yer buys the wine like a gent, though—like a real, high roller gent; anybody would 'a took yer fer a gent."

"Excuse me," said the preacher, "that wound on your forehead—the blood seems to be dripping on those engravings—allow me——"

"Keep your hankcher, reverend," said the being, as he raised a ragged coat tail and wiped the drops from his brow. "I won't spile yer pictures. I'll git offen yer carpet, and let some fresh air in in a minute. One time I could 'a told yer all about them pictures—dat's Una and de lion—dat one's the Venus of Milo—de other one's the disc thrower—you wouldn't believe, reverend, that I knowed de names, would you? One time I set in cheers like dat—I allus liked dat Spanish leather upholstering, but your wainscotin' ain't right. De carvin's allegorical and it don't suit de modern panels—'scuse me, reverend, dat ain't what I come to say. After you took in de Tenderloin, I got to tinkin' bout somethin' you said one night after I went wid you to de tough dance at Gilligan's. Dey was a cove dere dat twigged you as a parson and was about to biff you one on de ear, but he see'd my gun showin' down in my pocket, and den he see'd my eye, and changed his mind—but dat's all right. You says to yerself dat night, but I heard yer: 'De bruised reed he shall not

quench, and de smokin' flax he will not put out,' or somethin'
like dat, and I got ter studyin' over what a low down bum
I've been, and I says, 'I'm goin' to de big bug church, and
hear de bloke preach.'

*   *   *

"De boys an' de tinhorns gimme de laugh and called me
'Pious Jake', but today I went to der big church where you
preaches, reverend. I says to myself dat I showed you round
de Tenderloin, and stood by you when de rounders guyed
you, and never let de coves work de flimflam on yer, and
when I heard tell of the big sermons yer was preachin' and
de hot shot yer was shootin' into de tough gang, I was real
proud, and I felt like I kinder had a share in de business fen
havin' gone de round with yer. I says I'll hear dat cove
preach, and maybe de bruised reed'll git a chance to
straighten up—'scuse me, reverend, don't git skeared, I
ain't goin' to fall and spile yer carpet. I'm a little groggy.
That cut on my head is bled a heap, but I ain't drunk."

"Perhaps you would like—possibly, if you would sit—just
for a moment——"

"Thanks, reverend, I won't sit down. I've jest about
finished shootin' in my dye stuff. I goes to dat church and I
goes in. I hears music playin', and I suppose them was angels
singin' up in de peanut gallery, an' I smelt—such a smell ov
violets and stuff like de hay when we used to cut it in de
meanders when I wuz a kid. Dey wuz fine people in welvets
and folde-rols, and way over at de oder end was you,
reverend, standin' in de gran' stan', lookin' carm and fur
away like, jest as yer did at Gilligan's ball when de duck tried
to guy yer, and I went in fur to hear yer preach."

*   *   *

A flattering sentence from the report of his sermon in the
morning papers came to the preacher's mind:

"His wonderful, magnetic influence is as powerful to move
the hearts of his roughest, most unlettered hearer, as it is to

touch a responsive chord in the cultured brain of the man of refinement and taste."

"And my sermon," said the preacher, laying his delicate finger tips one against the other, and allowing the adulation even of this being to run with a slight exhilaration through his veins. "Did it awaken in you any remorse for the life of sin you have led, or bring any light of Divine pity and pardon to your soul, as He promises even unto the most degraded and wicked of creation?"

"Yer sermon, reverend?" asked the being, carrying a trembling hand to the disfiguring wounds upon his face. "Do you see them cuts and them bruises? Do you know where I got 'em? I never heard yer sermon. I got dese cuts on de rocks outside when de cop and yer usher fired me out de church. De bruised reed He will not quench, an' de smokin' flax He will not 'stinguish. Has you anything to say, reverend?"

28

Supply and Demand

FINCH keeps a hats-cleaned-by-electricity-while-you-wait establishment, nine feet by twelve, in Third Avenue. Once a customer, you are always his. I do not know his secret process, but every four days your hat needs to be cleaned again.

Finch is a leathern, sallow, slow-footed man, between twenty and forty. You would say he had been brought up a bushelman in Essex Street. When business is slack he likes to talk, so I had my hat cleaned even oftener than it deserved, hoping Finch might let me into some of the secrets of the sweat-shops.

One afternoon I dropped in and found Finch alone. He began to anoint my headpiece de Panama with his mysterious fluid that attracted dust and dirt like a magnet.

"They say the Indians weave 'em under water," said I, for a leader.

"Don't you believe it," said Finch. "No Indian or white man could stay under water that long. Say, do you pay much attention to politics? I see in the paper something about a law they've passed called 'the law of supply and demand'."

I explained to him as well as I could that the reference was to politico-economical law and not to a legal statute.

"I didn't know," said Finch. "I heard a good deal about it a year or so ago, but in a one-sided way."

"Yes," said I, "political orators use it a great deal. In fact, they never give it a rest. I suppose you heard some of those cart-tail fellows spouting on the subject over here on the east side."

"I heard it from a king," said Finch—"the white king of a tribe of Indians in South America."

I was interested but not surprised. The big city is like a mother's knee to many who have strayed far and found the roads rough beneath their uncertain feet. At dusk they come home and sit upon the doorstep. I know a piano player in a cheap café who has shot lions in Africa, a bell-boy who fought in the British army against the Zulus, an express-driver whose left arm had been cracked like a lobster's claw for a stewpot of Patagonian cannibals when the boat of his rescuers hove in sight. So a hat-cleaner who has been a friend of a king did not oppress me.

"A new band?" asked Finch, with his dry, barren smile.

"Yes," said I, "and half an inch wider." I had had a new band five days before.

"I meets a man one night," said Finch, beginning his story —"a man brown as snuff, with money in every pocket, eating schweiner-knuckel in Schlagel's. That was two years ago, when I was a hosecart driver for No. 98. His discourse runs to the subject of gold. He says that certain mountains in a country down South that he calls Gaudymala is full of it. He says the Indians wash it out of the streams in plural quantities.

"'Oh, Geronimo!' says I. 'Indians! There's no Indians in the South,' I tell him, 'except Elks, Maccabees, and the buyers for the fall dry-goods trade. The Indians are all on the reservations,' says I.

"'I'm telling you this with reservations,' says he. 'They ain't Buffalo Bill Indians; they're squattier and more pedigreed. They call 'em Inkers and Aspics, and they was old inhabitants when Mazuma was king of Mexico. They wash the gold out of the mountain streams,' says the brown man, 'and fill quills with it; and then they empty 'em into red jars till they are full; and then they pack it in buckskin sacks of one arroba each—an arroba is twenty-five pounds— and store it in a stone house, with an engraving of a idol with marcelled hair, playing a flute, over the door.'

"'How do they work off this unearth increment?' I asks.

"'They don't,' says the man. 'It's a case of "Ill fares the land with the great deal of velocity where wealth accumulates and there ain't any reciprocity."'

"After this man and me got through our conversation which left him dry of information, I shook hands with him and told him I was sorry I couldn't believe him. And a month afterward I landed on the coast of this Gaudymala with $1,300 that I had been saving up for five years. I thought I knew what Indians liked, and I fixed myself accordingly. I loaded down four pack-mules with red woollen blankets, wrought-iron pans, jewelled side-combs for the ladies, glass necklaces, and safety-razors. I hired a black mozo, who was supposed to be a mule-driver and an interpreter too. It turned out that he could interpret mules all right, but he drove the English language much too hard. His name sounded like a Yale key when you push it in wrong side up, but I called him McClintock, which was close to the noise.

"Well, this gold village was forty miles up in the mountains, and it took us nine days to find it. But one afternoon McClintock led the other mules and myself over a rawhide bridge stretched across a precipice five thousand feet deep, it seemed to me. The hoofs of the beasts drummed on it just like before George M. Cohan makes his first entrance on the stage.

"This village was built of mud and stone, and had no streets. Some few yellow-and-brown persons popped their heads out-of-doors, looking about like Welsh rabbits with Worcester sauce on 'em. Out of the biggest house, that had a kind of porch around it, steps a big white man, red as a beet in colour, dressed in fine tanned deerskin clothes, with a gold chain around his neck, smoking a cigar. I've seen United States Senators of his style of features and build, also head-waiters and cops.

"He walks up and takes a look at us, while McClintock disembarks and begins to interpret to the lead mule while he smokes a cigarette.

265

"'Hello, Buttinsky,' said the fine man to me. 'How did you get in the game? I didn't see you buy any chips. Who gave you the keys of the city?'

"'I'm a poor traveller,' says I. 'Especially mule-back. You'll excuse me. Do you run a hack line or only a bluff?'

"'Segregate yourself from your pseudo-equine quadruped,' says he, 'and come inside.'

"He raises a finger, and a villager runs up.

"'This man will take care of your outfit,' says he, 'and I'll take care of you.'

"He leads me into the biggest house, and sets out the chairs and a kind of a drink the colour of milk. It was the finest room I ever saw. The stone walls was hung all over with silk shawls, and there was red and yellow rugs on the floor, and jars of red pottery and Angora goat skins, and enough bamboo furniture to misfurnish half a dozen seaside cottages.

"'In the first place,' says the man, 'you want, to know who I am. I'm sole lessee and proprietor of this tribe of Indians. They call me the Grand Yacuma, which is to say King or Main Finger of the bunch. I've got more power here than a chargé d'affaires, a charge of dynamite, and a charge account at Tiffany's combined. In fact, I'm the Big Stick, with as many extra knots on it as there is on the record run of the *Lusitania*. Oh, I read the papers now and then,' says he. 'Now, let's hear your entitlements,' he goes on, 'and the meeting will be open.'

"'Well,' says I, 'I am known as one W. D. Finch. Occupation, capitalist. Address, 541 East Thirty-second——'

"'New York,' chips in the Noble Grand. 'I know,' says he, grinning. 'It ain't the first time you've seen it go down on the blotter. I can tell by the way you hand it out. Well, explain "capitalist".'

"I tells this boss plain what I come for and how I come to came.

"'Gold-dust?' says he, looking as puzzled as a baby that got a feather stuck on its molasses finger. 'That's funny. This ain't a gold-mining country. And you invested all your

266

capital on a stranger's story? Well, well! These Indians of
mine—they are the last of the tribe of Peches—are simple as
children. They know nothing of the purchasing power of
gold. I'm afraid you've been imposed on,' says he.

"'Maybe so,' says I, 'but it sounded pretty straight to me.'

"'W.D.,' says the King, all of a sudden, 'I'll give you a
square deal. It ain't often I get to talk to a white man, and
I'll give you a show for your money. It may be these con-
stituents of mine have a few grains of gold-dust hid away in
their clothes. To-morrow you may get out these goods you've
brought up and see if you can make any sales. Now, I'm
going to introduce myself unofficially. My name is Shane—
Patrick Shane. I own this tribe of Peche Indians by right of
conquest—single handed and unafraid. I drifted up here four
years ago, and won 'em by my size and complexion and
nerve. I learned their language in six weeks—it's easy; you
simply emit a string of consonants as long as your breath
holds out and then point at what you're asking for.

"'I conquered 'em, spectacularly,' goes on King Shane,
'and then I went at 'em with economical politics, law,
sleight-of-hand, and a kind of New England ethics and
parsimony. Every Sunday, or as near as I can guess at it, I
preach to 'em in the council-house (I'm the council) on
the law of supply and demand. I praise supply and knock
demand. I use the same text every time. You wouldn't think,
W.D.,' says Shane, 'that I had poetry in me, would you?'

"'Well,' says I, 'I wouldn't know whether to call it poetry
or not.'

"'Tennyson,' says Shane, 'furnishes the poetic gospel I
preach. I always considered him the boss poet. Here's the
way the text goes:

For, not to admire, if a man could learn it, were more
Than to walk all day like a Sultan of old in a garden of spice.

"'You see, I teach 'em to cut out demand—that supply is
the main thing. I teach 'em not to desire anything beyond
their simplest needs. A little mutton, a little cocoa, and a little

267

fruit brought up from the coast—that's all they want to make 'em happy. I've got 'em well trained. They make their own clothes and hats out of a vegetable fibre and straw, and they're a contented lot. It's a great thing,' winds up Shane, 'to have made a people happy by the incultivation of such simple institutions.'

"Well, the next day, with the King's permission, I has the McClintock open up a couple of sacks of my goods in the little plaza of the village. The Indians swarmed around by the hundred and looked the bargain-counter over. I shook red blankets at 'em, flashed finger-rings and ear-bobs, tried pearl necklaces and side-combs on the women, and a line of red hosiery on the men. 'Twas no use. They looked on like hungry graven images, but I never made a sale. I asked McClintock what was the trouble. Mac yawned three or four times, rolled a cigarette, made one or two confidential side remarks to a mule, and then condescended to inform me that the people had no money.

"Just then up strolls King Patrick, big and red, and royal as usual, with the gold chain over his chest and his cigar in front of him.

"'How's business, W.D.?' he asks.

"'Fine,' says I. 'It's a bargain-day rush. I've got one more line of goods to offer before I shut up shop. I'll try 'em with safety-razors. I've got two gross that I bought at a fire sale.'

"Shane laughs till some kind of mameluke or private secretary he carries with him has to hold him up.

"'O my sainted Aunt Jerusha!' says he, 'ain't you one of the Babes in the Goods, W.D.? Don't you know that no Indians ever shave? They pull out their whiskers instead.'

"'Well,' says I, 'that's just what these razors would do for 'em—they wouldn't have any kick coming if they used 'em once.'

"Shane went away, and I could hear him laughing a block, if there had been any block.

"'Tell 'em,' says I to McClintock, 'it ain't money I want—tell 'em I'll take gold-dust. Tell 'em I'll allow 'em sixteen dollars an ounce for it in trade. That's what I'm out for—the dust.'

"Mac interprets, and you'd have thought a squadron of cops had charged the crowd to disperse it. Every uncle's nephew and aunt's niece of 'em faded away inside of two minutes.

"At the royal palace that night me and the King talked it over.

"'They've got the dust hid out somewhere,' says I, 'or they wouldn't have been so sensitive about it.'

"'They haven't,' says Shane. 'What's this gag you've got about gold? You been reading Edward Allan Poe? They ain't got any gold.'

"'They put it in quills,' says I, 'and then they empty it in jars, and then into sacks of twenty-five pounds each. I got it straight.'

"'W.D.,' says Shane, laughing and chewing his cigar, 'I don't often see a white man, and I feel like putting you on. I don't think you'll get away from here alive, anyhow, so I'm going to tell you. Come over here.'

"He draws aside a silk fibre curtain in a corner of the room and shows me a pile of buckskin sacks.

"'Forty of 'em,' says Shane. 'One arroba in each one. In round numbers, $220,000 worth of gold-dust you see there. It's all mine. It belongs to the Grand Yacuma. They bring it all to me. Two hundred and twenty thousands dollars— think of that, you glass-bead peddler,' says Shane—'and all mine.'

"'Little good it does you,' says I, contemptuously and hatefully. 'And so you are the government depository of this gang of moneyless moneymakers? Don't you pay enough interest on it to enable one of your depositors to buy an Augusta (Maine) Pullman carbon diamond worth $200 for $4.85?'

"'Listen,' says Patrick Shane, with the sweat coming out on his brow. 'I'm confident with you, as you have, some-how, enlisted my regards. Did you ever,' he says, 'feel the

269

avoirdupois power of gold—not the troy weight of it, but the sixteen-ounces-to-the-pound force of it?'

"'Never,' says I. 'I never take in any bad money.'

"Shane drops down on the floor and throws his arms over the sacks of gold-dust.

"'I love it,' says he. 'I want to feel the touch of it day and night. It's my pleasure in life. I come in this room, and I'm a king and a rich man. I'll be a millionaire in another year. The pile's getting bigger every month. I've got the whole tribe washing out the sands in the creeks. I'm the happiest man in the world, W.D. I just want to be near this gold, and know it's mine and it's increasing every day. Now, you know,' says he, 'why my Indians wouldn't buy your goods. They can't. They bring all the dust to me. I'm their king. I've taught 'em not to desire or admire. You might as well shut up shop.'

"'I'll tell you what you are,' says I. 'You're a plain, contemptible miser. You preach supply and you forget demand. Now, supply,' I goes on, 'is never anything but supply. On the contrary,' says I, 'demand is a much broader syllogism and assertion. Demand includes the rights of our women and children, and charity and friendship, and even a little begging on the street corners. They've both got to harmonize equally. And I've got a few things up my commercial sleeve yet,' says I, 'that may jostle your preconceived ideas of politics and economy.'

"The next morning I had McClintock bring up another mule-load of goods to the plaza and open it up. The people gathered around the same as before.

"I got out the finest line of necklaces, bracelets, haircombs, and earrings that I carried, and had the women put 'em on. And then I played trumps.

"Out of my last pack I opened up a half gross of hand-mirrors, with solid tinfoil backs, and passed 'em around among the ladies. That was the first introduction of looking-glasses among the Peche Indians.

"Shane walks by with his big laugh.

" 'Business looking up any?' he asks.

" 'It's looking at itself right now,' says I.

"By and by a kind of a murmur goes through the crowd. The women had looked into the magic crystal and seen that they were beautiful, and was confiding the secret to the men. The men seemed to be urging the lack of money and the hard times just before the election, but their excuses didn't go.

"Then was my time.

"I called McClintock away from an animated conversation with his mules and told him to do some interpreting.

" 'Tell 'em,' says I, 'that gold-dust will buy for them these befitting ornaments for kings and queens of the earth. Tell 'em the yellow sand they wash out of the waters for the High Sanctified Yacomay and Chop Suey of the tribe will buy the precious jewels and charms that will make them beautiful and preserve and pickle them from evil spirits. Tell 'em the Pittsburg banks are paying four per cent interest on deposits by mail, while this get-rich-frequently custodian of the public funds ain't even paying attention. Keep telling 'em, Mac,' says I, 'to let the gold-dust family do their work. Talk to 'em like a born anti-Bryanite,' says I. 'Remind 'em that Tom Watson's gone back to Georgia,' says I.

"McClintock waves his hand affectionately at one of his mules, and then hurls a few stickfuls of minion type at the mob of shoppers.

"A gutta-percha Indian man, with a lady hanging on his arm, with three strings of my fish-scale jewellery and imitation marble beads around her neck, stands up on a block of stone and makes a talk that sounds like a man shaking dice in a box to fill aces and sixes.

" 'He says,' says McClintock, 'that the people not know that gold-dust will buy their things. The women very mad. The Grand Yacuma tell them it no good but for keep to make bad spirits keep away.'

" 'You can't keep bad spirits away from money,' says I.

" 'They say,' goes on McClintock, 'the Yacuma fool them. They raise plenty row.'

271

"'Going! Going!' says I. 'Gold-dust or cash takes the entire stock. The dust weighed before you, and taken at sixteen dollars the ounce—the highest price on the Gaudymala coast.'

"Then the crowd disperses all of a sudden, and I don't know what's up. Mac and me packs away the hand-mirrors and jewellery they had handed back to us, and we had the mules back to the corral they had set apart for our garage.

"While we was there we hear great noises of shouting, and down across the plaza runs Patrick Shane, hotfoot, with his clothes ripped half off, and scratches on his face like a cat had fought him hard for every one of its lives.

"'They're looting the treasury, W.D.,' he sings out. 'They're going to kill me and you, too. Unlimber a couple of mules at once. We'll have to make a getaway in a couple of minutes.'

"'They've found out,' says I, 'the truth about the law of supply and demand.'

"'It's the women, mostly,' says the King. 'And they used to admire me so!'

"'They hadn't seen looking-glasses then,' says I.

"'They've got knives and hatchets,' says Shane; 'hurry!'

"'Take that roan mule,' says I. 'You and your law of supply! I'll ride the dun, for he's two knots per hour the faster. The roan has a stiff knee, but he may make it,' says I. 'If you'd included reciprocity in your political platform I might have given you the dun,' says I.

"Shane and McClintock and me mounted our mules and rode across the rawhide bridge just as the Peches reached the other side and began firing stones and long knives at us. We cut the thongs that held up our end of the bridge and headed for the coast."

*   *   *

A tall, bulky policeman came into Finch's shop at that moment and leaned an elbow on the showcase. Finch nodded at him friendly.

"I heard down at Casey's," said the cop, in rumbling, husky tones, "that there was going to be a picnic of the Hat Cleaners' Union over at Bergen Beach, Sunday. Is that right?"

"Sure," said Finch. "There'll be a dandy time."

"Gimme five tickets," said the cop, throwing a five-dollar bill on the showcase.

"Why," said Finch, "ain't you going it a little too——"

"Go to h——!" said the cop. "You got 'em to sell, ain't you? Somebody's got to buy 'em. Wish I could go along."

I was glad to see Finch so well thought of in his neighbourhood.

And then in came a wee girl of seven, with dirty face and pure blue eyes and a smutched and insufficient dress.

"Mumma says," she recited shrilly, "that you must give me eighty cents for the grocer and nineteen for the milkman and five cents for me to buy hokey-pokey with—but she didn't say that,'' the elf concluded, with a hopeful but honest grin.

Finch shelled out the money, counting it twice, but I noticed that the total sum that the small girl received was one dollar and four cents.

"That's the right kind of a law," remarked Finch as he carefully broke some of the stitches of my hatband so that it would assuredly come off within a few days—"the law of supply and demand. But they've both got to work together. I'll bet," he went on, with his dry smile, "she'll get jelly beans with that nickel—she likes 'em. What's supply if there's no demand for it?"

"Whatever became of the King?" I asked, curiously.

"Oh, I might have told you," said Finch. "That was Shane came in and bought the tickets. He came back with me, and he's on the force now."

29

An Adjustment of Nature

IN an art exhibition the other day I saw a painting that had been sold for $5,000. The painter was a young scrub out of the West named Kraft, who had a favourite food and a pet theory. His pabulum was an unquenchable belief in the Unerring Artistic Adjustment of Nature. His theory was fixed around corned-beef hash with poached egg. There was a story behind the picture, so I went home and let it drip out of a fountain-pen. The idea of Kraft— but that is not the beginning of the story.

Three years ago Kraft, Bill Judkins (a poet), and I took our meals at Cypher's, on Eighth Avenue. I say "took". When we had money, Cypher got it "off of" us, as he expressed it. We had no credit; we went in, called for food and ate it. We paid or we did not pay. We had confidence in Cypher's sullenness and smouldering ferocity. Deep down in his sunless soul he was either a prince, a fool, or an artist. He sat at a worm-eaten desk, covered with files of waiters' checks so old that I was sure the bottomest one was for claims that Hendrik Hudson had eaten and paid for. Cypher had the power, in common with Napoleon III and the goggle-eyed perch, of throwing a film over his eyes, rendering opaque the windows of his soul. Once when we left him unpaid, with egregious excuses, I looked back and saw him shaking with inaudible laughter behind his film. Now and then we paid up back scores.

But the chief thing at Cypher's was Milly. Milly was a waitress. She was a grand example of Kraft's theory of the Artistic Adjustment of Nature. She belonged, largely, to waiting, as Minerva did to the art of scrapping, or Venus to

274

the science of serious flirtation. Pedestalled and in bronze she might have stood with the noblest of her heroic sisters as "Liver-and-Bacon Enlivening the World". She belonged to Cypher's. You expected to see her colossal figure loom through that reeking blue cloud of smoke from frying fat just as you expect the Palisades to appear through a drifting Hudson River fog. There amid the steam of vegetables and the vapours of acres of "ham and", the crash of crockery, the clatter of steel, the screaming of "short orders", the cries of the hungering and all the horrid tumult of feeding man, surrounded by swarms of the buzzing winged beasts bequeathed us by Pharaoh, Milly steered her magnificent way like some great liner cleaving among the canoes of howling savages.

Our Goddess of Grub was built on lines so majestic that they could be followed only with awe. Her sleeves were always rolled above her elbows. She could have taken us three musketeers in her two hands and dropped us out of the window. She had seen fewer years than any of us, but she was of such superb Evehood and simplicity that she mothered us from the beginning. Cypher's store of eatables she poured out upon us with royal indifference to price and quantity, as from a cornucopia that knew no exhaustion. Her voice rang like a great silver bell; her smile was many-toothed and frequent; she seemed like a yellow sunrise on mountain-tops. I never saw her but I thought of the Yosemite. And yet, somehow, I could never think of her as existing outside of Cypher's. There Nature had placed her, and she had taken root and grown mightily. She seemed happy, and took her few poor dollars on Saturday nights with the flushed pleasure of a child that receives an unexpected donation.

It was Kraft who first voiced the fear that each of us must have held latently. It came up apropos, of course, of certain questions of art at which we were hammering. One of us compared the harmony existing between a Hadyn symphony and pistache ice-cream to the exquisite congruity between Milly and Cypher's.

"There is a certain fate hanging over Milly," said Kraft, "and if it overtakes her she is lost to Cypher's and to us."

"She will grow fat?" asked Judkins fearsomely.

"She will go to night school and become refined?" I ventured anxiously.

"It is this," said Kraft, punctuating in a puddle of spilled coffee with a stiff forefinger. "Cæsar had his Brutus—'the cotton has its bollworm, the chorus girl has her Pittsburger, the summer boarder has his poison ivy, the hero has his Carnegie medal, art has its Morgan, the rose has its——"

"Speak," I interrupted, much perturbed. "You do not think that Milly will begin to lace?"

"One day," concluded Kraft solemnly, "there will come to Cypher's for a plate of beans a millionaire lumberman from Wisconsin, and he will marry Milly."

"Never!" exclaimed Judkins and I, in horror.

"A lumberman," repeated Kraft hoarsely.

"And a millionaire lumberman!" I sighed despairingly.

"From Wisconsin!" groaned Judkins.

We agreed that the awful fate seemed to menace her. Few things were less improbable. Milly, like some vast virgin stretch of pine woods, was made to catch the lumberman's eye. And well we knew the habits of the Badgers, once fortune smiled upon them. Straight to New York they hie, and lay their goods at the feet of the girl who serves them beans in a beanery. Why, the alphabet itself connives. The Sunday newspaper's headliner's work is cut for him.

"Winsome Waitress Wins Wealthy Wisconsin Woodsman."

For awhile we felt that Milly was on the verge of being lost to us.

It was our love of the unerring Artistic Adjustment of Nature that inspired us. We could not give her over to a lumberman, doubly accursed by wealth and provincialism. We shuddered to think of Milly, with her voice modulated and her elbows covered, pouring tea in the marble teepee of a tree murderer. No! In Cypher's she belonged—in the bacon

276

smoke, the cabbage perfume, the grand, Wagnerian chorus of hurled iron-stone china and rattling casters.

Our fears must have been prophetic, for on that same evening the wildwood discharged upon us Milly's pre-ordained confiscator—our fee to adjustment and order. But Alaska and not Wisconsin bore the burden of the visitation.

We were at our supper of beef stew and dried apples when he trotted in as if on the heels of a dog-team, and made one of the mess at our table. With the freedom of the camps he assaulted our ears and claimed the fellowship of men lost in the wilds of a hash-house. We embraced him as a specimen, and in three minutes we had all but died for one another as friends.

He was rugged and bearded, and wind-dried. He had just come off the "trail", he said, at one of the North River ferries. I fancied I could see the snow-dust of Chilcoot yet powdering his shoulders. And then he strewed the table with the nuggets, stuffed ptarmigans, bead work and seal pelts of the returned Klondiker, and began to prate to us of his millions.

"Bank drafts for two millions," was his summing up, "and a thousand a day piling up from my claims. And now I want some beef stew and canned peaches. I never got off the train since I mushed out of Seattle, and I'm hungry. The stuff the niggers feed you on Pullman's don't count. You gentlemen order what you want."

And then Milly loomed up with a thousand dishes on her bare arm—loomed up big and white and pink and awful as Mount Saint Elias—with a smile like day breaking in a gulch. And the Klondiker threw down his pelts and nuggets as dross, and let his jaw fall half-way, and stared at her. You could almost see the diamond tiaras on Milly's brow and the hand-embroidered silk Paris gowns that he meant to buy for her.

At last the bollworm had attacked the cotton—the poison ivy was reaching out its tendrils to entwine the summer

277

boarder—the millionaire lumberman, thinly disguised as the Alaskan miner, was about to engulf our Milly and upset Nature's adjustment.

Kraft was the first to act. He leaped up and pounded the Klondiker's back. "Come out and drink," he shouted. "Drink first and eat afterward." Judkins seized one arm and I the other. Gaily, roaringly, irresistibly, in jolly-good-fellow style, we dragged him from the restaurant to a café, stuffing his pockets with his embalmed birds and indigestible nuggets.

There he rumbled a roughly good-humoured protest. "That's the girl for my money," he declared. "She can eat out of my skillet the rest of her life. Why, I never see such a fine girl. I'm going back there and ask her to marry me. I guess she won't want to sling hash any more when she sees the pile of dust I've got."

"You'll take another whisky and milk now," Kraft persuaded, with Satan's smile. "I thought you up-country fellows were better sports."

Kraft spent his puny store of coin at the bar and then gave Judkins and me such an appealing look that we went down to the last dime we had in toasting our guest.

Then, when our ammunition was gone and the Klondiker, still somewhat sober, began to babble again of Milly, Kraft whispered into his ear such a polite, barbed insult relating to people who were miserly with their funds, that the miner crashed down handful after handful of silver and notes, calling for all the fluids in the world to drown the imputation.

Thus the work was accomplished. With his own guns we drove him from the field. And then we had him carted to a distant small hotel and put to bed with his nuggets and baby seal-skins stuffed around him.

"He will never find Cypher's again," said Kraft. "He will propose to the first white apron he sees in a dairy restaurant to-morrow. And Milly—I mean the Natural Adjustment—is saved!"

And back to Cypher's went we three, and, finding customers scarce, we joined hands and did an Indian dance with Milly in the centre.

This, I say, happened three years ago. And about that time a little luck descended upon us three, and we were enabled to buy costlier and less wholesome food than Cypher's. Our paths separated, and I saw Kraft no more and Judkins seldom.

But, as I said, I saw a painting the other day that was sold for $5,000. The title was "Boadicea", and the figure seemed to fill all out-of-doors. But of all the picture's admirers who stood before it, I believe I was the only one who longed for Boadicea to stalk from her frame, bringing me corned-beef hash with poached egg.

I hurried away to see Kraft. His satanic eyes were the same, his hair was worse tangled, but his clothes had been made by a tailor.

"I don't know," I said to him.

"We've bought a cottage in the Bronx with the money," said he. "Any evening at seven."

"Then," said I, "when you led us against the lumberman —the—Klondiker—it wasn't altogether on account of the Unerring Artistic Adjustment of Nature?"

"Well, not altogether," said Kraft, with a grin.

30

The Hypotheses of Failure

LAWYER GOOCH bestowed his undivided attention upon the engrossing arts of his profession. But one flight of fancy did he allow his mind to entertain. He was fond of likening his suite of office rooms to the bottom of a ship. The rooms were three in number, with a door opening from one to another. These doors could also be closed.

"Ships," Lawyer Gooch would say, "are constructed for safety, with separate, water-tight compartments in their bottoms. If one compartment springs a leak it fills with water; but the good ship goes on unhurt. Were it not for the separating bulkheads one leak would sink the vessel. Now it often happens that while I am occupied with clients, other clients with conflicting interests call. With the assistance of Archibald —an office boy with a future—I cause the dangerous influx to be diverted into separate compartments, while I sound with my legal plummet the depth of each. If necessary they may be baled into the hallway and permitted to escape by way of the stairs, which we may term the lee scuppers. Thus the good ship of business is kept afloat; whereas if the element that supports her were allowed to mingle freely in her hold we might be swamped—ha, ha, ha!"

The law is dry. Good jokes are few. Surely it might be permitted Lawyer Gooch to mitigate the bore of briefs, the tedium of torts, and the prosiness of processes with even so light a levy upon the good property of humour.

Lawyer Gooch's practice leaned largely to the settlement of marital infelicities. Did matrimony languish through complications, he mediated, soothed and arbitrated. Did it suffer from implications, he readjusted, defended and championed. Did it arrive at the extremity of duplications, he always got light sentences for his clients.

But not always was Lawyer Gooch the keen, armed, wily belligerent, ready with his two-edged sword to lop off the shackles of Hymen. He had been known to build up instead of demolishing, to reunite instead of severing, to lead erring and foolish ones back into the fold instead of scattering the flock. Often had he by his eloquent and moving appeals sent husband and wife, weeping, back into each other's arms. Frequently he had coached childhood so successfully that, at the plaintive pipe of "Papa, won't you tum home adain to me and muvver?" had won the day and upheld the pillars of a tottering home.

Unprejudiced persons admitted that Lawyer Gooch received as big fees from these reyoked clients as would have been paid him had the cases been contested in court. Prejudiced ones intimated that his fees were doubled, because the penitent couples always came back later for the divorce, anyhow.

There came a season in June when the legal ship of Lawyer Gooch (to borrow his own figure) was nearly becalmed. The divorce mill grinds slowly in June. It is the month of Cupid and Hymen.

Lawyer Gooch, then, sat idle in the middle room of his clientless suite. A small anteroom connected—or rather separated—this apartment from the hallway. Here was stationed Archibald, who wrested from visitors their cards or oral nomenclature which he bore to his master while they waited.

Suddenly, on this day, there came a great knocking at the outermost door.

Archibald, opening it, was thrust aside as superfluous by the visitor, who without due reverence at once penetrated to the office of Lawyer Gooch and threw himself with good-natured insolence into a comfortable chair facing that gentleman.

"You are Phineas C. Gooch, attorney-at-law?" said the

281

visitor, his tone of voice and inflection making his words at once a question, an assertion and an accusation.

Before commiting himself by a reply, the lawyer estimated his possible client in one of his brief but shrewd and calculating glances.

The man was of the emphatic type—large-sized, active, bold and debonair in demeanour, vain beyond a doubt, swaggering, ready and at ease. He was well-clothed, but with a shade too much ornateness. He was seeking a lawyer; but if that fact would seem to saddle him with troubles they were not patent in his beaming eye and courageous air.

"My name is Gooch," at length the lawyer admitted. Upon pressure he would also have confessed to the Phineas C. But he did not consider it good practice to volunteer information. "I did not receive your card," he continued, by way of rebuke, "so I——"

"I know you didn't," remarked the visitor coolly; "and you won't just yet. Light up?" He threw a leg over an arm of his chair, and tossed a handful of rich-hued cigars upon the table. Lawyer Gooch knew the brand. He thawed just enough to accept the invitation to smoke.

"You are a divorce lawyer," said the cardless visitor. This time there was no interrogation in his voice. Nor did his words consitute a simple assertion. They formed a charge— a denunciation—as one would say to a dog: "You are a dog." Lawyer Gooch was silent under the imputation.

"You handle," continued the visitor, "all the various ramifications of busted-up connubiality. You are a surgeon, we might say, who extracts Cupid's darts when he shoots 'em into the wrong parties. You furnish patent, incandescent lights for premises where the torch of Hymen has burned so low you can't light a cigar at it. Am I right, Mr. Gooch?"

"I have undertaken cases," said the lawyer guardedly, "in the line to which your figurative speech seems to refer. Do you wish to consult me professionally, Mr.——" The lawyer paused, with significance.

"Not yet," said the other, with an arch wave of his cigar, "not just yet. Let us approach the subject with the caution that should have been used in the original act that makes this pow-wow necessary. There exists a matrimonial jumble to be straightened out. But before I give you names I want your honest—well, anyhow, your professional opinion on the merits of the mix-up. I want you to size up the catastrophe—abstractly—you understand? I'm Mr. Nobody: and I've got a story to tell you. Then you say what's what. Do you get my wireless?"

"You want to state a hypothetical case?" suggested Lawyer Gooch.

"That's the word I was after. 'Apothecary' was the best shot I could make at it in my mind. The hypothetical goes. I'll state the case. Suppose there's a woman—a deuced fine-looking woman—who has run away from her husband and home? She's badly mashed on another man who went to her town to work up some real estate business. Now, we may as well call this woman's husband Thomas R. Billings, for that's his name. I'm giving you straight tips on the cognomens. The Lothario chap is Henry K. Jessup. The Billingses lived in a little town called Susanville—a good many miles from here. Now, Jessup leaves Susanville two weeks ago. The next day Mrs. Billings follows him. She's dead gone on this man Jessup; you can bet your law library on that."

Lawyer Gooch's client said this with such unctuous satisfaction that even the callous lawyer experienced a slight ripple of repulsion. He now saw clearly in his fatuous visitor the conceit of the lady-killer, the egoistic complacency of the successful trifler.

"Now," continued the visitor, "suppose this Mrs. Billings wasn't happy at home? We'll say she and her husband didn't gee worth a cent. They've got incompatibility to burn. The things she likes, Billings wouldn't have as a gift with trading-stamps. It's Tabby and Rover with them all the time. She's an educated woman in science and culture, and she reads things out loud at meetings. Billings is not on. He don't appreciate progress and obelisks and ethics, and things of that sort. Old Billings is simply a blink when it comes to such things. The lady is out and out above his class. Now, lawyer, don't it look like a fair equalization of rights and wrongs that a woman like that should be allowed to throw down Billings and take the man that can appreciate her?"

"Incompatibility," said Lawyer Gooch, "is undoubtedly the source of much marital discord and unhappiness. Where it is positively proved, divorce would seem to be the equitable remedy. Are you—excuse me—is this man Jessup one to whom the lady may safely trust her future?"

"Oh, you can bet on Jessup," said the client, with a confident wag of his head. "Jessup's all right. He'll do the square thing. Why, he left Susanville just to keep people from talking about Mrs. Billings. But she followed him up, and now, of course, he'll stick to her. When she gets a divorce, all legal and proper, Jessup will do the proper thing."

"And now," said Lawyer Gooch, "continuing the hypothesis, if you prefer, and supposing that my services should be desired in the case, what——"

The client rose impulsively to his feet.

"Oh, dang the hypothetical business," he exclaimed impatiently. "Let's let her drop, and get down to straight talk. You ought to know who I am by this time. I want that woman to have her divorce. I'll pay for it. The day you set Mrs. Billings free I'll pay you five hundred dollars."

Lawyer Gooch's client banged his fist upon the table to punctuate his generosity.

"If that is the case——" began the lawyer.

"Lady to see you, sir," bawled Archibald, bouncing in from his anteroom. He had orders to always announce immediately any client that might come. There was no sense in turning business away.

Lawyer Gooch took client number one by the arm and led him suavely into one of the adjoining rooms. "Favour me by remaining here a few minutes, sir," said he. "I will return and resume our consultation with the least possible delay. I am rather expecting a visit from a very wealthy old lady in connection with a will. I will not keep you waiting long."

The breezy gentleman seated himself with obliging acquiescence, and took up a magazine. The lawyer returned to the middle office, carefully closing behind him the connecting door.

"Show the lady in, Archibald," he said to the office boy, who was awaiting his order.

A tall lady, of commanding presence and sternly handsome, entered the room. She wore robes—robes; not clothes—ample and fluent. In her eye could be perceived the lambent flame of genius and soul. In her hand was a green bag of the capacity of a bushel, and an umbrella that also seemed to wear a robe, ample and fluent. She accepted a chair.

"Are you Mr. Phineas C. Gooch, the lawyer?" she asked, in formal and unconciliatory tones.

"I am," answered Lawyer Gooch, without circumlocution. He never circumlocuted when dealing with a woman. Women circumlocute. Time is wasted when both sides in debate employ the same tactics.

"As a lawyer, sir," began the lady, "you may have acquired some knowledge of the human heart. Do you believe that the pusillanimous and petty conventions of our artificial social life should stand as an obstacle in the way of a noble and affectionate heart when it finds its true mate among the miserable and worthless wretches in the world that are called men?"

"Madam," said Lawyer Gooch, in the tone that he used in curbing his female clients, "this is an office for conducting the practice of law. I am a lawyer, not a philosopher, nor the editor of an 'Answers to the Lovelorn' column of a newspaper. I have other clients waiting. I will ask you kindly to come to the point."

"Well, you needn't get so stiff around the gills about it," said the lady, with a snap of her luminous eyes and a startling gyration of her umbrella. "Business is what I've come for.

285

I want your opinion in the matter of a suit for divorce, as the vulgar would call it, but which is really only the readjustment of the false and ignoble conditions that the short-sighted laws of man have interposed between a loving——"

"I beg your pardon, madam," interrupted Lawyer Gooch, with some impatience, "for reminding you again that this is a law office. Perhaps Mrs. Wilcox——"

"Mrs. Wilcox is all right," cut in the lady, with a hint of asperity. "And so are Tolstoi, and Mrs. Gertrude Atherton, and Omar Khayyám, and Mr. Edward Bok. I've read 'em all. I would like to discuss with you the divine right of the soul as opposed to the freedom-destroying restrictions of a bigoted and narrow-minded society. But I will proceed to business. I would prefer to lay the matter before you in an impersonal way until you pass upon its merits. That is to describe it as a supposable instance, without——"

"You wish to state a hypothetical case?" said Lawyer Gooch.

"I was going to say that," said the lady sharply. "Now, suppose there is a woman who is all soul and heart and aspirations for a complete existence. This woman has a husband who is far below her in intellect, in taste—in everything. Bah! he is a brute. He despises literature. He sneers at the lofty thoughts of the world's great thinkers. He thinks only of real estate and such sordid things. He is no mate for a woman with soul. We will say that this unfortunate wife one day meets with her ideal—a man with brain and heart and force. She loves him. Although this man feels the thrill of a new-found affinity he is too noble, too honourable to declare himself. He flies from the presence of his beloved. She flies after him, trampling, with superb indifference, upon the fetters with which an unenlightened social system would bind her. Now, what will a divorce cost? Eliza Ann Timmins, the poetess of Sycamore Gap, got one for three hundred and forty dollars. Can I—I mean can this lady I speak of—get one that cheap?"

"Madam," said Lawyer Gooch, "your last two or three

sentences delight me with their intelligence and clearness. Can we not now abandon the hypothetical and come down to names and business?"

"I should say so," exclaimed the lady, adopting the practical with admirable readiness. "Thomas R. Billings is the name of the low brute who stands between the happiness of his legal—his legal, but not his spiritual—wife and Henry K. Jessup, the noble man whom nature intended for her mate. I," concluded the client, with an air of dramatic revelation, "am Mrs. Billings!"

"Gentleman to see you, sir," shouted Archibald, invading the room almost at a handspring. Lawyer Gooch arose from his chair.

"Mrs. Billings," he said courteously, "allow me to conduct you into the adjoining office apartment for a few minutes. I am expecting a very wealthy old gentleman on business connected with a will. In a very short while I will join you, and continue our consultation."

With his accustomed chivalrous manner, Lawyer Gooch ushered his soulful client into the remaining unoccupied room, and came out, closing the door with circumspection.

The next visitor introduced by Archibald was a thin, nervous, irritable-looking man of middle age, with a worried and apprehensive expression of countenance. He carried in one hand a small satchel, which he set down upon the floor beside the chair which the lawyer placed for him. His clothing was of good quality, but it was worn without regard to neatness or style, and appeared to be covered with the dust of travel.

"You make a speciality of divorce cases," he said, in an agitated but business-like tone.

"I may say," began Lawyer Gooch, "that my practice has not altogether avoided——"

"I know you do," interrupted client number three. "You needn't tell me. I've heard all about you. I have a case to lay before you without necessarily disclosing any connection that I might have with it—this is——"

"You wish," said Lawyer Gooch, "to state a hypothetical case."

"You may call it that. I am a plain man of business. I will be as brief as possible. We will first take up the hypothetical woman. We will say she is married uncongenially. In many ways she is a superior woman. Physically she is considered to be handsome. She is devoted to what she calls literature—poetry, and prose, and such stuff. Her husband is a plain man in the business walks of life. Their home has not been happy, although the husband has tried to make it so. Some time ago a man—a stranger—came to the peaceful town in which they lived and engaged in some real estate operations. This woman met him, and became unaccountably infatuated with him. Her attentions became so open that the man felt the community to be no safe place for him, so he left it. She abandoned husband and home, and followed him. She forsook her home, where she was provided with every comfort, to follow this man who had inspired her with such a strange affection. Is there anything more to be deplored," concluded the client, in a trembling voice, "than the wrecking of a home by a woman's uncalculating folly?"

Lawyer Gooch delivered the cautious opinion that there was not.

"This man she has gone to join," resumed the visitor, "is not the man to make her happy. It is a wild and foolish self-deception that makes her think he will. Her husband, in spite of their many disagreements, is the only one capable of dealing with her sensitive and peculiar nature. But this she does not realize now."

"Would you consider a divorce the logical cure in the case you present?" asked Lawyer Gooch, who felt that the conversation was wandering too far from the field of business.

"A divorce!" exclaimed the client feelingly—almost tearfully. "No, no—not that. I have read, Mr. Gooch, of many instances where your sympathy and kindly interest led you to act as a mediator between estranged husband and wife, and brought them together again. Let us drop the hypothetical case—I need conceal no longer that it is I who am the sufferer in this sad affair—the names you shall have—Thomas R. Billings and wife—and Henry K. Jessup, the man with whom she is infatuated."

Client number three laid his hand upon Mr. Gooch's arm. Deep emotion was written upon his careworn face. "For Heaven's sake," he said fervently, "help me in this hour of trouble. Seek out Mrs. Billings, and persuade her to abandon this distressing pursuit of her lamentable folly. Tell her, Mr. Gooch, that her husband is willing to receive her back to his heart and home—promise her anything that will induce her to return. I have heard of your success in these matters. Mrs. Billings cannot be very far away. I am worn out with travel and weariness. Twice during the pursuit I saw her, but various circumstances prevented our having an interview. Will you undertake this mission for me, Mr. Gooch, and earn my everlasting gratitude?"

"It is true," said Lawyer Gooch, frowning slightly at the other's last words, but immediately calling up an expression of virtuous benevolence, "that on a number of occasions I have been successful in persuading couples who sought the severing of their matrimonial bonds to think better of their rash intentions and return to their homes reconciled. But I assure you that the work is often exceedingly difficult. The amount of argument, perseverence, and, if I may be allowed to say it, eloquence that it requires would astonish you. But this is a case in which my sympathies would be wholly enlisted. I feel deeply for you, sir, and I would be most happy to see husband and wife reunited. But my time," concluded the lawyer, looking at his watch as if suddenly reminded of the fact, "is valuable."

"I am aware of that," said the client, "and if you will take the case and persuade Mrs. Billings to return home and leave the man alone that she is following—on that day I will pay you the sum of one thousand dollars. I have made a little money in real estate during the recent boom in Susanville, and I will not begrudge that amount."

"Retain your seat for a few minutes, please," said Lawyer Gooch, arising, and again consulting his watch. "I have another client waiting in an adjoining room whom I had very nearly forgotten. I will return in the briefest possible space."

The situation was now one that fully satisfied Lawyer Gooch's love of intricacy and complication. He revelled in cases that presented such subtle problems and possibilities. It pleased him to think that he was master of the happiness and fate of the three individuals, who sat unconscious of one another's presence, within his reach. His old figure of the ship glided into his mind. But now the figure failed, for to have filled every compartment of an actual vessel would have been to endanger her safety; while here, with his compartments full, his ship of affairs could but sail on to the advantageous port of a fine, fat fee. The thing for him to do, of course, was to wring the best bargain he could from someone of his anxious cargo.

First he called to the office boy: "Lock the outer door, Archibald, and admit no one." Then he moved with long, silent strides into the room in which client number one waited. That gentleman sat, patiently scanning the pictures in the magazine, with a cigar in his mouth and his feet upon a table.

"Well," he remarked cheerfully, as the lawyer entered, "have you made up your mind? Does five hundred dollars go for getting the fair lady a divorce?"

"You mean that as a retainer?" asked Lawyer Gooch, softly interrogative.

"Hey? No; for the whole job. It's enough, ain't it?"

"My fee," said Lawyer Gooch, "would be one thousand five hundred dollars. Five hundred dollars down, and the remainder upon issuance of the divorce."

A loud whistle came from client number one. His feet descended to the floor.

"Guess we can't close the deal," he said, arising. "I clinked up five hundred dollars in a little real estate dicker down in Susanville. I'd do anything I could to free the lady, but it outsizes my pile."

"Could you stand one thousand two hundred dollars?" asked the lawyer insinuatingly.

"Five hundred is my limit, I tell you. Guess I'll have to hunt up a cheaper lawyer." The client put on his hat.

"Out this way, please," said Lawyer Gooch, opening the door that led into the hallway.

As the gentleman flowed out of the compartment and down the stairs, Lawyer Gooch smiled to himself. "Exit Mr. Jessup," he murmured, as he fingered the Henry Clay tuft of hair at his ear. "And now for the forsaken husband." He returned to the middle office, and assumed a businesslike manner.

"I understand," he said to client number three, "that you agree to pay one thousand dollars if I bring about, or am instrumental in bringing about, the return of Mrs. Billings to her home, and her abandonment of her infatuated pursuit of the man for whom she has conceived such a violent fancy. Also that the case is now unreservedly in my hands on that basis. Is that correct?"

"Entirely," said the other eagerly. "And I can produce the cash any time at two hours' notice."

Lawyer Gooch stood up at his full height. His thin figure seemed to expand. His thumbs sought the arm-holes of his vest. Upon his face was a look of sympathetic benignity that he always wore during such undertakings.

"Then, sir," he said, in kindly tones, "I think I can promise you an early relief from your troubles. I have that much confidence in my powers of argument and persuasion, in the natural impulses of the human heart toward good, and in the strong influence of a husband's unfaltering love. Mrs. Billings, sir, is here—in that room——" The lawyer's long arm pointed to the door. "I will call her in at once; and our united pleadings——"

Lawyer Gooch paused, for client number three had

leaped from his chair as if propelled by steel springs, and clutched his satchel.

"What the devil," he exclaimed harshly, "do you mean? That woman in there! I thought I shook her off forty miles back."

He ran to the open window, looked out below, and threw one leg over the sill.

"Stop!" cried Lawyer Gooch, in amazement. "What would you do? Come, Mr. Billings, and face your erring but innocent wife. Our combined entreaties cannot fail to——"

"Billings!" shouted the now thoroughly moved client; "I'll Billings you, you old idiot!"

Turning, he hurled his satchel with fury at the lawyer's head. It struck that astounded peacemaker between the eyes, causing him to stagger backward a pace or two. When lawyer Gooch recovered his wits he saw that his client had disappeared. Rushing to the window, he leaned out, and saw the recreant gathering himself up from the top of a shed upon which he had dropped from the second-storey window. Without stopping to collect his hat he then plunged downward the remaining ten feet to the alley, up which he flew with prodigious celerity until the surrounding building swallowed him up from view.

Lawyer Gooch passed his hand tremblingly across his brow. It was an habitual act with him, serving to clear his thoughts. Perhaps also it now seemed to soothe the spot where a very hard alligator-hide satchel had struck.

The satchel lay upon the floor, wide open, with its contents spilled about. Mechanically Lawyer Gooch stooped to gather up the articles. The first was a collar; and the omniscient eye of the man of law perceived, wonderingly, the initial H. K. J. marked upon it. Then came a comb, a brush, a folded map and a piece of soap. Lastly a handful of old business letters, addressed—every one of them—to "Henry K. Jessup, Esq."

Lawyer Gooch closed the satchel, and set it upon the

table. He hesitated for a moment, and then put on his hat and walked into the office boy's anteroom.

"Archibald," he said mildly, as he opened the hall door, "I am going around to the Supreme Court rooms. In five minutes you may step into the inner office, and inform the lady who is waiting there that"—here Lawyer Gooch made use of the vernacular—"that there's nothing doing."

30

The Dissipated Jeweller

YOU will not find the name of Thomas Keeling in the
Houston city directory. It might have been there by
this time, if Mr. Keeling had not discontinued his business
a month or so ago and moved to other parts. Mr. Keeling
came to Houston about that time and opened up a small
detective bureau. He offered his services to the public as a
detective in rather a modest way. He did not aspire to be a
rival of the Pinkerton agency, but preferred to work along
less risky lines.

If an employer wanted the habits of a clerk looked into,
or a lady wanted an eye kept upon a somewhat too gay
husband, Mr. Keeling was the man to take the job. He was a
quiet, studious man with theories. He read Gaboriau and
Conan Doyle and hoped some day to take a higher place in
his profession. He had held a subordinate place in a large
detective bureau in the East, but as promotion was slow, he
decided to come West, where the field was not so well
covered.

Mr. Keeling had saved during several years the sum of
$900, which he deposited in the safe of a business man in
Houston to whom he had letters of introduction from a
common friend. He rented a small upstairs office on an
obscure street, hung out a sign stating his business and
burying himself in one of Doyle's Sherlock Holmes stories,
waited for customers.

Three days after he opened his bureau, which consisted
of himself, a client called to see him.

It was a young lady, apparently about twenty-six years of
age. She was slender and rather tall and neatly dressed. She

294

wore a thin veil which she threw back upon her black straw
hat after she had taken the chair Mr. Keeling offered her.
She had a delicate, refined face, with rather quick grey eyes,
and a slightly nervous manner.

*   *   *

"I came to see you, sir," she said in a sweet, but somewhat
sad, contralto voice, "because you are comparatively a
stranger, and I could not bear to discuss my private affairs
with any of my friends. I desire to employ you to watch the
movements of my husband. Humiliating as the confession is to
me, I fear that his affections are no longer mine. Before I
married him he was infatuated with a young woman connected with a family with whom he boarded. We have been
married five years, and very happily, but this young woman
has recently moved to Houston, and I have reasons to suspect
that he is paying her attentions. I want you to watch his
movements as closely as possible and report to me. I will
call here at your office every other day at a given time to
learn what you have discovered. My name is Mrs. R——,
and my husband is well known. He keeps a small jewellery
store on —— Street. I will pay you well for your services
and here is $20 to begin with."

The lady handed Mr. Keeling the bill and he took it
carelessly as if such things were very, very common in his
business.

He assured her that he would carry out her wishes faithfully, and asked her to call again the afternoon after the next
at four o'clock, for the first report.

The next day Mr. Keeling made the necessary inquiries
toward beginning operations. He found the jewellery store,
and went inside ostensibly to have the crystal of his watch
tightened. The jeweller, Mr. R——, was a man apparently
thirty-five years of age, of very quiet manners and industrious
ways. His store was small, but contained a nice selection of
goods and quite a large assortment of diamonds, jewellery
and watches. Further inquiry elicited the information that

Mr. R—— was a man of excellent habits, never drank and was always at work at his jeweller's bench.

Mr. Keeling loafed around near the door of the jewellery store for several hours that day and was finally rewarded by seeing a flashily dressed young woman with black hair and eyes enter the store. Mr. Keeling sauntered nearer the door, where he could see what took place inside. The young woman walked confidently to the rear of the store, leaned over the counter and spoke familiarly to Mr. R——. He rose from his bench and they talked in low tones for a few minutes. Finally, the jeweller handed her some coins, which Mr. Keeling heard clinking as they passed into her hands. The woman then came out and walked rapidly down the street.

Mr. Keeling's client was at his office promptly at the time agreed upon. She was anxious to know if he had seen anything to corroborate her suspicions. The detective told her what he had seen.

"That is she," said the lady, when he had described the young woman who had entered the store. "The brazen, bold thing! And so Charles is giving her money. To think that things should come to this pass."

The lady pressed her handkerchief to her eyes in an agitated way.

"Mrs. R.——," said the detective, "what is your desire in this matter? To what point do you wish me to prosecute inquiries?"

"I want to see with my own eyes enough to convince me of what I suspect. I also want witnesses, so I can instigate suit for divorce. I will not lead the life I am now living any longer."

She then handed the detective a ten-dollar bill.

On the day following the next, when she came to Mr. Keeling's office to hear his report, he said:

"I dropped into the store this afternoon on some trifling pretext. This young woman was already there, but she did not remain long. Before she left, she said: 'Charlie, we will

296

have a jolly little supper tonight as you suggest; then we will come around to the store and have a nice chat while you finish that setting for the diamond brooch with no one to interrupt us.' Tonight, Mrs. R——, I think, will be a good time for you to witness the meeting between your husband and the object of his infatuation, and satisfy your mind how matters stand."

"The wretch," cried the lady with flashing eyes.

"He told me at dinner that he would be detained late tonight with some important work. And this is the way he spends his time away from me!"

"I suggest," said the detective, "that you conceal yourself in the store, so you can hear what they say, and when you have heard enough you can summon witnesses and confront your husband before them."

"The very thing," said the lady. "I believe there is a policeman whose beat is along the street the store is on who is acquainted with our family. His duties will lead him to be in the vicinity of the store after dusk. Why not see him, explain the whole matter to him and when I have heard enough, let you and him appear as witnesses?"

"I will speak with him," said the detective, "and persuade him to assist us, and you will please come to my office a little before dark tonight, so we can arrange to trap them."

*   *   *

The detective hunted up the policeman and explained the situation.

"That's funny," said the guardian of the peace. "I didn't know R—— was a gay boy at all. But, then, you can never tell about anybody. So his wife wants to catch him to-night. Let's see, she wants to hide herself inside the store and hear what they say. There's a little room in the back of the store where R—— keeps his coal and old boxes. The door between is locked, of course, but if you can get her through that into the store she can hide somewhere. I don't like to mix up in these affairs, but I sympathize with the lady.

I've known her ever since we were children and don't mind helping her to do what she wants."

About dusk that evening the detective's client came hurriedly to his office. She was dressed plainly in black and wore a dark round hat and her face was covered with a veil.

"If Charlie should see me he will not recognize me," she said.

Mr. Keeling and the lady strolled down the street opposite the jewellery store, and about eight o'clock the young woman they were watching for entered the store. Immediately afterwards she came out with Mr. R——, took his arm, and they hurried away, presumably to their supper.

The detective felt the arm of the lady tremble.

"The wretch," she said bitterly. "He thinks me at home innocently waiting for him while he is out carousing with that artful, designing minx. Oh, the perfidy of man."

Mr. Keeling took the lady through an open hallway that led into the back yard of the store. The outer door of the back room was unlocked, and they entered.

"In the store," said Mrs. R——, "near the bench where my husband works is a large table, the cover of which hangs to the floor. If I could get under that I could hear every word that was said."

Mr. Keeling took a big bunch of skeleton keys from his pocket and in a few minutes found one that opened the door into the jewellery store. The gas was burning from one jet turned very low.

The lady stepped into the store and said: "I will bolt this door from the inside, and I want you to follow my husband and that woman. See if they are at supper, and if they are, when they start back, you must come back to this room, and let me know by tapping thrice on the door. After I listen to their conversation long enough I will unbolt the door, and we will confront the guilty pair together. I may need you to protect me, for I do not know what they might attempt to do to me."

*   *   *

The detective made his way softly out and followed the jeweller and the woman. He soon discovered that they had taken a private room in a little out of the way restaurant and had ordered supper. He lingered about until they came out and then hurried back to the store, and entering the back room, tapped three times on the door.

In a few minutes the jeweller entered with the woman and the detective saw the light shine more brightly through a crack in the door. He could hear the man and woman conversing familiarly and constantly, but could not distinguish their words. He slipped around again to the street, and looking through the window, could see Mr. R—— working away at his jeweller's bench, while the black-haired woman sat close to his side and talked.

"I'll give them a little time," thought Mr. Keeling, and he strolled down the street.

The policeman was standing on the corner.

The detective told him that Mrs. R——was concealed in the store, and that the scheme was working nicely.

"I'll drop back behind now," said Mr. Keeling, "so as to be ready when the lady springs her trap."

The policeman walked back with him, and took a look through the window.

"They seem to have made up all right," said he. "Where's the other woman gotten to?"

"Why, there she is sitting by him," said the detective.

"I'm talking about the girl R——had out to supper."

"So am I," said the detective.

"You seem to be mixed up," said the policeman. "Do you know that lady with R——?"

"That's the woman he was out with."

"That's R——'s wife," said the policeman. "I've known her for fifteen years."

"Then, who——?" gasped the detective. "Lord A'mighty, then who's under the table?"

Mr. Keeling began to kick at the door of the store.

Mr. R——came forward and opened it. The policeman and the detective entered.

"Look under that table, quick," yelled the detective. The policeman raised the cover and dragged out a black dress, a black veil and a woman's wig of black hair.

"Is this lady your w-w-wife?" asked Mr. Keeling excitedly, pointing out the dark-eyed young woman, who was regarding them in great surprise.

"Certainly," said the jeweller. "Now what the thunder are you looking under my table and kicking down my door for, if you please?"

"Look in your show cases," said the policeman, who began to size up the situation.

*   *   *

The diamond rings and watches that were missing amounted to $800, and the next day the detective settled the bill.

Explanations were made to the jeweller that night, and an hour later Mr. Keeling sat in his office busily engaged in looking over his albums of crooks' photos. At last he found one, and he stopped turning over the leaves and tore his hair. Under the picture of a smooth-faced young man, with delicate features, was the following description:

"JAMES H. MIGGLES, alias Slick Simon, alias The Weeping Widow, alias Bunco Kate, alias Jimmy the Sneak, General confidence man and burglar. Works generally in female disguises. Very plausible and dangerous. Wanted in Kansas City, Oshkosh, New Orleans and Milwaukee."

This is why Mr. Thomas Keeling did not continue his detective business in Houston.

32

Cabbages and Kings
The Poem: By the Carpenter

*T*HEY *will tell you in Anchuria that President Miraflores of that volatile republic died by his own hand in the coast town of Coralio; that he had reached thus far in flight from the inconveniences of an imminent revolution; and that one hundred thousand dollars, government funds, which he carried with him in an American leather valise as a souvenir of his tempestuous administration, was never afterward recovered.*

For a real, a boy will show you his grave. It is back of the town near a little bridge that spans a mangrove swamp. A plain slab of wood stands at its head. Some one has burned upon the headstone with a hot iron this inscription:

RAMON ANGEL DE LAS CRUZES
Y MIRAFLORES
PRESIDENTE DE LA REPUBLICA
DE ANCHURIA
QUE SEA SU JUEZ DIOS

It is characteristic of this buoyant people that they pursue no man beyond the grave. "Let God be his judge!"—Even with the hundred thousand unfound, though greatly coveted, the hue and cry went no further than that.

To the stranger or the guest the people of Coralio will relate the story of the tragic end of their former president: how he strove to escape from the country with the public funds and also with Doña Isabel Guilbert, the young American opera singer; and how, being apprehended by members of the opposing political party in Coralio, he shot himself through the head rather than give up the funds, and, in consequence, the Señorita *Guilbert. They will relate further that Doña Isabel, her adventurous bark of fortune shoaled by the simultaneous loss of her distinguished admirer and the souvenir hundred thousand, dropped anchor on this stagnant coast, awaiting a rising tide.*

They say in Coralio that she found a prompt and prosperous tide in the form of Frank Goodwin, an American resident of the town, an investor who had grown wealthy by dealing in the products of the country—a banana king, a rubber prince, a sarsaparilla, indigo, and mahogany baron. The Señorita *Guilbert, you will be told, married* Señor *Goodwin one month after the president's death, thus, in the very moment when Fortune had ceased to smile, wresting from her a gift greater than the prize withdrawn.*

Of the American, Don Frank Goodwin, and of his wife the natives have nothing but good to say. Don Frank has lived among them for years, and has compelled their respect. His lady is easily queen of what social life the sober coast affords. The wife of the governor of the district, herself, who was of the proud Castilian family of Monteleon y Dolorosa de los Santos y Mendez, feels honoured to unfold her napkin with olive-hued, ringed hands at the table of Señora *Goodwin. Were you to refer (with your northern prejudices) to the vicacious past of Mrs. Goodwin, when her audacious and gleeful abandon in light opera captured the mature president's fancy, or to her share in that statesman's downfall and malfeasance, the Latin shrug of the shoulder would be your only answer and rebuttal. What prejudices there were in Coralio concerning* Señora *Goodwin seemed now to be in her favour, whatever they had been in the past.*

It would seem that the story is ended, instead of begun; that the close of a tragedy and the climax of a romance have covered the ground of interest; but, to the more curious reader, it shall be some slight instruction to trace the close threads that underlie the ingenuous web of circumstances.

The headpiece, bearing the name of President Miraflores, is daily scrubbed with soap-bark and sand. An old half-breed Indian tends the grave with fidelity and the dawdling minuteness of inherited sloth. He chops down the weeds and ever-springing grass with his machete, he plucks ants and scorpions and beetles from it with his horny fingers, and sprinkles its turf with water from the plaza fountain. There is no grave anywhere so well kept and ordered.

Only by following out the underlying threads will it be made clear why the old Indian, Galvez, is secretly paid to keep green the grave of President Miraflores by one who never saw the unfortunate statesman in life or in death, and why that one was wont to walk in the twilight, casting from a distance looks of gentle sadness upon that unhonoured mound.

Elsewhere than at Coralio one learns of the impetuous career of Isabel Guilbert. New Orleans gave her birth and the mingled French and Spanish creole nature that tinctured her life with such turbulence and warmth. She had little education, but a knowledge of men and motives that seemed to have come by instinct. Far beyond the common woman was she endowed with intrepid rashness, with a love for the pursuit of adventure to the brink of danger, and with desire for the pleasures of life. Her spirit was one to chafe under any curb; she was Eve after the fall, but before the bitterness of it was felt. She wore life as a rose in her bosom.

Of the legion of men who had been at her feet it was said that but one was so fortunate as to engage her fancy. To President Miraflores, the brilliant but unstable ruler of Anchuria, she yielded the key to her resolute heart. How, then, do we find her (as the Coralians would have told you) the wife of Frank Goodwin, and happily living a life of dull and dreamy inaction?

The underlying threads reach far, stretching across the sea. Following them out it will be made plain why "Shorty" O'Day, of the Columbia Detective Agency, resigned his position. And, for a lighter pastime, it shall be a duty and a pleasing sport to wander with Momus beneath the tropic stars where Melpomene once stalked austere. Nor to cause laughter to echo from those lavish jungles and frowning crags, where formerly rang the cries of pirates' victims; to lay aside pike and cutlass and attack with quip and jollity; to draw one saving titter of mirth from the rusty casque of Romance—this were pleasant to do in the shade of the lemon-trees on that coast that is curved like lips set for smiling.

For there are yet tales of the Spanish Main. That segment of continent washed by the tempestuous Caribbean, and presenting to the sea a formidable border of tropical jungle topped by the over-weening Cordilleras, is still begirt by mystery and romance. In past times buccaneers and revolutionists roused the echoes of its cliffs, and the condor wheeled perpetually above where, in the green groves, they made food for him with their matchlocks and toledos. Taken and retaken by sea rovers, by adverse powers, and by sudden uprising of rebellious factions, the historic 300 miles of adventurous coast has scarcely known for hundreds of years whom rightly to call its master. Pizarro, Balboa, Sir Francis Drake, and Bolivar did what they could to make it a part of Christendom. Sir John Morgan, Lafitte and other eminent swashbucklers bombarded and pounded it in the name of Abaddon.

The game still goes on. The guns of the rovers are silenced, but the tintype man, the enlarged photograph brigand, the kodaking tourist and the scouts of the gentle brigade of fakirs have found it out, and carry on the work. The hucksters of Germany, France, and Sicily now bag its small change across their counters. Gentleman adventurers throng the waiting-rooms of its rulers with proposals for railways and concessions. The little opéra-bouffe *nations play at government and intrigue until some day a big, silent gunboat glides into the offing and warns them not to break their toys. And with these changes comes also the small adventurer, with empty pockets to fill, light of heart, busy-brained—the modern fairy prince, bearing an alarm clock with which, more surely than by the sentimental kiss, to awaken the beautiful tropics from their centuries' sleep. Generally he wears a shamrock, which he matches pridefully against the extravagant palms; and it is he who has driven Melpomene to the wings, and set Comedy to dancing before the footlights of the Southern Cross.*

So, there is a little tale to tell of many things. Perhaps to the promiscuous ear of the Walrus it shall come with most avail; for in it there are indeed shoes and ships and sealing-wax and cabbage-palms and presidents instead of kings.

Add to these a little love and counterplotting, and scatter everywhere through the maze a trail of tropical dollars—dollars warmed no more by the torrid sun than by the hot palms of the scouts of Fortune—and, after all, here seems to be Life itself, with talk enough to weary the most garrulous of Walruses.

33

"Fox-in-the-Morning"

CORALIO reclined, in the midday heat, like some vacuous beauty lounging in a guarded harem. The town lay at the sea's edge on a strip of alluvial coast. It was set like a little pearl in an emerald band. Behind it, and seeming almost to topple, imminent, above it, rose the sea-following range of the Cordilleras. In front the sea was spread, a smiling jailer, but even more incorruptible than the frowning mountains. The waves swished along the smooth beach; the parrots screamed in the orange and ceiba-trees; the palms waved their limber fronds foolishly, like an awkward chorus at the prima donna's cue to enter.

Suddenly the town was full of excitement. A native boy dashed down a grass-grown street, shrieking: *"Busca el Señor Goodwin. Ha venido un telégrafo por el!"*

The word passed quickly. Telegrams do not often come to anyone in Coralio. The cry for *Señor* Goodwin was taken up by a dozen officious voices. The main street running parallel to the beach became populated with those who desired to expedite the delivery of the dispatch. Knots of women with complexions varying from palest olive to deepest brown gathered at street corners and plaintively caroled: *"Un telégrafo por Señor Goodwin!"* The *comandante*, Don Señor el Coronel Encarnación Rios, who was loyal to the Ins and suspected Goodwin's devotion to the Outs, hissed "Aha!" and wrote in his secret memorandum book the accusive fact that *Señor* Goodwin had on that momentous date received a telegram.

In the midst of the hullabaloo a man stepped to the door of a small wooden building and looked out. Above the door was a sign that read "Keogh and Clancy"—a nomenclature that seemed not to be indigenous to that tropical soil. The man in the door was Billy Keogh, scout of fortune and progress, and latter-day rover of the Spanish Main. Tintypes and photographs were the weapons with which Keogh and Clancy were at that time assailing the hopeless shores. Outside the shop were set two large frames filled with specimens of their art and skill.

Keogh leaned in the doorway, his bold and humorous countenance wearing a look of interest at the unusual influx of life and sound into the street. When the meaning of the disturbance became clear to him he placed a hand beside his mouth and shouted: "Hey! Frank!" in such a robustious voice that the feeble clamour of the natives was drowned and silenced.

Fifty yards away, on the seaward side of the street, stood the abode of the consul for the United States. Out from the door of this building tumbled Goodwin at the call. He had been smoking with Willard Geddie, the consul, on the back porch of the consulate, which was conceded to be the coolest spot in Coralio.

"Hurry up," shouted Keogh. "There's a riot in town on account of a telegram that's come for you. You want to be careful about these things, my boy. It won't do to trifle with the feelings of the public this way. You'll be getting a pink note some day with violet scent on it; and then the country'll be steeped in the throes of a revolution."

Goodwin had strolled up the street and met the boy with the message. The ox-eyed women gazed at him with shy admiration, for his type drew them. He was big, blond, and jauntily dressed in white linen, with buckskin *zapatos*. His manner was courtly, with a sort of kindly truculence in it, tempered by a merciful eye. When the telegram had been delivered, and the bearer of it dismissed with a gratuity, the relieved populace returned to the contiguities of shade from which curiosity had drawn it—the women to their baking in the mud ovens under the orange-trees, or to the interminable combing of their long, straight hair; the men to their cigarettes and gossip in the cantinas.

Goodwin sat on Keogh's doorstep, and read his telegram. It was from Bob Englehart, an American, who lived in San Mateo, the capital city of Anchuria, eighty miles in the interior. Englehart was a gold miner, an ardent revolutionist and "good people". That he was a man of resource and imagination was proven by the telegram he had sent. It had been his task to send a confidential message to his friend in Coralio. This could not have been accomplished in either Spanish or English, for the eye politic in Anchuria was an active one. The Ins and the Outs were perpetually on their guard. But Englehart was a diplomatist. There existed but one code upon which he might make requisition with promise of safety—the great and potent code of Slang. So here is the message that slipped, unconstrued, through the fingers of curious officials, and came to the eye of Goodwin:

"His Nibs skedaddled yesterday per jack-rabbit line with all the coin in the kitty and the bundle of muslin he's spoony about. The boodle is six figures short. Our crowd in good shape, but we need the spondulicks. You collar it. The main guy and the dry goods are headed for the briny. You know what to do.

"Bob".

This screed, remarkable as it was, had no mystery for Goodwin. He was the most successful of the small advance-guard of speculative Americans that had invaded Anchuria, and he had not reached that enviable pinnacle without having well exercised the arts of foresight and deduction. He had taken up political intrigue as a matter of business. He was acute enough to wield a certain influence among the leading schemers, and he was prosperous enough to be able to purchase the respect of the petty office-holders. There was always a revolutionary party; and to it he had always allied himself; for the adherents of a new administration received the rewards of their labours. There was now a Liberal party seeking to overturn President Miraflores. If the wheel successfully revolved, Goodwin stood to win a concession to 30,000 manzanas of the finest coffee lands in the interior. Certain incidents in the recent career of President Miraflores had excited a shrewd suspicion in Goodwin's mind that the government was near a dissolution from another cause than that of a revolution, and now Englehart's telegram had come as a corroboration of his wisdom.

The telegram, which had remained unintelligible to the Anchurian linguists, who had applied to it in vain their knowledge of Spanish and elemental English, conveyed a stimulating piece of news to Goodwin's understanding. It informed him that the president of the republic had decamped from the capital city with the contents of the treasury. Furthermore, that he was accompanied in his flight by that winning adventuress, Isabel Guilbert, the opera singer, whose troupe of performers had been entertained by the president at San Mateo during the past month on a scale less modest than that with which royal visitors are often content. The reference of the "jack-rabbit line" could mean nothing else than the mule-back system of transport that prevailed between Coralio and the capital. The hint that the "boodle" was "six figures short" made the condition of the national treasury lamentably clear. Also it was convincingly true that the ingoing party—its way now made a pacific one—would need the "spondulicks". Unless its pledges should be fulfilled, and the spoils held for the delectation of the victors, precarious indeed would be the position of the new government. Therefore it was exceeding necessary to "collar the main guy", and recapture the sinews of war and government.

Goodwin handed the message to Keogh.

"Read that, Billy," he said. "It's from Bob Englehart. Can you manage the cipher?"

Keogh sat in the other half of the doorway, and carefully perused the telegram.

308

"'Tis not a cipher," he said, finally. "'Tis what they call literature, and that's a system of language put in the mouths of people that they've never been introduced to by writers of imagination. The magazines invented it, but I never knew before that President Norvin Green had stamped it with the seal of his approval. 'Tis now no longer literature, but language. The dictionaries tried, but they couldn't make it go for anything but dialect. Sure, now that the Western Union indorses it, it won't be long till a race of people will spring up that speaks it."

"You're running too much to philology, Billy," said Goodwin. "Do you make out the meaning of it?"

"Sure," replied the philosopher of Fortune. "All languages come easy to the man who must know 'em. I've even failed to misunderstand an order to evacuate in classical Chinese when it was backed up by the muzzle of a breech-loader. This little literary essay I hold in my hands means a game of 'Fox-in-the-Morning'. Ever play that, Frank, when you was a kid?"

"I think so," said Goodwin, laughing. "You join hands all 'round, and——"

"You do not," interrupted Keogh. "You've got a fine sporting game mixed up in your head with 'All Around the Rose-bush'. The spirit of 'Fox-in-the-Morning' is opposed to the holding of hands. I'll tell you how it's played. This president man and his companion in play, they stand up over in San Mateo, ready for the run, and shout: 'Fox-in-the-Morning!' Me and you, standing here, we say: 'Goose and the Gander!' They say: 'How many miles is it to London town?' We say: 'Only a few, if your legs are long enough. How many comes out?' They say: 'More than you're able to catch.' And then the game commences."

"I catch the idea," said Goodwin. "It won't do to let the goose and gander slip through our fingers, Billy; their feathers are too valuable. Our crowd is prepared and able to step into the shoes of the government at once; but with the treasury empty we'd stay in power about as long as a tenderfoot would stick on an untamed bronco. We must play the fox on every foot of the coast to prevent their getting out of the country."

"By the mule-back schedule," said Keogh, "it's five days down from San Mateo. We've got plenty of time to set our outposts. There's only three places on the coast where they can hope to sail from—here and Solitas and Alazan. They're the only points we'll have to guard. It's as easy as a chess problem—fox to play, and mate in three moves. Oh, goosey, goosey, gander, whither do you wander? By the blessing of the literary telegraph the boodle of this benighted fatherland shall be preserved to the honest political party that is seeking to overthrow it."

The situation had been justly outlined by Keogh. The down trail from the capital was at all times a weary road to travel. A jiggety-joggety journey it was; ice-cold and hot, wet and dry. The trail climbed appalling mountains, wound like a rotten string about the brows of breathless precipices, plunged through chilling snow-fed streams, and wriggled like a snake through sunless forests teeming with menacing insect and animal life. After descending to the foothills it turned to a trident, the central prong ending at Alazan. Another branched off to Coralio; the third penetrated to Solitas. Between the sea and the foothills stretched the five miles' breadth of alluvial coast. Here was the flora of the tropics in its rankest and most prodigal growth. Spaces here and there had been wrested from the jungle and planted with bananas and cane and orange groves. The rest was a riot of wild vegetation, the home of monkeys, tapirs, jaguars, alligators and prodigious reptiles and insects. Where no road was cut a serpent could scarcely make its way through the tangle of vines and creepers. Across the treacherous mangrove swamps few things without wings could safely pass. Therefore the fugitives could hope to reach the coast only by one of the routes named.

"Keep the matter quiet, Billy," advised Goodwin. "We don't want the Ins to know that the president is in flight. I suppose Bob's information is something of a scoop in the capital as yet. Otherwise he would not have tried to make his message a confidential one; and, besides, everybody would have heard the news. I'm going around now to see Dr. Zavalla, and start a man up the trail to cut the telegraph wire."

As Goodwin rose, Keogh threw his hat upon the grass by the door and expelled a tremendous sigh.

"What's the trouble, Billy?" asked Goodwin, pausing. "That's the first time I ever heard you sigh."

"'Tis the last," said Keogh. "With that sorrowful puff of wind I resign myself to a life of praiseworthy but harassing honesty. What are tintypes, if you please, to the opportunities of the great and hilarious class of ganders and geese? Not that I would be a president, Frank—and the boodle he's got is too big for me to handle—but in some ways I feel my conscience hurting me for addicting myself to photographing a nation instead of running away with it. Frank did you ever see the 'bundle of muslin' that His Excellency has wrapped up and carried off?"

"Isabel Guilbert?" said Goodwin, laughing. "No, I never did. From what I've heard of her, though, I imagine that she wouldn't stick at anything to carry her point. Don't get romantic, Billy. Sometimes I begin to fear that there's Irish blood in your ancestry."

"I never saw her either," went on Keogh; "but they say she's got all the ladies of mythology, sculpture, and fiction reduced to chromos. They say she can look at a man once, and he'll turn monkey and climb trees to pick coconuts for her. Think of that president man with Lord knows how many hundreds of thousands of dollars in one hand, and this muslin siren in the other, galloping downhill on a sympathetic mule amid songbirds and flowers! And here is Billy Keogh, because he is virtuous, condemned to the unprofitable swindle of slandering the faces of missing links on tin for an honest living! 'Tis an injustice of nature."

"Cheer up," said Goodwin. "You are a pretty poor fox

to be envying a gander. Maybe the enchanting Guilbert will take a fancy to you and your tintypes after we impoverish her royal escort."

"She could do worse," reflected Keogh; "but she won't. 'Tis not a tintype gallery, but the gallery of the gods that she's fitted to adorn. She's a very wicked lady, and the president man is in luck. But I hear Clancy swearing in the back room for having to do all the work." And Keogh plunged for the rear of the "gallery", whistling gaily in a spontaneous way that belied his recent sigh over the questionable good luck of the flying president.

Goodwin turned from the main street into a much narrower one that intersected it at a right angle.

These side streets were covered by a growth of thick, rank grass which was kept to a navigable shortness by the machetes of the police. Stone sidewalks, little more than a ledge in width, ran along the base of the mean and monotonous adobe houses. At the outskirts of the village these streets dwindled to nothing, and here were set the palm-thatched huts of the Caribs and the poorer natives, and the shabby cabins of negroes from Jamaica and the West India islands. A few structures raised their heads above the red-tiled roofs of the one-storey houses—the bell-tower of the *Calaboza*, the Hotel de los Estranjeros, the residence of the Vesuvius Fruit Company's agent, the store and residence of Bernard Brannigan, a ruined cathedral in which Columbus had once set foot, and, most imposing of all, the Casa Morena —the summer "White House" of the President of Anchuria. On the principal street running along the beach—the Broadway of Coralio—were the larger stores, the government *bodega* and post office, the *cuartel*, the rum-shops and the market-place.

On his way Goodwin passed the house of Bernard Brannigan. It was a modern wooden building, two storeys in height. The ground floor was occupied by Brannigan's store, the upper one contained the living apartments. A wide cool porch ran around the house half-way up its outer

312

walls. A handsome, vivacious girl neatly dressed in flowing white leaned over the railing and smiled down upon Goodwin. She was no darker than many an Andalusian of high descent; and she sparkled and glowed like a tropical moonlight.

"Good evening, Miss Paula," said Goodwin, taking off his hat, with his ready smile. There was little difference in his manner whether he addressed women or men. Everybody in Coralio liked to receive the salutation of the big American.

"Is there any news, Mr. Goodwin? Please don't say no. Isn't it warm? I feel just like Mariana in her moated grange —or was it a range?—it's hot enough."

"No, there's no news to tell, I believe," said Goodwin, with a mischievous look in his eye, "except that old Geddie is getting grumpier and crosser every day. If something doesn't happen to relieve his mind I'll have to quit smoking on his back porch—and there's no other place available that is cool enough."

"He isn't grumpy," said Paula Brannigan, impulsively, "when he——"

But she ceased suddenly, and drew back with a deepening colour; for her mother had been a *mestizo* lady, and the Spanish blood had brought to Paula a certain shyness that was an adornment to the other half of her demonstrative nature.

34

The Lotus and the Bottle

WILLARD GEDDIE, consul for the United States in Coralio, was working leisurely on his yearly report. Goodwin, who had strolled in as he did daily for a smoke on the much-coveted porch, had found him so absorbed in his work that he departed after roundly abusing the consul for his lack of hospitality.

"I shall complain to the civil service department," said Goodwin—"or is it a department?—perhaps it's only a theory. One gets neither civility nor service from you. You won't talk; and you won't set out anything to drink. What kind of a way is that of representing your government?"

Goodwin strolled out and across to the hotel to see if he could bully the quarantine doctor into a game on Coralio's solitary billiard-table. His plans were completed for the interception of the fugitives from the capital; and now it was but a waiting game that he had to play.

The consul was interested in his report. He was only 24; and he had not been in Coralio long enough for his enthusiasm to cool in the heat of the tropics—a paradox that may be allowed between Cancer and Capricorn.

So many thousand bunches of bananas, so many thousand oranges and coconuts, so many ounces of gold dust, pounds of rubber, coffee, indigo and sarsaparilla—actually, exports were 20 per cent. greater than for the previous year!

A little thrill of satisfaction ran through the consul. Perhaps, he thought, the State Department, upon reading his introduction, would notice—and then he leaned back in his chair and laughed. He was getting as bad as the others. For the moment he had forgotten that Coralio was an insignificant town in an insignificant republic lying along the by-ways of a second-rate sea. He thought of Gregg, the quarantine doctor, who subscribed for the London *Lancet*, expecting to find it quoting his reports to the home Board of Health concerning the yellow fever germ. The consul knew that not one in fifty of his acquaintances in the States had ever heard of Coralio. He knew that two men, at any rate, would have to read his report—some underling in the State Department and a compositor in the Public Printing Office. Perhaps the typesticker would note the increase of commerce in Coralio, and speak of it, over the cheese and beer, to a friend.

He had just written: "Most unaccountable is the supineness of the large exporters in the United States in permitting the French and German houses to practically control all trade interests of this rich and productive country"—when he heard the hoarse notes of a steamer's siren.

Geddie laid down his pen and gathered his Panama hat and umbrella. By the sound he knew it to be the *Valhalla*, one of the line of fruit vessels plying for the Vesuvius Company. Down to the *niños* of five years, every one in Coralio could name you each incoming steamer by the note of her siren. The consul sauntered by a roundabout, shaded way to the beach. By reason of long practice he gauged his stroll so accurately that by the time he arrived on the sandy shore the boat of the customs officials was rowing back from the steamer, which had been boarded and inspected according to the laws of Anchuria.

There is no harbour at Coralio. Vessels of the draught of the *Valhalla* must ride at anchor a mile from shore. When they take on fruit it is conveyed on lighters and freighter sloops. At Solitas, where there was a fine harbour, ships of many kinds were to be seen, but in the roadstead off Coralio scarcely any save the fruiters paused. Now and then a tramp coaster, or a mysterious brig from Spain, or a saucy French barque would hang innocently for a few days in the offing. Then the custom-house crew would become doubly vigilant

315

and wary. At night a sloop or two would be making strange trips in and out along the shore; and in the morning the stock of Three-Star Hennessey, wines and drygoods in Coralio would be found vastly increased. It has also been said that the customs officials jingled more silver in the pockets of their red-striped trousers, and that the record books showed no increase in import duties received.

The customs boat and the *Valhalla* gig reached the shore at the same time. When they grounded in the shallow water there was still five yards of rolling surf between them and dry sand. Then half-clothed Caribs dashed into the water, and brought in on their backs the *Valhalla*'s purser, and the little native officials in their cotton undershirts, blue trousers with red stripes, and flapping straw hats.

At college Geddie had been a treasure as a first-baseman. He now closed his umbrella, stuck it upright in the sand, and stooped, with his hands resting upon his knees. The purser, burlesquing the pitcher's contortions, hurled at the consul the heavy roll of newspaper, tied with a string, that the steamer always brought for him. Geddie leaped high and caught the roll with a sounding "thwack". The loungers on the beach—about a third of the population of the town—laughed and applauded delightedly. Every week they expected to see that roll of papers delivered and received in that same manner, and they were never disappointed. Innovations did not flourish in Coralio.

The consul re-hoisted his umbrella and walked back to the consulate.

This home of a great nation's representative was a wooden structure of two rooms, with a native-built gallery of poles, bamboo and nipa palm running on three sides of it. One room was the official apartment, furnished chastely with a flat-top desk, a hammock, and three uncomfortable cane-seated chairs. Engravings of the first and latest president of the country represented hung against the wall. The other room was the consul's living apartment.

It was eleven o'clock when he returned from the beach,

and therefore breakfast-time. Chanca, the Carib woman who
cooked for him, was just serving the meal on the side of the
gallery facing the sea—a spot famous as the coolest in
Coralio. The breakfast consisted of shark's fin soup, stew of
land crabs, breadfruit, a boiled iguana steak, aguacates, a
freshly-cut pineapple, claret and coffee.

Geddie took his seat, and unrolled with luxurious laziness
his bundle of newspapers. Here in Coralio for two days or
longer he would read of goings-on in the world very much as
we of the world read those whimsical contributions to inexact
science that assume to portray the doings of the Martians.
After he had finished with the papers they would be sent on
the rounds of the other English-speaking residents of the
town.

The paper that came first to his hand was one of those bulky
mattresses of printed stuff upon which the readers of certain
New York journals are supposed to take their Sabbath
literary nap. Opening this the consul rested it upon the table,
supporting its weight with the aid of the back of a chair.
Then he partook of his meal deliberately, turning the leaves
from time to time and glancing half idly at the contents.

Presently he was struck by something familiar to him in a
picture—a half-page, badly printed reproduction of a
photograph of a vessel. Languidly interested, he leaned for
a nearer scrutiny and a view of the florid headlines of the
column next to the picture.

Yes; he was not mistaken. The engraving was of the eight-
hundred-ton yacht *Idalia*, belonging to "that prince of good
fellows, Midas of the money market, and society's pink of
perfection, J. Ward Tolliver".

Slowly sipping his black coffee, Geddie read the column
of print. Following a listed statement of Mr. Tolliver's real
estate and bonds, came a description of the yacht's furnishings, and then the grain of news no bigger than a mustard
seed. Mr. Tolliver, with a party of favoured guests, would
sail the next day on a six weeks' cruise along the Central
American and South American coasts and among the

Bahama Islands. Among the guests were Mrs. Cumberland Payne and Miss Ida Payne, of Norfolk.

The writer, with the fatuous presumption that was demanded of him by his readers, had concocted a romance suited to their palates. He bracketed the names of Miss Payne and Mr. Tolliver until he had well-nigh read the marriage ceremony over them. He played coyly and insinuatingly with the strings of "*on dit*" and "Madame Rumour" and "a little bird" and "no one would be surprised", and ended with congratulations.

Geddie, having finished his breakfast, took his papers to the edge of the gallery, and sat there in his favourite steamer chair with his feet on the bamboo railing. He lighted a cigar, and looked out upon the sea. He felt a glow of satisfaction at finding he was so little disturbed by what he had read. He told himself that he had conquered the distress that had sent him, a voluntary exile, to this far land of the lotus. He could never forget Ida, of course; but there was no longer any pain in thinking about her. When they had had that misunderstanding and quarrel he had impulsively sought this consulship, with the desire to retaliate upon her by detaching himself from her world and presence. He had succeeded thoroughly in that. During the twelve months of his life in Coralio no word had passed between them, though he had sometimes heard of her through the dilatory correspondence with the few friends to whom he still wrote. Still he could not repress a little thrill of satisfaction at knowing that she had not yet married Tolliver or anyone else. But evidently Tolliver had not yet abandoned hope.

Well, it made no difference to him now. He had eaten of the lotus. He was happy and content in this land of perpetual afternoon. Those old days of life in the States seemed like an irritating dream. He hoped Ida would be as happy as he was. The climate as balmy as that of distant Avalon; the fetterless, idyllic round of enchanted days; the life among this indolent, romantic people—a life full of music, flowers, and low laughter, the influence of the imminent sea and mountains, and the many shapes of love and magic and beauty that bloomed in the white tropic nights—with all he was more than content. Also, there was Paula Brannigan.

Geddie intended to marry Paula—if, of course, she would consent; but he felt rather sure that she would do that. Somehow, he kept postponing his proposal. Several times he had been quite near to it; but a mysterious something always held him back. Perhaps it was only the unconscious, instinctive conviction that the act would sever the last tie that bound him to his old world.

He could be very happy with Paula. Few of the native girls could be compared with her. She had attended a convent school in New Orleans for two years; and when she chose to display her accomplishments no one could detect any difference between her and the girls of Norfolk and Manhattan. But it was delicious to see her at home dressed, as she sometimes was, in the native costume, with bare shoulders and flowing sleeves.

Bernard Brannigan was the great merchant of Coralio. Besides his store, he maintained a train of pack mules, and carried on a lively trade with the interior towns and villages. He had married a native lady of high Castilian descent, but with a tinge of Indian brown showing through her olive cheek. The union of the Irish and the Spanish had produced, as it so often has, an offshoot of rare beauty and variety. They were very excellent people indeed, and the upper storey of their house was ready to be placed at the service of Geddie and Paula as soon as he should make up his mind to speak about it.

By the time two hours were whiled away the consul tired of reading. The papers lay scattered about him on the gallery. Reclining there, he gazed dreamily out upon an Eden. A clump of banana plants interposed their broad shields between him and the sun. The gentle slope from the consulate to the sea was covered with the dark-green foliage of lemon-trees and orange-trees just bursting into bloom. A lagoon pierced the land like a dark, jagged crystal, and above it a pale ceiba-tree rose almost to the clouds. The waving coconut palms on the beach flared their decorative green leaves against the slate of an almost quiescent sea. His senses were cognizant of brilliant scarlet and ochres amid the vert of the coppice, of odours of fruit and bloom and the smoke from Chanca's clay oven under the calabash-tree; of the treble laughter of the native women in their huts, the song of the robin, the salt taste of the breeze, the diminuendo of the faint surf running along the shore—and, gradually, of a white speck, growing to a blur, that intruded itself upon the drab prospect of the sea.

Lazily interested, he watched this blur increase until it became the *Idalia* steaming at full speed, coming down the coast. Without changing his position he kept his eyes upon the beautiful white yacht as she drew slowly near, and came opposite to Coralio. Then, sitting upright, he saw her float steadily past and on. Scarcely a mile of sea had separated her from the shore. He had seen the frequent flash of her polished brass work and the stripes of her deck awnings——so much, and no more. Like a ship on a magic-lantern slide the *Idalia* had crossed the illuminated circle of the consul's little world, and was gone. Save for the tiny cloud of smoke that was left hanging over the brim of the sea, she might have been an immaterial thing, a chimera of his idle brain.

Geddie went into his office and sat down to dawdle over his report. If the reading of the article in the paper had left him unshaken, this silent passing of the *Idalia* had done for him still more. It had brought the calm and peace of a situation from which all uncertainty had been erased. He knew that men sometimes hope without being aware of it. Now, since she had come two thousand miles and had passed without a sign, not even his unconscious self need cling to the past any longer.

After dinner, when the sun was low behind the mountains, Geddie walked on the little strip of beach under the coconuts. The wind was blowing mildly landward, and the surface of the sea was rippled by tiny wavelets.

A miniature breaker, spreading with a soft "swish" upon
the sand, brought with it something round and shiny that
rolled back again as the wave receded. The next influx
beached it clear, and Geddie picked it up. The thing was a
long-necked wine bottle of colourless glass. The cork had
been driven in tightly to the level of the mouth, and the end
covered with dark-red sealing-wax. The bottle contained
only what seemed to be a sheet of paper, much curled from
the manipulation it had undergone while being inserted.
In the sealing-wax was the impression of a seal—probably
of a signet-ring, bearing the initials of a monogram; but the
impression had been hastily made, and the letters were past
anything more certain than a shrewd conjecture. Ida Payne
had always worn a signet-ring in preference to any other
finger decoration. Geddie thought he could make out the
familiar "I.P.", and a queer sensation of disquietude went
over him. More personal and intimate was this reminder of
her than had been the sight of the vessel she was doubtless
on. He walked back to his house, and set the bottle on his
desk.

Throwing off his hat and coat, and lighting a lamp—for
the night had crowded precipitately upon the brief twilight—
he began to examine his piece of sea salvage.

By holding the bottle near the light and turning it
judiciously, he made out that it contained a double sheet of
note-paper filled with close writing; further, that the paper
was of the same size and shade as that always used by Ida;
and that, to the best of his belief, the handwriting was hers.
The imperfect glass of the bottle so distorted the rays of light
that he could read no word of the writing; but certain capital
letters, of which he caught comprehensive glimpses, were
Ida's, he felt sure.

There was a little smile both of perplexity and amusement
in Geddie's eyes as he set the bottle down, and laid three
cigars side by side on his desk. He fetched his steamer chair
from the gallery, and stretched himself comfortably. He

would smoke those three cigars while considering the problem.

For it amounted to a problem. He almost wished that he had not found the bottle; but the bottle was there. Why should it have drifted in from the sea, whence come so many disquieting things, to disturb his peace?

In this dreamy land, where time seemed so redundant, he had fallen into the habit of bestowing much thought upon trifling matters.

He began to speculate upon many fanciful theories concerning the story of the bottle, rejecting each in turn.

Ships in danger of wreck or disablement sometimes cast forth such precarious messengers calling for aid. But he had seen the *Idalia* not three hours before, safe and speeding. Suppose the crew had mutinied and imprisoned the passengers below, and the message was one begging for succour! But, premising such an improbable outrage, would the agitated captives have taken the pains to fill four pages of note-paper with carefully penned arguments to their rescue?

Thus by elimination he soon rid the matter of the more unlikely theories, and was reduced—though aversely—to the less assailable one that the bottle contained a message to himself. Ida knew he was in Coralio; she must have launched the bottle while the yacht was passing and the wind blowing fairly toward the shore.

As soon as Geddie reached this conclusion a wrinkle came between his brows and a stubborn look settled around his mouth. He sat looking out through the doorway at the gigantic fireflies traversing the quiet streets.

If this was a message to him from Ida, what could it mean save an overture toward a reconciliation? And if that, why had she not used the sane methods of the post instead of this uncertain and even flippant means of communication? A note in an empty bottle, cast into the sea! There was something light and frivolous about it, if not actually contemptuous.

The thought stirred his pride and subdued whatever emotions had been resurrected by the finding of the bottle.

Geddie put on his coat and hat and walked out. He followed a street that led him along the border of the little plaza, where a band was playing and people were rambling, care-free and indolent. Some timorous *señoritas*, scurrying past with fireflies tangled in the jetty braids of their hair, glanced at him with shy, flattering eyes. The air was languorous with the scent of jasmine and orange-blossoms.

The consul stayed his steps at the house of Bernard Brannigan. Paula was swinging in a hammock on the gallery. She rose from it like a bird from its nest. The colour came to her cheek at the sound of Geddie's voice.

He was charmed at the sight of her costume—a flounced muslin dress, with a little jacket of white flannel, all made with neatness and style. He suggested a stroll, and they walked out to the old Indian well on the hill road. They sat on the curb, and there Geddie made the expected but long-deferred speech. Certain though he had been that she would not say him nay, he was thrilled with joy at the completeness and sweetness of her surrender. Here was surely a heart made for love and steadfastness. Here was no caprice or questionings or captious standards of convention.

When Geddie kissed Paula at the door that night he was happier than he had ever been before. "Here in this hollow lotus land, ever to live and lie reclined," seemed to him, as it has seemed to many mariners, the best as well as the easiest. His future would be an ideal one. He had attained a Paradise without a serpent. His Eve would be indeed a part of him, unbeguiled, and therefore more beguiling. He had made his decision to-night, and his heart was full of serene, assured content.

Geddie went back to his house whistling that finest and saddest love song, "La Golondrina". At the door his tame monkey leaped down from his shelf, chattering briskly. The consul turned to his desk to get him some nuts he usually kept there. Reaching in the half-darkness, his hand struck against the bottle. He started as if he had touched the cold rotundity of a serpent.

He had forgotten that the bottle was there.

He lighted the lamp and fed the monkey. Then, very deliberately, he lighted a cigar, and took the bottle in his hand, and walked down the path to the beach.

There was a moon, and the sea was glorious. The breeze had shifted, as it did each evening, and was now rushing steadily seaward.

Stepping to the water's edge, Geddie hurled the unopened bottle far out into the sea. It disappeared for a moment, and then shot upward twice its length. Geddie stood still, watching it. The moonlight was so bright that he could see it bobbing up and down with the little waves. Slowly it receded from the shore, flashing and turning as it went. The wind was carrying it out to sea. Soon it became a mere speck, doubtfully discerned at irregular intervals; and then the mystery of it was swallowed up by the greater mystery of the ocean. Geddie stood still upon the beach, smoking and looking out upon the water.

*   *   *

"Simon!—Oh, Simon!—wake up there, Simon!" bawled a sonorous voice at the edge of the water.

Old Simon Cruz was a half-breed fisherman and smuggler who lived in a hut on the beach. Out of his earliest nap Simon was thus awakened.

He slipped on his shoes and went outside. Just landing from one of the *Valhalla*'s boats was the third mate of that vessel, who was an acquaintance of Simon's, and three sailors from the fruiter.

"Go up, Simon," called the mate, "and find Dr. Gregg or Mr. Goodwin or anybody that's a friend to Mr. Geddie, and bring 'em here at once."

"Saints of the skies!" said Simon sleepily, "nothing has happened to Mr. Geddie?"

"He's under that tarpauling," said the mate, pointing

to the boat, "and he's rather more than half drownded. We seen him from the steamer nearly a mile out from shore, swimmin' like mad after a bottle that was floatin' in the water, outward bound. We lowered the gig and started for him. He nearly had his hand on the bottle, when he gave out and went under. We pulled him out in time to save him, maybe; but the doctor is the one to decide that."

"A bottle?" said the old man, rubbing his eyes. He was not yet fully awake. "Where is the bottle?"

"Driftin' along out there some'eres," said the mate, jerking his thumb toward the sea. "Get on with you, Simon."

35

Smith

GOODWIN and the ardent patriot, Zavalla, took all the precautions that their foresight could contrive to prevent the escape of President Miraflores and his companion. They sent trusted messengers up the coast to Solitas and Alazan to warn the local leaders of the flight, and to instruct them to patrol the water-line and arrest the fugitives at all hazards should they reveal themselves in that territory. After this was done there remained only to cover the district about Coralio and await the coming of the quarry. The nets were well spread. The roads were so few, the opportunities for embarkation so limited, and the two or three probable points of exit so well guarded that it would be strange indeed, if there should slip through the meshes so much of the country's dignity, romance, and collateral. The president would, without doubt, move as secretly as possible, and endeavour to board a vessel by stealth from some secluded point along the shore.

On the fourth day after the receipt of Englehart's telegram, the *Karlsefin*, a Norwegian steamer chartered by the New Orleans fruit trade, anchored off Coralio with three hoarse toots of her siren. The *Karlsefin* was not one of the line operated by the Vesuvius Fruit Company. She was something of a dilettante, doing odd jobs for a company that was scarcely important enough to figure as a rival to the Vesuvius. The movements of the *Karlsefin* were dependent upon the state of the market. Sometimes she would ply steadily between the Spanish Main and New Orleans in the regular transport of fruit; next she would be making erratic trips to Mobile or

Charleston, or even as far north as New York, according to the distribution of the fruit supply.

Goodwin lounged upon the beach with the usual crowd of idlers that had gathered to view the steamer. Now that President Miraflores might be expected to reach the borders of his abjured country at any time, the orders were to keep a strict and unrelenting watch. Every vessel that approached the shores might now be considered a possible means of escape for the fugitives; and an eye was kept even on the sloops and dories that belonged to the sea-going contingent of Coralio. Goodwin and Zavalla moved everywhere, but without ostentation, watching the loopholes of escape.

The customs officials crowded importantly into their boat and rowed out to the *Karlsefin*. A boat from the steamer landed her purser with his papers, and took out the quarantine doctor with his green umbrella and clinical thermometer. Next a swarm of Caribs began to load upon lighters the thousands of bunches of bananas heaped upon the shore and row them out to the steamer. The *Karlsefin* had no passenger list, and was soon done with the attention of the authorities. The purser declared that the steamer would remain at anchor until morning, taking on her fruit during the night. The *Karlsefin* had come, he said, from New York, to which port her latest cargo of oranges and coconuts had been conveyed. Two or three of the freighter sloops were engaged to assist in the work, for the captain was anxious to make a quick return in order to reap the advantage offered by a certain dearth of fruit in the States.

About four o'clock in the afternoon another of those marine monsters, not very familiar in those waters, hove in sight, following the fateful *Idalia*—a graceful steam yacht, painted a light buff, clean-cut as a steel engraving. The beautiful vessel hovered off-shore, see-sawing the waves as lightly as a duck in a rain barrel. A swift boat manned by a crew in uniform came ashore, and a stocky-built man leaped to the sands.

The new-comer seemed to turn a disapproving eye upon the rather motley congregation of native Anchurians, and made his way at once toward Goodwin, who was the most conspicuously Anglo-Saxon figure present. Goodwin greeted him with courtesy.

Conversation developed that the newly landed one was named Smith, and that he had come in a yacht. A meagre biography, truly; for the yacht was most apparent; and the "Smith" not beyond a reasonable guess before the revelation. Yet to the eye of Goodwin, who had seen several things, there was a discrepancy between Smith and his yacht. A bullet-headed man Smith was, with an oblique, dead eye and the moustache of a cocktail-mixer. And unless he had shifted costumes before putting off for shore he had affronted the deck of his correct vessel clad in a pearl-grey derby, a gay plaid suit and vaudeville neckwear. Men owning pleasure yachts generally harmonize better with them.

Smith looked business, but he was no advertiser. He commented upon the scenery, remarking upon its fidelity to the pictures in the geography; and then inquired for the United States consul. Goodwin pointed out the starred-and-striped bunting hanging above the little consulate, which was concealed behind the orange-trees.

"Mr. Geddie, the consul, will be sure to be there," said Goodwin. "He was very nearly drowned a few days ago while taking a swim in the sea, and the doctor has ordered him to remain indoors for some time."

Smith ploughed his way through the sand to the consulate, his haberdashery creating violent discord against the smooth tropical blues and greens.

Geddie was lounging in his hammock, somewhat pale of face and languid in pose. On that night when the *Valhalla*'s boat had brought him ashore, apparently drenched to death by the sea, Doctor Gregg and his other friends had toiled for hours to preserve the little spark of life that remained to him. The bottle, with its impotent message, was gone out to sea, and the problem that it had provoked was reduced to a simple sum in addition—one and one make two, by the rule of arithmetic; one by the rule of romance.

There is a quaint old theory that man may have two souls —a peripheral one which serves ordinarily, and a central one which is stirred only at certain times, but then with activity and vigour. While under the domination of the former a man will shave, vote, pay taxes, give money to his family, buy subscription books and comport himself on the average plan. But let the central soul suddenly become dominant, and he may, in the twinkling of an eye, turn upon the partner of his joys with furious execration; he may change his politics while you could snap your fingers; he may deal out deadly insult to his dearest friend; he may get him, instanter, to a monastery or a dance hall; he may elope, or hang himself—or he may write a song or poem, or kiss his wife unasked, or give his funds to the search of a microbe. Then the peripheral soul will return; and we have our safe, sane citizen again. It is but the revolt of the Ego against Order; and its effect is to shake up the atoms only that they may settle where they belong.

Geddie's revulsion had been a mild one—no more than a swim in a summer sea after so inglorious an object as a drifting bottle. And now he was himself again. Upon his desk, ready for the post, was a letter to his government tendering his resignation as consul, to be effective as soon as another could be appointed in his place. For Bernard Brannigan, who never did things in a half-way manner, was to take Geddie at once for a partner in his very profitable and various enterprises; and Paula was happily engaged in plans for refurnishing and decorating the upper storey of the Brannigan house.

The consul rose from his hammock when he saw the conspicuous stranger in his door.

"Keep your seat, old man," said the visitor, with an airy wave of his large hand. "My name's Smith; and I've come in a yacht. You are the consul—is that right? A big, cool guy on the beach directed me here. Thought I'd pay my respects to the flag."

"Sit down," said Geddie. "I've been admiring your craft ever since it came in sight. Looks like a fast sailer. What's her tonnage?"

"Search me!" said Smith. "I don't know what she weighs in at. But she's got a tidy gait. The *Rambler*—that's her name—don't take the dust of anything afloat. This is my first trip on her. I'm taking a squint along this coast just to get an idea of the countries where the rubber and red pepper and revolutions come from. I had no idea there was so much scenery down here. Why, Central Park ain't in it with this neck of the woods. I'm from New York. They get monkeys and coconuts, and parrots down here—is that right?"

"We have them all," said Geddie. "I'm quite sure that our fauna and flora would take a prize over Central Park."

"Maybe they would," admitted Smith cheerfully. "I haven't seen them yet. But I guess you've got us skinned on the animal and vegetation question. You don't have much travel here, do you?"

"Travel?" queried the consul. "I suppose you mean passengers on the steamers. No; very few people land in Coralio. An investor now and then—tourists and sightseers generally go farther down the coast to one of the larger towns where there is a harbour."

"I see a ship out there loading up with bananas," said Smith. "Any passengers on her?"

"That's the *Karlsefin*," said the consul. "She's a tramp fruiter—made her last trip to New York, I believe. No; she brought no passengers. I saw her boat come ashore, and there was no one. About the only exciting recreation we have here is watching steamers when they arrive; and a passenger on one of them generally causes the whole town to turn out. If you are going to remain in Coralio a while, Mr. Smith, I'll be glad to take you around to meet some people. There are four or five American chaps that are good to know, besides the native high-fliers."

"Thanks," said the yachtsman, "but I wouldn't put you to the trouble. I'd like to meet the guys you speak of, but I won't be here long enough to do much knocking around. That cool gent on the beach spoke of a doctor; can you tell me where I could find him? The *Rambler* ain't quite as steady on her feet as a Broadway hotel; and a fellow gets a touch of sea-sickness now and then. Thought I'd strike the croaker for a handful of the little sugar pills, in case I need 'em."

"You will be apt to find Dr. Gregg at the hotel," said the consul. "You can see it from the door—it's that two-storey building with the balcony, where the orange-trees are."

The Hotel de los Estranjeros was a dreary hostelry, in great disuse both by strangers and friends. It stood at a corner of the Street of the Holy Sepulchre. A grove of small orange-trees crowded against one side of it, enclosed by a low, rock wall over which a tall man might easily step. The house was of plastered adobe, stained a hundred shades of colour by the salt breeze and the sun. Upon its upper balcony opened a central door and two windows containing broad jalousies instead of sashes.

The lower floor communicated by two doorways with the narrow, rock-paved sidewalk. The *pulperia*—or drinking shop—of the proprietress, Madama Timotea Ortiz, occupied the ground floor. On the bottles of brandy, *anisada*, Scotch "smoke", and inexpensive wines behind the little counter, the dust lay thick, save where the fingers of infrequent customers had left irregular prints. The upper storey contained four or five guest-rooms which were rarely put to their destined use. Sometimes a fruitgrower, riding in from his plantation to confer with his agent, would pass a melancholy night in the dismal upper storey; sometimes a minor native official on some trifling government quest would have his pomp and majesty awed by Madama's sepulchral hospitality. But Madama sat behind her bar content, not desiring to quarrel with Fate. If anyone required meat, drink or lodging at the Hotel de los Estranjeros they had but to come, and be served. *Está bueno*. If they came not, why, then, they came not. *Está bueno*.

As the exceptional yachtsman was making his way down the precarious sidewalk of the Street of the Holy Sepulchre, the solitary permanent guest of that decaying hotel sat at its door, enjoying the breeze from the sea.

Dr. Gregg, the quarantine physician, was a man of fifty or sixty, with a florid face and the longest beard between Topeka and Terra del Fuego. He held his position by virtue of an appointment by the Board of Health of a seaport city in one of the Southern states. That city feared the ancient enemy of every Southern seaport—the yellow fever—and it was the duty of Dr. Gregg to examine crew and passengers of every vessel leaving Coralio for preliminary symptoms. The duties were light, and the salary, for one who lived in Coralio, ample. Surplus time there was in plenty; and the good doctor added to his gains by a large private practice among the residents of the coast. The fact that he did not know ten words of Spanish was no obstacle; a pulse could be felt and a fee collected without one being a linguist. Add to the description the facts that the doctor had a story to tell concerning the operation of trepanning which no listener had ever allowed him to conclude, and that he believed in brandy as a prophylactic; and the special points of interest possessed by Dr. Gregg will have become exhausted.

The doctor had dragged a chair to the sidewalk. He was coatless, and he leaned back against the wall and smoked, while he stroked his beard. Surprise came into his pale blue eyes when he caught sight of Smith in his unusual and prismatic clothes.

"You're Dr. Gregg—is that right?" said Smith, feeling the dog's-head pin in his tie. "The constable—I mean the consul, told me you hung out at this caravansary. My name's Smith; and I came in a yacht. Taking a cruise around, looking at the monkeys and pineapple trees. Come inside and have a drink,

Doc. This café looks on the blink, but I guess it can set out something wet."

"I will join you, sir, in just a taste of brandy," said Dr. Gregg, rising quickly. "I find that as a prophylactic a little brandy is almost a necessity in this climate."

As they turned to enter the *pulperia* a native man, barefoot, glided noiselessly up and addressed the doctor in Spanish. He was yellowish-brown, like an over-ripe lemon; he wore a cotton shirt and ragged linen trousers girded by a leather belt. His face was like an animal's, live and wary, but without promise of much intelligence. This man jabbered with animation and so much seriousness that it seemed a pity that his words were to be wasted.

Dr. Gregg felt his pulse.

"You sick?" he inquired.

"*Me mujer está enferma en la casa,*" said the man, thus endeavouring to convey the news in the only language open to him, that his wife lay ill in her palm-thatched hut.

The doctor drew a handful of capsules filled with a white powder from his trousers pocket. He counted out ten of them into the native's hand, and held up his forefinger impressively.

"Take one," said the doctor, "every two hours." He then held up two fingers, shaking them emphatically before the native's face. Next he pulled out his watch and ran his finger round its dial twice. Again the two fingers confronted the patient's nose. "Two—two—two hours," repeated the doctor.

"*Si, Señor,*" said the native, sadly.

He pulled a cheap silver watch from his own pocket and laid it in the doctor's hand. "Me bring," said he, struggling painfully with his scant English, "other watchy to-morrow." Then he departed down-heartedly with his capsules.

"A very ignorant race of people, sir," said the doctor, as he slipped the watch into his pocket. "He seems to have mistaken my directions for taking the physic for the fee. However, it is all right. He owes me an account, anyway. The chances are that he won't bring the other watch. You can't

333

depend on anything they promise you. About that drink, now? How did you come to Coralio, Mr. Smith? I was not aware that any boats except the *Karlsefin* had arrived for some days."

The two leaned against the deserted bar; and Madama set out a bottle without waiting for the doctor's order. There was no dust on it.

After they had drunk twice, Smith said:

"You say there were no passengers on the *Karlsefin*, Doc? Are you sure about that? It seems to me I heard somebody down on the beach say that there was one or two aboard."

"They were mistaken, sir. I myself went out and put all hands through a medical examination, as usual. The *Karlsefin* sails as soon as she gets her bananas loaded, which will be about daylight in the morning, and she got everything ready this afternoon. No, sir, there was no passenger list. Like that Three-Star? A French schooner landed two slooploads of it a month ago. If any customs duties on it went to the distinguished republic of Anchuria you may have my hat. If you won't have another, come out and let's sit in the cool a while. It isn't often we exiles get a chance to talk with some-body from the outside world."

The doctor brought out another chair to the side-walk for his new acquaintance. The two seated themselves.

"You are a man of the world," said Dr. Gregg; "a man of travel and experience. Your decision in a matter of ethics and, no doubt, on the point of equity, ability and professional probity should be of value. I would be glad if you will listen to the history of a case that I think stands unique in medical annals.

"About nine years ago, while I was engaged in the practice of medicine in my native city, I was called to treat a case of contusion of the skull. I made the diagnosis that a splinter of bone was pressing upon the brain, and that the surgical operation known as trepanning was required. However, as the patient was a gentleman of wealth and position, I called in for consultation Dr.——"

Smith rose from his chair, and laid a hand, soft with apology, upon the doctor's shirt sleeve.

"Say, Doc," he said, solemnly, "I want to hear that story. You've got me interested; and I don't want to miss the rest of it. I know it's a loola by the way it begins; and I want to tell it at the next meeting of the Barney O'Flynn Association, if you don't mind. But I've got one or two matters to attend to first. If I get 'em attended to in time I'll come right back and hear you spiel the rest before bedtime—is that right?"

"By all means," said the doctor, "get your business attended to, and then return. I shall wait up for you. You see, one of the most prominent physicians at the consultation diagnosed the trouble as a blood clot; another said it was an abscess, but I——"

"Don't tell me now, Doc. Don't spoil the story. Wait till I come back. I want to hear it as it runs off the reel—is that right?"

The mountains reached up their bulky shoulders to receive the level gallop of Apollo's homing steeds, the day died in the lagoons and in the shadowed banana groves and in the mangrove swamps, where the great blue crabs were beginning to crawl to land for the nightly ramble. And it died, at last, upon the highest peaks. Then the brief twilight, ephemeral as the flight of a moth, came and went; the Southern Cross peeped with its topmost eye above a row of palms, and the fire-flies heralded with their torches the approach of soft-footed night.

In the offing the *Karlsefin* swayed at anchor, her lights seeming to penetrate the water to countless fathoms with their shimmering, lanceolate reflections. The Caribs were busy loading her by means of the great lighters heaped full from the piles of fruit ranged upon the shore.

On the sandy beach, with his back against a coconut tree and the stubs of many cigars lying around him, Smith sat waiting, never relaxing his sharp gaze in the direction of the steamer.

The incongruous yachtsman had concentrated his interest upon the innocent fruiter. Twice had he been assured that no passengers had come to Coralio on board of her. And yet, with a persistence not to be attributed to an idling voyager, he had appealed the case to the higher court of his own eyesight. Surprisingly like some gay-coated lizard, he crouched at the foot of the coconut palm, and with the beady, shifting eyes of the selfsame reptile, sustained his espionage on the *Karlsefin.*

On the white sands a whiter gig belonging to the yacht was drawn up, guarded by one of the white-ducked crew. Not far away in a *pulperia* on the shore-following Calle Grande three other sailors swaggered with their cues around Coralio's solitary billiard-table. The boat lay there as if under orders to be ready for use at any moment. There was in the atmosphere a hint of expectation, of waiting for something to occur, which was foreign to the air of Coralio.

Like some passing bird of brilliant plumage, Smith alights on this palmy shore but to preen his wings for an instant and then to fly away upon silent pinions. When morning dawned there was no Smith, no waiting gig, no yacht in the offing. Smith left no intimation of his mission there, no footprints to show where he had followed the trail of his mystery on the sands of Coralio that night. He came; he spake his strange jargon of the asphalt and the cafés; he sat under the coconut tree, and vanished. The next morning Coralio, Smithless, ate its fried plantain and said: "The man of pictured clothing went himself away." With the *siesta* the incident passed, yawning, into history.

So, for a time, must Smith pass behind the scenes of the play. He comes no more to Coralio nor to Dr. Gregg, who sits in vain, wagging his redundant beard, waiting to enrich his derelict audience with his moving tale of trepanning and jealousy.

But prosperously to the lucidity of these loose pages, Smith shall flutter among them again. In the nick of time he shall come to tell us why he strewed so many anxious cigar

stumps around the coconut palm that night. This he must do;
for, when he sailed away before the dawn in his yacht
Rambler, he carried with him the answer to a riddle so big
and preposterous that few in Anchuria had ventured even to
propound it.

36

Caught

THE plans for the detention of the flying President
Miraflores and his companion at the coast line seemed
hardly likely to fail. Dr. Zavalla himself had gone to the port
of Alazan to establish a guard at that point. At Coralio the
Liberal patriot Varras could be depended upon to keep close
watch. Goodwin held himself responsible for the district
about Coralio.

The news of the president's flight had been disclosed to
no one in the coast towns save trusted members of the
ambitious political party that was desirous of succeeding to
power. The telegraph wire running from San Mateo to the
coast had been cut far up on the mountain trail by an emissary of Zavalla's. Long before this could be repaired and
word received along it from the capital the fugitives would
have reached the coast and the question of escape or capture
been solved.

Goodwin had stationed armed sentinels at frequent intervals along the shore for a mile in each direction from Coralio.
They were instructed to keep a vigilant lookout during the
night to prevent Miraflores from attempting to embark
stealthily by means of some boat or sloop found by chance
at the water's edge. A dozen patrols walked the streets of
Coralio unsuspected, ready to intercept the truant official
should he show himself there.

Goodwin was very well convinced that no precautions
had been overlooked. He strolled about the streets that bore
such high-sounding names and were but narrow, grass-
covered lanes, lending his own aid to the vigil that had been
entrusted to him by Bob Englehart.

The town had begun the tepid round of its nightly diversions. A few leisurely dandies, clad in white duck, with flowing neckties, and swinging slim bamboo canes, threaded the grassy by-ways toward the houses of their favoured *señoritas*. Those who wooed the art of music dragged tirelessly at whining concertinas, or fingered lugubrious guitars at doors and windows. An occasional soldier from the *cuartel*, with flapping straw hat, without coat or shoes, hurried by, balancing his long gun like a lance in one hand. From every density of the foliage the giant tree frogs sounded their loud and irritating clatter. Further out, where the by-ways perished at the brink of the jungle, the guttural cries of marauding baboons and the coughing of the alligators in the black estuaries fractured the vain silence of the wood.

By ten o'clock the streets were deserted. The oil lamps that had burned, a sickly yellow, at random corners, had been extinguished by some economical civil agent. Coralio lay sleeping calmly between toppling mountains and encroaching sea like a stolen babe in the arms of its abductors. Somewhere over in that tropical darkness—perhaps already threading the profundities of the alluvial lowlands—the high adventurer and his mate were moving toward land's end. The game of Fox-in-the-Morning should be soon coming to its close.

Goodwin, at his deliberate gait, passed the long, low *cuartel* where Coralio's contingent of Anchuria's military force slumbered, with its bare toes pointed heavenward. There was a law that no civilian might come so near the headquarters of that citadel of war after nine oc'clock, but Goodwin was always forgetting the minor statutes.

"*Quién vive?*" shrieked the sentinel, wrestling prodigiously with his lengthy musket.

"*Americano,*" growled Goodwin, without turning his head, and passed on, unhalted.

To the right he turned, and to the left up the street that ultimately reached the Plaza Nacional. When within the toss of a cigar stump from the intersecting Street of the Holy Sepulchre, he stopped suddenly in the pathway.

He saw the form of a tall man, clothed in black and carrying a large valise, hurry down the cross-street in the direction of the beach. And Goodwin's second glance made him aware of a woman at the man's elbow on the farther side, who seemed to urge forward, if not even to assist, her companion in their swift but silent progress. They were no Coralians, those two.

Goodwin followed at increased speed, but without any of the artful tactics that are so dear to the heart of the sleuth. The American was too broad to feel the instinct of the detective. He stood as an agent for the people of Anchuria, and but for political reasons he would have demanded then and there the money. It was the design of his party to secure the imperilled fund, to restore it to the treasury of the country, and to declare itself in power without bloodshed or resistance.

The couple halted at the door of the Hotel de los Estranjeros, and the man struck upon the wood with the impatience of one unused to his entry being stayed. Madama was long in response; but after a time her light showed, the door was opened, and the guests housed.

Goodwin stood in the quiet street, lighting another cigar. In two minutes a faint gleam began to show between the slates of the jalousies in the upper storey of the hotel. "They have engaged rooms," said Goodwin to himself. "So, then, their arrangements for sailing have yet to be made."

At that moment there came along one Estebán Delgado, a barber, an enemy to existing government, a jovial plotter against stagnation in any form. This barber was one of Coralio's saddest dogs, often remaining out of doors as late as eleven, post meridian. He was a partisan Liberal; and he greeted Goodwin with flatulent importance as a brother in the cause. But he had something important to tell.

"What think you, Don Frank!" he cried, in the universal tone of the conspirator. "I have to-night shaved *la baroa*—what you call the 'weeskers' of the *Presidente* himself, of this countree! Consider! He sent for me to come. In the poor *casita* of an old woman he awaited me—in a veree leetle house

340

in a dark place. *Carramba!— el Señor Presidente* to make himself thus secret and obscured! I think he desired not to be known—but, *carajo!* can you shave a man and not see his face? This gold piece he gave me, and said it was to be all quite still. I think, Don Frank, there is what you call a chip over the bug."

"Have you ever seen President Miraflores before?" asked Goodwin.

"But once," answered Estebán. "He is tall; and he had weeskers, verree black and sufficient."

"Was anyone else present when you shaved him?"

"An old Indian woman, *Señor,* that belonged with the *casa,* and one *señorita*—a ladee of so much beautee!—*ah, Dios!*"

"All right, Estebán," said Goodwin. "It's very lucky that you happened along with your tonsorial information. The new administration will be likely to remember you for this."

Then in a few words he made the barber acquainted with the crisis into which the affairs of the nation had culminated, and instructed him to remain outside, keeping watch upon the two sides of the hotel that looked upon the street, and observing whether anyone should attempt to leave the house by any door or window. Goodwin himself went to the door through which the guests had entered, opened it and stepped inside.

Madama had returned downstairs from her journey above to see after the comfort of her lodgers. Her candle stood upon the bar. She was about to take a thimbleful of rum as a solace for having her rest disturbed. She looked up without surprise or alarm as her third caller entered.

"Ah! It is the *Señor* Goodwin. Not often does he honour my poor house by his presence."

"I must come oftener," said Goodwin, with the Goodwin smile. "I hear that your cognac is the best between Belize to the north and Rio to the south. Set out the bottle, Madama, and let us have the proof in *un vasito* for each of us."

"My *aguardiente*," said Madama, with pride, "is the best. It grows, in beautiful bottles, in the dark places among the banana-trees. *Si, Señor*. Only at midnight can they be picked by sailor-men who bring them, before daylight comes, to your back door. Good *aguardiente* is a verree difficult fruit to handle, *Señor* Goodwin."

Smuggling, in Coralio, was much nearer than competition to being the life of trade. One spoke of it slyly, yet with a certain conceit, when it had been well accomplished.

"You have guests in the house to-night," said Goodwin, laying a silver dollar upon the counter.

"Why not?" said Madama, counting the change. "Two; but the smallest while finished to arrive. One *señor*, not quite old, and one *señorita*, of sufficient handsomeness. To their rooms they have ascended, not desiring the to-eat nor the to-drink. Two rooms—*Numero 9* and *Numero 10*."

"I was expecting that gentleman and that lady," said Goodwin. "I have important *negocios* that must be transacted. Will you allow me to see them?"

"Why not?" sighed Madama, placidly. "Why should not *Señor* Goodwin ascend and speak to his friends? *Está bueno*. Room *Numero* 9 and room *Numero* 10."

Goodwin loosened in his coat pocket the American revolver that he carried, and ascended the steep, dark stairway.

In the hallway above, the saffron light from a hanging lamp allowed him to select the gaudy numbers on the doors. He turned the knob of Number 9, entered and closed the door behind him.

If that was Isabel Guilbert seated by the table in that poorly furnished room, report had failed to do her charms justice. She rested her head upon one hand. Extreme fatigue was signified in every line of her figure; and upon her countenance a deep perplexity was written. Her eyes were grey-irised, and of that mould that seems to have belonged to the orbs of all the famous queens of hearts. Their whites were singularly clear and brilliant, concealed above the irises by heavy horizontal lids, and showing a snowy line below them. Such eyes denote great nobility, vigour, and, if you can conceive of it, a most generous selfishness. She looked up when the American entered, with an expression of surprised inquiry, but without alarm.

Goodwin took off his hat and seated himself, with his characteristic deliberate ease, upon a corner of the table. He held a lighted cigar between his fingers. He took this familiar course because he was sure that preliminaries would be wasted upon Miss Guilbert. He knew her history, and the small part that the conventions had played in it.

"Good evening," he said. "Now, madame, let us come to business at once. You will observe that I mention no names, but I know who is in the next room, and what he carries in that valise. That is the point which brings me here. I have come to dictate terms of surrender."

The lady neither moved nor replied, but steadily regarded the cigar in Goodwin's hand.

"We," continued the dictator, thoughtfully regarding the neat buckskin shoe on his gently-swinging foot—"I speak for a considerable majority of the people—demand the return of the stolen funds belonging to them. Our terms go very little further than that. They are very simple. As an accredited spokesman, I promise that our interference will cease if they are accepted. Give up the money, and you and your companion will be permitted to proceed wherever you will. In fact, assistance will be given you in the matter of securing a passage by any outgoing vessel you may choose. It is on my personal responsibility that I add congratulations to the gentleman in Number 10 upon his taste in feminine charms."

Returning his cigar to his mouth, Goodwin observed her, and saw that her eyes followed it and rested upon it with icy and significant concentration. Apparently she had not heard a word he had said. He understood, tossed the cigar out the window, and, with an amused laugh, slid from the table to his feet.

"That is better," said the lady. "It makes it possible for me

343

to listen to you. For a second lesson in good manners, you might now tell me by whom I am being insulted."

"I am sorry," said Goodwin, leaning one hand on the table, "that my time is too brief for devoting much of it to a course of etiquette. Come, now; I appeal to your good sense. You have shown yourself, in more than one instance, to be well aware of what is to your advantage. This is an occasion that demands the exercise of your undoubted intelligence. There is no mystery here. I am Frank Goodwin; and I have come for the money. I entered this room at a venture. Had I entered the other I would have had it before now. Do you want it in words? The gentleman in Number 10 has betrayed a great trust. He has robbed his people of a large sum, and it is I who will prevent their losing it. I do not say who that gentleman is; but if I should be forced to see him and he should prove to be a certain high official of the republic, it will be my duty to arrest him. The house is guarded. I am offering you liberal terms. It is not absolutely necessary that I confer personally with the gentleman in the next room. Bring me the valise containing the money, and we will call the affair ended."

The lady arose from her chair and stood for a moment, thinking deeply.

"Do you live here, Mr. Goodwin?" she asked, presently.

"Yes."

"What is your authority for this intrusion?"

"I am an instrument of the republic. I was advised by wire of the movements of the—gentleman in Number 10."

"May I ask you two or three questions? I believe you to be a man more apt to be truthful than—timid. What sort of a town is this—Coralio, I think they call it?"

"Not much of a town," said Goodwin, smiling. "A banana town, as they run. Grass huts, 'dobes, five or six two-storey houses, accommodations limited, population half-breed Spanish and Indian, Caribs and blackamoors. No sidewalks to speak of, no amusements. Rather unmoral. That's an offhand sketch, of course."

"Are there any inducements, say in a social or in a business way, for people to reside here?"

"Oh, yes," answered Goodwin, smiling broadly. "There are no afternoon teas, no hand-organs, no department stores —and there is no extradition treaty."

"He told me," went on the lady, speaking as if to herself, and with a slight frown, "that there were towns on this coast of beauty and importance; that there was a pleasing social order—especially an American colony of cultured residents."

"There is an American colony," said Goodwin, gazing at her in some wonder. "Some of the members are all right. Some are fugitives from justice from the States. I recall two exiled bank presidents, an army paymaster under a cloud, a couple of manslayers, and a widow—arsenic, I believe, was the suspicion in her case. I myself complete the colony, but, as yet, I have not distinguished myself by any particular crime."

"Do not lose hope," said the lady, dryly; "I see nothing in your actions to-night to guarantee you further obscurity. Some mistake has been made; I do not know just where. But *him* you shall not disturb to-night. The journey has fatigued him so that he has fallen asleep, I think, in his clothes. You talk of stolen money! I do not understand you. Some mistake has been made. I will convince you. Remain where you are and I will bring you the valise that you seem to covet so, and show it to you."

She moved toward the closed door that connected the two rooms, but stopped, and half turned and bestowed on Goodwin a grave, searching look that ended in a quizzical smile.

"You force my door," she said, "and you follow your ruffianly behaviour with the basest accusations; and yet"— she hesitated, as if to reconsider what she was about to say— "and yet—it is a puzzling thing—I am sure there has been some mistake."

She took a step toward the door, but Goodwin stayed her by a light touch upon her arm. I have said before that women turned to look at him in the streets. He was the viking sort of man, big, good-looking, and with an air of kindly truculence. She was dark and proud, glowing or pale as her mood moved her. I do not know if Eve were light or dark, but if such a woman had stood in the Garden I know that the apple would have been eaten. This woman was to be Goodwin's fate, and he did not know it; but he must have felt the first throes of destiny, for, as he faced her, the knowledge of what report named her turned bitter in his throat.

"If there has been any mistake," he said hotly, "it was yours. I do not blame the man who has lost his country, his honour, and is about to lose the poor consolation of his stolen riches, as much as I blame you, for, by heaven! I can very well see how he was brought to it. I can understand, and pity him. It is such women as you that strew this degraded coast with wretched exiles, that make men forget their trusts, that drag——"

The lady interrupted him with a weary gesture.

"There is no need to continue your insults," she said coldly. "I do not understand what you are saying, nor do I know what mad blunder you are making; but if the inspection of the contents of a gentleman's portmanteau will rid me of you, let us delay it no longer."

She passed quickly and noiselessly into the other room, and returned with the heavy leather valise, which she handed to the American with an air of patient contempt.

Goodwin set the valise quickly upon the table and began to unfasten the straps. The lady stood by, with an expression of infinite scorn and weariness upon her face.

The valise opened wide to a powerful, sidelong wrench. Goodwin dragged out two or three articles of clothing, exposing the bulk of its contents—package after package of tightly packed United States bank and treasury notes of large denomination. Reckoning from the high figures written upon the paper bands that bound them, the total must have come closely upon the hundred thousand mark.

346

Goodwin glanced swiftly at the woman, and saw, with surprise and a thrill of pleasure that he wondered at, that she had experienced an unmistakable shock. Her eyes grew wide, she gasped, and leaned heavily against the table. She had been ignorant, then, he inferred, that her companion had looted the government treasury. But why, he angrily asked himself should he be so well pleased to think this wandering and unscrupulous singer not so black as report had painted her?

A noise in the other room startled them both. The door swung open, and a tall, elderly, dark-complexioned man, recently shaven, hurried into the room.

All the pictures of President Miraflores represent him as the possessor of a luxuriant supply of dark and carefully tended whiskers; but the story of the barber, Estebán, had prepared Goodwin for the change.

The man stumbled in from the dark room, his eyes blinking at the lamplight, and heavy from sleep.

"What does this mean?" he demanded in excellent English, with a keen and perturbed look at the American—"robbery?"

"Very near it," answered Goodwin. "But I rather think I'm in time to prevent it. I represent the people to whom this money belongs, and I have come to convey it back to them." He thrust his hand into a pocket of his loose, linen coat.

The other man's hand went quickly behind him.

"Don't draw," called Goodwin sharply; "I've got you covered from my pocket."

The lady stepped forward, and laid one hand upon the shoulder of her hesitating companion. She pointed to the table. "Tell me the truth—the truth," she said, in a low voice. "Whose money is that?"

The man did not answer. He gave a deep, long-drawn sigh, leaned and kissed her on the forehead, stepped back into the other room and closed the door.

Goodwin foresaw his purpose, and jumped for the door,

but the report of the pistol echoed as his hand touched the knob. A heavy fall followed, and some one swept him aside and struggled into the room of the fallen man.

A desolation, thought Goodwin, greater than that derived from the loss of cavalier and gold must have been in the heart of the enchantress to have wrung from her, in that moment, the cry of one turning to the all-forgiving, all-comforting earthly consoler—to have made her call out from that bloody and dishonoured room—"Oh, mother, mother, mother!"

But there was an alarm outside. The barber, Estebán, at the sound of the shot, had raised his voice; and the shot itself had aroused half the town. A pattering of feet came up the street, and official orders rang out on the still air. Goodwin had a duty to perform. Circumstances had made him the custodian of his adopted country's treasure. Swiftly cramming the money into the valise, he closed it, leaned far out of the window and dropped it into a thick orange-tree in the little enclosure below.

*　　*　　*

They will tell you in Coralio, as they delight in telling the stranger, of the conclusion of that tragic fight. They will tell you how the upholders of the law came apace when the alarm was sounded—the *comandante* in red slippers and a jacket like a head waiter's, and girded sword, the soldiers with their interminable guns, followed by outnumbering officers struggling into their gold lace and epaulettes; the barefooted policemen (the only capables in the lot), and ruffled citizens of every hue and description.

They say that the countenance of the dead man was marred sadly by the effects of the shot; but he was identified as the fallen president by both Goodwin and the barber Estebán. One the next morning messages began to come over the mended telegraph wire; and the story of the flight from the capital was given out to the public. In San Mateo the revolutionary party had seized the sceptre of government without opposition, and the *vivas* of the mercurial populace quickly effaced the interest belonging to the unfortunate Miraflores.

They will relate to you how the new government sifted the towns and raked the roads to find the valise containing Anchuria's surplus capital, which the president was known to have carried with him, but all in vain. In Coralio *Señor* Goodwin himself led the searching party which combed that town as carefully as a woman combs her hair; but the money was not found.

So they buried the dead man, without honours, back of the town near the little bridge that spans the mangrove swamp; and for a *real* a boy will show you his grave. They say that the old woman, in whose hut the barber shaved the president, placed the wooden slab at his head, and burned the inscription upon it with a hot iron.

You will hear also that *Señor* Goodwin, like a tower of strength, shielded Doña Isabel Guilbert through those subsequent distressful days; and that his scruples as to her past career (if he had any) vanished; and her adventuresome waywardness (if she had any) left her, and they were wedded and were happy.

The American built a home on a little foothill near the town. It is a conglomerate structure of native woods that, exported, would be worth a fortune, and of brick, palm, glass, bamboo and adobe. There is a paradise of nature about it; and something of the same sort within. The natives speak of its interior with hands uplifted in admiration. There are floors polished like mirrors and covered with hand-woven Indian rugs of silk fibre, tall ornaments and pictures, musical instruments and papered walls—"figure-it-to-yourself!" they exclaim.

But they cannot tell you in Coralio (as you shall learn) what became of the money that Frank Goodwin dropped into the orange-tree. But that shall come later; for the palms are fluttering in the breeze, bidding us to sport and gaiety.

37

Cupid's Exile Number Two

THE United States of America, after looking over its stock of consular timber, selected Mr. John De Graffenreid Atwood, of Dalesburg, Alabama, for a successor to Willard Geddie, resigned.

Without prejudice to Mr. Atwood, it will have to be acknowledged that, in this instance, it was the man who sought the office. As with the self-banished Geddie, it was nothing less than the artful smiles of lovely woman that had driven Johnny Atwood to the desperate expedient of accepting office under a despised Federal Government so that he might go far, far away and never see again the false, fair face that had wrecked his young life. The consulship at Coralio seemed to offer a retreat sufficiently removed and romantic enough to inject the necessary drama into the pastoral scenes of Dalesburg life.

It was while playing the part of Cupid's exile that Johnny added his handiwork to the long list of casualties along the Spanish Main by his famous manipulation of the shoe market, and his unparalleled feat of elevating the most despised and useless weed in his own country from obscurity to be a valuable product in international commerce.

The trouble began, as trouble often begins instead of ending, with a romance. In Dalesburg there was a man named Elijah Hemstetter, who kept a general store. His family consisted of one daughter called Rosine, a name that atoned much for "Hemstetter". This young woman was possessed of plentiful attractions, so that the young men of the community were agitated in their bosoms. Among the more agitated was Johnny, the son of Judge Atwood, who lived in the big colonial mansion on the edge of Dalesburg.

It would seem that the desirable Rosine should have been pleased to return the affection of an Atwood, a name honoured all over the state long before and since the war. It does seem that she should have gladly consented to have been led into that stately but rather empty colonial mansion. But not so. There was a cloud on the horizon, a threatening, cumulous cloud, in the shape of a lively and shrewd young farmer in the neighbourhood who dared to enter the lists as a rival to the highborn Atwood.

One night Johnny propounded to Rosine a question that is considered of much importance by the young of the human species. The accessories were all there—moonlight, oleanders, magnolias, the mock-bird's song. Whether or no the shadow of Pinkney Dawson, the prosperous young farmer, came between them on that occasion is not known; but Rosine's answer was unfavourable. Mr. John De Graffenreid Atwood bowed till his hat touched the lawn grass, and went away with his head high, but with a sore wound in his pedigree and heart. A Hemstetter refuse an Atwood! Zounds!

Among other accidents of that year was a Democratic president. Judge Atwood was a warhorse of Democracy. Johnny persuaded him to set the wheels moving for some foreign appointment. He would go away—away. Perhaps in years to come Rosine would think how true, how faithful his love had been, and would drop a tear—maybe in the cream she would be skimming for Pink Dawson's breakfast.

The wheels of politics revolved; and Johnny was appointed consul to Coralio. Just before leaving he dropped in at Hemstetter's to say good-bye. There was a queer, pinkish look about Rosine's eyes; and had the two been alone, the United States might have had to cast about for another consul. But Pink Dawson was there, of course, talking about his 400-acre orchard, and the three-mile alfalfa tract, and the 200-acre pasture. So Johnny shook hands with Rosine as coolly as if he were only going to run up to Montgomery for a couple of days. They had the royal manner when they chose, those Atwoods.

"If you happen to strike anything in the way of a good investment down there, Johnny," said Pink Dawson, "Just let me know, will you? I reckon I could lay my hands on a few extra thousands 'most any time for a profitable deal."

"Certainly, Pink," said Johnny pleasantly. "If I strike anything of the sort I'll let you in with pleasure."

So Johnny went down to Mobile and took a fruit steamer for the coast of Anchuria.

When the new consul arrived in Coralio the strangeness of the scenes diverted him much. He was only twenty-two; and the grief of youth is not worn like a garment as it is by older men. It has its seasons when it reigns; and then it is unseated for a time by the assertion of the keen senses.

Billy Keogh and Johnny seemed to conceive a mutual friendship at once. Keogh took the new consul about town and presented him to the handful of Americans and the smaller number of French and Germans who made up the "foreign" contingent. And then, of course, he had to be more formally introduced to the native officials, and have his credentials transmitted through an interpreter.

There was something about the young Southerner that the sophisticated Keogh liked. His manner was simple almost to boyishness; but he possessed the cool carelessness of a man of far greater age and experience. Neither uniforms nor titles, red tape nor foreign languages, mountains nor sea weighed upon his spirits. He was heir to all the ages, an Atwood, of Dalesburg; and you might know every thought conceived in his bosom.

Geddie came down to the consulate to explain the duties and workings of the office. He and Keogh tried to interest the new consul in their description of the work that his government expected him to perform.

"It's all right," said Johnny from the hammock that he had set up as the official reclining place. "If anything turns up that has to be done I'll let you fellows do it. You can't expect a Democrat to work during his first term of holding office."

"You might look over these headings," suggested Geddie, "of the different lines of exports you will have to keep account of. The fruit is classified; and there are the valuable woods, coffee, rubber——"

"That last account sounds all right," interrupted Mr. Atwood. "Sounds as if it could be stretched. I want to buy a new flag, a monkey, a guitar and a barrel of pineapples. Will that rubber account stretch over 'em?"

"That's merely statistics," said Geddie, smiling. "The expense account is what you want. It is supposed to have a slight elasticity. The 'stationery' items are sometimes carelessly audited by the State Department."

"We're wasting our time," said Keogh. "This man was born to hold office. He penetrates to the root of the art at one step of his eagle eye. The true genius of government shows its hands in every word of his speech."

"I didn't take this job with any intention of working," explained Johnny, lazily. "I wanted to go somewhere in the world where they didn't talk about farms. There are none here, are there?"

"Not the kind you are acquainted with," answered the exconsul. "There is no such art here as agriculture. There never was a plough or a reaper within the boundaries of Anchuria."

"This is the country for me," murmured the consul, and immediately he fell asleep.

The cheerful tintypist pursued his intimacy with Johnny in spite of open charges that he did so to obtain a pre-emption on a seat in that coveted spot, the rear gallery of the consulate. But whether his designs were selfish or purely friendly, Keogh achieved that desirable privilege. Few were the nights on which the two could not be found reposing there in the seabreeze, with their heels on the railing, and the cigars and brandy conveniently near.

One evening they sat thus, mainly silent, for their talk

had dwindled before the stilling influence of an unusual night.

There was a great, full moon; and the sea was mother-of-pearl. Almost every sound was hushed, for the air was but faintly stirring; and the town lay panting, waiting for the night to cool. Offshore lay the fruit steamer *Andador*, of the Vesuvius line, full-laden and scheduled to sail at six in the morning. There were no loiterers on the beach. So bright was the moonlight that the two men could see the small pebbles shining on the beach where the gentle surf wetted them.

Then down the coast, tacking close to shore, slowly swam a little sloop, white-winged like some snowy sea-fowl. Its course lay within twenty points of the wind's eye; so it veered in and out again in long, slow strokes like the movements of a graceful skater.

Again the tactics of its crew brought it close inshore, this time nearly opposite the consulate; and then there blew from the sloop clear and surprising notes as if from a horn of elfland. A fairy bugle it might have been, sweet and silvery and unexpected, playing with spirit the familiar air of "Home, Sweet Home".

It was a scene set for the land of the lotus. The authority of the sea and the tropics, the mystery that attends unknown sails, and the prestige of drifting music on moonlit waters gave it an anodynous charm. Johnny Atwood felt it, and thought of Dalesburg; but as soon as Keogh's mind had arrived at a theory concerning the peripatetic solo he sprang to the railing, and his ear-rending yawp fractured the silence of Coralio like a cannon shot.

"Mel-lin-ger a-hoy!"

The sloop was now on its outward tack; but from it came a clear, answering hail:

"Good-bye, Billy . . . go-ing home—bye!"

The *Andador* was the sloop's destination. No doubt some passenger with a sailing permit from some up-the-coast point had come down in this sloop to catch the regular fruit steamer on its return trip. Like a coquettish pigeon the little boat tacked on its eccentric way until at last its white sail was lost to sight against the larger bulk of the fruiter's side.

"That's old H. P. Mellinger," explained Keogh, dropping back into his chair. "He's going back to New York. He was private secretary of the late hot-foot president of this grocery and fruit stand that they call a country. His job's over now; and I guess old Mellinger is glad."

"Why does he disappear to music, like Zozo the magic queen?" asked Johnny. "Just to show 'em that he doesn't care?"

"That noise you heard is a phonograph," said Keogh. "I sold him that. Mellinger had a graft in this country that was the only thing of its kind in the world. The tooting machine saved it for him once, and he always carried it around with him afterward."

"Tell me about it," demanded Johnny, betraying interest.

"I'm no disseminator of narratives," said Keogh. "I can use language for purposes of speech; but when I attempt a discourse the words come out as they will, and they may make sense when they strike the atmosphere, or they may not."

"I want to hear about that graft," persisted Johnny. "You've got no right to refuse. I've told you all about every man, woman and hitching post in Dalesburg."

"You shall hear it," said Keogh. "I said my instincts of narrative were perplexed. Don't you believe it. It's an art I've acquired along with many others of the graces and sciences."

38

The Phonograph and the Graft

"WHAT was this graft?" asked Johnny, with the impatience of the great public to whom tales are told.

"'Tis contrary to art and philosophy to give you the information," said Keogh calmly. "The art of narrative consists in concealing from your audience everything it wants to know until after you expose your favourite opinions on topics foreign to the subject. A good story is like a bitter pill with the sugar coating inside of it. I will begin, if you please, with a horoscope located in the Cherokee Nation; and end with a moral tune on the phonograph.

"Me and Henry Horsecollar brought the first phonograph to this country. Henry was a quarter-breed, quarter-back Cherokee, educated East in the idioms of football, and West in contraband whisky, and a gentleman, the same as you and me. He was easy and romping in his ways; a man about six foot, with a kind of rubber-tyre movement. Yes, he was a little man about five foot five, or five foot eleven. He was what you would call a medium tall man of average smallness. Henry had quit college once, and the Muscogee jail three times—the last-named institution on account of introducing and selling whisky in the territories. Henry Horsecollar never let any cigar stores come up and stand behind him. He didn't belong to that tribe of Indians.

"Henry and me met at Texarkana, and figured out this phonograph scheme. He had $360 which came to him out of a land allotment in the reservation. I had run down from Little Rock on account of a distressful scene I had witnessed on the street there. A man stood on a box and passed around some gold watches, screw case, stem-winders, Elgin move-

356

ment, very elegant. Twenty bucks they cost you over the counter. At three dolllars the crowd fought for the tickers. The man happened to find a valise full of them handy, and he passed them out like putting hot biscuits on a plate. The backs were hard to unscrew, but the crowd put its ear to the case, and they ticked mollifying and agreeable. Three of these watches were genuine tickers; the rest were only kickers. Hey? Why, empty cases with one of them horny black bugs kick off minutes and seconds industrious and beautiful. So, this man I was speaking of cleaned up $288; and then he went away, because he knew that when it came time to wind watches in Little Rock an entomologist would be needed, and he wasn't one.

"So, as I say, Henry had $360, and I had $288. The idea of introducing the phonograph to South America was Henry's; but I took to it freely, being fond of machinery of all kinds.

"'The Latin races,' says Henry, explaining easy in the idioms he learned at college, 'are peculiarly adapted to be victims of the phonograph. They have the artistic temperament. They yearn for music and colour and gaiety. They give wampum to the hand-organ man and the four-legged chicken in the tent when they're months behind with the grocery and the bread-fruit tree.'

"'Then,' says I, 'we'll export canned music to the Latins; but I'm mindful of Mr. Julius Cæsar's account of 'em where he says: "*Omnia Gallia in tres partes divisa est*"; which is the same as to say, "We will need all of our gall in devising means to tree them parties."'

"I hated to make a show of education; but I was disinclined to be overdone in syntax by a mere Indian, a member of a race to which we owe nothing except the land on which the United States is situated.

"We bought a fine phonograph in Texarkana—one of the best make—and half a trunkful of records. We packed up, and took the T. and P. for New Orleans. From that celebrated centre of molasses and disfranchised coon songs we took a steamer for South America.

"We landed at Solitas, forty miles up the coast from here. 'Twas a palatable enough place to look at. The houses were clean and white; and to look at 'em stuck around among the scenery they reminded you of hard-boiled eggs served with lettuce. There was a block of skyscraper mountains in the suburbs; and they kept pretty quiet, like they had crept up there and were watching the town. And the sea was remarking 'Sh-sh-sh' on the beach; and now and then a ripe coconut would drop kerblip in the sand; and that was all there was doing. Yes, I judge that town was considerably on the quiet. I judge that after Gabriel quits blowing his horn, and the car starts, with Philadelphia swinging to the last strap, and Pine Gully, Arkansas, hanging on to the rear step, this town of Solitas will wake up and ask if anybody spoke.

"The captain went ashore with us, and offered to conduct what he seemed to like to call the obsequies. He introduced Henry and me to the United States consul, and a roan man, the head of the Department of Mercenary and Licentious Dispositions, the way it read upon his sign.

"'I touch here again a week from to-day,' says the captain.

"'By that time,' we told him, 'we'll be amassing wealth in the interior towns with our galvanized prima donna and correct imitations of Sousa's band excavating a march from a tin mine.'

"'Ye'll not,' says the captain. 'Ye'll be hypnotised. Any gentleman in the audience who kindly steps upon the stage and looks this country in the eye will be converted to the hypothesis that he's but a fly in the Elgin creamery. Ye'll be standing knee deep in the surf waiting for me, and your machine for making Hamburger steak out of the hitherto respected art of music will be playing "There's no place like home".'

"Henry skinned a twenty off his roll, and received from the Bureau of Mercenary Dispositions a paper bearing a red seal and a dialect story, and no change.

"Then we got the consul full of red wine, and struck him for a horoscope. He was a thin, youngish kind of man, I should say past fifty, sort of French-Irish in his affections, and puffed up with disconsolation. Yes, he was a flattened kind of a man, in whom drink lay stagnant, inclined to corpulence and misery. Yes, I think he was a kind of Dutchman, being very sad and genial in his ways.

"'The marvellous invention,' he says, 'entitled the phonograph, has never invaded these shores. The people have never heard it. They would not believe it if they should. Simple-hearted children of nature, progress has never condemned them to accept the work of a can-opener as an overture, and ragtime might incite them to a bloody revolution. But you can try the experiment. The best chance you have is that the populace may not wake up when you play. There's two ways,' says the consul, 'they take it. They may become inebriated with attention, like an Atlanta colonel listening to "Marching Through Georgia", or they will get excited and transpose the key of the music with an axe and yourselves into a dungeon. In the latter case,' says the consul, 'I'll do my duty by cabling to the State Department, and I'll wrap the Stars and Stripes around you when you come to be shot, and threaten them with the vengeance of the greatest gold export and financial reserve nation on earth. The flag is full of bullet holes now,' says the consul, 'made in that way. Twice before,' says the consul, 'I have cabled our government for a couple of gunboats to protect American citizens. The first time the Department sent me a pair of gum boots. The other time was when a man named Pease was going to be executed here. They referred that appeal to the Secretary of Agriculture. Let us now disturb the *señor* behind the bar for a subsequence of the red wine.'

"Thus soliloquized the consul of Solitas to me and Henry Horsecollar.

"But, notwithstanding, we hired a room that afternoon in the Calle de los Angeles, the main street that runs along the shore, and put our trunks there. 'Twas a good-sized room, dark and cheerful, but small. 'Twas on a various street, diversified by houses and conservatory plants. The peasantry of the city passed to and fro on the fine pasturage between the sidewalks. 'Twas, for the world, like an opera chorus when the Royal Kafoozlum is about to enter.

"We were rubbing the dust off the machine and getting fixed to start business the next day, when a big, fine-looking white man in white clothes stopped at the door and looked in. We extended the invitations, and he walked inside and sized us up. He was chewing a long cigar, and wrinkling his eyes, meditative, like a girl trying to decide which dress to wear at the party.

"'New York?' he says to me finally.

"'Originally, and from time to time,' I says. 'Hasn't it rubbed off yet?'

"'It's simple,' says he, 'when you know how. It's the fit of the vest. They don't cut vests right anywhere else. Coats, maybe, but not vests.'

"The white man looks at Henry Horsecollar and hesitates.

"'Injun,' says Henry; 'tame Injun.'

"'Mellinger,' says the man—'Homer P. Mellinger. Boys, you're confiscated. You're babes in the wood without a chaperon or referee, and it's my duty to start you going. I'll knock out the props and launch you proper in the pellucid waters of this tropical mud puddle. You'll have to be christened, and if you'll come with me I'll break a bottle of wine across your bows, according to Hoyle.'

"Well, for two days Homer P. Mellinger did the honours. That man cut ice in Anchuria. He was It. He was the Royal Kafoozlum. If me and Henry was babes in the wood, he was a Robin Redbreast from the topmost bough. Him and me and Henry Horsecollar locked arms, and toted that phonograph around, and had wassail and diversions. Everywhere we found doors open we went inside and set the machine going, and Mellinger called upon the people to observe the artful music and his two lifelong friends, the *Señors* Americanos. The opera chorus was agitated with esteem, and fol-

lowed us from house to house. There was a different kind of
drink to be had with every tune. The natives had acquire-
ments of a pleasant thing in the way of a drink that gums
itself to the recollection. They chop off the end of a green
coconut, and pour in on the juice of it French brandy and
other adjuvants. We had them and other things.

"Mine and Henry's money was counterfeit. Everything
was on Homer P. Mellinger. That man could find rolls of
bills concealed in places on his person where Hermann the
Wizard couldn't have conjured out a rabbit or an omelette.
He could have founded universities, and made orchid collections, and then had enough left to purchase the coloured
vote of his country. Henry and me wondered what his graft
was. One evening he told us.

" 'Boys,' said he, 'I've deceived you. You think I'm a
painted butterfly; but in fact I'm the hardest worked man in
this country. Ten years ago I landed on its shores; and two
years ago on the point of its jaw. Yes, I guess I can get the
decision over this ginger cake commonwealth at the end of
any round I choose. I'll confide in you because you are my
countrymen and guests, even if you have assaulted my
adopted shores with the worst system of noises ever set to
music.

" 'My job is private secretary to the president of this
republic; and my duties are running it. I'm not headlined in
the bills, but I'm the mustard in the salad dressing just the
same. There isn't a law goes before Congress, there isn't a
concession granted, there isn't an import duty levied but
what H. P. Mellinger he cooks and seasons it. In the front
office I fill the president's inkstand and search visiting statesmen for dirks and dynamite; but in the back room I dictate
the policy of the government. You'd never guess in the world
how I got my pull. It's the only graft of its kind on earth.
I'll put you wise. You remember the old top-liner in the
copy-book—"Honesty is the Best Policy"? That's it. I'm
working honesty for a graft. I'm the only honest man in the
republic. The government knows it; the people know it; the

boodlers know it; the foreign investors know it. I make the government keep its faith. If a man is promised a job he gets it. If outside capital buys a concession it gets the goods. I run a monopoly of square dealing here. There's no competition. If Colonel Diogenes were to flash his lantern in this precinct he'd have my address inside of two minutes. There isn't big money in it, but it's a sure thing, and lets a man sleep of nights.'

"Thus Homer P. Mellinger made oration to me and Henry Horsecollar. And, later, he divested himself of this remark:

"'Boys, I'm to hold a *soirée* this evening with a gang of leading citizens, and I want your assistance. You bring the musical corn sheller and give the affair the outside appearance of a function. There's important business on hand, but it mustn't show. I can talk to you people. I've been pained for years on account of not having anybody to blow off and brag to. I get homesick sometimes, and I'd swap the entire perquisites of office for just one hour to have a stein and a caviare sandwich somewhere on Thirty-fourth Street, and stand and watch the street cars go by, and smell the peanut roaster at old Giuseppe's fruit stand.'

"'Yes,' said I, 'there's fine caviare at Billy Renfrow's café, corner of Thirty-fourth and——'

"'God knows it,' interrupts Mellinger, 'and if you'd told me you knew Billy Renfrow I'd have invented tons of ways of making you happy. Billy was my side-kicker in New York. There is a man who never knew what crooked was. Here I am working Honesty for a graft, but that man loses money on it. *Carrambos!* I get sick at times of this country. Everything's rotten. From the executive down to the coffee pickers. they're plotting to down each other and skin their friends. If a mule driver takes off his hat to an official, that man figures it out that he's a popular idol, and sets his pegs to stir up a revolution and upset the administration. It's one of my little chores as private secretary to smell out these revolutions and affix the kibosh before they break out, and scratch the paint off the government property. That's why I'm down here now in this mildewed coast town. The governor of the district and his crew are plotting to uprise. I've got every one of their names, and they're invited to listen to the phonograph to-night, compliments of H.P.M. That's the way I'll get them in a bunch, and things are on the programme to happen to them.'

"We three were sitting at table in the cantina of the Purified Saints. Mellinger poured out wine, and was looking some worried; I was thinking.

"'They're a sharp crowd,' he says, kind of fretful. 'They're capitalized by a foreign syndicate after rubber, and they're loaded to the muzzle for bribing. I'm sick,' goes on Mellinger, 'of comic opera. I want to smell East River and wear suspenders again. At times I feel like throwing up my job, but I'm d——n fool enough to be sort of proud of it. "There's Mellinger," they say here. "*Por Dios*! you can't touch him with a million." I'd like to take that record back and show it to Billy Renfrow some day; and that tightens my grip whenever I see a fat thing that I could corral just by winking one eye—and losing my graft. By ——, they can't monkey with me. They know it. What money I get I make honest and spend it. Some day I'll make a pile and go back and eat caviare with Billy. To-night I'll show you how to handle a bunch of corruptionists. I'll show them what Mellinger, private secretary, means when you spell it with the cotton and tissue paper off.'

"Mellinger appears shaky and breaks his glass against the neck of the bottle.

"I says to myself. 'White man, if I'm not mistaken there's been a bait laid out where the tail of your eye could see it.'

"That night, according to arrangements, me and Henry took the phonograph to a room in a 'dobe house in a dirty side street, where the grass was knee high. 'Twas a long room, lit with smoky oil lamps. There was plenty of chairs, and a table at the back end. We set the phonograph on the table.

Mellinger was there, walking up and down, disturbed in his predicaments. He chewed cigars and spat 'em out, and he bit the thumb nail of his left hand.

"By and by the invitations to the musicale came sliding in by pairs and threes and spade flushes. Their colour was of a diversity, running from a three-days' smoked meerschaum to a patent-leather polish. They were as polite as wax, being devastated with enjoyments to give *Señor* Mellinger the good evenings. I understood their Spanish talk—I ran a pumping engine two years in a Mexican silver mine, and had it pat—but I never let on.

"Maybe fifty of 'em had come, and was seated, when in slid the king bee, the governor of the district. Mellinger met him at the door, and escorted him to the grand stand. When I saw that Latin man I knew that Mellinger, private secretary, had all the dances on his card taken. That was a big, squashy man, the colour of a rubber overshoe, and he had an eye like a head waiter's.

"Mellinger explained, fluent in the Castilian idioms, that his soul was disconcerted with joy at introducing to his respected friends America's greatest invention, the wonder of the age. Henry got the cue and run on an elegant brass-band record and the festivities became initiated. The governor man had a bit of English under his hat, and when the music was choked off he says:

"'Ver-r-ree fine. *Gr-r-r-racias*, the American gentleemen, the so esplendeed moosic as to playee.'

"The table was a long one, and Henry and me sat at the end of it next the wall. The governor sat at the other end. Homer P. Mellinger stood at the side of it. I was just wondering how Mellinger was going to handle his crowd, when the home talent suddenly opened the services.

"That governor man was suitable for uprisings and policies. I judge he was a ready kind of man, who took his own time. Yes, he was full of attention and immediateness. He leaned his hands on the table and imposed his face toward the secretary man.

"'Do the American *señors* understand Spanish?' he asks in his native accents.

"'They do not,' says Mellinger.

"'Then listen,' goes on the Latin man, prompt. 'The musics are of sufficient prettiness, but not of necessity. Let us speak of business. I well know why we are here, since I observe my compratriots. You had a whisper yesterday, *Señor* Mellinger, of our proposals. To-night we will speak out. We know that you stand in the president's favour, and we know your influence. The government will be changed. We know the worth of your services. We esteem your friendship and aid so much that——' Mellinger raises his hand, but the governor man bottles him up. 'Do not speak until I have done.'

"The governor man then draws a package wrapped in paper from his pocket, and lays it on the table by Mellinger's hand.

"'In that you will find fifty thousand dollars in money of your country. You can do nothing against us, but you can be worth that for us. Go back to the capital and obey our instructions. Take that money now. We trust you. You will find with it a paper giving in detail the work you will be expected to do for us. Do not have the unwiseness to refuse.'

"The governor man paused, with his eyes fixed on Mellinger, full of expressions and observances. I looked at Mellinger, and was glad Billy Renfrow couldn't see him then. The sweat was popping out on his forehead, and he stood dumb, tapping the little package with the ends of his fingers. The colorado-maduro gang was after his graft. He had only to change his politics, and stuff five fingers in his inside pocket.

"Henry whispers to me and wants the pause in the programme interpreted. I whisper back: 'H. P. is up against a bribe, senator's size, and the coons have got him going.' I saw Mellinger's hand moving closer to the package. 'He's weakening,' I whispered to Henry. 'We'll remind him,' says

Henry, 'of the peanut-roaster on Thirty-fourth Street, New York.'

"Henry stooped down and got a record from the basketful we'd brought, slid it in the phonograph, and started her off. It was a cornet solo, very neat and beautiful, and the name of it was 'Home, Sweet Home'. Not one of them fifty odd men in the room moved while it was playing, and the governor man kept his eyes steady on Mellinger. I saw Mellinger's head go up little by little, and his hand came creeping away from the package. Not until the last note sounded did anybody stir. And then Homer P. Mellinger takes up the bundle of boodle and slams it in the governor man's face.

"'That's my answer,' says Mellinger, private secretary, 'and there'll be another in the morning. I have proofs of conspiracy against every man of you. The show is over, gentlemen.'

"'There's one more act,' puts in the governor man. 'You are a servant, I believe, employed by the president to copy letters and answer raps at the door. I am governor here. *Señors*, I call upon you in the name of the cause to seize this man.'

"That brindled gang of conspirators shoved back their chairs and advanced in force. I could see where Mellinger had made a mistake in massing his enemy so as to make a grand-stand play. I think he made another one, too; but we can pass that, Mellinger's idea of a graft and mine being different, according to estimations and points of view.

"There was only one window and door in that room, and they were in the front end. Here was fifty odd Latin men coming in a bunch to obstruct the legislation of Mellinger. You may say there were three of us, for me and Henry, simultaneous, declared New York City and the Cherokee Nation in sympathy with the weaker party.

"Then it was that Henry Horsecollar rose to a point of disorder and intervened, showing, admirable, the advantages of education as applied to the American Indian's natural intellect and native refinement. He stood up and smoothed

366

back his hair on each side with his hands as you have seen little girls do when they play.

"'Get behind me, both of you,' says Henry.

"'What's it to be, chief?' I asked.

"'I'm going to buck centre,' says Henry, in his football idioms. 'There isn't a tackle in the lot of them. Follow me close, and rush the game.'

"Then that cultured Red Man exhaled an arrangement of sounds with his mouth that made the Latin aggregation pause, with thoughtfulness and hesitations. The matter of his proclamation seemed to be a co-operation of the Carlisle war-whoop with the Cherokee college yell. He went at the chocolate team like a bean out of a little boy's nigger shooter. His right elbow laid out the governor man on the grid-iron, and he made a lane the length of the crowd so wide that a woman could have carried a step-ladder through it without striking against anything. All Mellinger and me had to do was to follow.

"It took us just three minutes to get out of that street around to military headquarters, where Mellinger had things his own way. A colonel and a battalion of bare-toed infantry turned out and went back to the scene of the musicale with us, but the conspirator gang was gone. But we recaptured the phonograph with honours of war, and marched back to the *cuartel* with it playing 'All Coons Look Alike to Me'.

"The next day Mellinger takes me and Henry to one side, and begins to shed tens and twenties.

"'I want to buy that phonograph,' says he. 'I liked that last tune it played at the *soirée*.'

"'This is more money than the machine is worth,' says I.

"''Tis government expense money,' says Mellinger. 'The government pays for it, and it's getting the tune-grinder cheap.'

"Me and Henry knew that pretty well. We knew that it had saved Homer P. Mellinger's graft when he was on the point of losing it; but we never let him know we knew it.

"'Now you boys better slide off further down the coast for

a while,' says Mellinger, 'till I get the screws put on these fellows here. If you don't they'll give you trouble. And if you ever happen to see Billy Renfrow again before I do, tell him I'm coming back to New York as soon as I can make a stake —honest.'

"Me and Henry laid low until the day the steamer came back. When we saw the captain's boat on the beach we went down and stood in the edge of the water. The captain grinned when he saw us.

"'I told you you'd be waiting,' he says. 'Where's the Hamburger machine?'

"'It stays behind,' I says, 'to play "Home, Sweet Home".'

"'I told you so,' says the captain again. 'Climb in the boat.'

"And that," said Keogh, "is the way me and Henry Horsecollar introduced the phonograph into this country. Henry went back to the States, but I've been rummaging around in the tropics ever since. They say Mellinger never travelled a mile after that without his phonograph. I guess it kept him reminded about his graft whenever he saw the siren voice of the boodler tip him the wink with a bribe in its hand."

"I suppose he's taking it home with him as a souvenir," remarked the consul.

"Not as a souvenir," said Keogh. "He'll need two of 'em in New York, running day and night."

39

Money Maze

THE new administration of Anchuria entered upon its
duties and privileges with enthusiasm. Its first act was
to send an agent to Coralio with imperative orders to recover,
if possible, the sum of money ravished from the treasury by the
ill-fated Miraflores.

Colonel Emilio Falcon, the private secretary of Losada,
the new president, was dispatched from the capital upon this
important mission.

The position of private secretary to a tropical president is
a responsible one. He must be a diplomat, a spy, a ruler of
men, a bodyguard to his chief, and a smeller-out of plots and
nascent revolutions. Often he is the power behind the throne,
the dictator of policy; and a president chooses him with a
dozen times the care with which he selects a matrimonial
mate.

Colonel Falcon, a handsome and urbane gentleman of
Castilian courtesy and debonair manners, came to Coralio
with the task before him of striking upon the cold trail of the
lost money. There he conferred with the military authorities,
who had received instructions to co-operate with him in the
search.

Colonel Falcon established his headquarters in one of the
rooms of the Casa Morena. Here for a week he held informal
sittings—much as if he were a kind of unified grand jury—and
summoned before him all those whose testimony might
illumine the financial tragedy that had accompanied the less
momentous one of the late president's death.

Two or three who were thus examined, among whom was

369

the barber Estebán, declared that they had identified the body of the president before its burial.

"Of a truth," testified Estebán before the mighty secretary, "it was he, the president. Consider!—how could I shave a man and not see his face? He sent for me to shave him in a small house. He had a beard very black and thick. Had I ever seen the president before? Why not? I saw him once ride forth in a carriage from the *vapor* in Solitas. When I shaved him he gave me a gold piece, and said there was to be no talk. But I am a Liberal—I am devoted to my country—and I spake of these things to *Señor* Goodwin."

"It is known," said Colonel Falcon, smoothly, "that the late President took with him an American leather valise, containing a large amount of money. Did you see that?"

"*De veras*—no," Estebán answered. "The light in the little house was but a small lamp by which I could scarcely see to shave the President. Such a thing there may have been, but I did not see it. No. Also in the room was a young lady—a *señorita* of much beauty—that I could see even in so small a light. But the money, *señor*, or the thing in which it was carried —that I did not see."

The *comandante* and other officers gave testimony that they had been awakened and alarmed by the noise of a pistol-shot in the Hotel de los Estranjeros. Hurrying thither to protect the peace and dignity of the republic, they found a man lying dead, with a pistol clutched in his hand. Beside him was a young woman, weeping sorely. *Señor* Goodwin was also in the room when they entered it. But of the valise of money they saw nothing.

Madame Timotea Ortiz, the proprietress of the hotel in which the game of Fox-in-the-Morning had been played out, told of the coming of the two guests to her house.

"To my house they came," said she—"one *señor*, not quite old, and one *señorita* of sufficient handsomeness. They desired not to eat or to drink—not even of my *aguardiente*, which is the best. To their rooms they ascended—*Numero*

Nueve and *Numero Diez.* Later came *Señor* Goodwin, who ascended to speak with them. Then I heard a great noise like that of a *canon*, and they said that the *pobre Presidente* had shot himself. *Està bueno.* I saw nothing of money or of the thing you call veliz that you say he carried it in."

Colonel Falcon soon came to the reasonable conclusion that if anyone in Coralio could furnish a clue to the vanished money, Frank Goodwin must be the man. But the wise secretary pursued a different course in seeking information from the American. Goodwin was a powerful friend to the new administration, and one who was not to be carelessly dealt with in respect to either his honesty or his courage. Even the private secretary of His Excellency hesitated to have this rubber prince and mahogany baron haled before him as a common citizen of Anchuria. So he sent Goodwin a flowery epistle, each word-petal dripping with honey, requesting the favour of an interview. Goodwin replied with an invitation to dinner at his own house.

Before the hour named the American walked over to the Casa Morena, and greeted his guest frankly and friendly. Then the two strolled in the cool of the afternoon, to Goodwin's home in the environs.

The American left Colonel Falcon in a big, cool, shadowed room with a floor of inlaid and polished woods that any millionaire in the States would have envied, excusing himself for a few minutes. He crossed a *patio*, shaded with deftly arranged awnings and plants, and entered a long room looking upon the sea in the opposite wing of the house. The broad jalousies were opened wide, and the ocean breeze flowed in through the room, an invisible current of coolness and health. Goodwin's wife sat near one of the windows, making a water-colour sketch of the afternoon seascape.

Here was a woman who looked to be happy. And more— she looked to be content. Had a poet been inspired to pen just similes, concerning her favour, he would have likened her full, clear eyes, with their white-encircled, grey irises, to moonflowers. With none of the goddesses whose traditional charms have become coldly classic would the discerning rhymester have compared her. She was purely Paradisaic, not Olympian. If you can imagine Eve, after the eviction, beguiling the flaming warriors and serenely re-entering the Garden, you will have her. Just so human, and still so harmonious with Eden seemed Mrs. Goodwin.

When her husband entered she looked up, and her lips curved and parted; her eyelids fluttered twice or thrice—a movement remindful (Poesy forgive us!) of the tail-wagging of a faithful dog—and a little ripple went through her like the commotion set up in a weeping willow by a puff of wind. Thus she ever acknowledged his coming, were it twenty times a day. If they who sometimes sat over their wine in Coralio, reshaping old, diverting stories of the madcap career of Isabel Guilbert, could have seen the wife of Frank Goodwin that afternoon in the estimable aura of her happy wifehood, they might have disbelieved, or have agreed to forget, those graphic annals of the life of the one for whom their president gave up his country and his honour.

"I have brought a guest to dinner," said Goodwin. "One Colonel Falcon, from San Mateo. He is come on government business. I do not think you will care to see him, so I prescribe for you one of those convenient and indisputable feminine headaches."

"He has come to inquire about the lost money, has he not?" asked Mrs. Goodwin, going on with her sketch.

"A good guess!" acknowledged Goodwin. "He has been holding an inquisition among the natives for three days. I am next on his list of witnesses, but as he feels shy about dragging one of Uncle Sam's subjects before him, he consents to give it the outward appearance of a social function. He will apply the torture over my own wine and provender."

"Has he found anyone who saw the valise of money?"

"Not a soul. Even Madama Ortiz, whose eyes are so sharp for the sight of a revenue official, does not remember that there was any baggage."

Mrs. Goodwin laid down her brush and sighed.

"I am so sorry, Frank," she said, "that they are giving you so much trouble about the money. But we can't let them know about it, can we?"

"Not without doing our intelligence a great injustice," said Goodwin, with a smile and a shrug that he had picked up from the natives. "*Americano* though I am, they would have me in the *calaboza* in half an hour if they knew we had appropriated that valise. No; we must appear as ignorant about the money as the other ignoramuses in Coralio."

"Do you think that this man they have sent suspects you?" she asked, with a little pucker of her brows.

"He'd better not," said the American, carelessly. "It's lucky that no one caught a sight of the valise except myself. As I was in the rooms when the shot was fired, it is not surprising that they should want to investigate my part in the affair rather closely. But there's no cause for alarm. This colonel is down on the list of events for a good dinner, with a dessert of American 'bluff' that will end the matter, I think."

Mrs. Goodwin rose and walked to the window; Goodwin followed and stood by her side. She leaned to him, and rested in the protection of his strength, as she had always rested since that dark night on which he had first made himself her tower of refuge. Thus they stood for a little while.

Straight through the lavish growth of tropical branch and leaf and vine that confronted them had been cunningly trimmed a vista, that ended at the cleared environs of Coralio, on the banks of the mangrove swamp. At the other end of the aerial tunnel they could see the grave and wooden headpiece that bore the name of the unhappy President Miraflores. From this window when the rains forbade the open, and from the green and shady slopes of Goodwin's fruitful lands when the skies were smiling, his wife was wont to look upon that grave with a gentle sadness that was now scarcely a mar to her happiness.

"I loved him so, Frank!" she said, "even after that terrible flight and its awful ending. And you have been so good to me, and have made me so happy. It has all grown into such a strange puzzle. If they were to find out that we got the money, do you think they would force you to make the amount good to the government?"

"They would undoubtedly try," answered Goodwin. "You are right about its being a puzzle. And it must remain a puzzle to Falcon and all his countrymen until it solves itself. You and I, who know more than anyone else, only know half of the solution. We must not let even a hint about this money get abroad. Let them come to the theory that the president concealed it in the mountains during his journey, or that he found means to ship it out of the country before he reached Coralio. I don't think that Falcon suspects me. He is making a close investigation, according to his orders, but he will find out nothing."

Thus they spake together. Had anyone overheard or overseen them as they discussed the lost funds of Anchuria there would have been a second puzzle presented. For upon the faces and in the bearing of each of them was visible (if countenances are to be believed) Saxon honesty and pride and honourable thoughts. In Goodwin's steady eye and firm lineaments, moulded into material shape by the inward spirit of kindness and generosity and courage, there was nothing reconcilable with his words.

As for his wife, physiognomy championed her even in the face of their accusive talk. Nobility was in her guise; purity was in her glance. The devotion that she manifested had not even the appearance of that feeling that now and then inspires a woman to share the guilt of her partner out of the pathetic greatness of her love. No, there was a discrepancy here between what the eye would have seen and the ear have heard.

Dinner was served to Goodwin and his guest in the *patio*, under cool foliage and flowers. The American begged the illustrious secretary to excuse the absence of Mrs. Goodwin, who was suffering, he said, from a headache brought on by a slight *calentura*.

After the meal they lingered, according to the custom, over their coffee and cigars. Colonel Falcon, with true Castilian delicacy, waited for his host to open the question that they had met to discuss. He had not long to wait. As soon as the cigars were lighted, the American cleared the way by inquiring whether the secretary's investigations in the town had furnished him with any clue to the lost funds.

"I have found no one yet," admitted Colonel Falcon, "who even had sight of the valise or the money. Yet I have persisted. It has been proven in the capital that President Miraflores set out from San Mateo with one hundred thousand dollars belonging to the government, accompanied by *Señorita* Isabel Guilbert, the opera singer. The government, officially and personally, is loath to believe," concluded Colonel Falcon, with a smile, "that our late President's tastes would have permitted him to abandon on the route, as excess baggage, either of the desirable articles with which his flight was burdened."

"I suppose you would like to hear what I have to say about the affair," said Goodwin, coming directly to the point. "It will not require many words.

"On that night, with others of our friends here, I was keeping a lookout for the president, having been notified of his flight by a telegram in our national cipher from Englehart, one of our leaders in the capital. About ten o'clock that night I saw a man and a woman hurrying along the streets. They went to the Hotel de los Estranjeros, and engaged rooms. I followed them upstairs, leaving Estebán, who had come up, to watch outside. The barber had told me that he had shaved the beard from the president's face that night; therefore I was prepared, when I entered the rooms, to find him with a smooth face. When I approached him in the name of the people he drew a pistol and shot himself instantly. In a few minutes many officers and citizens were on the spot. I suppose you have been informed of the subsequent facts."

Goodwin paused. Losada's agent maintained an attitude of waiting, as if he expected a continuance.

"And now," went on the American, looking steadily into the eyes of the other man, and giving each word a deliberate emphasis, "you will oblige me by attending carefully to what I have to add. I saw no valise or receptacle of any kind, or any money belonging to the Republic of Anchuria. If President Miraflores decamped with any funds belonging to the treasury of this country, or to himself, or to anyone else, I saw no trace of it in the house or elsewhere, at that time or at any other. Does that statement cover the ground of the inquiry you wished to make of me?"

Colonel Falcon bowed, and described a fluent curve with his cigar. His duty was performed. Goodwin was not to be disputed. He was a loyal supporter of the government, and enjoyed the full confidence of the new president. His rectitude had been the capital that had brought him fortune in Anchuria, just as it had formed the lucrative "graft" of Mellinger, the secretary of Miraflores.

"I thank you, *Señor* Goodwin," said Falcon, "for speaking plainly. Your word will be sufficient for the president. But, *Señor* Goodwin, I am instructed to pursue every clue that presents itself in this matter. There is one that I have not yet touched upon. Our friends in France, *señor*, have a saying *'Cherchez la femme'*, when there is a mystery without a clue. But here we do not have to search. The woman who accompanied the late President in his flight must surely——"

"I must interrupt you there," interposed Goodwin. "It is true when I entered the hotel for the purpose of intercepting President Miraflores I found a lady there. I must beg of you to remember that that lady is now my wife. I speak for her as I do for myself. She knows nothing of the fate of the valise or of the money that you are seeking. You will say to his excellency, that I guarantee her innocence. I do not need to add to you, Colonel Falcon, that I do not care to have her questioned or disturbed."

Colonel Falcon bowed again.

"*Por supuesto*, no!" he cried. And to indicate that the inquiry was ended he added: "And now, *señor*, let me beg of you to show me that sea view from your *galeria* of which you spoke. I am a lover of the sea."

In the early evening Goodwin walked back to the town with his guest, leaving him at the corner of the Calle Grande. As he was returning homeward one "Beelzebub" Blythe, with the air of courtier and the outward aspect of a scarecrow, pounced upon him hopefully from the door of a *pulperia*.

Blythe had been re-christened "Beelzebub" as an acknowledgment of the greatness of his fall. Once in some distant Paradise Lost, he had forgathered with the angels of the earth. But Fate had hurled him headlong down to the tropics, where flamed in his bosom a fire that was seldom quenched. In Coralio they called him a beachcomber; but he was, in reality, a categorical idealist who strove to anamorphosize the dull verities of life by the means of brandy and rum. As Beelzebub, himself, might have held in his clutch with unwitting tenacity his harp or crown during his tremendous fall, so his namesake had clung to his gold-rimmed eyeglasses as the only souvenir of his lost estate. These he wore with impressiveness and distinction while he combed beaches and extracted toll from his friends. By some mysterious means he kept his drink-reddened face always smoothly shaven. For the rest he sponged gracefully upon whomsoever he could for enough to keep him pretty drunk, and sheltered from the rains and night dews.

"Hallo, Goodwin!" called the derelict, airily. "I was hoping I'd strike you. I wanted to see you particularly. Suppose we go where we can talk. Of course you know there's a chap down here looking up the money old Miraflores lost."

"Yes," said Goodwin, "I've been talking with him. Let's go into Espada's place. I can spare you ten minutes."

They went into the *pulperia* and sat at a little table upon stools with rawhide tops.

"Have a drink?" said Goodwin.

377

"They can't bring it too quickly," said Blythe. "I've been in a drought ever since morning. Hi—*muchacho!—el aguardiente por acà.*"

"Now, what do you want to see me about?" asked Goodwin, when the drinks were before them.

"Confound it, old man," drawled Blythe, "why do you spoil a golden moment like this with business? I wanted to see you—well, this has the preference." He gulped down his brandy, and gazed longingly into the empty glass.

"Have another?" suggested Goodwin.

"Between gentlemen," said the fallen angel, "I don't quite like your use of that word 'another'. It isn't quite delicate. But the concrete idea that the word represents is not displeasing."

The glasses were refilled. Blythe sipped blissfully from his, as he began to enter the state of a true idealist.

"I must trot along in a minute or two," hinted Goodwin. "Was there anything in particular?"

Blythe did not reply at once.

"Old Losada would make it a hot country," he remarked at length, "for the man who swiped that grip-sack of treasury boodle, don't you think?"

"Undoubtedly he would," agreed Goodwin calmly, as he rose leisurely to his feet. "I'll be running over to the house now, old man. Mrs. Goodwin is alone. There was nothing important you had to say, was there?"

"That's all," said Blythe. "Unless you wouldn't mind sending in another drink from the bar as you go out. Old Espada has closed my account to profit and loss. And pay for the lot, will you, like a good fellow?"

"All right," said Goodwin. "*Buenas noches.*"

"Beelzebub" Blythe lingered over his cups, polishing his eyeglasses with a disreputable handkerchief.

"I thought I could do it, but I couldn't," he muttered to himself after a time. "A gentleman can't blackmail the man that he drinks with."

378

40

The Admiral

SPILLED milk draws few tears from an Anchurian administration. Many are its lacteal sources; and the clock's hands point for ever to milking time. Even the rich cream skimmed from the treasury by the bewitched Miraflores did not cause the newly-installed patriots to waste time in unprofitable regrets. The government philosophically set about supplying the deficiency by increasing the import duties and by "suggesting" to wealthy private citizens that contributions according to their means would be considered patriotic and in order. Prosperity was expected to attend the reign of Losada, the new president. The ousted office-holders and military favourites organized a new "Liberal" party, and began to lay their plans for a re-succession. Thus the game of Anchurian politics began, like a Chinese comedy, to unwind slowly its serial length. Here and there Mirth peeps for an instant from the wings and illumines the florid lines.

A dozen quarts of champagne in conjunction with an informal sitting of the president and his cabinet led to the establishment of the navy and the appointment of Felipe Carrera as its admiral.

Next to the champagne the credit of the appointment belongs to Don Sabas Placido, the newly confirmed Minister of War.

The president had requested a convention of his cabinet for the discussion of questions politic and for the transaction of certain routine matters of state. The session had been signally tedious; the business and the wine prodigiously dry. A sudden, prankish humour of Don Sabas, impelling him to

379

the deed, spiced the grave affairs of state with a whiff of agreeable playfulness.

In the dilatory order of business had come a bulletin from the coast department of Orilla del Mar reporting the seizure by the custom-house officers at the town of Coralio of the sloop *Estrella del Noche* and her cargo of dry goods, patent medicines, granulated sugar and three-star brandy. Also six Martini rifles and a barrel of American whisky. Caught in the act of smuggling, the sloop with its cargo was now, according to law, the property of the republic.

The Collector of Customs, in making his report, departed from the conventional forms so far as to suggest that the confiscated vessel be converted to the use of the government. The prize was the first capture to the credit of the department in ten years. The collector took opportunity to pat his department.

It often happened that government officers required transportation from point to point along the coast, and means were usually lacking. Furthermore, the sloop could be manned by a loyal crew and employed as a coast-guard to discourage the pernicious art of smuggling. The collector also ventured to nominate one to whom the charge of the boat could be safely entrusted—a young man of Coralio, Felipe Carrera—not, be it understood, one of extreme wisdom, but loyal and the best sailor along the coast.

It was upon this hint that the Ministry of War acted, executing a rare piece of drollery that so enlivened the tedium of executive session.

In the constitution of this small, maritime banana republic was a forgotten section that provided for the maintenance of a navy. This provision—with many other wiser ones—had lain inert since the establishment of the republic. Anchuria had no navy and had no use for one. It was characteristic of Don Sabas—a man at once merry, learned whimsical and audacious—that he should have disturbed the dust of this musty and sleeping statute to increase the humour of the world by so much as a smile from his indulgent colleagues.

With delightful mock seriousness the Minister of War proposed the creation of a navy. He argued its need and the glories it might achieve with such gay and witty zeal that the travesty overcame with its humour even the swart dignity of President Losada himself.

The champagne was bubbling trickily in the veins of the mercurial statesmen. It was not the custom of the grave governors of Anchuria to enliven their sessions with a beverage so apt to cast a veil of disparagement over sober affairs. The wine had been a thoughtful compliment tendered by the agent of the Vesuvius Fruit Company as a token of amicable relations—and certain consummated deals—between that company and the republic of Anchuria.

The jest was carried to its end. A formidable, official document was prepared, encrusted with chromatic seals and jaunty with fluttering ribbons, bearing the florid signatures of state. This commission conferred upon *el Señor* Don Felipe Carrera the title of Flag Admiral of the Republic of Anchuria. Thus within the space of a few minutes and the dominion of a dozen "extra dry" the country took its place among the naval powers of the world, and Felipe Carrera became entitled to a salute of nineteen guns whenever he might enter port.

The southern races are lacking in that particular kind of humour that finds entertainment in the defects and misfortunes bestowed by Nature. Owing to this defect in their constitution they are not moved to laughter (as are their northern brothers) by the spectacle of the deformed, the feeble-minded or the insane.

Felipe Carrera was sent upon earth with but half his wits. Therefore, the people of Coralio called him "*El pobrecito loco*" —"the poor little crazed one"—saying that God had sent but half of him to earth, retaining the other half.

A sombre youth, glowering, and speaking only at the rarest times, Felipe was but negatively "loco". On shore he generally refused all conversation. He seemed to know that he was badly handicapped on land, where so many kinds

of understanding are needed; but on the water his one talent
set him equal with most men. Few sailors whom God had
carefully and completely made could handle a sail-boat as
well. Five points nearer the wind than the best of them he
could sail his sloop. When the elements raged and set other
men to cowering, the deficiencies of Felipe seemed of little
importance. He was a perfect sailor, if an imperfect man. He
owned no boat, but worked among the crews of the schooners
and sloops that skimmed the coast, trading and freighting
fruit out to the steamers where there was no harbour. It was
through his famous skill and boldness on the sea, as well as
for the pity felt for his mental imperfections, that he was
recommended by the collector as a suitable custodian of the
captured sloop.

When the outcome of Don Sabas' little pleasantry arrived
in the form of the imposing and preposterous commission,
the collector smiled. He had not expected such prompt and
overwhelming response to his recommendation. He des-
patched a *muchacho* at once to fetch the future admiral.

The collector waited in his official quarters. His office was
in the Calle Grande, and the sea-breezes hummed through
its windows all day. The collector, in white linen and canvas
shoes, philandered with papers on an antique desk. A parrot,
perched on a pen rack, seasoned the official tedium with a
fire of choice Castilian imprecations. Two rooms opened into
the collector's. In one the clerical force of young men of
variegated complexions transacted with glitter and parade,
their several duties. Through the open door of the other room
could be seen a bronze babe, guiltless of clothing, that
rollicked upon the floor. In a grass hammock a thin woman,
tinted a pale lemon, played a guitar and swung contentedly
in the breeze. Thus surrounded by the routine of his high
duties and the visible tokens of agreeable domesticity, the
collector's heart was further made happy by the power placed
in his hands to brighten the fortunes of the "innocent"
Felipe.

Felipe came and stood before the collector. He was a lad

of twenty, not ill-favoured in looks, but with an expression of distant and pondering vacuity. He wore white cotton trousers, down the seams of which he had sewn red stripes with some vague aim of military decoration. A flimsy blue shirt fell open at his throat; his feet were bare; he held in his hand the cheapest of straw hats from the States.

"*Señor* Carrera," said the collector, gravely, producing the showy commission, "I have sent for you at the president's bidding. This document that I present to you confers upon you the title of Admiral of this great republic, and gives you absolute command of the naval forces and fleet of our country. You may think, friend Felipe, that we have no navy—but yes! The sloop the *Estrella del Noche*, that my brave men captured from the coast smugglers, is to be placed under your command. The boat is to be devoted to the services of your country. You will be ready at all times to convey officials of the government to points along the coast where they may be obliged to visit. You will also act as a coast-guard to prevent, as far as you may be able, the crime of smuggling. You will uphold the honour and prestige of your country at sea, and endeavour to place Anchuria among the proudest naval powers of the world. These are your instructions as the Minister of War desires me to convey them to you. *Por Dios!* I do not know how all this is to be accomplished, for not one word did the letter contain in respect to a crew or to the expenses of this navy. Perhaps you are to provide a crew yourself, *Señor* Admiral—I do not know—but it is a very high honour that has descended upon you. I now hand you your commission. When you are ready for the boat I will give orders that she shall be made over into your charge. That is as far as my instructions go."

Felipe took the commission that the collector handed to him. He gazed through the open window at the sea for a moment, with his customary expression of deep but vain pondering. Then he turned without having spoken a word, and walked swiftly away through the hot sand of the street.

"*Pobrecito loco!*" sighed the collector; and the parrot on the pen racks screeched "Loco!—loco!—loco!"

The next morning a strange procession filed through the streets to the collector's office. At its head was the admiral of the navy. Somewhere Felipe had raked together a pitiful semblance of a military uniform—a pair of red trousers, a dingy blue short jacket heavily ornamented with gold braid, and an old fatigue cap that must have been cast away by one of the British soldiers in Belize and brought away by Felipe on one of his coasting voyages. Buckled around his waist was an ancient ship's cutlass contributed to his equipment by Pedro Lafitte, the baker, who proudly asserted its inheritance from his ancestor, the illustrious buccaneer. At the Admiral's heels tagged his newly-shipped crew—three grinning, glossy, black Caribs, bare to the waist, the sand spurting in showers from the spring of their naked feet.

Briefly and with dignity Felipe demanded his vessel of the collector. And now a fresh honour awaited him. The collector's wife, who played the guitar and read novels in the hammock all day, had more than a little romance in her placid, yellow bosom. She had found in an old book an engraving of a flag that purported to be the naval flag of Anchuria. Perhaps it had so been designed by the founders of the nation; but, as no navy had ever been established, oblivion had claimed the flag. Laboriously with her own hands she had made a flag after the pattern—a red cross upon a blue-and-white ground. She presented it to Felipe with these words: "Brave sailor, this flag is of your country. Be true and defend it with your life. Go you with God."

For the first time since his appointment the admiral showed a flicker of emotion. He took the silken emblem, and passed his hand reverently over its surface. "I am an admiral," he said to the collector's lady. Being on land he could bring himself to no more exuberant expression of sentiment. At sea with the flag at the masthead of his navy, some more eloquent exposition of feelings might be forthcoming.

Abruptly the admiral departed with his crew. For the

next three days they were busy giving the *Estrella del Noche* a new coat of white paint trimmed with blue. And then Felipe further adorned himself by fastening a handful of brilliant parrot's plumes in his cap. Again he tramped with his faithful crew to the collector's office and formally notified him that the sloop's name had been changed to *El Nacional*.

During the next few months the navy had its troubles. Even an admiral is perplexed to know what to do without any orders. But none came. Neither did any salaries. *El Nacional* swung idly at anchor.

When Felipe's little store of money was exhausted he went to the collector and raised the question of finances.

"Salaries!" exclaimed the collector, with hands raised; "*Valgame Dios!* Not one *centavo* of my own pay have I received for the last seven months. The pay of an admiral, do you ask? *Quién sabe?* Should it be less than three thousand *pesos? Mira!* You will see a revolution in this country very soon. A good sign of it is when the government calls all the time for *pesos, pesos, pesos,* and pays none out."

Felipe left the collector's office with a look almost of content on his sombre face. A revolution would mean fighting, and then the government would need his services. It was rather humiliating to be an admiral without anything to do, and have a hungry crew at your heels begging for *reales* to buy plantains and tobacco with.

When he returned to where his happy-go-lucky Caribs were waiting they sprang up and saluted, as he had drilled them to do.

"Come, *muchachos*," said the admiral; "it seems that the government is poor. It has no money to give us. We will earn what we need to live upon. Thus we will serve our country. Soon"—his heavy eyes almost lighted up—"it may gladly call upon us for help."

Thereafter *El Nacional* turned out with the other coast craft and became a wage-earner. She worked with the lighters freighting bananas and oranges out to the fruit steamers that could not approach nearer than a mile from the shore. Surely a self-supporting navy deserves red letters in the budget of any nation.

After earning enough at freighting to keep himself and his crew in provisions for a week, Felipe would anchor the navy and hang about the little telegraph office, looking like one of the chorus of an insolvent comic opera troupe besieging the manager's den. A hope for orders from the capital was always in his heart. That his services as admiral had never been called into requirement hurt his pride and patriotism. At every call he would inquire, gravely and expectantly, for dispatches. The operator would pretend to make a search, and then reply:

"Not yet, it seems, *Señor el Almirante—poco tiempo!*"

Outside in the shade of the lime-trees the crew chewed sugar-cane or slumbered, well content to serve a country that was contented with so little service.

One day in the early summer the revolution predicted by the collector flamed out suddenly. It had long been smouldering. At the first note of alarm the admiral of the navy force and fleet made all sail for a larger port on the coast of a neighbouring republic, where he traded a hastily collected cargo of fruit for its value in cartridges for the five Martini rifles, the only guns that the navy could boast. Then to the telegraph office sped the admiral. Sprawling in his favourite corner, in his fast-decaying uniform, with his prodigious sabre distributed between his red legs, he waited for the long-delayed, but now soon expected, orders.

"Not yet, *Señor el Almirante*," the telegraph clerk would call to him—"*poco tiempo!*"

At the answer the admiral would plump himself down with a great rattling of scabbard to await the infrequent tick of the little instrument on the table.

"They will come," would be his unshaken reply; "I am the admiral."

41

The Flag Paramount

A T the head of the insurgent party appeared that Hector and learned Theban of the southern republics, Don Sabas Placido. A traveller, a soldier, a poet, a scientist, a statesman and a connoisseur—the wonder was that he could content himself with the petty, remote life of his native country.

"It is a whim of Placido's," said a friend who knew him well, "to take up political intrigue. It is not otherwise than as if he had come upon a new *tempo* in music, a new bacillus in the air, a new scent, or rhyme, or explosive. He will squeeze this revolution dry of sensations, and a week afterward will forget it, skimming the seas of the world in his brigantine to add to his already world-famous collections. Collections of what? *Por Dios!* of everything from postage stamps to prehistoric stone idols."

But, for a mere dilettante, the æsthetic Placido seemed to be creating a lively row. The people admired him; they were fascinated by his brilliancy and flattered by his taking an interest in so small a thing as his native country. They rallied to the call of his lieutenants in the capital, where (somewhat contrary to arrangements) the army remained faithful to the government. There was also lively skirmishing in the coast towns. It was rumoured that the revolution was aided by the Vesuvius Fruit Company, the power that for ever stood with chiding smile and uplifted finger to keep Anchuria in the class of good children. Two of its steamers, the *Traveler* and the *Salvador*, were known to have conveyed insurgent troops from point to point along the coast.

As yet there had been no actual uprising in Coralio.

Military law prevailed, and the ferment was bottled for the time. And then came the word that everywhere the revolutionists were encountering defeat. In the capital the president's forces triumphed; and there was a rumour that the leaders of the revolt had been forced to fly, hotly pursued.

In the little telegraph office at Coralio there was always a gathering of officials and loyal citizens, awaiting news from the seat of government. One morning the telegraph key began clicking, and presently the operator called, loudly: "One telegram for *el Almirante*, Don *Señor* Felipe Carrera!"

There was a shuffling sound, a great rattling of tin scabbard, and the admiral, prompt at his spot of waiting, leaped across the room to receive it.

The message was handed to him. Slowly spelling it out, he found it to be his first official order—thus running:

Proceed immediately with your vessel to mouth of Rio Ruiz; transport beef and provisions to barracks at Alforan.

MARTINEZ, *General.*

Small glory, to be sure, in this, his country's first call. But it had called, and joy surged in the admiral's breast. He drew his cutlass belt to another buckle hole, roused his dozing crew, and in a quarter of an hour *El Nacional* was tacking swiftly down-coast in a stiff landward breeze.

The Rio Ruiz is a small river, emptying into the sea ten miles below Coralio. That portion of the coast is wild and solitary. Through a gorge in the Cordilleras rushes the Rio Ruiz, cold and bubbling, to glide, at last, with breadth and leisure, through an alluvial morass into the sea.

In two hours *El Nacional* entered the river's mouth. The banks were crowded with a disposition of formidable trees. The sumptuous undergrowth of the tropics overflowed the land, and drowned itself in the fallow waters. Silently the sloop entered there, and met a deeper silence. Brilliant with greens and ochres and floral scarlets, the umbrageous mouth of the Rio Ruiz furnished no sound or movement save of the sea-going water as it purled against the prow of the vessel. Small chance there seemed of wresting beef or provisions from that empty solitude.

The admiral decided to cast anchor, and, at the chain's rattle, the forest was stimulated to instant and resounding uproar. The mouth of the Rio Ruiz had only been taking a morning nap. Parrots and baboons screeched and barked in the trees; a whirring and a hissing and a booming marked the awakening of animal life; a dark-blue bulk was visible for an instant as a startled tapir fought his way through the vines.

The navy, under orders, hung in the mouth of the little river for hours. The crew served the dinner of shark's-fin soup, plantains, crab gumbo and sour wine. The admiral, with a three-foot telescope, closely scanned the impervious foliage fifty yards away.

It was nearly sunset when a reverberating "hallo-o-o!" came from the forest to their left. It was answered; and three men, mounted upon mules, crashed through the tropic tangle to within a dozen yards of the river's bank. There they dismounted; and one, unbuckling his belt, struck each mule a violent blow with his sword scabbard, so that they, with a fling of heels, dashed back again into the forest.

Those were strange-looking men to be conveying beef and provisions. One was a large and exceedingly active man, of striking presence. He was of the purest Spanish type, with curling, grey-besprinkled, dark hair, blue, sparkling eyes, and the pronounced air of a *caballero grande*. The other two were small, brown-faced men, wearing white military uniforms, high riding-boots and swords. The clothes of all were drenched, bespattered and rent by the thicket. Some stress of circumstance must have driven them, *diable à quatre*, through flood, mire and jungle.

"*Oh-hé! Señor Almirante*," called the large man. "Send to us your boat."

The dory was lowered, and Felipe, with one of the Caribs, rowed toward the left bank.

The large man stood near the water's brink, waist deep in the curling vines. As he gazed upon the scarecrow figure in the stern of the dory a sprightly interest beamed upon his mobile face.

Months of wageless and thankless service had dimmed the admiral's splendour. His red trousers were patched and ragged. Most of the bright buttons and yellow braid were gone from his jacket. The visor of his cap was torn, and depended almost to his eyes. The admiral's feet were bare.

"Dear admiral," cried the large man, and his voice was like a blast from a horn, "I kiss your hands. I knew we could build upon your fidelity. You had our dispatch—from General Martinez. A little nearer with your boat, dear admiral. Upon these devils of shifting vines we stand with the smallest security."

Felipe regarded him with a stolid face.

"Provisions and beef for the barracks at Alforan," he quoted.

"No fault of the butchers, *Almirante mio*, that the beef awaits you not. But you are come in time to save the cattle. Get us aboard your vessel, *señor*, at once. You first, *caballeros—à priesa*! Come back for me. The boat is too small."

The dory conveyed the two officers to the sloop, and returned for the large man.

"Have you so gross a thing as food, good admiral?" he cried, when aboard. "And, perhaps, coffee? Beef and provisions! *Nombre de Dios!* a little longer and we could have eaten one of those mules that you, Colonel Rafael, saluted so feelingly with your sword scabbard at parting. Let us have food; and then we will sail—for the barracks at Alforan—no?"

The Caribs prepared a meal, to which the three passengers of *El Nacional* set themselves with famished delight. About sunset, as was its custom, the breeze veered and swept back from the mountains, cool and steady, bringing a taste of the stagnant lagoons and mangrove swamps that guttered the lowlands. The mainsail of the sloop was hoisted and swelled to it, and at that moment they heard shouts and a waxing clamour from the bosky profundities of the shore.

"The butchers, my dear admiral," said the large man, smiling, "too late for the slaughter."

Further than his orders to the crew, the admiral was saying nothing. The topsail and jib were spread, and the sloop glided out of the estuary. The large man and his companions had bestowed themselves with what comfort they could about the bare deck. Belike, the thing big in their minds had been their departure from that critical shore; and now that the hazard was so far reduced their thoughts were loosed to the consideration of further deliverance. But when they saw the sloop turn and fly up-coast again they relaxed, satisfied with the course the admiral had taken.

The large man sat at ease, his spirited blue eye engaged in the contemplation of the navy's commander. He was trying to estimate this sombre and fantastic lad, whose impenetrable stolidity puzzled him. Himself a fugitive, his life sought, and chafing under the smart of defeat and failure, it was characteristic of him to transfer instantly his interest to the study of a thing new to him. It was like him, too, to have conceived and risked all upon this last desperate and madcap scheme—this message to a poor crazed *fanatico* cruising about with his grotesque uniform and his farcical title. But his companions had been at their wits' end; escape had seemed incredible; and now he was pleased with the success of the plan they had called crack-brained and precarious.

The brief tropic twilight seemed to slide swiftly into the pearly splendour of a moonlit night. And now the lights of Coralio appeared, distributed against the darkening shore to their right. The admiral stood, silent, at the tiller; the Caribs, like black panthers, held the sheets, leaping noiselessly at his short commands. The three passengers were watching intently the sea before them, and when at length they came in sight of the bulk of a steamer lying a mile out from the town, with her lights radiating deep into the water, they held a sudden voluble and close-headed converse. The sloop was speeding as if to strike midway between ship and shore.

The large man suddenly separated from his companions and approached the scarecrow at the helm.

"My dear admiral," he said, "the government has been exceedingly remiss. I feel all the shame for it that only its ignorance of your devoted service has prevented it from sustaining. An inexcusable oversight has been made. A vessel, a uniform and a crew worthy of your fidelity shall be furnished you. But just now, dear admiral, there is business of moment afoot. The steamer lying there is the *Salvador*. I and my friends desire to be conveyed to her, where we are sent on the government's business. Do us the favour to shape your course accordingly."

Without replying, the admiral gave a short command, and put the tiller hard to port. *El Nacional* swerved and headed straight as an arrow's course for the shore.

"Do me the favour," said the large man, a trifle restively, "to acknowledge, at least, that you catch the sound of my words." It was possible that the fellow might be lacking in senses as well as intellect.

The admiral emitted a croaking, harsh laugh, and spake.

"They will stand you," he said, "with your face to a wall and shoot you dead. That is the way they kill traitors. I knew you when you stepped into my boat. I have seen your picture in a book. You are Sabas Placido, traitor to your country. With your face to a wall. So, you will die. I am the admiral, and I will take you to them. With your face to a wall. Yes."

Don Sabas half turned and waved his hand, with a ringing laugh, toward his fellow-fugitives. "To you, *caballeros*, I have related the history of that session when we issued that O! so ridiculous commission. Of a truth our jest has been turned against us. Behold the Frankenstein's monster we have created!"

Don Sabas glanced toward the shore. The lights of Coralio

were drawing near. He could see the beach, the warehouse of the *Bodega Nacional*, the long, low *cuartel* occupied by the soldiers, and, behind that, gleaming in the moonlight, a stretch of high adobe wall. He had seen men stood with their faces to that wall and shot dead.

Again he addressed the extravagant figure at the helm.

"It is true," he said, "that I am fleeing the country. But, receive the assurance that I care very little for that. Courts and camps everywhere are open to Sabas Placido. *Vaya!* what is this molehill of a republic—this pig's head of a country—to a man like me? I am a *paisano* of everywhere. In Rome, in London, in Paris, in Vienna, you will hear them say: 'Welcome back, Don Sabas.' Come!—*tonto*—baboon of a boy—admiral, whatever you call yourself, turn your boat. Put us on board the *Salvador*, and here is your pay— five hundred *pesos* in money of the *Estados Unidos*—more than your lying government will pay you in twenty years."

Don Sabas pressed a plump purse against the youth's hand. The admiral gave no heed to the words or the move- ment. Braced against the helm, he was holding the sloop dead on her shoreward course. His dull face was lit almost to intelligence by some inward conceit that seemed to afford him joy, and found utterance in another parrot-like cackle.

"That is why they do it," he said—"so that you will not see the guns. They fire—boom!—and you fall dead. With your face to the wall. Yes."

The admiral called a sudden order to his crew. The lithe, silent Caribs made fast the sheets they held, and slipped down the hatchway into the hold of the sloop. When the last one had disappeared Don Sabas, like a big, brown leopard, leaped forward, closed and fastened the hatch and stood smiling.

"No rifles, if you please, dear admiral," he said. "It was a whimsey of mine once to compile a dictionary of the Carib *lengua*. So I understood your order. Perhaps now you will——"

He cut short his words, for he heard the dull "swish" of iron scraping along tin. The admiral had drawn the cutlass of Pedro Lafitte, and was darting upon him. The blade descended, and it was only by a display of surprising agility that the large man escaped, with only a bruised shoulder, the glancing weapon. He was drawing his pistol as he sprang, and the next instant he shot the admiral down.

Don Sabas stooped over him, and rose again.

"In the heart," he said briefly. "*Señores*, the navy is abolished."

Colonel Rafael sprang to the helm, and the other officer hastened to loose the mainsail sheets. The boom swung round; *El Nacional* veered and began to tack industriously for the *Salvador*.

"Strike that flag, *señor*," called Colonel Rafael. "Our friends on the steamer will wonder why we are sailing under it."

"Well said," cried Don Sabas. Advancing to the mast he lowered the flag to the deck, where lay its too loyal supporter. Thus ended the Minister of War's little piece of after-dinner drollery, and by the same hand that began it.

Suddenly Don Sabas gave a great cry of joy, and ran down the slanting deck to the side of Colonel Rafael. Across his arm he carried the flag of the extinguished navy.

"*Mire! mire! señor*. Ah, *Dios!* Already can I hear that great bear of an *Oestreicher* shout, '*Du hast mein herz gebrochen!*' *Mire!* Of my friend, Herr Grunitz of Vienna, you have heard me relate. That man has travelled to Ceylon for an orchid—to Patagonia for a headdress—to Benares for a slipper—to Mozambique for a spearhead to add to his famous collections. Thou knowest, also, *amigo* Rafael, that I have been a gatherer of curios. My collection of battle flags of the world's navies was most complete in existence until last year. Then Herr Grunitz secured two, O! such rare specimens. One of a Barbary state, and one of the Makarooroos, a tribe on the west coast of Africa. I have not those, but they can be procured. But this flag, *señor*—do you know what it is? Name of

God! do you know? See that red cross upon the blue-and-white ground! You never saw it before? *Seguramente no.* It is the naval flag of your country. *Mire!* This rotten tub we stand upon is its navy—that dead cockatoo lying there was its commander—that stroke of cutlass and single pistol shot a sea battle. All a piece of absurd foolery, I grant you—but authentic. There has never been another flag like this, and there never will be another. No. It is unique in the whole world. Yes. Think of what that means to a collector of flags! Do you know, *Coronel mio,* how many golden crowns Herr Grunitz would give for this flag? Ten thousand, likely. Well, a hundred thousand would not buy it. Beautiful flag! Only flag! Little devil of a most heaven-born flag! *O-hé!* old grumbler beyond the ocean. Wait till Don Sabas comes again to the Königin Strasse. He will let you kneel and touch the folds of it with one finger. *O-hé!* old spectacled ransacker of the world!"

Forgotten was the important revolution, the danger, the loss, the gall of defeat. Possessed solely by the inordinate and unparalleled passion of the collector, he strode up and down the little deck clasping to his breast with one hand the paragon of a flag. He snapped his fingers triumphantly toward the east. He shouted the pæan to his prize in trumpet tones, as though he would make old Grunitz hear in his musty den beyond the sea.

They were waiting, on the *Salvador,* to welcome them. The sloop came close alongside the steamer, where her sides were sliced almost to the lower deck for the loading of fruit. The sailors of the *Salvador* grappled and held her there.

Captain McLeod leaned over the side.

"Well, *señor,* the jig is up, I'm told."

"The jig is up?" Don Sabas looked perplexed for a moment. "That revolution—ah, yes!" With a shrug of his shoulders he dismissed the matter.

The captain learned of the escape and the imprisoned crew.

"Caribs?" he said; "no harm in them." He slipped down

into the sloop and kicked loose the hasp of the hatch. The black fellows came tumbling up, sweating but grinning.

"Hey! black boys!" said the captain, in a dialect of his own; "you sabe, catchy boat and vamos back same place quick."

They saw him point to themselves, the sloop and Coralio. "Yas, yas!" they cried, with broader grins and many nods.

The four—Don Sabas, the two officers and the captain— moved to quit the sloop. Don Sabas lagged a little behind, looking at the still form of the late admiral, sprawled in his paltry trappings.

"*Pobrecito loco,*" he said softly.

He was a brilliant cosmopolite and a *cognoscente* of high rank; but, after all, he was of the same race and blood and instinct as this people. Even as the simple *paisanos* of Coralio had said it, so said Don Sabas. Without a smile, he looked, and said, "The poor little crazed one!"

Stooping, he raised the limp shoulders, drew the priceless and induplicable flag under them and over the breast, pinning it there with the diamond star of the Order of San Carlos that he took from the collar of his own coat.

He followed after the others, and stood with them upon the deck of the *Salvador*. The sailors that steadied *El Nacional* shoved her off. The jabbering Caribs hauled away at the rigging; the sloop headed for the shore.

And Herr Grunitz's collection of naval flags was still the finest in the world.

42

The Shamrock and the Palm

ONE night when there was no breeze, and Coralio seemed closer than ever to the gratings of Avernus, five men were grouped about the door of the photograph establishment of Keogh and Clancy. Thus, in all the scorched and exotic places of the earth, Caucasians meet when the day's work is done to preserve the fullness of their heritage by the aspersion of alien things.

Johnny Atwood lay stretched upon the grass in the undress uniform of a Carib, and prated feebly of cool water to be had in the cucumber-wood pumps of Dalesburg. Dr. Gregg, through the prestige of his whiskers and as a bribe against the relation of his imminent professional tales, was conceded the hammock that was swung between the door jamb and a calabash-tree. Keogh had moved out upon the grass a little table that held the instrument for burnishing completed photographs. He was the only busy one of the group. Industriously from between the cylinders of the burnisher rolled the finished depictments of Coralio's citizens. Blanchard, the French mining engineer, in his cool linen, viewed the smoke of his cigarette through his clam glasses, impervious to the heat. Clancy sat on the steps, smoking his short pipe. His mood was the gossip's; the others were reduced, by the humidity, to the state of disability desirable in an audience.

Clancy was an American with an Irish diathesis and cosmopolitan proclivities. Many businesses had claimed him, but not for long. The roadster's blood was in his veins. The voice of the tintype was but one of the many callings that had wooed him upon so many roads. Sometimes he could be persuaded to oral construction of his voyages into the informal and egregious. To-night there were symptoms of divulgement in him.

"''Tis elegant weather for filibusterin','" he volunteered. "It reminds me of the time I struggled to liberate a nation from the poisonous breath of a tyrant's clutch. 'Twas hard work. 'Tis strainin' to the back and makes corns on the hands."

"I didn't know you had ever lent your sword to an oppressed people," murmured Atwood, from the grass.

"I did," said Clancy; "and they turned it into a plough-share."

"What country was so fortunate as to secure your aid?" airily inquired Blanchard.

"Where's Kamchatka?" asked Clancy, with seeming irrelevance.

"Why, off Siberia, somewhere in the Arctic regions," somebody answered, doubtfully.

"I thought that was the cold one," said Clancy, with a satisfied nod. "I'm always gettin' the two names mixed. 'Twas Guatemala, then—the hot one—I've been filibusterin' with. Ye'll find that country on the map. 'Tis in the district known as the tropics. By the foresight of Providence, it lies on the coast, so the geography man could run the names of the towns off into the water. They're an inch long, small type, composed of Spanish dialects, and, 'tis my opinion, of the same system of syntax that blew up the *Maine*. Yes, 'twas that country I sailed against, single-handed, and endeavoured to liberate it from a tyrannical government with a single-barrelled pickaxe, unloaded at that. Ye don't understand, of course. 'Tis a statement demandin' elucidation and apologies.

"''Twas in New Orleans one morning about the first of June; I was standin' down on the wharf lookin' about at the ships in the river. There was a little steamer moored right opposite me that seemed about ready to sail. The funnels of it were throwin' out smoke, and a gang of roustabouts were carryin' aboard a pile of boxes that was stacked up on the wharf. The boxes were about two feet square, and somethin' like four feet long, and they seemed to be pretty heavy.

"I walked over, careless, to the stack of boxes. I saw one of them had been broken in handlin'. 'Twas curiosity made me pull up the loose top and look inside. The box was packed full of Winchester rifles. 'So, so,' says I to myself; 'somebody's gettin' a twist on the neutrality laws. Somebody's aidin' with munitions of war. I wonder where the popguns are goin'?'

"I heard somebody cough, and I turned round. There stood a little, round, fat man with a brown face and white clothes, a first-class-looking little man, with a four-carat diamond on his finger and his eye full of interrogations and respects. I judged he was a kind of foreigner—maybe from Russia or Japan or the archipelagos.

"'Hist!' says the round man, full of concealments and confidences. 'Will the *señor* respect the discoveryments he has made, that the mans on the ship shall not be acquaint? The *señor* will be a gentleman that shall not expose one thing that by accident occur.'

"'Monseer,' says I—for I judged him to be a kind of Frenchman—'receive my most exasperated assurances that your secret is safe with James Clancy. Furthermore, I will go so far as to remark, Veev la Liberty—veev it good and strong. Whenever you hear of a Clancy obstructin' the abolishment of existin' governments you may notify me by return mail.'

"'The *señor* is good,' says the dark, fat man, smilin' under his black moustache. 'Wish you to come aboard my ship and drink of wine a glass.'

"Bein' a Clancy, in two minutes me and the foreigner man was seated at a table in the cabin of the steamer, with a bottle between us. I could hear the heavy boxes bein' dumped into the hold. I judged that cargo must consist of at least 2,000 Winchesters. Me and the brown man drank the bottle of stuff, and he called the steward to bring another. When you amalgamate a Clancy with the contents of a bottle you practically instigate secession. I had heard a good deal about these revolutions in them tropical localities, and I begun to want a hand in it.

"'You goin' to stir up things in your country, ain't you, monseer?' says I, with a wink to let him know I was on.

"'Yes, yes,' said the little man, pounding his fist on the table. 'A change of the greatest will occur. Too long have the people been oppressed with the promises and the never-to-happen things to become. The great work it shall be carry on. Yes. Our forces shall in the capital city strike of the soonest. *Carrambos!*'

"'*Carrambos* is the word,' says I, beginning to invest myself with enthusiasm and more wine, 'likewise veeva, as I said before. May the shamrock of old—I mean the banana-vine or the pie-plant, or whatever the imperial emblem may be of your downtrodden country, wave for ever.'

"'A thousand thank-yous,' says the round man, 'for your emission of amicable utterances. What our cause needs of the very most is mans who will the work do, to lift it along. Oh, for one thousands strong, good mans to aid the General De Vega that he shall to his country bring those success and glory! It is hard—oh, so hard to find good mans to help in the work.'

"'Monseer,' says I, leanin' over the table and graspin' his hand, 'I don't know where your country is, but me heart bleeds for it. The heart of a Clancy was never deaf to the sight of an oppressed people. The family is filibusterers by birth, and foreigners by trade. If you can use James Clancy's arms and his blood in denudin' your shores of the tyrant's yoke they're yours to command.'

"General De Vega was overcome with joy to confiscate my condolence of his conspiracies and predicaments. He tried to embrace me across the table, but his fatness, and the wine that had been in the bottles, prevented. Thus was I welcomed into the ranks of filibustery. Then the general man told me his country had the name of Guatemala, and was the greatest nation laved by any ocean whatever anywhere.

400

He looked at me with tears in his eyes, and from time to time he would emit the remark, 'Ah! big, strong, brave mans! That is what my country need.'

"General De Vega, as was the name by which he denounced himself, brought out a document for me to sign, which I did, makin' a fine flourish and curly-cue with the tail of the 'y'.

"'Your passage money,' says the general, businesslike, 'shall from your pay be deduct.'

"'Twill not,' says I haughtily. 'I'll pay my own passage.' A hundred and eighty dollars I had in my inside pocket, and 'twas no common filibuster I was goin' to be, filibusterin' for me board and clothes.

"The steamer was to sail in two hours, and I went ashore to get some things together I'd need. When I came aboard I showed the general with pride the outfit. 'Twas a fine Chinchilla overcoat, Arctic overshoes, fur cap and earmuffs, with elegant fleece-lined gloves and woollen muffler.

"'*Carrambos!*' says the little general. 'What clothes are these that shall go to the tropic?' And then the little spalpeen laughs, and he calls the captain, and the captain calls the purser, and they pipe up the chief engineer, and the whole gang leans against the cabin and laughs at Clancy's wardrobe for Guatemala.

"I reflects a bit, serious, and asks the general again to denominate the terms by which his country is called. He tells me, and I see then that 'twas the t'other one, Kamchatka, I had in mind. Since then I've had difficulty in separatin' the two nations in name, climate and seographic disposition.

"I paid my passage—twenty-four dollars, first cabin—and ate at table with the officer crowd. Down on the lower deck was a gang of second-class passengers, about forty of them, seemin' to be Dagoes and the like. I wondered what so many of them were goin' along for.

"Well, then, in three days we sailed alongside that Guatemala. 'Twas a blue country, and not yellow as 'tis miscoloured on the map. We landed at a town on the coast, where a train of cars was waitin' for us on a dinky little railroad. The boxes on the steamer were brought ashore and loaded on the cars. The gang of Dagoes got aboard, too, the general and me in the front car. Yes, me and General De Vega headed the revolution, as it pulled out of the seaport town. That train travelled about as fast as a policeman goin' to a riot. It penetrated the most conspicuous lot of fuzzy scenery ever seen outside a geography. We run some forty miles in seven hours, and the train stopped. There was no more railroad. 'Twas a sort of camp in a damp gorge full of wildness and melancholies. They were gradin' and choppin' out the forests ahead to continue the road. 'Here,' says I to myself, 'is the romantic haunt of the revolutionists. Here will Clancy, by the virtue that is in a superior race and the inculcation of Fenian tactics, strike a tremendous blow for liberty.'

"They unloaded the boxes from the train and begun to knock the tops off. From the first one that was open I saw General De Vega take the Winchester rifles and pass them around to a squad of morbid soldiery. The other boxes was opened next, and, believe me or not, divil another gun was to be seen. Every other box in the load was full of pickaxes and spades.

"And then—sorrow be upon them tropics—the proud Clancy and the dishonoured Dagoes, each one of them, had to shoulder a pick or a spade, and march away to work on that dirty little railroad. Yes; 'twas that the Dagoes shipped for, and 'twas that the filibusterin' Clancy signed for, though unbeknownst to himself at the time. In after days I found out about it. It seems 'twas hard to get hands to work on that road. The intelligent natives of the country was too lazy to work. Indeed, the saints know, 'twas unnecessary. By stretchin' out one hand, they could seize the most delicate and costly fruits of the earth, and by stretchin' out the other, they could sleep for days at a time without hearin' a seven-o'clock whistle or the footsteps of the rent man upon the stairs. So, regular, the steamers travelled to the United States to seduce labour. Usually the imported spade-slingers died in two or three months from eatin' the over-ripe water and breathin' the violent tropical scenery. Wherefore they made them sign contracts for a year, when they hired them, and put an armed guard over the poor divils to keep them from runnin' away.

"'Twas thus I was double-crossed by the tropics through a family failin' of goin' out of the way to hunt disturbances.

"They gave me a pick, and I took it, meditatin' an insurrection on the spot; but there was the guards handlin' the Winchesters careless, and I come to the conclusion that discretion was the best part of filibusterin'. There was about a hundred of us in the gang startin' out to work, and the word was given to move. I steps out of the ranks and goes up to that General De Vega man, who was smokin' a cigar and gazin' upon the scene with satisfactions and glory. He smiles at me polite and devilish. 'Plenty work,' says he, 'for big, strong mans in Guatemala. Yes. T'irty dollars in the month. Good pay. Ah, yes. You strong, brave man. Bimeby we push those railroad in the capital very quick. They want you go work now. *Adios*, strong mans.'

"'Monseer,' says I, lingerin', 'will you tell a poor little Irishman this: When I set foot on your cockroachy steamer, and breathed liberal and revolutionary sentiments into your sour wine, did you think I was conspirin' to sling a pick on your contemptuous little railroad? And when you answered me with patriotic recitations, humping up the star-spangled cause of liberty, did you have meditations of reducin' me to the ranks of the stump-grubbin' Dagoes in the chain-gangs of your vile and grovellin' country?'

"The general man expanded his rotundity and laughed considerable. Yes, he laughed very long and loud, and I, Clancy, stood and waited.

"'Comical mans!' he shouts, at last. 'So you will kill me from the laughing. Yes; it is hard to find the brave, strong mans to aid my country. Revolutions? Did I speak of r-r-revolutions? Not one word. I say, big, strong mans is need in Guatemala. So. The mistake is of you. You have looked in those one box containing those gun for the guard. You think all boxes is contain gun? No.

"'There is not war in Guatemala. But work? Yes. Good. T'irty dollars in the month. You shall shoulder one pickaxe, *señor*, and dig for the liberty and prosperity of Guatemala. Off to your work. The guard waits for you.'

"'Little, fat, poodle dog of a brown man,' says I, quiet, but full of indignations and discomforts, 'things shall happen to you. Maybe not right away, but as soon as J. Clancy can formulate somethin' in the way of repartee.'

"The boss of the gang orders us to work. I tramps off with the Dagoes, and I hears the distinguished patriot and kidnapper laughin' hearty as we go.

"'Tis a sorrowful fact, for eight weeks I built railroads for that misbehavin' country. I filibustered twelve hours a day with a heavy pick and spade, choppin' away the luxurious landscape that grew upon the right of way. We worked in swamps that smelled like there was a leak in the gas mains, trampin' down a fine assortment of the most expensive hothouse plants and vegetables. The scene was tropical beyond the wildest imagination of the geography man. The trees was all sky-scrapers; the underbrush was full of needles and pins; there was monkeys jumpin' around and crocodiles and pink-tailed mockin'-birds, and ye stood knee-deep in the rotten water and grabbled roots for the liberation of Guatemala. Of rights we would build smudges in camp to discourage the mosquitoes, and sit in the smoke, with the guards pacin' all around us. There was two hundred men workin' on the road—mostly Dagoes, nigger-men, Spanish-men and Swedes. Three or four were Irish.

"One old man named Halloran—a man of Hibernian entitlements and discretions—explained it to me. He had been workin' on the road a year. Most of them died in less than six months. He was dried up to gristle and bone, and shook with chills every third night.

"'When you first come,' says he, 'ye think ye'll leave right away. But they hold out your first month's pay for your passage over, and by that time the tropics has its grip on ye. Ye're surrounded by a ragin' forest full of disreputable beasts —lions and baboons and anacondas—waiting to devour ye. The sun strikes ye hard, and it melts the marrow in your bones. Ye get similar to the lettuce-eaters the poetry-book speaks about. Ye forget the elevated sintiments of life, such as patriotism, revenge, disturbances of the peace and the dacint love of a clane shirt. Ye do your work, and ye swallow the kerosene ile and rubber pipe-stems dished up to ye by the Dago cook for food. Ye light your pipeful, and say to yoursilf, "Nixt week I'll break away," and ye go to sleep and call yersilf a liar, for ye know ye'll never do it.'

"'Who is this general man,' asks I, 'that calls himself De Vega?'

"''Tis the man,' says Halloran, 'who is tryin' to complete the finishin' of the railroad. 'Twas the project of a private corporation, but it busted, and then the government took it up. De Vegy is a big politician, and wants to be president. The people want the railroad completed, as they're taxed mighty on account of it. The De Vegy man is pushin' it along as a campaign move.'

"''Tis not my way,' says I, 'to make threats against any man, but there's an account to be settled between the railroad man and James O'Dowd Clancy.'

"''Twas that way I thought, mesilf, at first,' Halloran says, with a big sigh, 'until I got to be a lettuce-eater. The fault's wid these tropics. They rejuices a man's system. 'Tis a land, as the poet says, "Where it always seems to be after dinner." I does me work and smokes me pipe and sleeps. There's little else in life, anyway. Ye'll get that way yersilf, mighty soon. Don't be harbourin' any sintiments at all, Clancy.'

"'I can't help it,' says I; 'I'm full of 'em. I enlisted in the revolutionary army of this dark country in good faith to fight for its liberty, honours and silver candlesticks; instead of which I am set to amputatin' its scenery and grubbin' its roots. 'Tis the general man will have to pay for it.'

"Two months I worked on that railroad before I found a chance to get away. One day a gang of us was sent back to the end of the completed line to fetch some picks that had been sent down to Port Barrios to be sharpened. They were brought on a hand-car, and I noticed when I started away that the car was left there on the track.

"That night, about twelve, I woke up Halloran and told him my scheme.

"'Run away?' says Halloran. 'Good Lord, Clancy, do ye mean it? Why, I ain't got the nerve. It's too chilly, and I ain't slept enough. Run away? I told you, Clancy, I've eat the lettuce. I've lost my grip. 'Tis the tropics that's done it. 'Tis like the poet says: "Forgotten are our friends that we have left behind; in the hollow lettuce-land we will live and lay reclined." You had better go on, Clancy. I'll stay, I guess. It's too early and cold, and I'm sleepy.'

"So I had to leave Halloran. I dressed quiet, and slipped out of the tent we were in. When the guard came along I knocked him over, like a ninepin, with a green coconut I had, and made for the rail-road. I got on that hand-car and made it fly. 'Twas yet awhile before daybreak when I saw the lights of Port Barrios about a mile away. I stopped the hand-car there and walked to the town. I stepped inside the corporations of that town with care and hesitations. I was not afraid of the army of Guatemala, but me soul quaked at the prospect of a hand-to-hand struggle with its employment bureau. 'Tis a country that hires its help easy and keeps 'em long. Sure I can fancy Missis America and Missis Guatemala passin' a bit of gossip some fine, still night across the mountains. 'Oh, dear,' says Missis America, 'and it's a lot of trouble I'm havin' ag'in with the help, *señora*, ma'am.' 'Laws, now!' says Missis Guatemala, 'you don't say so, ma'am! Now, mine never think of leavin' me—te-he! ma'am,' snickers Missis Guatemala.

"I was wonderin' how I was goin' to move away from

them tropics without bein' hired again. Dark as it was, I could see a steamer ridin' in the harbour, with smoke emergin' from her stacks. I turned down a little grass street that run down to the water. On the beach I found a little brown nigger-man just about to shove off in a skiff.

"'Hold on, Sambo,' says I, 'savve English?'

"'Heap plenty, yes,' says he, with a pleasant grin.

"'What steamer is that?' I asks him, 'and where is it going? And what's the news, and the good word and the time of day?'

"'That steamer the *Conchita*,' said the brown man, affable and easy, rollin' a cigarette. 'Him come from New Orleans for load banana. Him got load last night. I think him sail in one, two hour. Verre nice day we shall be goin' have. You hear some talkee' bout big battle, maybe so? You think catchee General De Vega, *señor*? Yes? No?'

"'How's that, Sambo?' says I. 'Big battle? What battle? Who wants catchee General De Vega? I've been up at my old gold mines in the interior for a couple of months, and haven't heard any news.'

"'Oh,' says the nigger-man, proud to speak the English, 'verree great revolution in Guatemala one week ago. General De Vega, him try be president. Him raise armee—one—five—ten thousand mans for fight at the government. Those one government send five—forty—hundred thousand soldier to suppress revolution. They fight big battle yesterday at Lomagrande—that about nineteen or fifty mile in the mountain. That government soldier wheep General De Vega—ah, most bad. Five hundred—nine hundred—two thousand of his mans is kill. That revolution is smash, suppress—bust—very quick. General De Vega, him r-r-run away fast on one big mule. Yes, *carrambos*! The general, him r-r-run away, and his armee is kill. That government soldier, they try find General De Vega verree much. They want catchee him for shoot. You think they catchee that general, *señor*?'

"'Sain'ts grant it!' says I. ''Twould be the judgment of

Providence for settin' the warlike talent of a Clancy to gradin' the tropics with a pick and shovel. But 'tis not so much a question of insurrections now, me little man, as 'tis of the hired-man problem. 'Tis anxious I am to resign a situation of responsibility and trust with the white wings department of your great and degraded country. Row me in your little boat out to that steamer, and I'll give ye five dollars—sinker pacers—sinker pacers,' says I, reducin' the offer to the language and denomination of the tropic dialects.

"'*Cinco pesos*,' repeats the little man. 'Five dollee, you give?'

"'Twas not such a bad little man. He had hesitations at first, sayin' that passengers leavin' the country had to have papers and passports, but at last he took me out alongside the steamer.

"Day was just breakin' as we struck her, and there wasn't a soul to be seen on board. The water was very still, and the nigger-man gave me a lift from the boat, and I climbed on to the steamer where her side was sliced to the deck for loadin' fruit. The hatches were open, and I looked down and saw the cargo of bananas that filled the hold to within six feet of the top. I thinks to myself, 'Clancy, you better go as a stowaway. It's safer. The steamer men might hand you back to the employment bureau. The tropic'll get you, Clancy, if you don't watch out.'

"So I jumps down easy among the bananas, and digs out a hole to hide in among the bunches. In an hour or so I could hear the engines goin', and feel the steamer rockin', and I knew we were off to sea. They left the hatches open for ventilation, and pretty soon it was light enough in the hold to see fairly well. I got to feelin' a bit hungry, and thought I'd have a light fruit lunch, by way of refreshment. I creeped out of the hole I'd made and stood up straight. Just then I saw another man crawl up about ten feet away and reach out and skin a banana and stuff it into his mouth. 'Twas a dirty man, black-faced and ragged and disgraceful of aspect. Yes, the man was a ringer for the pictures of the fat Weary Willie in the funny papers. I looked again, and saw it was my general man—De Vega, the great revolutionist, mule-rider and pick-axe importer. When he saw me the general hesitated with his mouth filled with banana and his eyes the size of coconuts.

"'Hist!' I says. 'Not a word, or they'll put us off and make us walk. "Veev la Liberty!"'" I adds, copperin' the sentiment by shovin' a banana into the source of it. I was certain the general wouldn't recognize me. The nefarious work of the tropics had left me lookin' different. There was half an inch of roan whiskers coverin' me face, and me costume was a pair of blue overalls and a red shirt.

"'How you come in the ship, *señor*?' asked the general as soon as he could speak.

"'By the back door—whist!' says I. ''Twas a glorious blow for liberty we struck,' I continues: 'but wes powered by numbers. Let us accept our defeat like brave men and eat another banana.'

"'Were you in the cause of liberty fightin', *señor*?' says the general, sheddin' tears on the cargo.

"'To the last,' says I. ''Twas I led the last desperate charge against the minions of the tyrant. But it made them mad, and we was forced to retreat. 'Twas I, general, pro-cured the mule upon which you escaped. Could you give that ripe bunch a little boost this way, general? It's a bit out of my reach. Thanks.'

"'Say you so, brave patriot?' said the general, again weepin'. 'Ah, *Dios*! And I have not the means to reward your devotion. Barely did I my life bring away. *Carrambos!* what a devil's animal was that mule, *señor!* Like ships in one storm was I dashed about. The skin on myself was ripped away with the thorns and vines. Upon the bark of a hundred trees did that beast of the infernal bump, and cause outrage to the legs of mine. In the night to Port Barrios I came. I dispossess myself of that mountain of mule and hasten along the water shore. I find a little boat to be tied. I launch myself and row to the steamer. I cannot see any mans on board, so I climbed one rope which hang at the side. I then hide in the bananas. Surely, I say, if the ship captains view me, they shall throw me again to those Guatemala. Those things are not good. Guatemala will shoot General De Vega. Therefore, I am hide and remain silent. Life itself is glorious. Liberty, it is pretty good; but so good as life I do not think.'

"Three days, as I said, was the trip to New Orleans. The general man and me got to be cronies of the deepest dye. Bananas we ate until they were distasteful to the sight and an eyesore to the palate; but to bananas alone was the bill of fare reduced. At night I crawls out, careful, on the lower deck, and gets a bucket of fresh water.

"That General De Vega was a man inhabited by an engorgement of words and sentences. He added to the mono-tony of the voyage by divestin' himself of conversation. He believed I was a revolutionist of his own party, there bein', as he told me, a good many Americans and other foreigners in its ranks. 'Twas a braggart and a conceited little gabbler it was, though he considered himself a hero. 'Twas on himself he wasted all his regrets at the failin' of his plot. Not a word did the little balloon have to say about the other misbehavin' idiots that had been shot, or run themselves to death in his revolution.

"The second day out he was feelin' pretty braggy and uppish for a stowed-away conspirator that owed his existence to a mule and stolen bananas. He was tellin' me about the great railroad he had been buildin', and he relates what he calls a comic incident about a fool Irishman he inveigled from New Orleans to sling a pick on his little morgue of a narrow-gauge line. 'Twas sorrowful to hear the little, dirty general tell the opprobrious story of how he put salt upon the tail of that reckless and silly bird, Clancy. Laugh, he did, hearty and long. He shook with laughin', the black-faced rebel and outcast, standin' neck deep in bananas, without friends or country.

"'Ah, *señor*,' he snickers, 'to the death you would have laughed at that drollest Irish. I say to him: "Strong, big mans is need very much in Guatemala." "I will blows strike

410

for your down-pressed country," he says. "That shall you do," I tell him. Ah! it was an Irish so comic. He sees one box break upon the wharf that contain for the guard a few gun. He think there is gun in all the box. But that is all pickaxe. Yes. Ah! *señor*, could you the face of that Irish have seen when they set him to the work!'

"'Twas thus the ex-boss of the employment bureau contributed to the tedium of the trip with merry jests and anecdote. But now and then he would weep upon the bananas and make oration about the lost cause of liberty and the mule.

"'Twas a pleasant sound when the steamer bumped against the pier in New Orleans. Pretty soon we heard the pat-a-pat of hundreds of bare feet, and the Dago gang that unloads the fruit jumped on the deck and down into the hold. Me and the general worked awhile at passin' up the bunches, and they thought we were part of the gang. After about an hour we managed to slip off the steamer on to the wharf.

"'Twas a great honour on the hands of an obscure Clancy, havin' the entertainment of the representative of a great foreign filibusterin' power. I first bought for the general and myself many long drinks and things to eat that were not bananas. The general man trotted along at my side, leavin' all the arrangements to me. I led him up to Lafayette Square and set him on a bench in the little park. Cigarettes I had bought for him, and he humped himself down on the seat like a little, fat, contented hobo. I look over him as he sets there, and what I see pleases me. Brown by nature and instinct, he is now brindled with dirt and dust. Praise to the mule, his clothes is mostly strings and flaps. Yes, the looks of the general man is agreeable to Clancy.

"I asks him, delicate, if, by any chance, he brought away anybody's money with him from Guatemala. He sighs and humps his shoulders against the bench. Not a cent. All right. Maybe, he tells me, some of his friends in the tropic outfit will send him funds later. The general was as clear a case of no visible means as I ever saw.

"I told him not to move from the bench, and then I went

411

up to the corner of Poydras and Carondelet. Along there is O'Hara's beat. In five minutes along comes O'Hara, a big, fine man, red-faced, with shinin' buttons, swingin' his club. 'Twould be a fine thing for Guatemala to move into O'Hara's precinct. 'Twould be a fine bit of recreation for Danny to suppress revolutions and uprisin's once or twice a week with his club.

"'Is 5046 workin' yet, Danny?' says I, walkin' up to him.

"'Overtime,' says O'Hara, lookin' over me suspicious. 'Want some of it?'

"Fifty-forty-six is the celebrated city ordinance authorizin' arrest, conviction and imprisonment of persons that succeed in concealing their crimes from the police.

"'Don't ye know Jimmy Clancy?' says I. 'Ye pink-gilled monster.' So, when O'Hara recognized me beneath the scandalous exterior bestowed upon me by the tropics, I backed him into a doorway and told him what I wanted, and why I wanted it. 'All right, Jimmy,' says O'Hara. 'Go back and hold the bench. I'll be along in ten minutes.'

"In that time O'Hara strolled through Lafayette Square and spied two Weary Willies disgracin' one of the benches. In ten minutes more J. Clancy and General De Vega, late candidate for the presidency of Guatemala, was in the station house. The general is badly frightened, and calls upon me to proclaim his distinguishments and rank.

"'The man,' says I to the police, 'used to be a railroad man. He's on the bum now. 'Tis a little bug-house he is, on account of losin' his job.'

"'*Carrambos!*' says the general, fizzin' like a little soda-water fountain, 'you fought, *señor*, with my forces in my native country. Why do you say the lies? You shall say I am the General De Vega, one soldier, one *caballero*——'

"'Railroader,' says I again. 'On the hog. No good. Been livin' for three days on stolen bananas. Look at him. Ain't that enough?'

"Twenty-five dollars or sixty days, was what the recorder gave the general. He didn't have a cent, so he took the time.

412

They let me go, as I knew they would, for I had the money to show, and O'Hara spoke for me. Yes; sixty days he got. 'Twas just so long that I slung a pick for the great country of Kam—Guatemala."

Clancy paused. The bright starlight showed a reminiscent look of happy content on his seasoned features. Keogh leaned in his chair and gave his partner a slap on his thinly-clad back that sounded like the crack of the surf on the sands.

"Tell 'em, ye divil," he chuckled, "how you got even with the tropical general in the way of agricultural manœuvrings."

"Havin' no money," concluded Clancy, with unction, "they set him to work his fine out with a gang from the parish prison clearing Ursulines Street. Around the corner was a saloon decorated genially with electric fans and cool merchandise. I made that me headquarters, and every fifteen minutes I'd walk around and take a look at the little man filibusterin' with a rake and shovel. 'Twas just such a hot broth of a day as this has been. And I'd call at him 'Hey monseer!' and he'd look at me black, with the damp showin' through his shirt in places.

"'Fat, strong mans,' says I to General De Vega, 'is needed in New Orleans. Yes. To carry on the good work. *Carrambos!* Erin go bragh!'"

43

The Remnants of the Code

B REAKFAST in Coralio was at eleven. Therefore the people
did not go to market early. The little wooden market-
house stood on a patch of short-trimmed grass, under the
vivid green foliage of a bread-fruit tree.

Thither one morning the venders leisurely convened, bringing their wares with them. A porch or platform six feet wide
encircled the building, shaded from the mid-morning sun
by the projecting, grass-thatched roof. Upon this platform
the venders were wont to display their goods—newly-killed
beef, fish, crabs, fruit of the country, cassava, eggs, *dulces*
and high, tottering stacks of native tortillas as large around
as the sombrero of a Spanish grandee.

But on this morning those whose stations lay on the seaward
side of the market-house, instead of spreading their merchandise formed themselves into a softly jabbering and gesticulating group. For there upon their space of the platform was
sprawled, asleep, the unbeautiful figure of "Beelzebub"
Blythe. He lay upon a ragged strip of coco matting, more
than ever a fallen angel in appearance. His suit of coarse
flax, soiled, bursting at the seams, crumpled into a thousand
diversified wrinkles and creases, inclosed him absurdly, like
the garb of some effigy that had been stuffed in sport and
thrown there after indignity had been wrought upon it. But
firmly upon the high bridge of his nose reposed his gold-
rimmed glasses, the surviving badge of his ancient glory.

The sun's rays, reflecting quiveringly from the rippling
sea upon his face, and the voices of the market-men woke
"Beelzebub" Blythe. He sat up, blinking, and leaned his
back against the wall of the market. Drawing a blighted silk

handkerchief from his pocket, he assiduously rubbed and burnished his glasses. And while doing this he became aware that his bedroom had been invaded, and that polite brown and yellow men were beseeching him to vacate in favour of their market stuff.

If the *señor* would have the goodness—a thousand pardons for bringing to him molestation—but soon would come the *compradores* for the day's provisions—surely they had ten thousand regrets at disturbing him!

In this manner they expanded to him the intimation that he must clear out and cease to clog the wheels of trade.

Blythe stepped from the platform with the air of a prince leaving his canopied couch. He never quite lost that air, even at the lowest point of his fall. It is clear that the college of good breeding does not necessarily maintain a chair of morals within its walls.

Blythe shook out his wry clothing, and moved slowly up the Calle Grande through the hot sand. He moved without a destination in his mind. The little town was languidly stirring to its daily life. Golden-skinned babies tumbled over one another in the grass. The sea-breeze brought him appetite, but nothing to satisfy it. Throughout Coralio were its morning odours—those from the heavily fragrant tropical flowers and from the bread baking in the outdoor ovens of clay and the pervading smoke of their fires. When the smoke cleared, the crystal air, with some of the efficacy of faith, seemed to remove the mountains almost to the sea, bringing them so near that one might count the scarred glades on their wooded sides. The light-footed Caribs were swiftly gliding to their tasks at the waterside. Already along the bosky trails from the banana grove files of horses were slowly moving, concealed, except for their nodding heads and plodding legs, by the bunches of green-golden fruit heaped upon their backs. On doorsills sat women combing their long, black hair and calling, one to another, across the narrow thoroughfares. Peace reigned in Coralio—arid and bald peace; but still peace.

On that bright morning when Nature seemed to be offering the lotus on the Dawn's golden platter "Beelzebub" Blythe had reached rock bottom. Further descent seemed impossible. That last night's slumber in a public place had done for him. As long as he had had a roof to cover him there had remained, unbridged, the space that separates a gentleman from the beasts of the jungle and the fowls of the air. But now he was little more than a whimpering oyster led to be devoured on the sands of a Southern sea by the artful walrus, Circumstance, and the implacable carpenter, Fate.

To Blythe money was now but a memory. He had drained his friends of all that their good-fellowship had to offer; then he had squeezed them to the last drop of their generosity; and at the last, Aaron-like, he had smitten the rock of their hardening bosoms for the scattering, ignoble drops of Charity itself.

He had exhausted his credit to the last *real*. With the minute keenness of the shameless sponger he was aware of every source in Coralio from which a glass of rum, a meal or a piece of silver could be wheedled. Marshalling each such source in his mind, he considered it with all the thoroughness and penetration that hunger and thirst lent him for the task. All his optimism failed to thresh a grain of hope from the chaff of his postulations. He had played out the game. That one night in the open had shaken his nerves. Until then there had been left to him at least a few grounds upon which he could base his unblushing demands upon his neighbour's stores. Now he must beg instead of borrowing. The most brazen sophistry could not dignify by the name of "loan" the coin contemptuously flung to a beachcomber who slept on the bare boards of the public market.

But on this morning no beggar would have more thankfully received a charitable coin, for the demon thirst had him by the throat—the drunkard's matutinal thirst that requires to be slaked at each morning station on the road to Tophet.

Blythe walked slowly up the street, keeping a watchful

416

eye for any miracle that might drop manna upon him in his wilderness. As he passed the popular eating house of Madama Vasquez, Madama's boarders were just sitting down to freshly-baked bread, *aguacates*, pines and delicious coffee that sent forth odorous guarantee of its quality upon the breeze. Madama was serving; she turned her shy, stolid, melancholy gaze for a moment out of the window, she saw Blythe, and her expression turned more shy and embarrassed. "Beelzebub" owed her twenty *pesos*. He bowed as he had once bowed to less embarrassed dames to whom he owed nothing and passed on.

Merchants and their clerks were throwing open the solid wooden doors of their shops. Polite but cool were the glances they cast upon Blythe as he lounged tentatively by with the remains of his old jaunty air; for they were his creditors almost without exception.

At the little fountain in the plaza he made an apology for a toilet with his wetted handkerchief. Across the open square filed the dolorous line of friends to the prisoners in the *calaboza*, bearing the morning meal of the immured. The food in their hands aroused small longing in Blythe. It was drink that his soul craved, or money to buy it.

In the streets he met with many with whom he had been friends and equals, and whose patience and liberality he had gradually exhausted. Willard Geddie and Paula cantered past him with the coolest of nods, returning from their daily horseback ride along the old Indian road. Keogh passed him at another corner, whistling cheerfully and bearing a prize of newly-laid eggs for the breakfast of himself and Clancy. The jovial scout of Fortune was one of Blythe's victims who had plunged his hand oftenest into his pocket to aid him. But now it seemed that Keogh, too, had fortified himself against further invasions. His curt greeting and the ominous light in his full, grey eye quickened the steps of "Beelzebub", whom desperation had almost incited to attempt an additional "loan".

Three drinking shops the forlorn one next visited in

o

succession. In all of these his money, his credit and his welcome had long since been spent; but Blythe felt that he would have fawned in the dust at the feet of an enemy that morning for one draught of *aguardiente*. In two of the *pulperias* his courageous petition for drink was met with a refusal so polite that it stung worse than abuse. The third establishment had acquired something of American methods; and here he was seized bodily and cast out upon his hands and knees.

This physical indignity caused a singular change in the man. As he picked himself up and walked away, an expression of absolute relief came upon his features. The specious and conciliatory smile that had been graven there was succeeded by a look of calm and sinister resolve. "Beelzebub" had been floundering in the sea of improbity, holding by a slender life-line to the respectable world that had cast him overboard. He must have felt that with this ultimate shock the line had snapped, and have experienced the welcome ease of the drowning swimmer who has ceased to struggle.

Blythe walked to the next corner and stood there while he brushed the sand from his garments and repolished his glasses.

"I've got to do it—oh, I've got to do it," he told himself, aloud. "If I had a quart of rum, I believe I could stave it off yet—for a little while. But there's no more rum for—'Beelzebub', as they call me. By the flames of Tartarus! if I'm to sit at the right hand of Satan somebody has got to pay the court expenses. You'll have to pony up, Mr. Frank Goodwin. You're a good fellow; but a gentleman must draw the line at being kicked into the gutter. Blackmail isn't a pretty word, but it's the next station on the road I'm travelling."

With purpose in his steps Blythe now moved rapidly through the town by way of its landward environs. He passed through the squalid quarters of the improvident negroes and on beyond the picturesque shacks of the poorer *mestizos*. From many points along his course he could see, through the umbrageous glades, the house of Frank Goodwin on its wooded hill. And as he crossed the little bridge over the lagoon he saw the old Indian, Galvez, scrubbing at the wooded slab that bore the name of Miraflores. Beyond the lagoon the lands of Goodwin began to slope gently upward. A grassy road, shaded by a munificent and diverse array of tropical flora, wound from the edge of an outlying banana grove to the dwelling. Blythe took this road with long and purposeful strides.

Goodwin was seated on his coolest gallery, dictating letters to his secretary, a sallow and capable native youth. The household adhered to the American plan of breakfast; and that meal had been a thing of the past for the better part of an hour.

The castaway walked to the steps, and flourished a hand.

"Good morning, Blythe," said Goodwin, looking up. "Come in and have a chair. Anything I can do for you?"

"I want to speak to you in private."

Goodwin nodded at his secretary, who strolled out under a mango tree and lit a cigarette. Blythe took the chair that he had left vacant.

"I want some money," he began, doggedly.

"I'm sorry," said Goodwin, with equal directness, "but you can't have any. You're drinking yourself to death, Blythe. Your friends have done all they could to help you to brace up. You won't help yourself. There's no use furnishing you with money to ruin yourself with any longer."

"Dear man," said Blythe, tilting back his chair, "it isn't a question of social economy now. It's past that. I like you, Goodwin; and I've come to stick a knife between your ribs. I was kicked out of Espada's saloon this morning; and Society owes me reparation for my wounded feelings."

"I didn't kick you out."

"No; but in a general way you represent Society; and in a particular way you represent my last chance. I've had to come down to it, old man—I tried to do it a month ago when Losada's man was here turning things over; but I couldn't do

419

it then. Now it's different. I want a thousand dollars, Goodwin; and you'll have to give it to me."

"Only last week," said Goodwin, with a smile, "a silver dollar was all you were asking for."

"An evidence," said Blythe, flippantly, "that I was still virtuous—though under heavy pressure. The wages of sin should be something higher than a *peso* worth forty-eight cents. Let's talk business. I am the villain in the third act; and I must have my merited, if only temporary, triumph. I saw you collar the late president's valiseful of boodle. Oh, I know it's blackmail; but I'm liberal about the price. I know I'm a cheap villain—one of the regular saw-mill-drama kind —but you're one of my particular friends, and I don't want to stick you hard."

"Suppose you go into the details," suggested Goodwin, calmly arranging his letters on the table.

"All right," said "Beelzebub". "I like the way you take it. I despise histrionics; so you will please prepare yourself for the facts without any red fire, calcium or grace notes on the saxophone.

"On the night that His Fly-by-Night Excellency arrived in town I was very drunk. You will excuse the pride with which I state that fact; but it was quite a feat for me to attain that desirable state. Somebody had left a cot out under the orange trees in the yard of Madama Ortiz's hotel. I stepped over the wall, laid down upon it, and fell asleep. I was awakened by an orange that dropped from the tree upon my nose, and I laid there for a while cursing Sir Isaac Newton, or whoever it was that invented gravitation, for not confining his theory to apples.

"And then along came Mr. Miraflores and his true-love with the treasury in a valise, and went into the hotel. Next you hove in sight, and held a pow-wow with the tonsorial artist who insisted upon talking shop after hours. I tried to slumber again; but once more my rest was disturbed—this time by the noise of the popgun that went off upstairs. Then that valise came crashing down into an orange tree just above my head; and I arose from my couch, not knowing when it might begin to rain Saratoga trunks. When the army and the constabulary began to arrive, with their medals and decorations hastily pinned to their pyjamas, and their snicker-snees drawn, I crawled into the welcome shadow of a banana plant. I remained there for an hour, by which time the excitement and the people had cleared away. And then, my dear Goodwin—excuse me—I saw you sneak back and pluck that ripe and juicy valise from the orange tree. I followed you, and saw you take it to your own house. A hundred-thousand-dollar crop from one orange tree in a season about breaks the record of the fruit-growing industry.

"Being a gentleman at that time, of course I never mentioned the incident to anyone. But this morning I was kicked out of a saloon, my code of honour is all out at the elbows, and I'd sell my mother's prayer-book for three fingers of *aguardiente*. I'm not putting on the screws hard. It ought to be worth a thousand to you for me to have slept on that cot through the whole business without waking up and seeing anything."

Goodwin opened two more letters, and made memoranda in pencil on them. Then he called "Manuel!" to his secretary, who came, spryly.

"The *Ariel*—when does she sail?" asked Goodwin.

"*Señor*," answered the youth, "at three this afternoon. She drops down coast to Punta Soledad to complete her cargo of fruit. From there she sails for New Orleans without delay."

"*Bueno!*" said Goodwin. "These letters may wait yet awhile."

The secretary returned to his cigarette under the mango tree.

"In round numbers," said Goodwin, facing Blythe squarely, "how much money do you owe in this town, not including the sums you have 'borrowed' from me?"

"Five hundred—at a rough guess," answered Blythe, lightly.

"Go somewhere in the town and draw up a schedule of

your debts," said Goodwin. "Come back here in two hours, and I will send Manuel with the money to pay them. I will also have a decent outfit of clothing ready for you. You will sail on the *Ariel* at three. Manuel will accompany you as far as the deck of the steamer. There he will hand you one thousand dollars in cash. I suppose that we needn't discuss what you will be expected to do in return."

"Oh, I understand," piped Blythe, cheerily. "I was asleep all the time on the cot under Madama Ortiz's orange trees; and I shall shake off the dust of Coralio for ever. I'll play fair. No more of the lotus for me. Your proposition is O.K. You're a good fellow, Goodwin; and I let you off light. I'll agree to everything. But in the meantime—I've a devil of a thirst on, old man——"

"Not a *centavo*," said Goodwin, firmly, "until you are on board the *Ariel*. You would be drunk in thirty minutes if you had money now."

But he noticed the blood-streaked eyeballs, the relaxed form and the shaking hands of "Beelzebub"; and he stepped into the dining-room through the low window, and brought out a glass and a decanter of brandy.

"Take a bracer, anyway, before you go," he proposed, even as a man to the friend whom he entertains.

"Beelzebub" Blythe's eyes glistened at the sight of the solace for which his soul burned. To-day for the first time his poisoned nerves had been denied their steadying dose; and their retort was a mounting torment. He grasped the decanter and rattled its crystal mouth against the glass in his trembling hand. He flushed the glass, and then stood erect, holding it aloft for an instant. For one fleeting moment he held his head above the drowning waves of his abyss. He nodded easily at Goodwin, raised his brimming glass and murmured a "health" that men had used in his ancient Paradise Lost. And then so suddenly that he spilled the brandy over his hand, he set down his glass, untasted.

"In two hours," his dry lips muttered to Goodwin, as he marched down the steps and turned his face toward the town.

In the edge of the cool banana grove "Beelzebub" halted, and snapped the tongue of his belt buckle into another hole.

"I couldn't do it," he explained, feverishly, to the waving banana fronds. "I wanted to, but I couldn't. A gentleman can't drink with the man that he blackmails."

44

Shoes

JOHN DE GRAFFENREID ATWOOD ate of the lotus, root, stem, and flower. The tropics gobbled him up. He plunged enthusiastically into his work, which was to try to forget Rosine.

Now, they who dine on the lotus rarely consume it plain. There is a sauce *au diable* that goes with it; and the distillers are the chefs who prepare it. And on Johnny's menu card it read "brandy". With a bottle between them, he and Billy Keogh would sit on the porch of the little consulate at night and roar out great, indecorous songs, until the natives, slipping hastily past, would shrug a shoulder and mutter things to themselves about the "*Americanos diablos*".

One day Johnny's *mozo* brought the mail and dumped it on the table. Johnny leaned from his hammock, and fingered the four or five letters dejectedly. Keogh was sitting on the edge of the table chopping lazily with a paper knife at the legs of a centipede that was crawling among the stationery. Johnny was in that phase of lotus-eating when all the world tastes bitter in one's mouth.

"Same old thing!" he complained. "Fool people writing for information about the country. They want to know all about raising fruit, and how to make a fortune without work. Half of 'em don't even send stamps for a reply. They think a consul hasn't anything to do but write letters. Slit those envelopes for me, old man, and see what they want. I'm feeling too rocky to move."

Keogh, acclimated beyond all possibility of ill humour, drew his chair to the table with smiling compliance on his rose-pink countenance, and began to slit open the letters.

Four of them were from citizens in various parts of the United States who seemed to regard the consul at Coralio as a cyclopædia of information. They asked long lists of questions, numerically arranged, about the climate, products, possibilities, laws, business chances, and statistics of the country in which the consul had the honour of representing his own government.

"Write 'em, please, Billy," said the inert official, "just a line, referring them to the latest consular report. Tell 'em the State Department will be delighted to furnish the literary gems. Sign my name. Don't let your pen scratch, Billy; it'll keep me awake."

"Don't snore," said Keogh, amiably, "and I'll do your work for you. You need a corps of assistants, anyhow. Don't see how you ever get out a report. Wake up a minute!—here's one more letter—it's from your own town, too—Dalesburg."

"That so?" murmured Johnny, showing a mild and obligatory interest. "What's it about?"

"Postmaster writes," explained Keogh. "Says a citizen of that town wants some fact and advice from you. Says the citizen has an idea in his head of coming down where you are and opening a shoe store. Wants to know if you think the business would pay. Says he's heard of the boom along this coast, and wants to get in on the ground floor."

In spite of the heat and his bad temper, Johnny's hammock swayed with his laughter. Keogh laughed too; and the pet monkey on the top shelf of the bookcase chattered in shrill sympathy with the ironical reception of the letter from Dalesburg.

"Great bunions!" exclaimed the consul. "Shoe store! What'll they ask about next, I wonder? Overcoat factory, I reckon. Say, Billy—of our three thousand citizens, how many do you suppose ever had a pair of shoes?"

Keogh reflected judicially.

"Let's see—there's you and me and——"

"Not me," said Johnny, promptly and incorrectly, holding

425

up a foot encased in a disreputable deerskin *zapato*. "I haven't been a victim to shoes in months."

"But you've got 'em, though," went on Keogh. "And there's Goodwin and Blanchard and Geddie and old Lutz and Doc Gregg and that Italian that's agent for the banana company, and there's old Delgado—no; he wears sandals. And, oh, yes; there's Madama Ortiz, 'what kapes the hotel' —she had on a pair of red kid slippers at the *baile* the other night. And Miss Pasa, her daughter, that went to school in the States—she brought back some civilized notions in the way of footgear. And there's the *comandante*'s sister that dresses up her feet on feast-days—and Mrs. Geddie, who wears a two with a Castilian instep—and that's about all the ladies. Let's see—don't some of the soldiers at the *cuartel*—no: that's so; they're allowed shoes only when on the march. In barracks they turn their little toeses out to grass."

"'Bout right," agreed the consul. "Not over twenty out of the three thousand ever felt leather on their walking arrangements. Oh, yes; Coralio is just the town for an enterprising shoe store—that doesn't want to part with its goods. Wonder if old Patterson is trying to jolly me! He always was full of things he called jokes. Write him a letter, Billy. I'll dictate it. We'll jolly him back a few."

Keogh dipped his pen, and wrote at Johnny's dictation. With many pauses, filled in with smoke and sundry travellings of the bottle and glasses, the following reply to the Dalesburg communication was perpetrated:

MR. OBADIAH PATTERSON,
        Dalesburg, Ala.

DEAR SIR,—In reply to your favour of July 2nd, I have the honour to inform you that, according to my opinion, there is no place on the habitable globe that presents to the eye stronger evidence of the need of a first-class shoe store than does the town of Coralio. There are 3,000 inhabitants in the place, and not a single shoe store! The situation speaks for itself. This coast is rapidly becoming the goal of enterprising business men, but the shoe business is one that has been sadly overlooked or neglected. In fact there are a considerable number of our citizens actually without shoes at present.

Besides the want above mentioned, there is also a crying need for a brewery, a college of higher mathematics, a coal yard, and a clean and intellectual Punch and Judy Show. I have the honour to be, sir,

Your Obt. Servant,
JOHN DE GRAFFENREID ATWOOD,
U.S. Consul at Coralio.

P.S.—Hello! Uncle Obadiah. How's the old burg racking along? What would the government do without you and me? Look out for a green-headed parrot and a bunch of bananas soon, from your old friend,

JOHNNY.

"I throw in that postscript," explained the consul, "so Uncle Obadiah won't take offence at the official tone of the letter! Now, Billy, you get that correspondence fixed up, and send Pancho to the post office with it. The *Ariadne* takes the mail out to-morrow if they make up that load of fruit to-day."

The night programme in Coralio never varied. The recreations of the people were soporific and flat. They wandered about, barefoot and aimless, speaking lowly and smoking cigar or cigarette. Looking down on the dimly lighted ways one seemed to see a threading maze of brunette ghosts tangled with a procession of insane fireflies. In some houses the thrumming of lugubrious guitars added to the depression of the *triste* night. Giant tree-frogs rattled in the foliage as loudly as the end man's "bones" in a minstrel troupe. By nine o'clock the streets were almost deserted.

Nor at the consulate was there often a change of bill. Keogh would come there nightly, for Coralio's one cool place was the little seaweed porch of that official residence.

The brandy would be kept moving; and before midnight sentiment would begin to stir in the heart of the self-exiled consul. Then he would relate to Keogh the story of his ended romance. Each night Keogh would listen patiently to the tale, and be ready with untiring sympathy.

"But don't you think for a minute"—thus Johnny would always conclude his woeful narrative—"that I'm grieving about that girl, Billy. I've forgotten her. She never enters my mind. If she were to enter that door right now, my pulse wouldn't gain a beat. That's all over long ago."

"Don't I know it?" Keogh would answer. "Of course you've forgotten her. Proper thing to do. Wasn't quite O.K. of her to listen to the knocks that—er—Dink Pawson kept giving you."

"Pink Dawson!"—a word of contempt would be in Johnny's tones—"Poor white trash! That's what he was. Had five hundred acres of farming land, though; and that counted. Maybe I'll have a chance to get back at him some day. The Dawsons weren't anybody. Everybody in Alabama knows the Atwoods. Say, Billy—did you know my mother was a De Graffenreid?"

"Why, no," Keogh would say; "is that so?" He had heard it some three hundred times.

"Fact. The De Graffenreids of Hancock County. But I never think of that girl any more, do I Billy?"

"Not for a minute, my boy," would be the last sounds heard by the conqueror of Cupid.

At this point Johnny would fall into a gentle slumber, and Keogh would saunter out to his own shack under the calabash tree at the edge of the plaza.

In a day or two the letter from the Dalesburg postmaster and its answer had been forgotten by the Coralio exiles. But on the 26th day of July the fruit of the reply appeared upon the tree of events.

The *Andador*, a fruit steamer that visited Coralio regularly, drew into the offing and anchored. The beach was lined with spectators while the quarantine doctor and the custom-house crew rowed out to attend to their duties.

An hour later Billy Keogh lounged into the consulate, clean and cool in his linen clothes, and grinning like a pleased shark.

"Guess what?" he said to Johnny, lounging in his hammock.

"Too hot to guess," said Johnny, lazily.

"Your shoe-store man's come," said Keogh, rolling the sweet morsel on his tongue, "with a stock of goods big enough to supply the continent as far down as Terra del Fuego. They're carting his cases over to the custom-house now. Six barges full they brought ashore and have paddled back for the rest. Oh, ye saints in glory! won't there be regalements in the air when he gets on to the joke and has an interview with Mr. Consul? It'll be worth nine years in the tropics just to witness that one joyful moment."

Keogh loved to take his mirth easily. He selected a clean place on the matting and lay upon the floor. The walls shook with his enjoyment. Johnny turned half over and blinked.

"Don't tell me," he said, "that anybody was fool enough to take that letter seriously."

"Four-thousand-dollar stock of goods!" gasped Keogh, in ecstasy. "Talk about coals to Newcastle! Why didn't he take a shipload of palm-leaf fans to Spitzbergen while he was about it? Saw the old codger on the beach. You ought to have been there when he put on his specs and squinted at the five hundred or so barefooted citizens standing around."

"Are you telling the truth, Billy?" asked the consul, weakly.

"Am I? You ought to see the buncoed gentleman's daughter he brought along. Looks! She makes the brick-dust *señoritas* here look like tar-babies."

"Go on," said Johnny, "if you can stop that asinine giggling. I hate to see a grown man make a laughing hyena of himself."

"Name is Hemstetter," went on Keogh. "He's a——
Hello! what's the matter now?"

Johnny's moccasined feet struck the floor with a thud as
he wriggled out of his hammock.

"Get up, you idiot," he said, sternly, "or I'll brain you
with this inkstand. That's Rosine and her father. Gad!
what a drivelling idiot old Patterson is! Get up, here, Billy
Keogh, and help me. What the devil are we going to do? Has
all the world gone crazy?"

Keogh rose and dusted himself. He managed to regain a
decorous demeanour.

"Situation has got to be met, Johnny," he said, with some
success at seriousness. "I didn't think about its being your
girl until you spoke. First thing to do is to get them comfortable quarters. You go down and face the music, and I'll
trot out to Goodwin's and see if Mrs. Goodwin won't take
them in. They've got the decentest house in town."

"Bless you, Billy!" said the consul. "I knew you wouldn't
desert me. The world's bound to come to an end, but maybe
we can stave it off for a day or two."

Keogh hoisted his umbrella and set out for Goodwin's
house. Johnny put on his coat and hat. He picked up the
brandy bottle, but set it down again without drinking, and
marched bravely down to the beach.

In the shade of the custom-house walls he found Mr.
Hemstetter and Rosine surrounded by a mass of gaping
citizens. The customs officers were ducking and scraping,
while the captain of the *Andador* interpreted the business of
the new arrivals. Rosine looked healthy and very much
alive. She was gazing at the strange scenes around her with
amused interest. There was a faint blush upon her round
cheek as she greeted her old admirer. Mr. Hemstetter shook
hands with Johnny in a very friendly way. He was an oldish,
impractical man—one of that numerous class of erratic
business men who are for ever dissatisfied, and seeking a
change.

"I am very glad to see you, John—may I call you John?"

430

he said. "Let me thank you for your prompt answer to our postmaster's letter of inquiry. He volunteered to write to you on my behalf. I was looking about for something different in the way of business in which the profits would be greater. I had noticed in the papers that this coast was receiving much attention from investors. I am extremely grateful for your advice to come. I sold out everything that I possess, and invested the proceeds in as fine a stock of shoes as could be bought in the North. You have a picturesque town here, John. I hope business will be as good as your letter justifies me in expecting."

Johnny's agony was abbreviated by the arrival of Keogh, who hurried up with the news that Mrs. Goodwin would be much pleased to place rooms at the disposal of Mr. Hemstetter and his daughter. So there Mr. Hemstetter and Rosine were at once conducted and left to recuperate from the fatigue of the voyage, while Johnny went down to see that the cases of shoes were safely stored in the customs warehouse pending their examination by the officials. Keogh, grinning like a shark, skirmished about to find Goodwin, to instruct him not to expose to Mr. Hemstetter the true state of Coralio as a shoe market until Johnny had been given a chance to redeem the situation, if such a thing were possible.

That night the consul and Keogh held a desperate consultation on the breezy porch of the consulate.

"Send 'em back home," began Keogh, reading Johnny's thoughts.

"I would," said Johnny, after a little silence; "but I've been lying to you, Billy."

"All right about that," said Keogh, affably.

"I've told you hundreds of times," said Johnny, slowly, "that I had forgotten that girl, haven't I?"

"About three hundred and seventy-five," admitted the monument of patience.

"I lied," repeated the consul, "every time. I never forgot her for one minute. I was an obstinate ass for running away just because she said 'No' once. And I was too proud a fool

431

to go back. I talked with Rosine a few minutes this evening up at Goodwin's. I found out one thing. You remember that farmer fellow who was always after her?"

"Dink Pawson?" asked Keogh.

"Pink Dawson. Well, he wasn't a hill of beans to her. She says she didn't believe a word of the things he told her about me. But I'm sewed up now, Billy. That tomfool letter we sent ruined whatever chance I had left. She'll despise me when she finds out that her old father has been made the victim of a joke that a decent schoolboy wouldn't have been guilty of. Shoes! Why, he couldn't sell twenty pairs of shoes in Coralio if he kept store here for twenty years. You put a pair of shoes on one of these Caribs or Spanish brown boys and what'd he do? Stand on his head and squeal until he'd kicked 'em off. None of 'em ever wore shoes, and they never will. If I send 'em back home, I'll have to tell the whole story, and what'll she think of me? I want that girl worse than ever, Billy, and now when she's in reach, I lost her for ever because I tried to be funny when the thermometer was at 102."

"Keep cheerful," said the optimistic Keogh. "And let 'em open the store. I've been busy myself this afternoon. We can stir up a temporary boom in footgear anyhow. I'll buy six pairs when the doors open. I've been around and seen all the fellows and explained the catastrophe. They'll all buy shoes like they was centipedes. Frank Goodwin will take cases of 'em. The Geddies want about eleven pairs between 'em. Clancy is going to invest the savings of weeks, and even old Doc Gregg wants three pairs of alligator hide slippers if they've got any tens. Blanchard got a look at Miss Hemstetter; and as he's a Frenchman, no less than a dozen pairs will do for him."

"A dozen customers," said Johnny, "for a $4,000 stock of shoes! It won't work. There's a big problem here to figure out. You go home, Billy, and leave me alone. I've got to work at it all by myself. Take that bottle of three-star along with you—no, sir; not another ounce of booze for the United States consul. I'll sit here to-night and pull out the think stop. If there's a soft place on this proposition anywhere I'll land on it. If there isn't, there'll be another wreck to the credit of the gorgeous tropics."

Keogh left, feeling that he could be of no use. Johnny laid a handful of cigars on a table and stretched himself in a steamer chair. When the sudden daylight broke, silvering the harbour ripples, he was still sitting there. Then he got up, whistling a little tune, and took his bath.

At nine o'clock he walked down to the dingy little cable office and hung up for half an hour over a blank. The result of his application was the following message, which he signed and had transmitted at a cost of $33:

To PINKNEY DAWSON,
 Dalesburg, Ala.

Draft for $100 comes to you next mail. Ship me immediately 500 pounds stiff, dry cockleburrs. New use here in arts. Market price twenty cents pound. Further orders likely. Rush.

45

Ships

WITHIN a week a suitable building had been secured in the Calle Grande, and Mr. Hemstetter's stock of shoes arranged upon their shelves. The rent of the store was moderate; and the stock made a fine showing of neat white boxes, attractively displayed.

Johnny's friends stood by him loyally. On the first day Keogh strolled into the store in a casual kind of way about once every hour, and bought shoes. After he had purchased a pair each of extension soles, congress gaiters, button kids, low-quartered calfs, dancing pumps, rubber boots, tans of various hues, tennis shoes and flowered slippers, he sought out Johnny to be prompted as to the names of other kinds that he might inquire for. The other English-speaking residents also played their parts nobly by buying often and liberally. Keogh was grand marshal, and made them distribute their patronage, thus keeping up a fair run of custom for several days.

Mr. Hemstetter was gratified by the amount of business done thus far; but expressed surprise that the natives were so backward with their custom.

"Oh, they're awfully shy," explained Johnny, as he wiped his forehead nervously. "They'll get the habit pretty soon. They'll come with a rush when they do come."

One afternoon Keogh dropped into the consul's office, chewing an unlighted cigar thoughtfully.

"Got anything up your sleeve?" he inquired of Johnny. "If you have it's about time to show it. If you can borrow some gent's hat in the audience, and make a lot of customers for an idle stock of shoes come out of it, you'd better spiel.

The boys have all laid in enough footgear to last 'em for ten years; and there's nothing doing in the shoe store but dolcy far nienty. I just came by there. Your venerable victim was standing in the door, gazing through his specs at the bare toes passing by his emporium. The natives have got the true artistic temperament. He and Clancy took eighteen tintypes this morning in two hours. There's been but one pair of shoes sold all day. Blanchard went in and bought a pair of fur-lined house-slippers because he thought he saw Miss Hemstetter go into the store. I saw him throw the slippers into the lagoon afterwards."

"There's a Mobile fruit steamer coming in to-morrow or next day," said Johnny. "We can't do anything until then."

"What are you going to do—try to create a demand?"

"Political economy isn't your strong point," said the consul, impudently. "You can't create a demand. But you can create a necessity for a demand. That's what I am going to do."

Two weeks after the consul sent his cable, a fruit steamer brought him a large, mysterious brown bale of some unknown commodity. Johnny's influence with the custom-house people was sufficiently strong for him to get the goods turned over to him without the usual inspection. He had the bale taken to the consulate and snugly stowed in the back corner.

That night he ripped open a corner of it and took out a handful of the cockleburrs. He examined them with the care with which a warrior examines his arms before he goes forth to battle for his lady-love and life. The burrs were the ripe August product, as hard as filberts, and bristling with pines as tough and sharp as needles. Johnny whistled softly a little tune, and went out to find Billy Keogh.

Later in the night, when Coralio was steeped in slumber, he and Billy went forth into the deserted streets with their coats bulging like balloons. All up and down the Calle Grande they went, sowing the sharp burrs, carefully in the sand, along the narrow sidewalks, in every foot of grass

between the silent houses. And then they took the side streets
and byways, missing none. No place where the foot of man,
woman or child might fall was slighted. Many trips they made
to and from the prickly hoard. And then, nearly at the dawn,
they laid themselves down to rest calmly, as great generals
do after planning a victory according to the revised tactics,
and slept, knowing that they had sowed with the accuracy
of Satan sowing tares and the perseverance of Paul planting.

With the rising sun came the purveyors of fruits and meats,
and arranged their wares in and around the little market-
house. At the end of the town near the seashore the market-
house stood; and the sowing of the burrs had not been carried
that far. The dealers waited long past the hour when their
sales usually began. None came to buy. "*Qué hay?*" they
began to exclaim, one to another.

At their accustomed time, from every 'dobe and palm
hut and grass-thatched shack and dim *patio* glided women—
black women, brown women, lemon-coloured women,
women dun and yellow and tawny. They were the marketers
starting to purchase the family supply of cassava, plantains,
meat, fowls, and tortillas. *Décolleté* they were and bare-armed
and bare-footed, with a single skirt reaching below the knee.
Stolid and ox-eyed, they stepped from their doorways into
the narrow paths or upon the soft grass of the streets.

The first to emerge uttered ambiguous squeals, and raised
one foot quickly. Another step and they sat down, with shrill
cries of alarm, to pick at the new and painful insects that
had stung them upon the feet. "*Qué picadores diablos!*" they
screeched to one another across the narrow ways. Some tried
the grass instead of the paths, but there they were also stung
and bitten by the strange little prickly balls. They plumped
down in the grass, and added their lamentations to those of
their sisters in the sandy paths. All through the town was
heard the plaint of the feminine jabber. The venders in the
market still wondered why no customers came.

Then men, lords of the earth, came forth. They, too, began
to hop, to dance, to limp, and to curse. They stood stranded

436

and foolish, or stooped to pluck at the scourge that attacked their feet and ankles. Some loudly proclaimed the pest to be poisonous spiders of an unknown species.

And then the children ran out for their morning romp. And now to the uproar was added the howls of limping infants and cockleburred childhood. Every minute the advancing day brought forth fresh victims.

Doña Maria Castillas y Buenventura de las Casas stepped from her honoured doorway, as was her daily custom, to procure fresh bread from the *panaderia* across the street. She was clad in a skirt of flowered yellow satin, a chemise of ruffled linen, and wore a purple mantilla from the looms of Spain. Her lemon-tinted feet, alas! were bare. Her progress was majestic, for were not her ancestors hidalgos of Aragon? Three steps she made across the velvety grass, and set her aristocratic sole upon a bunch of Johnny's burrs. Doña Maria Castillas y Buenventura de las Casas emitted a yowl even as a wild-cat. Turning about, she fell upon hands and knees, and crawled—ay, like a beast of the field she crawled back to her honourable door-sill.

Don Señor Ildefonso Federico Valdazar, *Juez de la Paz*, weighing twenty stone, attempted to convey his bulk to the *pulperia* at the corner of the plaza in order to assuage his matutinal thirst. The first plunge of his unshod foot into the cool grass struck a concealed mine. Don Ildefonso fell like a crumpled cathedral, crying out that he had been fatally bitten by a deadly scorpion. Everywhere were the shoeless citizens hopping, stumbling, limping, and picking from their feet the venomous insects that had come in a single night to harass them.

The first to perceive the remedy was Estebán Delgado, the barber, a man of travel and education. Sitting upon a stone, he plucked burrs from his toes, and made oration:

"Behold, my friends, these bugs of the devil! I know them well. They soar through the skies in swarms like pigeons. These are dead ones that fell during the night. In Yucatan I have seen them as large as oranges. Yes! There they hiss like serpents, and have wings like bats. It is the shoes—the shoes that one needs! *Zapatos—zapatos para mi!*"

Estebán hobbled to Mr. Hemstetter's store, and bought shoes. Coming out, he swaggered down the street with impunity, reviling loudly the bugs of the devil. The suffering ones sat up and stood upon one foot and beheld the immune barber. Men, women and children took up the cry: "*Zapatos! zapatos!*"

The necessity for the demand had been created. The demand followed. That day Mr. Hemstetter sold three hundred pairs of shoes.

"It is really surprising," he said to Johnny, who came up in the evening to help to straighten out the stock, "how trade is picking up. Yesterday I made but three sales."

"I told you they'd whoop things up when they got started," said the consul.

"I think I shall order a dozen more cases of goods, to keep the stock up," said Mr. Hemstetter, beaming through his spectacles.

"I wouldn't send in any orders yet," advised Johnny. "Wait till you see how the trade holds up."

Each night Johnny and Keogh sowed the crop that grew dollars by day. At the end of ten days two-thirds of the stock of shoes had been sold; and the stock of cockleburrs was exhausted. Johnny cabled to Pink Dawson for another 500 pounds, paying twenty cents per pound as before. Mr. Hemstetter carefully made up an order for $1,500 worth of shoes from Northern firms. Johnny hung about the store until this order was ready for the mail, and succeeded in destroying it before it reached the post office.

That night he took Rosine under the mango tree by Goodwin's porch, and confessed everything. She looked him in the eye, and said: "You are a very wicked man. Father and I will go back home. You say it was a joke? I think it is a very serious matter."

But at the end of half an hour's argument the conversation had been turned upon a different subject. The two were considering the respective merits of pale blue and pink wallpaper with which the old colonial mansion of the Atwoods in Dalesburg was to be decorated after the wedding.

On the next morning Johnny confessed to Mr. Hemstetter. The shoe merchant put on his spectacles, and said through them: "You strike me as being a most extraordinary young scamp. If I had not managed this enterprise with good business judgment my entire stock of goods might have been a complete loss. Now, how do you propose to dispose of the rest of it?"

When the second invoice of cockleburrs arrived Johnny loaded them and the remainder of the shoes into a schooner, and sailed down the coast to Alazan.

There, in the same dark and diabolical manner, he repeated his success; and came back with a bag of money and not so much as a shoestring.

And then he besought his great Uncle of the waving goatee and starred vest to accept his resignation, for the lotus no longer lured him. He hankered for the spinach and cress of Dalesburg.

The services of Mr. William Terence Keogh as acting consul, *pro tem.*, were suggested and accepted, and Johnny sailed with the Hemstetters back to his native shores.

Keogh slipped into the sinecure of the American consul-ship with the ease that never left him even in such high places. The tintype establishment was soon to become a thing of the past, although its deadly work along the peaceful and helpless Spanish Main was never effaced. The restless partners were about to be off again, scouting ahead of the slow ranks of Fortune. But now they would take different ways. There were rumours of a promising uprising in Peru; and thither the martial Clancy would turn his adventurous steps. As for Keogh, he was figuring in his mind and on quires of Government letter-heads a scheme that dwarfed the art of misrepresenting the human countenance upon tin.

"What suits me," Keogh used to say, "in the way of a

business proposition is something diversified that looks like a longer shot than it is—something in the way of a genteel graft that isn't worked enough for the correspondence schools to be teaching it by mail. I take the long end; but I like to have at least as good a chance to win as a man learning to play poker on an ocean steamer, or running for governor of Texas on the Republican ticket. And when I cash in my winnings, I don't want to find any widows' and orphans' chips in my stack."

The grass-grown globe was the green table on which Keogh gambled. The games he played were of his own invention. He was no grubber after the diffident dollar. Nor did he care to follow it with horn and hounds. Rather he loved to coax it with egregious and brilliant flies from its habitat in the waters of strange streams. Yet Keogh was a business man; and his schemes, in spite of their singularity, were as solidly set as the plans of a building contractor. In Arthur's time Sir William Keogh would have been a Knight of the Round Table. In these modern days he rides abroad, seeking the Graft instead of the Grail.

Three days after Johnny's departure, two small schooners appeared off Coralio. After some delay a boat put off from one of them, and brought a sunburned young man ashore. This young man had a shrewd and calculating eye; and he glanced with amazement at the strange things that he saw. He found on the beach some one who directed him to the consul's office; and thither he made his way at a nervous gait.

Keogh was sprawled in the official chair, drawing caricatures of his Uncle's head on an official pad of paper. He looked up at his visitor.

"Where's Johnny Atwood?" inquired the sunburned young man, in a business tone.

"Gone," said Keogh, working carefully at Uncle Sam's necktie.

"That's just like him," remarked the nut-brown one, leaning against the table. "He always was a fellow to gallivant round instead of 'tending to business. Will he be in soon?"

"Don't think so," said Keogh, after a fair amount of deliberation.

"I s'pose he's out at some of his tomfoolery," conjectured the visitor, in a tone of virtuous conviction. "Johnny never would stick to anything long enough to succeed. I wonder how he manages to run his business here, and never be 'round to look after it."

"I'm looking after the business just now," admitted the *pro tem.* consul.

"Are you?—then, say!—where's the factory?"

"What factory?" asked Keogh, with a mildly polite interest.

"Why, the factory where they use them cockleburrs. Lord knows what they use 'em for, anyway! I've got the basements of both them ships out there loaded with 'em. I'll give you a bargain in this lot. I've had every man, woman and child around Dalesburg that wasn't busy pickin' 'em for a month. I hired these ships to bring 'em over. Everybody thought I was crazy. Now, you can have this lot for fifteen cents a pound, delivered on land. And if you want more I guess old Alabam' can come up to the demand. Johnny told me when he left home that if he struck anything down here that there was any money in he'd let me in on it. Shall I drive the ships in and hitch?"

A look of supreme, almost incredulous, delight dawned in Keogh's ruddy countenance. He dropped his pencil. His eyes turned upon the sunburned young man with joy in them mingled with fear lest his ecstasy should prove a dream.

"For God's sake tell me," said Keogh, earnestly, "are you Dink Pawson?"

"My name is Pinkney Dawson," said the cornerer of the cockleburr market.

Billy Keogh slid rapturously and gently from his chair to his favourite strip of matting on the floor.

There were not many sounds in Coralio on that sultry

441

afternoon. Among those that were may be mentioned a noise of enraptured and unrighteous laughter from a prostrate Irish-American, while a sunburned young man, with a shrewd eye, looked on him with wonder and amazement. Also the "tramp, tramp, tramp", of many well-shod feet in the streets outside. Also the lonesome wash of the waves that beat along the historic shores of the Spanish Main.

46

Masters of Arts

A TWO-INCH stub of blue pencil was the wand with which Keogh performed the preliminary acts of his magic. So, with this he covered paper with diagrams and figures, while he waited for the United States of America to send down to Coralio a successor to Atwood, resigned.

The new scheme that his mind had conceived, his stout heart indorsed, and his blue pencil corroborated, was laid around the characteristics and human frailties of the new president of Anchuria. These characteristics, and the situation out of which Keogh hoped to wrest a golden tribute, deserve chronicling contributive to the clear order of events.

President Losada—many called him Dictator—was a man whose genius would have made him conspicuous even among Anglo-Saxons, had not that genius been intermixed with other traits that were petty and subversive. He had some of the lofty patriotism of Washington (the man he most admired), the force of Napoleon, and much of the wisdom of the sages. These characteristics might have justified him in the assumption of the title of "The Illustrious Liberator", had they not been accompanied by a stupendous and amazing vanity that kept him in the less worthy ranks of the dictators.

Yet he did his country great service. With a mighty grasp he shook it nearly free from the shackles of ignorance and sloth and the vermin that fed upon it, and all but made it a power in the council of nations. He established schools and hospitals, built roads, bridges, railroads and palaces, and bestowed generous subsidies upon the arts and sciences. He was the absolute despot and the idol of his people. The wealth of the country poured into his hands. Other presidents had been rapacious without reason. Losada amassed enormous wealth, but his people had their share of the benefits.

The joint in his armour was his insatiate passion for monuments and tokens commemorating his glory. In every town he caused to be erected statues of himself bearing legends in praise of his greatness. In the walls of every public edifice, tablets were fixed reciting his splendour and the gratitude of his subjects. His statuettes and portraits were scattered throughout the land in every house and hut. One of the sycophants in his court painted him as St. John, with a halo and a train of attendants in full uniform. Losada saw nothing incongruous in this picture, and had it hung in a church in the capital. He ordered from a French sculptor a marble group including himself with Napoleon, Alexander the Great, and one or two others whom he deemed worthy of the honour.

He ransacked Europe for decorations, employing policy, money and intrigue to cajole the orders he coveted from kings and rulers. On state occasions his breast was covered from shoulder to shoulder with crosses, stars, golden roses, medals and ribbons. It was said that the man who could contrive for him a new decoration, or invent some new method of extolling his greatness, might plunge a hand deep into the treasury.

This was the man upon whom Billy Keogh had his eye. The gentle buccaneer had observed the rain of favours that fell upon those who ministered to the president's vanities, and he did not deem it his duty to hoist his umbrella against the scattering drops of liquid fortune.

In a few weeks the new consul arrived, releasing Keogh from his temporary duties. He was a young man fresh from college, who lived for botany alone. The consulate at Coralio gave him the opportunity to study tropical flora. He wore smoked glasses, and carried a green umbrella. He filled the cool, back porch of the consulate with plants and specimens so that space for a bottle and chair was not to be found.

444

Keogh gazed on him sadly, but without rancour, and began to pack his gripsack. For his new plot against stagnation along the Spanish Main required of him a voyage overseas.

Soon came the *Karlsefin* again—she of the trampish habits —gleaning a cargo of coconuts for a speculative descent upon the New York market. Keogh was booked for a passage on the return trip.

"Yes, I'm going to New York," he explained to the group of his countrymen that had gathered on the beach to see him off. "But I'll be back before you miss me. I've undertaken the art education of this piebald country, and I'm not the man to desert it while it's in the early throes of tintypes."

With this mysterious declaration of his intentions Keogh boarded the *Karlsefin*.

Ten days later, shivering, with the collar of his thin coat turned high, he burst into the studio of Carolus White at the top of a tall building in Tenth Street, New York City.

Carolus White was smoking a cigarette and frying sausages over an oil stove. He was only twenty-three, and had noble theories about art.

"Billy Keogh!" exclaimed White, extending the hand that was not busy with the frying pan. "From what part of the uncivilized world, I wonder?"

"Hallo, Carry," said Keogh, dragging forward a stool, and holding his fingers close to the stove. "I'm glad I found you so soon. I've been looking for you all day in the directories and art galleries. The free-lunch man on the corner told me where you were, quick. I was sure you'd be painting pictures yet."

Keogh glanced about the studio with the shrewd eye of a connoisseur in business.

"Yes, you can do it," he declared with many gentle nods of his head. "That big one in the corner with the angels and green clouds and band-wagon is just the sort of thing we want. What would you call that, Carry—scene from Coney Island, ain't it?"

445

"That," said White, "I had intended to call 'The Translation of Elijah', but you may be nearer right than I am."

"Name doesn't matter," said Keogh, largely; "it's the frame and the varieties of paint that does the trick. Now, I can tell you in a minute what I want. I've come on a little voyage of two thousand miles to take you in with me on a scheme. I thought of you as soon as the scheme showed itself to me. How would you like to go back with me and paint a picture? Ninety days for the trip, and five thousand dollars for the job."

"Cereal food or hair-tonic posters?" asked White.

"It isn't an ad."

"What kind of a picture is it to be?"

"It's a long story," said Keogh.

"Go ahead with it. If you don't mind, while you talk I'll just keep my eye on these sausages. Let 'em get one shade deeper than a Vandyke brown and you spoil 'em."

Keogh explained his project. They were to return to Coralio, where White was to pose as a distinguished American portrait painter who was touring in the tropics as a relaxation from his arduous and remunerative professional labours. It was not an unreasonable hope, even to those who trod in the beaten paths of business, that an artist with so much prestige might secure a commission to perpetuate upon canvas the lineaments of the president, and secure a share of the *pesos* that were raining upon the caterers to his weaknesses.

Keogh had set his price at ten thousand dollars. Artists had been paid more for portraits. He and White were to share the expenses of the trip and divide the possible profits. Then he laid the scheme before White, whom he had known in the West before one declared for Art and the other became a Bedouin.

Before long the two machinators abandoned the rigour of the bare studio for a snug corner of a café. There they sat far into the night, with old envelopes and Keogh's stub of blue pencil between them.

446

At twelve o'clock White doubled up in his chair, with his chin on his fist, and shut his eyes at the unbeautiful wallpaper.

"I'll go you, Billy," he said, in the quiet tones of decision. "I've got two or three hundred saved up for sausages and rent; and I'll take the chance with you. Five thousand! It will give me two years in Paris and one in Italy. I'll begin to pack to-morrow."

"You'll begin in ten minutes," said Keogh. "It's to-morrow now. The *Karlsefin* starts back at four p.m. Come on to your painting shop, and I'll help you."

For five months in the year Coralio is the Newport of Anchuria. Then only does the town possess life. From November to March it is practically the seat of government. The president with his official family sojourns there; and society follows him. The pleasure-loving people make the season one long holiday of amusement and rejoicing. *Fiestas*, balls, games, sea bathing, processions and small theatres contribute to their enjoyment. The famous Swiss band from the capital plays in the little plaza every evening, while the fourteen carriages and vehicles in the town circle in funereal but complacent procession. Indians from the interior mountains, looking like prehistoric stone idols, come down to peddle their handiwork in the streets. The people throng the narrow ways, a chattering, happy, careless stream of buoyant humanity. Preposterous children, rigged out with the shortest of ballet skirts and gilt wings, howl, underfoot, among the effervescent crowds. Especially is the arrival of the presidential party, at the opening of the season, attended with pomp, show and patriotic demonstrations of enthusiasm and delight.

When Keogh and White reached their destination, on the return trip of the *Karlsefin*, the gay winter season was well begun. As they stepped upon the beach they could hear the band playing in the plaza. The village maidens, with fireflies already fixed in their dark locks, were gliding, barefoot and coy-eyed, along the paths. Dandies in white linen, swinging their canes, were beginning their seductive strolls. The air was full of human essence, of artificial excitement, of coquetry, indolence, pleasure—the man-made sense of existence.

The first two or three days after their arrival were spent in preliminaries. Keogh escorted the artist about town, introducing him to the little circle of English-speaking residents, and pulling whatever wires he could to effect the spreading of White's fame as a painter. And then Keogh planned a more spectacular demonstration of the idea he wished to keep before the public.

He and White engaged rooms in the Hotel de los Estranjeros. The two were clad in new suits of immaculate duck, with American straw hats, and carried canes of remarkable uniqueness and inutility. Few *caballeros* in Coralio—even the gorgeously uniformed officers of the Anchurian army— were as conspicuous for ease and elegance of demeanour as Keogh and his friend, the great American painter, *Señor* White.

White set up his easel on the beach and made striking sketches of the mountain and sea views. The native population formed at his rear in a vast, chattering semicircle to watch his work. Keogh, with his care for details, had arranged for himself a pose which he carried out with fidelity. His rôle was that of friend to the great artist, a man of affairs and leisure. The visible emblem of his position was a pocket camera.

"For branding the man who owns it," said he, "a genteel dilettante with a bank account and an easy conscience, a steam yacht ain't in it with a camera. You see a man doing nothing but loafing around making snapshots, and you know right away he reads up well in 'Bradstreet'. You notice these old millionaire boys—soon as you get through taking everything else in sight they go to taking photographs. People are more impressed by a kodak than they are by a title or a four-carat scar-pin." So Keogh strolled blandly about Coralio, snapping the scenery and the shrinking *señoritas* while White posed conspicuously in the higher regions of art.

Two weeks after their arrival, the scheme began to bear

fruit. An aide-de-camp of the president drove to the hotel in a dashing victoria. The president desired that *Señor* White come to the Casa Morena for an informal interview.

Keogh gripped his pipe tightly between his teeth. "Not a cent less than ten thousand," he said to the artist—"remember the price. And in gold or its equivalent—don't let him stick you with this bargain-counter stuff they call money here."

"Perhaps it isn't that he wants," said White.

"Get out!" said Keogh, with splendid confidence. "I know what he wants. He wants his picture painted by the celebrated young American painter and filibuster now sojourning in his downtrodden country. Off you go."

The victoria sped away with the artist. Keogh walked up and down, puffing great clouds of smoke from his pipe, and waited. In an hour the victoria swept again to the door of the hotel, deposited White, and vanished. The artist dashed up the stairs, three at a step. Keogh stopped smoking, and became a silent interrogation point.

"Landed," exclaimed White, with his boyish face flushed with elation. "Billy, you are a wonder. He wants a picture. I'll tell you all about it. By heavens! that dictator chap is a corker! He's a dictator clear down to his finger-ends. He's a kind of combination of Julius Cæsar, Lucifer, and Chauncey Depew done in sepia. Polite and grim—that's his way. The room I saw him in was about ten acres big, and looked like a Mississippi steamboat with its gilding and mirrors and white paint. He talks English better than I can ever hope to. The matter of the price came up. I mentioned ten thousand. I expected him to call the guard and have me taken out and shot. He didn't move an eyelash. He just waved one of his chestnut hands in a careless way and said, 'Whatever you say.' I am to go back to-morrow and discuss with him the details of the picture."

Keogh hung his head. Self-abasement was easy to read in his downcast countenance.

"I'm failing, Carry," he said, sorrowfully. "I'm not fit to

handle these man's-size schemes any longer. Peddling oranges in a push-cart is about the suitable graft for me. When I said ten thousand, I swear I thought I had sized up that brown man's limit to within two cents. He'd have melted down for fifteen thousand just as easy. Say—Carry—you'll see old Keogh safe in some nice, quiet idiot asylum, won't you, if he makes a break like that again?"

The Casa Morena, although only one storey in height, was a building of brown stone, luxurious as a palace in its interior. It stood on a low hill in a walled garden of splendid tropical flora at the upper edge of Coralio. The next day the president's carriage came again for the artist. Keogh went out for a walk along the beach, where he and his "picture box" were now familiar sights. When he returned to the hotel White was sitting in a steamer chair on the balcony.

"Well," said Keogh, "did you and His Nibs decide on the kind of chromo he wants?"

White got up and walked back and forth on the balcony a few times. Then he stopped, and laughed strangely. His face was flushed, and his eyes were bright with a kind of angry amusement.

"Look here, Billy," he said, somewhat roughly, "when you first came to me in my studio and mentioned a picture, I thought you wanted a Smashed Oats or a Hair Tonic poster painted on a range of mountains or the side of a continent. Well, either of those jobs would have been Art in its highest form compared to the one you've steered me against. I can't paint that picture, Billy. You've got to let me out. Let me try to tell you what that barbarian wants. He had it all planned out, and even a sketch made of his idea. The old boy doesn't draw badly at all. But, ye goddesses of Art! listen to the monstrosity of his idea. He wants himself in the centre of the canvas, of course. He is to be painted as Jupiter sitting on Olympus, with the clouds at his feet. At one side of him stands George Washington, in full regimentals, with his hand on the president's shoulder. An angel with outstretched wings hovers overhead, crowning him—Queen of the May,

I suppose. In the background is to be cannon, more angels and soldiers. The man who would paint that picture would have to have the soul of a dog, and would deserve to go down into oblivion without even a tin can tied to his tail to sound his memory."

Little beads of moisture crept out all over Billy Keogh's brow. The stub of his blue pencil had not figured out a contingency like this. The machinery of his plan had run with flattering smoothness until now. He dragged another chair upon the balcony, and got White back to his seat. He lit his pipe with apparent calm.

"Now, sonny," he said, with gentle grimness, "you and me will have an Art to Art talk. You've got your art and I've got mine. Yours is the real Pierian stuff that turns up its nose at bock-beer signs and oleographs of the Old Mill. Mine's the art of Business. This was my scheme, and it worked out like two-and-two. Paint that president man as Old King Cole, or Venus, or a landscape, or a fresco, or a bunch of lilies, or anything he thinks he looks like. But get the paint on the canvas and collect the spoils. You wouldn't throw me down, Carry, at this stage of the game. Think of that ten thousand."

"I can't help thinking of it," said White, "and that's what hurts. I'm tempted to throw every ideal I ever had down in the mire, and steep my soul in infamy by painting that picture. That five thousand meant three years of foreign study to me, and I'd almost sell my soul for that."

"Now it ain't as bad as that," said Keogh, soothingly. "It's a business proposition. It's so much paint and time against money. I don't fall in with your idea that that picture would so everlastingly jolt the art side of the question. George Washington was all right, you know, and nobody could say a word against the angel. I don't think so bad of that group. If you was to give Jupiter a pair of epaulettes and a sword, and kind of work the clouds around to look like a blackberry patch, it wouldn't make such a bad battle scene. Why, if we hadn't already settled on the price, he

451

ought to pay an extra thousand for Washington, and the angel ought to raise it five hundred."

"You don't understand, Billy," said White, with an uneasy laugh. "Some of us fellows who try to paint have big notions about Art. I wanted to paint a picture some day that people would stand before and forget that it was made of paint. I wanted it to creep into them like a bar of music and mushroom there like a soft bullet. And I wanted 'em to go away and ask, 'What else has he done?' And I didn't want 'em to find a thing; not a protrait nor a magazine cover nor an illustration nor a drawing of a girl—nothing but *the* picture. That's why I've lived on fried sausages, and tried to keep true to myself. I persuaded myself to do this portrait for the chance it might give me to study abroad. But this howling, screaming caricature! Good Lord! can't you see how it is?"

"Sure," said Keogh, as tenderly as he would have spoken to a child, and he laid a long forefinger on White's knee. "I see. It's bad to have your art all slugged up like that. I know. You wanted to paint a big thing like a panorama of the battle of Gettysburg. But let me kalsomine you a little mental sketch to consider. Up to date we're out $385.50 on this scheme. Our capital took every cent both of us could raise. We've got about enough left to get back to New York on. I need my share of that ten thousand. I want to work a copper deal in Idaho, and make a hundred thousand. That's the business end of the thing. Come down off your art perch, Carry, and let's land that hatful of dollars."

"Billy," said White, with an effort, "I'll try. I won't say I'll do it, but I'll try. I'll go at it, and put it through if I can."

"That's business," said Keogh, heartily. "Good boy! Now, here's another thing—rush that picture—crowd it through as quick as you can. Get a couple of boys to help you mix the paint if necessary. I've picked up some pointers around town. The people here are beginning to get sick of Mr. President. They say he's been too free with concessions; and they accuse him of trying to make a dicker with England to sell out the country. We want that picture done and paid for before there's any row."

In the great *patio* of Casa Morena, the president caused to be stretched a huge canvas. Under this White set up his temporary studio. For two hours each day the great man sat to him.

White worked faithfully. But, as the work progressed, he had seasons of bitter scorn, of infinite self-contempt, of sullen gloom and sardonic gaiety. Keogh, with the patience of a great general, soothed, coaxed, argued—kept him at the picture.

At the end of a month White announced that the picture was completed—Jupiter, Washington, angels, clouds, cannon and all. His face was pale and his mouth drawn straight when he told Keogh. He said the president was much pleased with it. It was to be hung in the National Gallery of Statesmen and Heroes. The artist had been requested to return to Casa Morena on the following day to receive payment. At the appointed time he left the hotel, silent under his friend's joyful talk of their success.

An hour later he walked into the room where Keogh was waiting, threw his hat on the floor, and sat upon the table.

"Billy," he said, in strained and labouring tones, "I've a little money out West in a small business that my brother is running. It's what I've been living on while I've been studying art. I'll draw out my share and pay you back what you've lost on this scheme."

"Lost!" exclaimed Keogh, jumping up. "Didn't you get paid for the picture?"

"Yes, I got paid," said White. "But just now there isn't any picture, and there isn't any pay. If you care to hear about it, here are the edifying details. The president and I were looking at the painting. His secretary brought a bank draft on New York for ten thousand dollars and handed it to me. The moment I touched it I went wild. I tore it into little pieces and threw them on the floor. A workman was repainting the pillars inside the *patio*. A bucket of his paint happened to be convenient. I picked up his brush and slapped a quart of blue paint all over that ten-thousand-dollar nightmare. I bowed and walked out. The president didn't move or speak. That was one time he was taken by surprise. It's tough on you, Billy, but I couldn't help it."

There seemed to be excitement in Coralio. Outside there was a confused, rising murmur pierced by high-pitched cries. "*Bajo el traidor—Muerte el traidor!*" were the words they seemed to form.

"Listen to that!" exclaimed White, bitterly; "I know that much Spanish. They're shouting 'Down with the traitor!' I heard them before. I felt that they meant me. I was a traitor to Art. The picture had to go."

"'Down with the blank fool' would have suited your case better," said Keogh, with fiery emphasis. "You tear up ten thousand dollars like an old rag because the way you've spread on five dollars' worth of paint hurts your conscience. Next time I pick a side-partner in a scheme the man has got to go before a notary and swear he never even heard the word 'ideal' mentioned."

Keogh strode from the room, white-hot. White paid little attention to his resentment. The scorn of Billy Keogh seemed a trifling thing beside the greater self-scorn he had escaped.

In Coralio the excitement waxed. An outburst was imminent. The cause of this demonstration of displeasure was the presence in the town of a big, pink-cheeked Englishman, who, it was said, was an agent of his government come to clinch the bargain by which the president placed his people in the hands of a foreign power. It was charged that not only had he given away priceless concessions, but that the public debt was to be transferred into the hands of the English, and the custom-houses turned over to them as a guarantee. The long-enduring people had determined to make their protest felt.

On that night, in Coralio and in other towns, their ire found vent. Yelling mobs, mercurial but dangerous, roamed the streets. They overthrew the great bronze statue of the president that stood in the centre of the plaza, and hacked it to shapeless pieces. They tore from public buildings the tablets set there proclaiming the glory of the "Illustrious Liberator". His pictures in the government offices were demolished. The mobs even attacked the Casa Morena, but were driven away by the military, which remained faithful to the executive. All the night terror reigned.

The greatness of Losada was shown by the fact that by noon the next day order was restored, and he was still absolute. He issued proclamations denying positively that any negotiation of any kind had been entered into with England. Sir Stafford Vaughan, the pink-cheeked Englishman, also declared in placards and in public print that his presence there had no international significance. He was a traveller without guile. In fact (so he stated), he had not even spoken with the president or been in his presence since his arrival.

During this disturbance, White was preparing for his homeward voyage in the steamship that was to sail within two or three days. About noon, Keogh, the restless, took his camera out with the hope of speeding the lagging hours. The town was now as quiet as if peace had never departed from her perch on the red-tiled roofs.

About the middle of the afternoon, Keogh hurried back to the hotel with something decidedly special in the air. He retired to the little room where he developed his pictures.

Later on he came out to White on the balcony, with a luminous, grim, predatory smile on his face.

"Do you know what that is?" he asked, holding up a 4 by 5 photograph mounted on cardboard.

"Snapshot of a *señorita* sitting in the sand—alliteration unintentional," guessed White, lazily.

"Wrong," said Keogh with shining eyes. "It's a slung-shot. It's a can of dynamite. It's a gold-mine. It's a sight-draft on your president man for twenty thousand dollars— yes, sir—twenty thousand this time, and no spoiling the picture. No ethics of art in the way. Art! You with your smelly little tubes! I've got you skinned to death with a kodak. Take a look at that."

White took the picture in his hand, and gave a long whistle.

"Jove!" he exclaimed, "but wouldn't that stir up a row in the town if you let it be seen. How in the world did you get it, Billy?"

"You know that high wall around the president man's back garden? I was up there trying to get a bird's-eye of the town. I happened to notice a chink in the wall where a stone and a lot of plaster had slid out. Thinks I, I'll take a peep through to see how Mr. President's cabbages are growing. The first thing I saw was him and this Sir Englishman sitting at a little table about twenty feet away. They had the table all spread over with documents, and they were hobnobbing over them as thick as two pirates. 'Twas a nice corner of the garden, all private and shady with palms and orange-trees, and they had a pail of champagne set by handy in the grass. I knew then was the time for me to make my big hit in art. So I raised the machine up to the crack, and pressed the button. Just as I did so them old boys shook hands on the deal— you see they took that way in the picture."

Keogh put on his coat and hat.

"What are you going to do with it?" asked White.

"Me," said Keogh in a hurt tone, "why, I'm going to tie a pink ribbon to it and hang it on the whatnot, of course. I'm surprised at you. But while I'm out you just try to figure out what gingercake potentate would be most likely to want to buy this work of art for his private collection—just to keep it out of circulation."

The sunset was reddening the tops of the coconut palms when Billy Keogh came back from Casa Morena. He nodded to the artist's questioning gaze, and lay down on a cot with his hands under the back of his head.

"I saw him. He paid the money like a little man. They didn't want to let me in at first. I told 'em it was important. Yes, that president man is on the plenty-able list. He's got a beautiful business system about the way he uses his brains. All I had to do was to hold up the photograph so he could see it, and name the price. He just smiled, and walked over to a safe to get the cash. Twenty one-thousand-dollar brand-new United States Treasury notes he laid on the table, like I'd pay out a dollar and a quarter. Fine notes, too—they crackled with a sound like burning the brush of a ten-acre lot."

"Let's try the feel of one," said White, curiously. "I never saw a thousand-dollar bill." Keogh did not immediately respond.

"Carry," he said, in an absent-minded way, "you think a heap of your art, don't you?"

"More," said White, frankly, "than has been for the financial good of myself and my friends."

"I thought you were a fool the other day," went on Keogh, quietly, "and I'm not sure now that you wasn't. But if you was, so am I. I've been in some funny deals, Carry, but I've always managed to scramble fair, and match my brains and capital against the other fellow's. But when it comes to—well, when you've got the other fellow cinched, and the screws on him, and he's got to put up—why, it don't strike me as being a man's game. They've got a name for it, you know; it's—confound you, don't you understand? A fellow feels—it's something like that blamed art of yours—he—well, I tore that photograph up and laid the pieces on that stack of money, and shoved the whole business back across the table. 'Excuse me, Mr. Losada,' I said, 'but I guess I've made a mistake in the price. You get the photo for nothing.' Now, Carry, you get out the pencil, and we'll do some more figuring. I'd like to save enough out of our capital for you to have some fried sausages in your joint when you get back to New York."

47

Dicky

THERE is little consecutiveness along the Spanish Main. Things happen there intermittently. Even Time seems to hang his scythe daily on the branch of an orange-tree while he takes a siesta and a cigarette.

After the ineffectual revolt against the administration of President Losada, the country settled again in quiet toleration of the abuses with which he had been charged. In Coralio old political enemies went arm-in-arm, lightly, eschewing for the time all differences of opinion.

The failure of the art expedition did not stretch the cat-footed Keogh upon his back. The ups and downs of Fortune made smooth travelling for his nimble steps. His blue pencil stub was at work again before the smoke of the steamer on which White sailed had cleared away from the horizon. He had but to speak a word to Geddie to find his credit negotiable for whatever goods he wanted from the store of Brannigan & Company. On the same day on which White arrived in New York, Keogh, at the rear of a train of five pack mules loaded with hardware and cutlery, set his face toward the grim, interior mountains. There the Indian tribes wash gold-dust from the auriferous streams; and when a market is brought to them trading is brisk and *muy bueno* in the Cordilleras.

In Coralio, Time folded his wings and paced wearily along his drowsy path. They who had most cheered the torpid hours were gone. Clancy had sailed on a Spanish barque for Colon, contemplating a cut across the isthmus and then a further voyage to end at Callao, where the fighting was said to be on. Geddie, whose quiet and genial

458

nature had once served to mitigate the frequent dull reaction of lotus eating, was now a home-man, happy with his bright orchid, Paula, and never even dreaming of or regretting the unsolved, sealed and monogramed Bottle whose contents, now inconsiderable, were held safely in the keeping of the sea.

Well may the Walrus, most discerning and eclectic of beasts, place sealing-wax midway on his programme of topics that fall pertinent and diverting upon the ear.

Atwood was gone—he of the hospitable back porch and ingenuous cunning. Dr. Gregg, with his trepanning story smouldering within him, was a whiskered volcano, always showing signs of imminent eruption, and was not to be considered in the ranks of those who might contribute to the amelioration of ennui. The new consul's note chimed with the sad sea waves and the violent tropical greens—he had not a bar of Scheherezade or of the Round Table in his lute. Goodwin was employed with large projects; what time he was loosed from them found him at his home, where he loved to be. Therefore it will be seen that there was a dearth of fellowship and entertainment among the foreign contingent of Coralio.

And then Dicky Maloney dropped down from the clouds upon the town, and amused it.

Nobody knew where Dicky Maloney hailed from or how he reached Coralio. He appeared there one day; and that was all. He afterward said that he came on the fruit steamer *Thor*; but an inspection of the *Thor*'s passenger lists of that date was found to be Maloneyless. Curiosity, however, soon perished, and Dicky took his place among the odd fish cast up by the Caribbean.

He was an active, devil-may-care, rollicking fellow with an engaging grey eye, the most irresistible grin, a rather dark or much sunburned complexion, and a head of the fiercest red hair ever seen in that country. Speaking the Spanish language as well as he spoke English, and seeming always to have plenty of silver in his pockets, it was not long before he was a welcome companion whithersoever he went. He had an extreme fondness for *vino blanco*, and gained the reputation of being able to drink more of it than any three men in town. Everybody called him "Dicky"; everybody cheered up at the sight of him—especially the natives, to whom his marvellous red hair and his free-and-easy style were a constant delight and envy. Wherever you went in the town you would soon see Dicky or hear his genial laugh, and find around him a group of admirers who appreciated him both for his good nature and the white wine he was always so ready to buy.

A considerable amount of speculation was had concerning the object of his sojourn there, until one day he silenced this by opening a small shop for the sale of tobacco, *dulces* and the handiwork of the interior Indians—fibre-and-silk-woven goods, deerskin *zapatos* and basketwork of *tule* reeds. Even then he did not change his habits; for he was drinking and playing cards half the day and night with the *comandante*, the collector of customs, the *Jefe Politico* and other gay dogs among the native officials.

One day Dicky saw Pasa, the daughter of Madama Ortiz, sitting in the side door of the Hotel des los Estranjeros. He stopped in his tracks, still, for the first time in Coralio; and then he sped, swift as a deer, to find Vasquez, a gilded native youth, to present him.

The young men had named Pasa "*La Santita Naranjadita*". *Naranjadita* is a Spanish word for a certain colour that you must go to more trouble to describe in English. By saying "The little saint, tinted the most beautiful-delicate-slightly orange-golden", you will approximate the description of Madama Ortiz's daughter.

La Madama Ortiz sold rum in addition to other liquors. Now, you must know that the rum expiates whatever opprobrium attends upon the other commodities. For rum-making, mind you, is a government monopoly; and to keep a government dispensary assures respectability if not pre-eminence. Moreover, the saddest of precisians could find no fault with the conduct of the shop. Customers drank there in the lowest of spirits and fearsomely, as in the shadow of the dead; for Madama's ancient and vaulted lineage counteracted even the rum's behest to be merry. For, was she not of the Inglesias, who landed with Pizarro? And had not her deceased husband been *comisionado de caminos y puentes* for the district?

In the evening Pasa sat by the window in the room next to the one where they drank, and strummed dreamily upon her guitar. And then, by twos and threes, would come visiting young *caballeros* and occupy the prim line of chairs set against the wall of this room. They were there to besiege the heart of "*La Santita*". Their method (which is not proof against intelligent competition) consisted of expanding the chest, looking valorous, and consuming a gross or two of cigarettes. Even saints delicately oranged prefer to be wooed differently.

Doña Pasa would tide over the vast chasms of nicotinized silence with music from her guitar, while she wondered if the romances she had read about gallant and more—more contiguous cavaliers were all lies. At somewhat regular intervals Madama would glide in from the dispensary with a sort of drought-suggesting gleam in her eyes, and there would be a rustling of stiffly starched white trousers as one of the *caballeros* would propose an adjournment to the bar.

That Dicky Maloney would, sooner or later, explore this field was a thing to be foreseen. There were few doors in Coralio into which his red head had not been poked.

In an incredibly short space of time after his first sight of her he was there, seated close beside her rocking chair. There were no back-against-the-wall poses in Dicky's theory of wooing. His plan of subjection was an attack at close range. To carry the fortress with one concentrated, ardent, eloquent, irresistible *escalade*—that was Dicky's way.

Pasa was descended from the proudest Spanish families in the country. Moreover, she had had unusual advantages. Two years in a New Orleans school had elevated her ambitions, and fitted her for a fate above the ordinary maidens of her native land. And yet here she succumbed to the first red-haired scamp with a glib tongue and a charming smile that came along and courted her properly.

Very soon Dicky took her to the little church on the corner of the plaza, and "Mrs. Maloney" was added to her string of distinguished names.

And it was her fate to sit, with her patient, saintly eyes and figure like a bisque Psyche, behind the sequestered counter of the little shop, while Dicky drank and philandered with his frivolous acquaintances.

The women, with their naturally fine instinct, saw a chance for vivisection, and delicately taunted her with his habits. She turned upon them in a beautiful, steady blaze of sorrowful contempt.

"You meat-cows," she said, in her level, crystal-clear tones; "you know nothing of a man. Your men are *maromeros*. They are only fit to roll cigarettes in the shade until the sun strikes and shrivels them up. They drone in your hammocks and you comb their hair and feed them with fresh fruit. My man is of no such blood. Let him drink of the wine. When he has taken sufficient of it to drown one of your *flaccitos* he will come home to me more of a man than one thousand of your *pobrecitos*. *My* hair he smooths and braids; to me he sings; he himself removes my *zapatos*, and there, there, upon each instep leaves a kiss. He holds—Oh, you will never understand! Blind ones who have never known a *man.*"

Sometimes mysterious things happened at night about Dicky's shop. While the front of it was dark in the little room back of it Dicky and a few of his friends would sit about a table carrying on some kind of very quiet *negocios* until quite late. Finally he would let them out of the front door very carefully, and go upstairs to his little saint. These visitors were generally conspirator-like men with dark clothes and hats. Of course, these dark doings were noticed after awhile, and talked about.

Dicky seemed to care nothing at all for the society of the

alien residents of the town. He avoided Goodwin, and his skilful escape from the trepanning story of Dr. Gregg is still referred to, in Coralio, as a masterpiece of lightning diplomacy.

Many letters arrived, addressed to "Mr. Dicky Maloney", or "*Señor* Dickee Maloney", to the considerable pride of Pasa. That so many people should desire to write to him only confirmed her own suspicion that the light from his red head shone around the world. As to their contents she never felt curiosity. There was a wife for you!

The one mistake Dicky made in Coralio was to run out of money at the wrong time. Where his money came from was a puzzle, for the sales of the shop were next to nothing; but that source failed, and at a peculiarly unfortunate time. It was when the *comandante*, Don Señor el Coronel Encarnacion Rios, looked upon the little saint seated in the shop and felt his heart go pit-a-pat.

The *comandante*, who was versed in all the intricate arts of gallantry, first delicately hinted at his sentiments by donning his dress uniform and strutting up and down fiercely before her window. Pasa, glancing demurely with her saintly eyes, instantly perceived the resemblance to her parrot, Chichi, and was diverted to the extent of a smile. The *comandante* saw the smile, which was not intended for him. Convinced of an impression made, he entered the shop, confidently, and advanced to open compliment. Pasa froze; he pranced; she flamed royally; he was charmed to injudicious persistence; she commanded him to leave the shop; he tried to capture her hand, and—Dicky entered, smiling broadly, full of white wine and the devil.

He spent five minutes in punishing the *comandante* scientifically and carefully, so that the pain might be prolonged as far as possible. At the end of that time he pitched the rash wooer out the door upon the stones of the street, senseless.

A barefooted policeman, who had been watching the affair from across the street, blew a whistle. A squad of four soldiers came running from the *cuartel* around the corner. When they saw that the offender was Dicky, they stopped, and blew more whistles, which brought out reinforcements of eight. Deeming the odds against them sufficiently reduced, the military advanced upon the disturber.

Dicky, being thoroughly imbued with the martial spirit, stooped and drew the *comandante*'s sword, which was girded about him, and charged his foe. He chased the standing army four squares, playfully prodding its squealing rear and hacking at its ginger-coloured heels.

But he was not so successful with the civic authorities. Six muscular, nimble policemen overpowered him and conveyed him, triumphantly but warily, to jail. "*El Diablo Colorado*" they dubbed him, and derided the military for its defeat.

Dicky, with the rest of the prisoners, could look out through the barred door at the grass of the little plaza, at a row of orange-trees and the red-tile roofs and 'dobe walls of a line of insignificant stores.

At sunset along a path across this plaza came a melancholy procession of sad-faced women bearing plantains, cassava, bread and fruit—each coming with food to some wretch behind those bars to whom she still clung and furnished the means of life. Twice a day—morning and evening—they were permitted to come. Water was furnished to her compulsory guests by the republic, but no food.

That evening Dicky's name was called by the sentry, and he stepped before the bars of the door. There stood his little saint, a black mantilla draped about her head and shoulders, her face like glorified melancholy, her clear eyes gazing longingly at him as if they might draw him between the bars to her. She brought a chicken, some oranges, *dulces* and a loaf of white bread. A soldier inspected the food, and passed it in to Dicky. Pasa spoke calmly, as she always did, briefly, in her thrilling, flutelike tones. "Angel of my life," she said, "let it not be long that thou art away from me. Thou knowest that life is not a thing to be endured with thou not at my side. Tell me if I can do aught in this matter. If not, I will wait—a little while. I come again in the morning."

Dicky, with his shoes removed so as not to disturb his fellow-prisoners, tramped the floor of the jail half the night condemning his lack of money and the cause of it—whatever that might have been. He knew very well that money would have bought his release at once.

For two days succeeding Pasa came at the appointed times and brought him food. He eagerly inquired each time if a letter or package had come for him, and she mournfully shook her head.

On the morning of the third day she brought only a small loaf of bread. There were dark circles under her eyes. She seemed as calm as ever.

"By Jingo," said Dicky, who seemed to speak in English or Spanish as the whim seized him, "this is dry provender, *muchachita*. Is this the best you can dig up for a fellow?"

Pasa looked at him as a mother looks at a beloved but capricious babe.

"Think better of it," she said, in a low voice; "since for the next meal there will be nothing. The last *centavo* is spent." She pressed closer against the grating.

"Sell the goods in the shop—take anything for them."

"Have I not tried? Did I not offer them for one-tenth their cost? Not even one *peso* would anyone give. There is not one *real* in this town to assist Dickee Malonee."

Dick clenched his teeth grimly. "That's the *comandante*," he growled. "He's responsible for that sentiment. Wait, oh, wait till the cards are all out."

Pasa lowered her voice to almost a whisper. "And listen, heart of my heart," she said, "I have endeavoured to be brave, but I cannot live without thee. Three days now——"

Dicky caught the faint gleam of steel from the folds of her mantilla. For once she looked in his face and saw it without a smile, stern, menacing and purposeful. Then he suddenly raised his hand and his smile came back like a gleam of sunshine. The hoarse signal of an incoming steamer's siren

465

sounded in the harbour. Dicky called to the sentry who was pacing before the door: "What steamer comes?"

"The *Catarina*."

"Of the Vesuvius line?"

"Without doubt, of that line."

"Go you, *picarilla*," said Dicky joyously to Pasa, "to the American consul. Tell him I wish to speak with him. See that he comes at once. And look you! let me see a different look in those eyes, for I promise your head shall rest upon this arm to-night."

It was an hour before the consul came. He held his green umbrella under his arm, and mopped his forehead impatiently.

"Now, see here, Maloney," he began, captiously, "you fellows seem to think you can cut up any kind of row, and expect me to pull you out of it. I'm neither the War Department nor a gold-mine. This country has its laws, you know, and there's one against pounding the senses out of the regular army. You Irish are for ever getting into trouble. I don't see what I can do. Anything like tobacco, now, to make you comfortable—or newspapers——"

"Son of Eli," interrupted Dicky, gravely, "you haven't changed an iota. That is almost a duplicate of the speech you made when old Koen's donkeys and geese got into the chapel loft, and the culprits wanted to hide in your room."

"Oh, heavens!" exclaimed the consul, hurriedly adjusting his spectacles. "Are you a Yale man too? Were you in that crowd? I don't seem to remember anyone with red—anyone named Maloney. Such a lot of college men seem to have misused their advantages. One of the best mathematicians of the class of '91 is selling lottery tickets in Belize. A Cornell man dropped off here last month. He was second steward on a guano boat. I'll write to the department if you like, Maloney. Or if there's any tobacco, or newspa——"

"There's nothing," interrupted Dicky, shortly, "but this. You go tell the captain of the *Catarina* that Dicky Maloney

466

wants to see him as soon as he can conveniently come. Tell him where I am. Hurry. That's all."

The consul, glad to be let off so easily, hurried away. The captain of the *Catarina*, a stout man, Sicilian born, soon appeared, shoving, with little ceremony, through the guards to the jail door. The Vesuvius Fruit Company had a habit of doing things that way in Anchuria.

"I am exceeding sorry—exceeding sorry," said the captain, "to see this occur. I place myself at your service, Mr. Maloney. What you need shall be furnished. Whatever you say shall be done."

Dicky looked at him unsmilingly. His red hair could not detract from his attitude of severe dignity as he stood, tall and calm, with his now grim mouth forming a horizontal line.

"Captain De Lucco, I believe I still have funds in the hands of your company—ample and personal funds. I ordered a remittance last week. The money has not arrived. You know what is needed in this game. Money and money and more money. Why has it not been sent?"

"By the *Cristobal*," replied De Lucco, gesticulating, "it was dispatched. Where is the *Cristobal*? Off Cape Antonio I spoke her with a broken shaft. A tramp coaster was towing her back to New Orleans. I brought money ashore thinking your need for it might not withstand delay. In this envelope is one thousand dollars. There is more if you need it, Mr. Maloney."

"For the present it will suffice," said Dicky, softening as he crinkled the envelope and looked down at the half-inch thickness of smooth dingy bills.

"The long green!" he said, gently, with a new reverence in his gaze. "Is there anything it will not buy, Captain?"

"I had three friends," said De Lucco, who was a bit of a philosopher, "who had money. One of them speculated in stocks and made ten million; another is in heaven, and the third married a poor girl whom he loved."

"The answer, then," said Dicky, "is held by the Almighty, Wall Street and Cupid. So, the question remains."

"This," queried the captain, including Dicky's surroundings in a significant gesture of his hand, "is it—it is not—it is not connected with the business of your little shop? There is no failure in your plans?"

"No, no," said Dicky. "This is merely the result of a little private affair of mine, a digression from the regular line of business. They say for a complete life a man must know poverty, love and war. But they don't go well together, *capitán mio*. No; there is no failure in my business. The little shop is doing very well."

When the captain had departed Dicky called the sergeant of the jail squad and asked:

"Am I *preso* by the military or by the civil authority?"

"Surely there is no martial law in effect now, *señor*."

"*Bueno*. Now go or send to the alcalde, the *Juez de la Paz* and the *Jefe de los Policios*. Tell them I am prepared at once to satisfy the demands of justice." A folded bill of the "long green" slid into the sergeant's hand.

Then Dicky's smile came back again, for he knew that the hours of his captivity were numbered; and he hummed, in time with the sentry's tread:

> *They're hanging men and women now,*
> *For lacking of the green.*

So, that night Dicky sat by the window of the room over his shop and his little saint sat close by, working at something silken and dainty. Dicky was thoughtful and grave. His red hair was in an unusual state of disorder. Pasa's fingers often ached to smooth and arrange it, but Dicky would never allow it. He was poring, to-night, over a great litter of maps and books and papers on his table until that perpendicular line came between his brows that always distressed Pasa. Presently she went and brought his hat, and stood with it until he looked up, inquiringly.

"It is sad for you here," she explained. "Go out and drink *vino blanco*. Come back when you get that smile you used to wear. That is what I wish to see."

Dicky laughed and threw down his papers. "The *vino blanco* stage is past. It has served its turn. Perhaps, after all, there was less entered my mouth and more my ears than people thought. But, there will be no more maps or frowns to-night. I promise you that. Come."

They sat upon a reed *silleta* at the window and watched the quivering gleams from the lights of the *Catarina* reflected in the harbour.

Presently Pasa rippled out one of her infrequent chirrups of audible laughter.

"I was thinking," she began, anticipating Dicky's question, "of the foolish things girls have in their minds. Because I went to school in the States I used to have ambitions. Nothing less than to be the president's wife would satisfy me. And, look, thou red picaroon, to what obscure fate thou hast stolen me!"

"Don't give up hope," said Dicky, smiling. "More than one Irishman has been the ruler of a South American counrey. There was a dictator of Chili named O'Higgins. Why not a President Maloney, of Anchuria? Say the word, *santita mia*, and we'll make the race."

"No, no, no, thou red-haired, reckless one!" sighed Pasa; "I am content"—she laid her head against his arm—"here."

48

Rouge et Noir

IT has been indicated that disaffection followed the elevation of Losada to the presidency. This feeling continued
to grow. Throughout the entire republic there seemed to be
a spirit of silent, sullen discontent. Even the old Liberal
party, to which Goodwin, Zavalla and other patriots had
lent their aid, was disappointed. Losada had failed to become
a popular idol. Fresh taxes, fresh import duties and, more
than all, his tolerance of the outrageous oppression of citizens
by the military, had rendered him the most obnoxious president since the despicable Alforan. The majority of his own
cabinet were out of sympathy with him. The army, which he
had courted by giving it licence to tyrannize, had been his
main, and thus far adequate, support.

But the most impolitic of the administration's moves had
been when it antagonized the Vesuvius Fruit Company, an
organization plying twelve steamers and with a cash capital
somewhat larger than Anchuria's surplus and debt combined.

Reasonably, an established concern like the Vesuvius
would become irritated at having a small retail republic
with no rating at all attempt to squeeze it. So, when the
government proxies applied for a subsidy they encountered
a polite refusal. The president at once retaliated by clapping
an export duty of one *real* per bunch on bananas—a thing
unprecedented in fruit-growing countries. The Vesuvius
Company had invested large sums in wharves and plantations
along the Anchurian coast, their agents had erected fine
homes in the towns where they had their headquarters, and
heretofore had worked with the republic in goodwill and

with advantage to both. It would lose an immense sum if compelled to move out. The selling price of bananas from Vera Cruz to Trinidad was three *reales* per bunch. This new duty of one *real* would have ruined the fruit growers in Anchuria and have seriously discommoded the Vesuvius Company had it declined to pay it. But for some reason, the Vesuvius continued to buy Anchurian fruit, paying four *reales* for it; and not suffering the growers to bear the loss.

This apparent victory deceived His Excellency; and he began to hunger for more of it. He sent an emissary to request a conference with a representative of the fruit company. The Vesuvius sent Mr. Franzoni, a little, stout, cheerful man, always cool, and whistling airs from Verdi's operas. *Señor* Espirition, of the office of the Minister of Finance, attempted the sandbagging in behalf of Anchuria. The meeting took place in the cabin of the *Salvador* of the Vesuvius line.

Señor Espirition opened negotiations by announcing that the government contemplated the building of a railroad to skirt the alluvial coast lands. After touching upon the benefits such a road would confer upon the interests of the Vesuvius, he reached the definite suggestion that a contribution to the road's expenses of, say, fifty thousand *pesos* would not be more than an equivalent to benefits received.

Mr. Franzoni denied that his company would receive any benefits from a contemplated road. As its representative he must decline to contribute fifty thousand *pesos*. But he would assume the responsibility of offering twenty-five.

Did *Señor* Espirition understand *Señor* Franzoni to mean twenty-five thousand *pesos*?

By no means. Twenty-five *pesos*. And in silver; not in gold.

"Your offer insults my government," cried *Señor* Espirition, rising, with indignation.

"Then," said Mr. Franzoni, in warning tone, "*we will change it.*"

471

The offer was never changed. Would Mr. Franzoni have meant the government?

This was the state of affairs in Anchuria when the winter season opened at Coralio at the end of the second year of Losada's administration. So, when the government and society made its annual exodus to the seashore it was evident that the presidential advent would not be celebrated by unlimited rejoicing. The tenth of November was the day set for the entrance into Coralio of the gay company from the capital. A narrow-gauge railroad runs twenty miles into the interior from Solitas. The government party travels by carriage from San Mateo to this road's terminal point, and proceeds by train to Solitas. From here they march in grand procession to Coralio where, on the day of their coming, festivities and ceremonies abound. But this season saw an ominous dawning of the tenth of November.

Although the rainy season was over, the day seemed to hark back to reeking June. A fine drizzle of rain fell all during the forenoon. The procession entered Coralio amid a strange silence.

President Losada was an elderly man, grizzly bearded, with a considerable ratio of Indian blood revealed in his cinnamon complexion. His carriage headed the procession, surrounded and guarded by Captain Cruz and his famous troop of one hundred light horse, "*El Ciento Huilando*". Colonel Rocas followed, with a regiment of the regular army.

The president's sharp, beady eyes glanced about him for the expected demonstration of welcome; but he faced a stolid, indifferent array of citizens. Sightseers the Anchurians are by birth and habit, and they turned out to their last able-bodied unit to witness the scene; but they maintained an accusive silence. They crowded the streets to the very wheel ruts; they covered the red-tile roofs to the eaves, but there was never a "*viva*" from them. No wreaths of palm and lemon branches or gorgeous strings of paper roses hung from the windows and balconies as was the custom. There was an

472

apathy, a dull, dissenting disapprobation, that was the more ominous because it puzzled. No one feared an outburst, a revolt of the discontents, for they had no leader. The president and those loyal to him had never even heard whispered a name among them capable of crystallizing the dissatisfaction into opposition. No, there could be no danger. The people always procured a new idol before they destroyed an old one.

At length, after a prodigious galloping and curveting of red-sashed majors, gold-laced colonels and epauletted generals, the procession formed for its annual progress down the Calle Grande to the Casa Morena, where the ceremony of welcome to the visiting president always took place.

The Swiss band led the line of march. After it pranced the local *comandante*, mounted, and a detachment of his troops. Next came a carriage with four members of the cabinet, conspicuous among them the Minister of War, old General Pilar, with his white moustache and his soldierly bearing. Then the president's vehicle, containing also the Ministers of Finance and State; and surrounded by Captain Cruz's light horse formed in a close double file of fours. Following them, the rest of the officials of state, the judges and distinguished military and social ornaments of public and private life.

As the band struck up, and the movement began, like a bird of ill-omen the *Valhalla*, the swiftest steamship of the Vesuvius line, glided into the harbour in plain view of the president and his train. Of course, there was nothing menacing about its arrival—a business firm does not go to war with a nation—but it reminded *Señor* Espirition and others in those carriages that the Vesuvius Fruit Company was undoubtedly carrying something up its sleeve for them.

By the time the van of the procession had reached the government building, Captain Cronin, of the *Valhalla*, and Mr. Vincenti, member of the Vesuvius Company, had landed, and were pushing their way, bluff, hearty and nonchalant,

473

through the crowd on the narrow sidewalk. Clad in white linen, big, debonair, with the air of good-humoured authority, they made conspicuous figures among the dark mass of unimposing Anchurians, as they penetrated to within a few yards of the steps of the Casa Morena. Looking easily above the heads of the crowd, they perceived another that towered above the undersized natives. It was the fiery poll of Dicky Maloney against the wall close by the lower step; and his broad, seductive grin showed that he recognized their presence.

Dicky had attired himself becomingly for the festive occasion in a well-fitting black suit. Pasa was close by his side, her head covered with the ubiquitous black mantilla.

Mr. Vincenti looked at her attentively.

"Botticelli's Madonna," he remarked, gravely. "I wonder when she got into the game. I don't like his getting tangled with the women. I hoped he would keep away from them."

Captain Cronin's laugh almost drew attention from the parade.

"With that head of hair! Keep away from the women! And a Maloney! Hasn't he got a licence? But, nonsense aside, what do you think of the prospects? It's a species of filibustering out of my line."

Vincenti glanced again at Dicky's head and smiled.

"*Rouge et noir*," he said. "There you have it. Make your play, gentlemen. Our money is on the red."

"The lad's game," said Cronin, with a commending look at the tall, easy figure by the steps. "But 'tis all like fly-by-night theatricals to me. The talk's bigger than the stage; there's a smell of gasolene in the air, and they're their own audience and scene-shifters."

They ceased talking, for General Pilar had descended from the first carriage and had taken his stand upon the top step of Casa Morena. As the oldest member of the cabinet, custom had decreed that he should make the address of welcome, presenting the keys of the official residence to the president at its close.

474

General Pilar was one of the most distinguished citizens of the republic. Hero of three wars and innumerable revolutions, he was an honoured guest at European camps and courts. An eloquent speaker and a friend to the people, he represented the highest type of the Anchurians.

Holding in his hand the gilt keys of Casa Morena, he began his address in a historical form, touching upon each administration and the advance of civilization and prosperity from the first dim striving after liberty down to the present times. Arriving at the regime of President Losada, at which point, according to precedent, he should have delivered a eulogy upon its wise conduct and the happiness of the people, General Pilar paused. Then he silently held up the bunch of keys high above his head, with his eyes closely regarding it. The ribbon with which they were bound fluttered in the breeze.

"It still blows," cried the speaker, exultantly. "Citizens of Anchuria, give thanks to the saints this night that our air is still free."

Thus disposing of Losada's administration, he abruptly reverted to that of Olivarra, Anchuria's most popular ruler. Olivarra had been assassinated nine years before while in the prime of life and usefulness. A faction of the Liberal party led by Losada himself had been accused of the deed. Whether guilty or not, it was eight years before the ambitious and scheming Losada had gained his goal.

Upon this theme General Pilar's eloquence was loosed. He drew the picture of the beneficent Olivarra with a loving hand. He reminded the people of the peace, the security and the happiness they had enjoyed during that period. He recalled in vivid detail and with significant contrast the last winter sojourn of President Olivarra in Coralio, when his appearance at their *fiestas* was the signal for thundering *vivas* of love and approbation.

The first public expression of sentiment from the people that day followed. A low, sustained murmur went along them like the surf rolling along the shore.

"Ten dollars to a dinner at the Saint Charles," remarked Mr. Vincenti, "that *rouge* wins."

"I never bet against my own interests." said Captain Cronin, lighting a cigar. "Long-winded old boy, for his age. What's he talking about?"

"My Spanish," replied Vincenti, "runs about ten words to the minute; his is something around two hundred. Whatever he's saying, he's getting them warmed up."

"Friends and brothers," General Pilar was saying, "could I reach out my hand this day across the lamentable silence of the grave to Olivarra 'the Good', to the ruler who was one of you, whose tears fell when you sorrowed, and whose smile followed your joy—I would bring him back to you, but —Olivarra is dead—dead at the hands of a craven assassin!"

The speaker turned and gazed boldly into the carriage of the president. His arm remained extended aloft as if to sustain peroration. The president was listening, aghast, at this remarkable address of welcome. He was sunk back upon his seat, trembling with rage and dumb surprise, his dark hands tightly gripping the carriage cushions.

Half rising, he extended one arm toward the speaker, and shouted a harsh command at Captain Cruz. The leader of the "Flying Hundred" sat his horse, immovable, with folded arms, giving no sign of having heard. Losada sank back again, his dark features distinctly paling.

"Who says that Olivarra is dead?" suddenly cried the speaker, his voice, old as he was, sounding like a battle trumpet. "His body lies in the grave, but to the people he loved he has bequeathed his spirit—yes, more—his learning, his courage, his kindness—yes, more—his youth, his image— people of Anchuria, have you forgotten Ramon, the son of Olivarra?"

Cronin and Vincenti, watching closely, saw Dicky Maloney suddenly raise his hat, tear off his shock of red hair, leap up the steps and stand at the side of General Pilar. The Minister of War laid his arm across the young man's shoulders. All who had known President Olivarra saw again the same lion-like pose, the same frank, undaunted expression, the same high forehead with the peculiar line of the clustering, crisp black hair.

General Pilar was an experienced orator. He seized the moment of breathless silence that preceded the storm.

"Citizens of Anchuria," he trumpeted, holding aloft the keys to Casa Morena, "I am here to deliver these keys—the keys to your homes and liberty—to your chosen president. Shall I deliver them to Enrico Olivarra's assassin, or to his son?"

"Olivarra! Olivarra!" the crowd shrieked and howled. All vociferated the magic name—men, women, children and the parrots.

And the enthusiasm was not confined to the blood of the plebs. Colonel Rocas ascended the steps and laid his sword theatrically at young Ramon Olivarra's feet. Four members of the cabinet embraced him. Captain Cruz gave a command, and twenty of *El Ciento Huilando* dismounted and arranged themselves in a cordon about the steps of Casa Morena.

But Ramon Olivarra seized the moment to prove himself a born genius and politician. He waved those soldiers aside, and descended the steps to the street. There, without losing his dignity or the distinguished elegance that the loss of the red hair brought him, he took the proletariat to his bosom—the barefooted, the dirty, the Indians, Caribs, babies, beggars, old, young, saints, soldiers and sinners—he missed none of them.

While this act of the drama was being presented, the scene-shifters had been busy at the duties that had been assigned to them. Two of Cruz's dragoons had seized the bridle reins of Losada's horses; others formed a close guard around the carriage; and they galloped off with the tyrant and his two unpopular Ministers. No doubt a place had been prepared for them. There are a number of well-barred stone apartments in Coralio.

"*Rouge* wins," said Mr. Vincenti, calmly lighting another cigar.

Captain Cronin had been intently watching the vicinity of the steps for some time.

"Good boy!" he exclaimed suddenly, as if relieved. "I wondered if he was going to forget his Kathleen Mavourneen."

Young Olivarra had reascended the steps and spoken a few words to General Pilar. Then that distinguished veteran descended to the ground and approached Pasa, who still stood, wonder-eyed, where Dicky had left her. With his plumed hat in his hand, and his medals and decorations shining on his breast, the general spoke to her and gave her his arm, and they went up the stone steps of the Casa Morena together. And then Ramon Olivarra stepped forward and took both her hands before all the people.

And while the cheering was breaking out afresh everywhere, Captain Cronin and Mr. Vincenti turned and walked back to the shore where the gig was waiting for them.

"There'll be another '*presidente proclamada*' in the morning," said Mr. Vincenti, musingly. "As a rule they are not as reliable as the elected ones, but this youngster seems to have some good stuff in him. He planned and manœuvred the entire campaign. Olivarra's widow, you know, was wealthy. After her husband was assassinated she went to the States, and educated her son at Yale. The Vesuvius Company hunted him up, and backed him in the little game."

"It's a glorious thing," said Cronin, half jestingly, "to be able to discharge a government, and insert one of your own choosing, in these days."

"Oh, it is only a matter of business," said Vincenti, stopping and offering the stump of his cigar to a monkey that swung down from a lime-tree; "and that is what moves the world of to-day. That extra *real* on the price of bananas had to go. We took the shortest way of removing it."

49

Two Recalls

THERE remains three duties to be performed before the curtain falls upon this patched comedy. Two have been promised; the third is no less obligatory.

It was set forth in the programme of this tropic vaudeville that it would be made known why Shorty O'Day, of the Columbia Detective Agency, lost his position. Also that Smith should come again to tell us what mystery he followed that night on the shores of Anchuria, when he strewed so many cigar stumps around the coconut palm during his lonely night vigil on the beach. These things were promised; but a bigger thing yet remains to be accomplished—the clearing up of a seeming wrong that has been done according to the array of chronicled facts (truthfully set forth) that have been presented. And one voice, speaking, shall do these three things.

Two men sat on a stringer of a North River pier in the City of New York. A steamer from the tropics had begun to unload bananas and oranges on the pier. Now and then a banana or two would fall from an over-ripe bunch, and one of the two men would shamble forward, seize the fruit and return to share it with his companion.

One of the men was in the ultimate stage of deterioration. As far as rain and wind and sun could wreck the garments he wore, it had been done. In his person the ravages of drink were as plainly visible. And yet, upon his high-bridged, rubicund nose was jauntily perched a pair of shining and flawless gold-rimmed glasses.

The other man was not so far gone upon the descending Highway of the Incompetents. Truly, the flower of his manhood had gone to seed—seed that, perhaps, no soil might sprout. But there were still cross-cuts along where he travelled through which he might yet regain the pathway of usefulness without disturbing the slumbering Miracles. This man was short and compactly built. He had an oblique, dead eye, like that of a sting-ray, and the moustache of a cocktail-mixer. We know the eye and the moustache; we know that Smith of the luxurious yacht, the gorgeous raiment, the mysterious mission, the magic disappearance, has come again, though shorn of the accessories of his former state.

At his third banana, the man with the nose glasses spat it from him with a shudder.

"Deuce take all fruit!" he remarked, in a patrician tone of disgust. "I lived for two years where these things grow. The memory of their taste lingers with you. The oranges are not so bad. Just see if you can gather a couple of them, O'Day, when the next broken crate comes up."

"Did you live down with the monkeys?" asked the other, made tepidly garrulous by the sunshine and the alleviating meal of juicy fruit. "I was down there once, myself. But only for a few hours. That was when I was with the Columbia Detective Agency. The monkey people did me up. I'd have my job yet if it hadn't been for them. I'll tell you about it.

"One day the chief sent a note around to the office that read: 'Send O'Day here at once for a big piece of business.' I was the crack detective of the agency at that time. They always handed me the big jobs. The address the chief wrote from was down in the Wall Street district.

"When I got there I found him in a private office with a lot of directors who were looking pretty fuzzy. They stated the case. The president of the Republic Insurance Company had skipped with about a tenth of a million dollars in cash. The directors wanted him back pretty bad, but they wanted the money worse. They said they needed it. They had traced the old gent's movements to where he boarded a tramp fruit steamer bound for South America that same morning with his daughter and a big gripsack—all the family he had.

"One of the directors had his steam yacht coaled and with steam up, ready for a trip; and he turned her over to me, cart blongsh. In four hours I was on board of her, and hot on the trail of the fruit tub. I had a pretty good idea where old Wahrfield—that was his name, J. Churchill Wahrfield— would head for. At that time we had a treaty with about every foreign country except Belgium and that banana republic, Anchuria. There wasn't a photo of old Wahrfield to be had in New York—he had been foxy there—but I had his description. And besides, the lady with him would be a dead-give-away anywhere. She was one of the high-flyers in Society—not the kind that have their pictures in the Sunday papers—but the real sort that open chrysanthemum shows and christen battleships.

"Well, sir, we never got a sight of that fruit tub on the road. The ocean is a pretty big place; and I guess we took different paths across it. But we kept going toward this Anchuria, where the fruiter was bound for.

"We struck the monkey coast one afternoon about four. There was a ratty-looking steamer off-shore taking on bananas. The monkeys were loading her up with big barges. It might be the one the old man had taken, and it might not. I went ashore to look around. The scenery was pretty good. I never saw any finer on the New York stage. I struck an American on shore, a big, cool chap, standing around with the monkeys. He showed me the consul's office. The consul was a nice young fellow. He said the fruiter was the *Karlsefin*, running generally to New Orleans, but took her last cargo to New York. Then I was sure my people were on board, although everybody told me that no passengers had landed. I didn't think they would land until after dark, for they might have been shy about it on account of seeing that yacht of mine hanging around. So, all I had to do was to wait and nab 'em when they came ashore. I couldn't arrest old Wahrfield without extradition papers, but my play was to get the cash. They generally give up if you strike 'em when they're tired and rattled and short on nerve.

"After dark I sat under a coconut-tree on the beach for a while, and then I walked around and investigated that town some, and it was enough to give you the lions. If a man could stay in New York and be honest, he'd better do it than to hit that monkey town with a million.

"Dinky little mud houses; grass over your shoe-tops in the streets; ladies in low-neck-and-short-sleeves walking around smoking cigars; tree frogs rattling like a hose cart going to a ten blow; big mountains dropping gravel in the back yards, and the sea licking the paint off in front—no, sir—a man had better be in God's country living on free lunch than there.

"The main street ran along the beach, and I walked down it, and then turned up a kind of lane where the houses were made of poles and straw. I wanted to see what the monkeys did when they weren't climbing coconut-trees. The very first shack I looked in I saw my people. They must have come ashore while I was promenading. A man about fifty, smooth face, heavy eyebrows, dressed in black broadcloth, looking like he was just about to say, 'Can any little boy in the Sunday school answer that?' He was freezing on to a grip that weighed like a dozen gold bricks, and a swell girl—a regular peach, with a Fifth Avenue cut—was sitting on a wooden chair. An old black woman was fixing some coffee and beans on a table. The light they had came from a lantern hung on a nail. I went and stood in the door, and they looked at me, and I said:

"'Mr. Wahrfield, you are my prisoner. I hope, for the lady's sake, you will take the matter sensibly. You know why I want you.'

"'Who are you?' says the old gent.

"'O'Day,' says I, 'of the Columbia Detective Agency. And now, sir, let me give you a piece of good advice, You go back and take your medicine like a man. Hand 'em back the boodle; and maybe they'll let you off light. Go back easy, and I'll put in a word for you. I'll give you five minutes to decide.' I pulled out my watch and waited.

"Then the young lady chipped in. She was one of the genuine high-steppers. You could tell by the way her clothes fit and the style she had that Fifth Avenue was made for her.

"'Come inside,' she says. 'Don't stand in the door and disturb the whole street with that suit of clothes. Now, what is it you want?'

"'Three minutes gone,' I said. 'I'll tell you again while the other two tick off.

"'You'll admit being the president of the Republic, won't you?'

"'I am,' says he.

"'Well, then,' says I, 'it ought to be plain to you. Wanted, in New York, J. Churchill Wahrfield, president of the Republic Insurance Company.

"'Also the funds belonging to said company, now in that grip, in the unlawful possession of said J. Churchill Wahr- field.'

"'Oh-h-h-h!' says the young lady, as if she was thinking, 'you want to take us back to New York?'

"'To take Mr. Wahrfield. There's no charge against you, miss. There'll be no objection, of course, to your returning with your father.'

"Of a sudden the girl gave a tiny scream and grabbed the old boy round the neck. 'Oh, father, father!' she says, kind of contralto, 'can this be true? Have you taken money that is not yours? Speak, father!' It made you shiver to hear the tremolo stop she put on her voice.

"The old boy looked pretty bughouse when she first grappled him but she went on, whispering in his ear and patting his off shoulder till he stood still, but sweating a little.

"She got him to one side and they talked together a minute, and then he put on some gold eyeglasses and walked up and handed me the grip.

"'Mr. Detective,' he says, talking a little broken, 'I conclude to return with you. I have finished to discover that

life on this desolate and displeased coast would be worse than
to die, itself. I will go back and hurl myself upon the mercy of
the Republic Company. Have you brought a sheep?'

"'Sheep!' says I; 'I haven't a single——'

"'Ship,' cut in the young lady. 'Don't get funny. Father
is of German birth, and doesn't speak perfect English. How
did you come?'

"The girl was all broke up. She had a handkerchief to her
face, and kept saying every little bit, 'Oh, father, father!'
She walked up to me and laid her lily-white hand on the
clothes that had pained her at first. I smelt a milllion violets.
She was a lulu. I told her I came in a private yacht.

"'Mr. O'Day,' she says. 'Oh, take us away from this
horrid country at once. Can you? Will you? Say you will.'

"'I'll try,' I said, concealing the fact that I was dying to
get them on salt water before they could change their mind.

"One thing they both kicked against was going through
the town to the boat landing. Said they dreaded publicity,
and now that they were going to return, they had a hope
that the thing might yet be kept out of the papers. They
swore they wouldn't go unless I got them out to the yacht
without anyone knowing it, so I agreed to humour them.

"The sailors who rowed me ashore were playing billiards
in a bar-room near the water, waiting for orders, and I proposed to have them take the boat down the beach half a mile
or so, and take us up there. How to get them word was the
question, for I couldn't leave the grip with the prisoner, and
I couldn't take it with me, not knowing but that the monkeys
might stick me up.

"The young lady says the old coloured woman would
take them a note. I sat down and wrote it, and gave it to the
dame with plain directions what to do, and she grins like a
baboon and shakes her head.

"Then Mr. Wahrfield handed her a string of foreign
dialect, and she nods her head and says, 'See, *señor*,' maybe
fifty times, and lights out with the note.

"'Old Augusta only understands German,' said Miss

Wahrfield, smiling at me. 'We stopped in her house to ask where we could find lodging, and she insisted upon our having coffee. She tells us she was raised in a German family in San Domingo.'

"'Very likely,' I said. 'But you can search me for German words, except *nix verstay* and *noch einst*. I would have called that "See, *señor*" French, though, on a gamble.'

"Well, we three made a sneak around the edge of town so as not to be seen. We got tangled in vines and ferns and the banana bushes and tropical scenery a good deal. The monkey suburbs was as wild as places in Central Park. We came out on the beach a good half-mile below. A brown chap was lying asleep under a coconut-tree, with a ten-foot musket beside him. Mr. Wahrfield takes up the gun and pitches it into the sea. 'The coast is guarded,' he says. 'Rebellion and plots ripen like fruit.' He pointed to the sleeping man, who never stirred. 'Thus,' he says, 'they perform trusts. Children!'

"I saw our boat coming, and I struck a match and lit a piece of newspaper to show them where we were. In thirty minutes we were on board the yacht.

"The first thing, Mr. Wahrfield and his daughter and I took the grip into the owner's cabin, opened it up, and took an inventory. There was one hundred and five thousand dollars, United States treasury notes, in it, besides a lot of diamond jewellery and a couple of hundred Havana cigars. I gave the old man the cigars and a receipt for the rest of the lot, as agent for the company, and locked the stuff up in my private quarters.

"I never had a pleasanter trip than that one. After we got to sea the young lady turned out to be the jolliest ever. The very first time we sat down to dinner, and the steward filled her glass with champagne—that director's yacht was a regular floating Waldorf-Astoria—she winks at me and says, 'What's the use to borrow trouble, Mr. Fly Cop? Here's hoping you may live to eat the hen that scratches on your grave.' There was a piano on board, and she sat down to it and sung better than you give up two cases to hear plenty times. She knew about nine operas clear through. She was sure enough *bon ton* and swell. She wasn't one of the 'among others present' kind; she belonged on the special mention list!

"The old man, too, perked up amazingly on the way. He passed cigars, and says to me once, quite chipper, out of a cloud of smoke, 'Mr. O'Day, somehow I think the Republic Company will not give me the much trouble. Guard well the gripvalise of the money, Mr. O'Day, for that it must be returned to them that it belongs when we finish to arrive.'

"When we landed in New York I 'phoned to the chief to meet us in that director's office. We got in a cab and went there. I carried the grip, and we walked in, and I was pleased to see that the chief had got together the same old crowd of moneybugs with pink faces and white vests to see us march in. I set the grip on the table. 'There's the money,' I said.

"'And your prisoner?' said the chief.

"I pointed to Mr. Wahrfield, and he stepped forward and says:

"'The honour of a word with you, sir, to explain.'

"He and the chief went into another room and stayed ten minutes. When they came back the chief looked as black as a ton of coal.

"'Did this gentleman,' he says to me, 'have this valise in his possession when you first saw him?'

"'He did,' said I.

"The chief took up the grip and handed it to the prisoner with a bow, and says to the director crowd: 'Do any of you recognize this gentleman?'

"They all shook their pink faces.

"'Allow me to present,' he goes on, '*Señor* Miraflores, president of the republic of Anchuria. The *señor* has generously consented to overlook this outrageous blunder, on condition that we undertake to secure him against the annoyance of public comment. It is a concession on his part to overlook an insult for which he might claim international redress.

I think we can gratefully promise him secrecy in the matter.'

"They gave him a pink nod all round.

"'O'Day,' he says to me. 'As a private detective you're wasted. In a war, where kidnapping governments is in the rules, you'd be invaluable. Come down to the office at eleven.'

"I knew what that meant.

"'So that's the president of the monkeys,' says I. 'Well, why couldn't he have said so?'

"Wouldn't it jar you?"

50

The Vitagraphoscope

VAUDEVILLE is intrinsically episodic and discontinuous. Its audiences do not demand dénouements. Sufficient unto each "turn" is the evil thereof. No one cares how many romances the singing comédienne may have had if she can capably sustain the limelight and a high note or two. The audiences reck not if the performing dogs get to the pound the moment they have jumped through their last hoop. They do not desire bulletins about the possible injuries received by the comic bicyclist who retires head first from the stage in a crash of (property) chinaware. Neither do they consider that their seat coupons entitle them to be instructed whether or no there is a sentiment between the lady solo banjoist and the Irish monologist.

Therefore, let us have no lifting of the curtain upon a tableau of the united lovers, backgrounded by defeated villainy and derogated by the comic, osculating maid and butler, thrown in as a sop to the Cerberi of the fifty-cent seats.

But our programme ends with a brief "turn" or two; and then to the exits. Whoever sits the show out may find, if he will, the slender thread that binds together, though ever so slightly, the story that, perhaps, only the Walrus will understand.

Extracts from a letter from the first vice-president of the Republic Insurance Company, of New York City, to Frank Goodwin, of Coralio, Republic of Anchuria.

MY DEAR MR. GOODWIN—Your communication per Messrs. Howland and Fourchet, of New Orleans, has reached us. Also their draft on N.Y. for $100,000, the amount abstracted from the funds of this company by the late J. Churchill Wahrfield, its former president. . . . The officers and directors unite in requesting me to express to you their sincere esteem and thanks for your prompt and much appreciated return of the entire missing sum within two weeks from the time of its disappearance. . . . Can assure you that the matter will not be allowed to receive the least publicity. . . . Regret exceedingly the distressing death of Mr. Wahrfield by his own hand, but . . . congratulations on your marriage to Miss Wahrfield . . . many charms, winning manners, noble and womanly nature and envied position in the best metropolitan society. . . .

Cordially yours,

Lucius E. Applegate,

First Vice-President the Republic Insurance Company.

The Vitagraphoscope

(Moving Pictures)

The Last Sausage

SCENE—*An Artist's Studio.* The artist, a young man of prepossessing appearance, sits in a dejected attitude, amid a litter of sketches, with his head resting upon his hand. An oil stove stands on a pine box in the centre of the studio. The artist rises, tightens his waist-belt to another hole, and lights the stove. He goes to a tin bread-box, half-hidden by a screen, takes out a solitary link of sausage, turns the box upside-down to show that there is no more, and chucks the sausage into a frying-pan, which he sets upon the stove. The flame of the stove goes out, showing that there is no more oil. The artist, in evident despair, seizes the sausage, in a sudden access of rage, and hurls it violently from him. At the same time a door opens, and a man who enters receives the sausage forcibly against his nose. He seems to cry out; and is observed to make a step dance or two, vigorously. The new-comer is a ruddy-faced, keen-looking man, apparently of Irish ancestry.

489

Next he is observed to laugh immoderately; he kicks over the stove; he claps the artist (who is vainly striving to grasp his hand) vehemently upon the back. Then he goes through a pantomime which to the sufficiently intelligent spectator reveals that he has acquired large sums of money by trading pot-metal hatchets and razors to the Indians of the Cordillera Mountains for gold dust. He draws a roll of money as large as a small loaf of bread from his pocket and waves it above his head, while at the same time he makes a pantomime of drinking from a glass. The artist hurriedly secures his hat, and the two leave the studio together.

The Writing on the Sands

SCENE—*The Beach at Nice.* A woman, beautiful, still young, exquisitely clothed, complacent, poised, reclines near the water, idly scrawling letters in the sand with the staff of her silken parasol. The beauty of her face is audacious; her languid pose is one that you feel to be impermanent—you wait, expectant, for her to spring or glide or crawl, like a panther that has unaccountably become stock-still. She idly scrawls in the sand; and the word that she always writes is "Isabel". A man sits a few yards away. You can see that they are companions, even if no longer comrades. His face is dark and smooth, and almost inscrutable—but not quite. The two speak little together. The man also scratches on the sand with his cane. And the word that he writes is "Anchuria". And then he looks out where the Mediterranean and the sky intermingle, with death in his gaze.

The Wilderness and Thou

SCENE—*The Borders of a Gentleman's Estate in a Tropical Land.* An old Indian, with a mahogany-coloured face, is trimming the grass on a grave by a mangrove swamp. Presently he rises to his feet and walks slowly toward a grove that is shaded by the gathering, brief twilight. In the edge of the grove stand a man who is stalwart, with a kind and courteous air, and a woman of a serene and clear-cut love-

490

liness. When the old Indian comes up to them the man drops money in his hand. The grave-tender, with the stolid pride of his race, takes it as his due, and goes his way. The two in the edge of the grove turn back along the dim pathway, and walk close, close—for, after all, what is the world at its best but a little round field of the moving pictures with two walking together in it?

CURTAIN

51

Out of Nazareth

O KOCHEE, in Georgia, had a boom, and J. Pinkney Bloom came out of it with a "wad". Okochee came out of it with a half-million-dollar debt, a two and a half per cent. city property tax, and a city council that showed a propensity for travelling the back streets of the town. These things came about through a fatal resemblance of the river Cooloosa to the Hudson, as set forth and expounded by a Northern tourist. Okochee felt that New York should not be allowed to consider itself the only alligator in the swamp, so to speak. And then that harmless, but persistent, individual so numerous in the South—the man who is always clamouring for more cotton mills, and is ready to take a dollar's worth of stock, provided he can borrow the dollar—that man added his daily work to the tourist's innocent praise, and Okochee fell.

The Cooloosa River winds through a range of small mountains, passes Okochee, and then blends its waters trippingly, as fall the mellifluous Indian syllables, with the Chattahoochee.

Okochee rose, as it were, from its sunny seat on the post-office stoop, hitched up its suspender, and threw a granite dam two hundred and forty feet long and sixty feet high across the Cooloosa one mile above the town. Thereupon, a dimpling, sparkling lake backed up twenty miles among the little mountains. Thus in the great game of municipal rivalry did Okochee match that famous drawing card, the Hudson. It was conceded that nowhere could the Palisades be judged superior in the way of scenery and grandeur. Following the picture card was played the ace of commercial importance.

Fourteen thousand horsepower would this dam furnish. Cotton mills, factories, and manufacturing plants would rise up as the green corn after a shower. The spindle and the fly-wheel and turbine would sing the shrewd glory of Okochee. Along the picturesque heights above the lake would rise in beauty the costly villas and the splendid summer residences of capital. The naphtha launch of the millionaire would spit among the romantic coves; the verdured hills would take formal shapes of terrace, lawn, and park. Money would be spent like water in Okochee, and water would be turned into money.

The fate of the good town is quickly told. Capital decided not to invest. Of all the great things promised, the scenery alone came to fulfilment. The wooded peaks, the impressive promontories of solemn granite, the beautiful green slants of bank and ravine did all they could to reconcile Okochee to the delinquency of miserly gold. The sunsets gilded the dreamy draws and coves with a minting that should charm away heart-burning. Okochee, true to the instinct of its blood and clime, was lulled by the spell. It climbed out of the arena, loosed its suspender, sat down again on the post-office stoop, and took a chew. It consoled itself by drawling sarcasms at the city council which was not to blame, causing the fathers, as has been said, to seek back streets and figure perspiringly on the sinking fund and the appropriation for interest due.

The youth of Okochee—they who were to carry into the rosy future the burden of the debt—accepted failure with youth's uncalculating joy. For here was sport, aquatic and nautical, added to the meagre round of life's pleasures. In yachting caps and flying neckties they pervaded the lake to its limits. Girls wore silk waists embroidered with anchors in blue and pink. The trousers of the young men widened at the bottom, and their hands were proudly calloused by the oft-plied oar. Fishermen were under the spell of a deep and tolerant joy. Sailboats and rowboats furrowed the lenient waves, popcorn and ice-cream booths sprang up about the little wooden pier. Two small excursion steamboats were built, and plied the delectable waters. Okochee philosophically gave up the hope of eating turtle soup with a gold spoon, and settled back, not ill content, to its regular diet of lotus and fried hominy. And out of this slow wreck of great expectations rose up J. Pinkney Bloom with his "wad" and his prosperous, cheery smile.

Needless to say, J. Pinkney was no product of Georgia soil. He came out of that flushed and capable region known as the "North". He called himself a "promoter"; his enemies had spoken of him as a "grafter"; Okochee took a middle course, and held him to be no better nor no worse than a "Yank".

Far up the lake—eighteen miles above the town—the eye of this cheerful camp-follower of booms had spied out a graft. He purchased there a precipitous tract of five hundred acres at forty-five cents per acre; and this he laid out and subdivided as the city of skyland—the Queen City of the Switzerland of the South. Streets and avenues were surveyed; parks designed; corners of central squares reserved for the "proposed" opera house, board of trade, lyceum, market, public schools, and "Exposition Hall". The price of lots ranged from five to five hundred dollars. Positively, no lot would be priced higher than five hundred dollars.

While the boom was growing in Okochee, J. Pinkney's circulars, maps, and prospectuses were flying through the mails to every part of the country. Investors sent in their money by post, and the Skyland Real Estate Company (J. Pinkney Bloom) returned to each a deed, duly placed on record, to the best lot, at the price, on hand that day. All this time the catamount screeched upon the reserved lot of the Skyland Board of Trade, the opposum swung by his tail over the site of the Exposition Hall, and the owl hooted a melancholy recitative to his audience of young squirrels in opera house square. Later, when the money was coming in fast, J. Pinkney caused to be erected in the coming city half a dozen cheap box houses, and persuaded a contingent of

494

indigent natives to occupy them, thereby assuming the rôle of "population" in subsequent prospectuses, which became, accordingly, more seductive and remunerative.

So, when the dream faded and Okochee dropped back to digging bait and nursing its two and a half per cent. tax, J. Pinkney Bloom (unloving of cheques and drafts and the cold interrogatories of bankers) strapped about his fifty-two-inch waist a soft leather belt containing eight thousand dollars in big bills and said that all was very good.

One last trip he was making to Skyland before departing to other salad fields. Skyland was a regular post office, and the steamboat, *Dixie Belle*, under contract, delivered the mail bag (generally empty) twice a week. There was a little business there to be settled—the postmaster was to be paid off for his light but lonely services, and the "inhabitants" had to be furnished with another month's homely rations, as per agreement. And then Skyland would know J. Pinkney Bloom no more. The owners of these precipitous, barren, useless lots might come and view the scene of their invested credulity, or they might leave them to their fit tenants, the wild hog and the browsing deer. The work of the Skyland Real Estate Company was finished.

The little steamboat *Dixie Belle* was about to shove off on her regular up-the-lake trip, when a rickety hired carriage rattled up to the pier, and a tall, elderly gentleman, in black, stepped out, signalling courteously but vivaciously for the boat to wait. Time was of the least importance in the schedule of the *Dixie Belle*; Captain MacFarland gave the order, and the boat received its ultimate two passengers. For, upon the arm of the tall, elderly gentleman, as he crossed the gangway, was a little elderly lady, with a grey curl depending quaintly forward on her left ear.

Captain MacFarland was at the wheel; therefore it seemed to J. Pinkney Bloom, who was the only other passenger, that it should be his to play the part of host to the boat's new guests, who were, doubtless, on a scenery-viewing expedition. He stepped forward, with that translucent, child-candid

smile upon his fresh, pink countenance, with that air of
unaffected sincerity that was redeemed from bluffness only
by its exquisite calculation, with that promptitude and
masterly decision of manner that so well suited his calling—
all his stock in trade well to the front, he stepped forward to
receive Colonel and Mrs. Peyton Blaylock. With the grace
of a grand marshal or a wedding usher, he escorted the two
passengers to a side of the upper deck, from which the
scenery was supposed to present itself to the observer in
increased quantity and quality. There in comfortable steamer
chairs, they sat and began to piece together the random lines
that were to form an intelligent paragraph in the big history
of little events.

"Our home, sir," said Colonel Blaylock, removing his
wide-brimmed, rather shapeless black felt hat, "is in Holly
Springs—Holly Springs, Georgia. I am very proud to make
your acquaintance, Mr. Bloom. Mrs. Blaylock and myself
have just arrived in Okochee this morning, sir, on business—
business of importance in connection with the recent rapid
march of progress in this section of our state."

The Colonel smoothed back, with a sweeping gesture, his
long, smooth, grey locks. His dark eyes, still fiery under the
heavy, black brows, seemed inappropriate to the face of a
business man. He looked rather to be an old courtier handed
down from the reign of Charles, and reattired in a modern
suit of fine, but ravelling and seam-worn, broadcloth.

"Yes, sir," said Mr. Bloom, in his heartiest prospectus
voice, "things have been whizzing around Okochee. Biggest
industrial revival and waking up to natural resources
Georgia ever had. Did you happen to squeeze in on the
ground floor in any of the gilt-edged grafts, Colonel?"

"Well, sir," said the Colonel, hesitating in courteous
doubt, "if I understood your question, I may say that I took
the opportunity to make an investment that I believe will
prove quite advantageous—yes, sir, I believe it will result
in both pecuniary profit and agreeable occupation."

"Colonel Blaylock," said the little elderly lady, shaking her gay curl and smiling indulgent explanation at J. Pinkney Bloom, "is so devoted to business. He has such a talent for financiering and markets and investments and those kind of things. I think myself extremely fortunate in having secured him for a partner on life's journey—I am so unversed in those formidable but very useful branches of learning."

Colonel Blaylock rose and made a bow—a bow that belonged with silk stockings and lace ruffles and velvet.

"Practical affairs," he said, with a wave of his hand toward the promoter, "are, if I may use the comparison, the garden walks upon which we tread through life, viewing upon either side of us the flowers which brighten that journey. It is my pleasure to be able to lay out a walk or two. Mrs. Blaylock, sir, is one of those fortunate higher spirits whose mission it is to make the flowers grow. Perhaps, Mr. Bloom, you have perused the lines of Lorella, the Southern poetess. That is the name above which Mrs. Blaylock has contributed to the press of the South for many years."

"Unfortunately," said Mr. Bloom, with a sense of the loss clearly written upon his frank face, "I'm like the Colonel— in the walk-making business myself—and I haven't had time even to take a sniff at the flowers. Poetry is a line I never dealt in. It must be nice, though—quite nice."

"It is the region," smiled Mrs. Blaylock, "in which my soul dwells. My shawl, Peyton, if you please—the breeze comes a little chilly from yon verdured hills."

The Colonel drew from the tail pocket of his coat a small shawl of knitted silk and laid it solicitously about the shoulders of the lady. Mrs. Blaylock sighed contentedly, and turned her expressive eyes—still as clear and unworldly as a child's—upon the steep slopes that were slowly slipping past. Very fair and stately they looked in the clear morning air. They seemed to speak in familiar terms to the responsive spirit of Lorella. "My native hills!" she murmured dreamily. "See how the foliage drinks the sunlight from the hollows and dells."

"Mrs. Blaylock's maiden days," said the Colonel, interpreting her mood to J. Pinkney Bloom, "were spent among the mountains of northern Georgia. Mountain air and mountain scenery recall to her those days. Holly Springs, where we have lived for twenty years, is low and flat. I fear that she may have suffered in health and spirits by so long a residence there. That is one potent reason for the change we are making. My dear, can you not recall those lines you wrote— entitled, I think, 'The Georgia Hills'—the poem that was so extensively copied by the Southern press and praised so highly by the Atlanta critics?"

Mrs. Blaylock turned a glance of speaking tenderness upon the Colonel, fingered for a moment the silvery curl that drooped upon her bosom, then looked again toward the mountains. Without preliminary or affectation or demurral she began, in rather thrilling and more deeply pitched tones, to recite these lines:

> The Georgia hills, the Georgia hills!—
>   Oh, heart, why dost thou pine?
> Are not these sheltered lowlands fair
>   With mead and bloom and vine?
> Ah! as the slow-paced river here
>   Broods on its natal rills
> My spirit drifts, in longing sweet,
>   Back to the Georgia hills.
>
> And through the close-drawn, curtained night
>   I steal on sleep's slow wings
> Back to my heart's ease—slopes of pine—
>   Where end my wanderings.
> Oh, heaven seems nearer from their tops—
>   And farther earthly ills—
> Even in dreams, if I may but
>   Dream of my Georgia hills.
>
> The grass upon their orchard sides
>   Is a fine couch to me;

The common note of each small bird
    Passes all minstrelsy.
It would not seem so dread a thing
    If, when the Reaper wills,
He might come there and take my hand
    Up in the Georgia hills.

"That's great stuff, ma'am," said J. Pinkney Bloom, enthusiastically, when the poetess had concluded. "I wish I had looked up poetry more than I have. I was raised in the pine hills myself."

"The mountains ever call to their children," murmured Mrs. Blaylock. "I feel that life will take on the rosy hue of hope again in among these beautiful hills. Peyton—a little taste of the currant wine, if you will be so good. The journey, though delightful in the extreme, slightly fatigues me."

Colonel Blaylock again visited the depths of his prolific coat, and produced a tightly corked, rough, black bottle. Mr. Bloom was on his feet in an instant. "Let me bring a glass, ma'am. You come along, Colonel—there's a little table we can bring too. Maybe we can scare up some fruit or a cup of tea on board. I'll ask Mac."

Mrs. Blaylock reclined at ease. Few royal ladies have held their royal prerogative with the serene grace of the petted Southern woman. The Colonel, with an air as gallant and assiduous as in the days of his courtship, and J. Pinkney Bloom, with a ponderous agility half professional and half directed by some resurrected, unnamed, long-forgotten sentiment, formed a diversified but attentive court. The currant wine—wine home-made from the Holly Springs fruit—went round; and then J. Pinkney began to hear something of Holly Springs life.

It seemed (from the conversation of the Blaylocks) that the Springs was decadent. A third of the population had moved away. Business—and the Colonel was an authority on business—had dwindled to nothing. After carefully studying the field of opportunities open to capital he had sold his little property there for eight hundred dollars and invested it in one of the enterprises opened up by the book in Okochee.

"Might I inquire, sir," said Mr. Bloom, "in what particular line of business you inserted your coin? I know that town as well as I know the regulations for illegal use of the mails. I might give you a hunch as to whether you can make the game go or not."

J. Pinkney, somehow, had a kindly feeling toward these unsophisticated representatives of bygone days. They were so simple, impractical, and unsuspecting. He was glad that he happened not to have a gold brick or a block of that western Bad Boy Silver Mine stock along with him. He would have disliked to unload on people he liked so well as he did these; but there are some temptations too enticing to be resisted.

"No, sir," said Colonel Blaylock, pausing to arrange the queen's wrap. "I did not invest in Okochee. I had made an exhaustive study of business conditions, and I regard old settled towns as unfavourable fields in which to place capital that is limited in amount. Some months ago, through the kindness of a friend, there came into my hands a map and description of this new town of Skyland that has been built upon the lake. The description was so pleasing, the future of the town set forth in such convincing arguments, and its increasing prosperity portrayed in such an attractive style that I decided to take advantage of the opportunity it offered. I carefully selected a lot in the centre of the business district, although its price was the highest in the schedule— five hundred dollars—and made the purchase at once."

"Are you the man—I mean, did you pay five hundred dollars for a lot in Skyland?" asked J. Pinkney Bloom.

"I did, sir," answered the Colonel, with the air of a modest millionaire explaining his success; "a lot most excellently situated on the same square with the opera house, and only two squares from the board of trade. I consider the purchase a most fortuitous one. It is my intention to erect a small building upon it at once, and open a modest book and stationery store. During past years I have met with many pecuniary reverses, and I now find it necessary to engage in some commercial occupation that will furnish me with a livelihood. The book and stationery business, though a humble one, seems to me not inapt nor altogether uncongenial. I am a graduate of the University of Virginia; and Mrs. Blaylock's really wonderful acquaintance with belles-lettres and poetic literature should go far toward insuring success. Of course, Mrs. Blaylock would not personally serve behind the counter. With the nearly three hundred dollars I have remaining I can manage the building of a house, by giving a lien on the lot. I have an old friend in Atlanta who is a partner in a large book store, and he has agreed to furnish me with a stock of goods on credit, on extremely easy terms. I am pleased to hope, sir, that Mrs. Blaylock's health and happiness will be increased by the change of locality. Already I fancy I can perceive the return of those roses that were once the hope and despair of Georgia cavaliers."

Again followed that wonderful bow, as the Colonel lightly touched the pale cheek of the poetess. Mrs. Blaylock, blushing like a girl, shook her curl and gave the Colonel an arch, reproving tap. Secret of eternal youth—where art thou? Every second the answer comes—"Here, here, here." Listen to thine own heartbeats, O weary seeker after external miracles.

"Those years," said Mrs. Blaylock, "in Holly Springs were long, long, long. But now is the promised land in sight. Skyland!—a lovely name."

"Doubtless," said the Colonel, "we shall be able to secure comfortable accommodation at some modest hotel at reasonable rates. Our trunks are in Okochee, to be forwarded when we shall have made permanent arrangements."

J. Pinkney Bloom excused himself, went forward, and stood by the captain at the wheel.

"Mac," said he, "do you remember my telling you once that I sold one of those five-hundred-dollar lots in Skyland?"

"Seems I do," grinned Captain MacFarland.

"I'm not a coward, as a general rule," went on the promoter, "but I always said that if I ever met the sucker that bought that lot I'd run like a turkey. Now, you see that old babe-in-the-wood over there? Well, he's the boy that drew the prize. That was the only five-hundred-dollar lot that went. The rest ranged from ten dollars to two hundred. His wife writes poetry. She's invented one about the high grounds of Georgia, that's way up in G. They're going to Skyland to open a book store."

"Well," said MacFarland, with another grin, "it's a good thing you are along, J.P.; you can show 'em around town until they begin to feel at home."

"He's got three hundred dollars left to build a house and store with," went on J. Pinkney, as if he were talking to himself. "And he thinks there's an opera house up there."

Captain MacFarland released the wheel long enough to give his leg a roguish slap.

"You old fat rascal!" he chuckled, with a wink.

"Mac, you're a fool," said J. Pinkney Bloom, coldly. He went back and joined the Blaylocks, where he sat, less talkative, with that straight furrow between his brows, that always stood as a signal of schemes being shaped within.

"There's a good many swindles connected with these booms," he said presently. "What if this Skyland should turn out to be one—that is, suppose business should be sort of dull there, and no special sale for books?"

"My dear sir," said Colonel Blaylock, resting his hand upon the back of his wife's chair, "three times I have been reduced to almost penury by the duplicity of others, but I have not yet lost faith in humanity. If I have been deceived again, still we may glean health and content, if not wordly profit. I am aware that there are dishonest schemers in the world who set traps for the unwary, but even they are not altogether bad. My dear, can you recall those verses entitled, 'He Giveth the Increase', that you composed for the choir of our church in Holly Springs?"

"That was four years ago," said Mrs. Blaylock; "perhaps I can repeat a verse or two.

> The lily springs from the rotting mould;
>   Pearls from the deep sea slime;
> Good will come out of Nazareth
>   All in God's own time.
>
> To the hardest heart the softening grace
>   Cometh, at last, to bless;
> Guiding it right to help and cheer
>   And succour in distress.

"I cannot remember the rest. The lines were not ambitious. They were written to the music composed by a dear friend."

"It's a fine rhyme, just the same," declared Mr. Bloom. "It seems to ring the bell, all right. I guess I gather the sense of it. It means that the rankest kind of a phony will give you the best end of it once in a while."

Mr. Bloom strayed thoughtfully back to the captain, and stood meditating.

"Ought to be in sight of the spires and gilded domes of Skyland now in a few minutes," chirruped MacFarland, shaking with enjoyment.

"Go to the devil," said Mr. Bloom, still pensive.

And now, upon the left bank, they caught a glimpse of a white village, high up on the hills, smothered among green trees. That was Cold Branch—no boom town, but the slow growth of many years. Cold Branch lay on the edge of the grape and corn lands. The big country road ran just back of the heights. Cold Branch had nothing in common with the frisky ambition of Okochee with its impertinent lake.

"Mac," said J. Pinkney suddenly, "I want you to stop at Cold Branch. There's a landing there that they made to use sometimes when the river was up."

"Can't," said the captain, grinning more broadly. "I've got the United States mails on board. Right to-day this boat's in the government service. Do you want to have the poor old captain keelhauled by Uncle Sam? And the great city of Skyland, all disconsolate, waiting for its mail? I'm ashamed of your extravagance, J.P."

"Mac," almost whispered J. Pinkney, in his danger-line voice, "I looked into the engine-room of the *Dixie Belle* a while ago. Don't you know of somebody that needs a new boiler? Cement and black Japan can't hide flaws from me. And then, those shares of building and loan that you traded for repairs—they were all yours, of course. I hate to mention these things, but——"

"Oh, come now, J.P.," said the captain. "You know I was just fooling. I'll put you off at Cold Branch, if you say so."

"The other passengers get off there, too," said Mr. Bloom.

Further conversation was held, and in ten minutes the *Dixie Belle* turned her nose toward a little, cranky wooden pier on the left bank, and the captain relinquishing the wheel to a roustabout came to the passenger deck and made the remarkable announcement: "All out for Skyland."

The Blaylocks and J. Pinkney Bloom disembarked and the *Dixie Belle* proceeded on her way up the lake. Guided by the indefatigable promoter, they slowly climbed the steep hillside, pausing often to rest and admire the view. Finally they entered the village of Cold Branch. Warmly both the Colonel and his wife praised it for its homelike and peaceful beauty. Mr. Bloom conducted them to a two-storey building on a shady street that bore the legend, "Pinetop Inn". Here he took his leave, receiving the cordial thanks of the two for his attentions, the Colonel remarking that he thought they would spend the remainder of the day in rest, and take a look at his purchase on the morrow.

J. Pinkney Bloom walked down Cold Branch's main street. He did not know this town, but he knew towns, and his feet did not falter. Presently he saw a sign over a door: "Frank E. Cooly, Attorney-at-Law and Notary Public." A young man was Mr. Cooly, and awaiting business.

"Get your hat, son," said Mr. Bloom, in his breezy way, "and a blank deed, and come along. It's a job for you."

"Now," he continued, when Mr. Cooly had responded with alacrity, "is there a book store in town?"

"One," said the lawyer. "Henry Williams's."

"Get there," said Mr. Bloom. "We're going to buy it."

Henry Williams was behind his counter. His store was a small one, containing a mixture of books, stationery, and fancy rubbish. Adjoining it was Henry's home—a decent cottage, vine-embowered and cosy. Henry was lank and soporific, and not inclined to rush his business.

"I want to buy your house and store," said Mr. Bloom. "I haven't got time to dicker—name your price."

"It's worth eight hundred," said Henry, too much dazed to ask more than its value.

"Shut that door," said Mr. Bloom to the lawyer. Then he tore off his coat and vest, and began to unbutton his shirt.

"Wanter fight about it, do yer?" said Henry Williams, jumping up and cracking his heels together twice. "All right, hunky—sail in and cut yer capers."

"Keep your clothes on," said Mr. Bloom. "I'm only going down to the bank."

He drew eight one-hundred-dollar bills from his money belt and planked them down on the counter. Mr. Cooly showed signs of future promise, for he already had the deed spread out, and was reaching across the counter for the ink bottle. Never before or since was such quick action had in Cold Branch.

"Your name, please?" asked the lawyer.

"Make it out to Peyton Blaylock," said Mr. Bloom. "God knows how to spell it."

Within thirty minutes Henry Williams was out of business, and Mr. Bloom stood on the brick sidewalk with Mr. Cooly, who held in his hand the signed and attested deed.

"You'll find the party at the Pinetop Inn," said J. Pinkney Bloom. "Get it recorded, and take it down and give it to him. He'll ask you a hell's mint of questions; so here's ten dollars for the trouble you'll have in not being able to answer 'em. Never run much to poetry, did you, young man?"

"Well," said the really talented Cooly, who even yet retained his right mind, "now and then."

"Dig into it," said Mr. Bloom, "it'll pay you. Never heard a poem, now, that run something like his, did you?—

> A good thing out of Nazareth
> Comes up sometimes, I guess,
> On hand, all right, to help and cheer
> A sucker in distress.

"I believe not," said Mr. Cooly.

"It's a hymn," said J. Pinkney Bloom. "Now, show me the way to a livery stable, son, for I'm going to hit the dirt road back to Okochee."

S

T

...turned on or before the last ... Fines,
...rged ...

3